CHIRAL MAD

2

CHIRAL MAD

2

ANTHOLOGY OF
PSYCHOLOGICAL HORROR

[edited by michael bailey]

WWW.NETTIRW.COM

Published by Written Backwards

Cover artwork by Michael Bailey.

"The Counselor" first appeared on the *Horror World* website. Copyright © 2011, Mort Castle

"Orange is for Anguish, Blue for Insanity" first appeared in *Prime Evil*, by NAL Books / New American Library (ed. Douglas E. Winter). Copyright © 1988, David Morrell
1998 Bram Stoker Award - Superior Achievement in Long Fiction (winner)

"Empathy" first appeared in *Demons: Encounters with the Devil and his Minions, Fallen Angels, and the Possessed,* by Black Dog & Leventhal (ed. John Skipp). Copyright © 2011, John Skipp
2011 Bram Stoker Award – Superior Achievement in an Anthology (winner)

"The Word" first appeared in *Revelations*, by HarperPrism (ed. Douglas E. Winter).
Copyright © 1997, Ramsey Campbell
1997 International Horror Guild Award – Best Long Form (nomination)
1997 Bram Stoker Award – Superior Achievement in Long Fiction (nomination)
1998 British Fantasy Award – Best Short Story (nomination)

FIRST EDITION

ISBN-10: 1.4942.3997.3
ISBN-13: 978.1.4942.3997.8

CONTENTS

DEDICATION

FOR THOSE WITH 46 HELPING THOSE WITH 47
FOR THOSE WITH 47 HELPING THOSE WITH 46

CAUSE

Reading this page means you have either purchased this book, or it was purchased for you; either way, all proceeds from the sale of this book went directly to Down syndrome charities.

If you received this book as a gift, please consider purchasing a copy for a friend to continue spreading the love.

Thank you, readers, writers and artists.

INTRO

MICHAEL BAILEY

I, CHIRAL MAD 2, HEREBY EXIST. I am the second volume of something spectacular. I'll admit to that. My predecessor (let's call her CM1 for short) was nominated for various accolades, won some awards and recognition and whatnot. As of my printing, CM1 has raised around five thousand dollars for Down syndrome charities. Not bad. Hopefully my existence will increase that number. All stories in the first volume were donated; none of the contributors received payment; yet everyone involved (writers and readers alike) seemed to want the anthology to exist. Everyone shared a desire to help raise some serious dough, for a good cause. That's love.

Another year later and here I am, exposing my pages. And I'm another beast altogether. I can do better. I know I can, and the crazy editor who pieced me together must think the same. This time around (I guess you can call me CM2 for short), this Michael Bailey fellow decided to pay the writers, and not only in contributor copies, but by paying them professional rates. He's either crazy, or has serious faith in me, the writers involved, my readers, and most importantly, the cause. It's a damn good cause. I'll admit to that, too.

Here's how I really came to be: people asked for me, specifically. "When's *Chiral Mad 2* coming out?" readers asked. "When does *Chiral Mad 2* open for submissions?" writers asked. Well, I can tell you this: my creator isn't a fan of sequels, or serial volumes. Supply vs. Demand must have gotten the better of him, however. Demand was high. And Supply wasn't considered when people started asking about me. Readers wanted to read the book. Writers wanted to write for the book. And, according to my editor (how else would I know these things?), a follow-up anthology wasn't planned.

So thank you. Yes, you: the person reading my pages. You are the reason I exist. You asked for me.

Now, I'm a rather large book. 424 pages: a palindrome number (how fitting). Twenty-eight contributors, similar to my predecessor. Word counts vary between 400 and 15,000. Within are magnificent literary works (flash fiction, short stories, long fiction, and a novelette) from the well-known, the relatively-known and the unknown, twenty-four of those original and four reprints. If you want more information on these fine folks, you can read all about them in the Outro toward the end of the book, but know that all this creativity sparked from a single, loose theme of chirality.

What is chirality? If you've read CM1, you already know. If you went out of order and started with me (which is not a problem, but may spark you to buy my predecessor), then you will soon discover chirality as you work your way through the stories, one by one.

It took a lot of hard work to get to where I am today. It wasn't simply a process of finding twenty-four stories, placing them alongside one another, slapping on a fancy-looking cover, and calling me a book. No, I am much more than that. Everyone and their mother (and possibly a cousin or two) wanted in this anthology. Suddenly, out of the ether, a viral submission call appeared. As stated before, people asked for a second *Chiral Mad* the moment the first volume found print. This is not an exaggeration. Overnight, stories flooded in, and within a few days, a simple blog post from the editor spread across the internet like an SMTD (social media transmitted disease). In ten days, there were nearly a hundred stories submitted, and by the end, around 650, from twenty-eight countries. Over five million words total were considered for this book. That's love.

So here we are. You hold me now, along with the twenty-eight writers/stories carefully selected for this anthology. You leave behind your oily fingerprints on my glossy cover. Sure, you may wipe them off with the back of your sleeve or a napkin or something to make me all pretty again, but they'll be back, every time you pick me up. I was purposefully made that way, you know, so you could be a part of me. We are one. You. Me. All the writers involved and their unforgettable words. You've broken my spine to take a peek, but that's okay. I'm flexible. You've possibly smelled my pages. If not, do it now. Take a whiff. I smell great. Digital books, they've got nothin' on me! No smell, no pages to thumb through, no earmarks, no spine, no history, no fingerprints. Just a bunch of 1's and 0's, those guys. More than that, I've got bite because I've got teeth; twenty-eight of them, to be exact, all different shapes and sizes and sharpnesses. These teeth were pulled from various people around the world who wanted to share their stories with you. Will you get bitten? Yes, and I can only hope you let them sink in deep. Once they do, the virus will spread. You will hand me over to another, perhaps, or purchase a new copy of me for a friend. And the virus spreads and spreads and spreads...

So, now that we're acquainted, perhaps I can hold *you* now, until you turn the last page. I can make you laugh, I can make you cry, and I can make you set me down every once in a while, just long enough to catch your breath...

ANOTHER MAN'S BONES

MASON IAN BUNDSCHUH

"I had three large mirrors in my room when I was a boy and I felt very acutely afraid of them, because I saw myself in the dim light... thrice over, and I was very afraid that perhaps the three shapes would begin moving by themselves."

- Jorge Luis Borges

I FEEL FOR THE GUN in my pocket and wait. I dare not sit with my back to the door. He is almost here so I ought to say I don't have much time, but I know better. The window is boarded up and shards of the shattered mirror crackle like electricity under my feet. I check the time absently then ignore the flicking numbers. We always forget that time doesn't really mean anything anyway. We. The word makes me tired and sick. I am scattered like light through a prism.

The machine works, isn't that a triumph? Now I must be a murderer.

No, not a murderer; there can only be one self, and the past and future are utterly separated by time. You are either here or there or in between. Nothing should be allowed to exist in two places simultaneously. But that isn't how it really works. I know it not from an abstract theory, but from blood-drenched experience.

I feel the reassuring weight in my coat pocket one more time. I won't leave this room again. No, it won't be me—I need to re-member that it's not me. Once they are dead they'll just be another man's bones.

But I'm ahead of myself. All this is five days from now.

In the present I am moving across the street. I forgot how good the sunlight feels. It isn't autumn yet, but it's close. The end is in the past, but I haven't got there yet...

This is harder than I thought it would be. Time is slipperier than I remembered.

I walk somewhere. I can't remember where I am going. It is important that I get there. An old woman is coughing on a bus stop bench. I think she must know me, but she looks past me in the deep selfishness of her ominous cough. I pause at a window shaded by a green awning. It is a restaurant—I have been here before. I do not look at the menu or my reflection; mirrors are abominations because they multiply an individual.

I am supposed to wait here for a second. Not much more.

The car screeches around the corner. I remember that it's a kid stealing for the first time. I'd known that somehow. The kid isn't important, just the hurtling steel and plastic.

A man walks out of the restaurant. I don't have to see him to know who he is. All I need to do is turn and face him. Not now, in a second. The old woman on the bench coughs again, almost a death rattle.

The man I have scarcely waited for turns towards the sound. I face him, like a plant to the sun. He recognizes me and I smile, putting my hand meaningfully into my too-bulky coat. I know I'm supposed to do that right at this moment.

He bolts. Just as I remember he would.

The kid in the stolen car crushes him and tumbles him and breaks him in one red moment. I don't move because I'm trying to notice if I feel any different.

"Someone call an ambulance," a guy shouts from across the street. I know it'll do no good.

The kid in the stolen car stops. He is so shocked that his mouth is frozen in a grin. I know that he will drive off in horror and pounding adrenaline soon, but enough people have already taken pictures with their cell phones that he doesn't get away with it. None of that matters because he's done his part.

I stand on the curb, then step into the street. I don't want to look at the body but I know I must. A cyclist is already stooping over the mangled thing that had so recently been alive and running. I'd almost forgotten how bright yellow the bike shorts look against the red blood. Those kinds of details are lost in the shuffle of time sometimes.

I look. I have not forgotten how hard it is to see their faces in death. But you always have to look. The cyclist looks up at me from the dead man's face. He should be past shock, but he still has room for a little more.

"Do you know this man?"

I tell him no.

It's time for me to leave.

As I turn away and walk back towards the coughing old woman I hear him still asking questions.

"Is he your brother?"

I veer into an alley. I know I'm not going to be sick, but it feels like it. The brick wall is rough against my hands, but solid enough to support my shaking weight. There isn't much time to waste. But again I am reminded that this is not really true. To my left, amid the broken pallets and piss-stained refuse, is a battered steel door. I am also supposed to wait here.

Almost a minute passes before I remember that I am actually supposed to be somewhere else. But the moment is upon me and I reach into my pocket for the gun. It is when I hear the percussive shot muffled by the heavy door that I remember that my pockets are empty. I run but the alley is a dead end.

That was four days ago in someone else's future, but my past. For now.

I keep remembering that I should have left it all alone. But I didn't. None of us did.

This time my heart is pounding as I run through a corridor. I don't recall why I am running, but I know that if I stop he'll get me instead of the other way around. The right way around. One of us has the gun, I don't remember which. The hall is going to end soon. There is the faint outline of a door. I know I'm supposed to go through it into the alley, but I don't. If you want to stay alive you have to go against time; against fate. Only then can you sneak around and chip away at the duplicity of your failure.

Instead I turn right. I had not done that before.

Not in this corridor.

But suddenly I am facing a mirror. I watch my hand come up with a gun. I raise my own, but there is no weapon in it. I remembered that I should have gone straight but it's too late.

The gun goes off. That was three days from now.

I am sitting in a small café. I've forgotten that I have no money to pay for my meal. I am not as embarrassed as I once would have been before this madness took me in its teeth and shook me. I wish I'd have junked the infernal machine.

I still have no money.

The waiter is busy with a table full of young women. They will grow old, fall in love, have kids, lose their dreams, struggle to find meaning—all within the happy confines of linear time. While I have to worry about remembering all that hasn't happened yet so I don't echo through the past like two mirrors facing one another.

I sidle out of the booth and keep my head down as I push out the door. My heart is pounding. There is a sharp, ugly cough and I turn reflexively—afraid, because all of a sudden I remember. Standing just behind me, waiting by the doorway, is the one I feared.

He reaches deliberately into his pocket. I have no choice but to run. As I do, I remember that this is the wrong choice: I am the one who has the gun.

Before I can stop myself I hear the car and see a bicyclist on the other side of the street. His yellow shorts make me sad even as everything flies to shreds and time ends.

That was two days ago. The future for everyone else.

I am waiting in the hallway. He will run this way soon. I don't know if it will feel any different, him being the last one.

Or am I the last one?

Who now could say which of us is the original? I suppose the answer is at best, purely academic. They say that the instinct to survive is the strongest one we have, and once I have killed them, that which is me still survives.

My existentialist masturbation is interrupted by furtive footsteps. I almost don't have time to pull the gun out of my pocket before the other one peels around the corner. I hate looking into my own face as I pull the trigger. The silence afterwards is deafening. I laugh once because I realize that it feels like time has slowed. But I know it never slows.

I cut through the alley and walk back to the dirty hotel, pretending not to hurry. I don't feel any more whole, but I doubted I ever would. My pocket is strangely light after ditching the gun in the dumpster. I pass the ratty man who always lurks in the lobby. He says "Hello again," and suddenly I am afraid.

In the hall outside my door I play back the twists and turns since that fateful night—recalling with vertiginous dread that that was actually tomorrow. No ends were left open. I had closed all the loops, cut off all the threads of fate.

My hand clenches the doorknob and I enter my squalid little room. The windows are boarded up and I am surprised to see that I am waiting. And then I remember something: I do not have anything in my pocket.

"You dropped your gun a few days ago," the figure in the shadows says to me.

"That was just a minute ago," I answer automatically. There is nothing else to do.

"It's the same thing."

And then the gun spoke for us both.

MNEMONICIDE

JAMES CHAMBERS

ANGIE HOLDS the gun while you tie a humiliating old memory to the chair.

You bind his hands behind the wooden back, fasten his ankles to the chair legs, the coarse rope scratching your fingers. An August breeze flows through the open garage doorway and tickles the sweat on the back of your neck. The memory's name is Robert. He stares at you with wide, watery eyes, terrified Angie will shoot him if he makes a sound. Dirt and grime streak his crooked tie and tailored suit. Blood trickles down his face from a gash where his head cracked against the hood of your trunk. His face is your humiliation, his eyes witnesses to your shame, his existence a lifeline for a cold shadow from your past, a distant moment you want to erase.

With the memory secured, you step outside and collect the padded moving blankets that dropped from Robert's body when you and Angie walked him in from your car. You toss them back in the trunk. Spots of Robert's blood shine on the edge of the hood as you shut it. You roll the tension from your shoulders, take a deep breath. Maple leaves flutter above you. Bulrushes sway at the edge of the clearing around the old municipal garage, an ivy-covered, brick building no one has used in years. A weedy dirt road leads away into the thin shade of the tangled woods. The lapping of surf lilts through the air. Somewhere a seagull caws. From across the bay on the far side of the trees come the broken-down hum and groan of the old city, the buzz of helicopters flitting past tired skyscrapers. It's so good to live in the moment, in the bright, wonderful present, even if only for a few seconds before the past drags you back to it.

It's a taste of the life ahead of you.

You return to the garage, pull down the door. Sunlight drops from Robert's face, leaving him pale with terror in the gloom. A trembling memory. Too scared to speak.

Robert, who you described as "never at a loss for words."

His eyes beg for answers.

You tell him, "You can talk now."

Angie lowers the gun and paces. Her attention jumps between you and Robert, who eyes the gun like it's a trap waiting to spring.

"Don't worry about Angie," you say. "She's here to remember for me."

Quavering, Robert says, "Why... why are you doing this? We're friends for God's sake. We've known each other for twenty fucking years. What did I ever do to you... to deserve *this*?"

You grab a battered folding chair propped against the wall, open it across from Robert, and sit, wobbling on its uneven legs. "We *are* friends." You squeeze Robert's shoulder, reassure him. "You're a good friend. But you remember the night Mary dumped me."

"...Mary?" Robert says.

"Mary Lawson. Junior year."

Robert's face puckers. "That was... so long ago."

"You remember," you say. "I heard it in your voice when I called you yesterday. The first thing that came to mind when you heard me on the phone, wasn't it? That night she dumped me? How could you forget, right? She broke my heart. Shattered it. Bad enough she did it in front of my friends but then naming off all the times she'd cheated on me, boasting about what she'd done... I nearly killed myself that night."

"That was... I had no idea," Robert says.

You shrug. "I can tell you now because you won't remember it for long."

"What... what the hell does that mean?" Robert asks. "Please let me go... Please... Please... Whatever this is, whatever you need, say the word. I can get you help, okay? Doctors. Or a lawyer. I know the best. I swear. You need a job, right? I can get you a job, a good one. I can give you money. Just don't... take me away from my kids. Please."

"I climbed up to the observatory on top of the student center. I knew the lock was broken from volunteering there with the local kids who came in for the enrichment programs. I stood by the telescope for two hours trying to talk myself into jumping into the alley. A hundred-foot drop, at least. But I couldn't do it. I wanted to forget, not die. If I could've pushed a button in my mind and reset everything how it was one day before, I would've. I'd have pressed it over and over to scrub the humiliation and the *hurt* from my mind. But nothing can ever unhappen. We can't bury anything deep enough to ever really forget it. You know why?"

"I'm sorry," Robert says. "Shit, man, whatever I did, *I'm sorry*. I should've been there for you that night—that it? I felt awful for you—but you ran from Pria's room... disappeared from campus for three days."

"Stop," you say. "Answer my question. Do you know why we can't forget?"

Robert comes up empty, shaking his head. "No. I don't know."

"Something always reminds us," you say. "I can forget, but then what? A song, a picture, a place, or a smell dredges up the memory. The hurt comes rushing back as fresh as it was that night. Songs, pictures, places, *things*, though—their power dies out, but people *know*. They keep memories alive. You were *there* that night, and even if I make myself forget like it never took place, *you* sustain the memory when *I* suffocate and kill it. I see you, or talk to you, or think about you or the others, it surges back to life in me. You, Eduardo, Selena, Pria—especially Mary. You won't let me forget that pain."

"I... I never brought it up after that night," Robert says.

"You think about it, though," you say. "You thought about it when I called you. You're thinking about it now."

"No, I swear I'm not," Robert says.

"I *want* you to think about it now," you tell him.

You reach toward Angie. She sniffles as she hands you the gun, warm and moist from her sweaty palm, its weight solid, deadly. You rest your hand and the gun on your leg and slide them forward till the barrel bumps Robert's left knee, and he flinches.

"Remember it," you say. "Right now. *Think of that night.*"

"O-okay. Pria's lava lamp was on. It was late. We'd come back from the bars. We were drinking—"

"Don't talk. Remember."

Robert nods, slips into the memory, and the parasite you share with him—that you shared with the others—consumes his face. A memory that senses it has nowhere left to hide. You've killed it inside yourself over and again, until you realized the only way to stop it growing back was to kill it in everyone else who remembered it. Eduardo. Pria. Selena. *Mary.* Only you and Robert remember now.

"That night was awful for you," Robert says, his voice rising out of the muddled, shifting shape of the memory eclipsing his face. "I felt so bad for you, man. But *Mary* hurt you. *She* was wrong. *She* was a total bitch. *I* didn't hurt you!"

"But you won't let me forget the pain," you say. "We each have our own memory of that night, diverging from the same point in the past, but mine shaped by pain, yours by compassion. We're the last two reflections of what happened. You know what formed the others' memories? For Eduardo, contempt. He was one of Mary's lovers. Pria pitied me. The whole scene disgusted Selena. And Mary—she *wanted* to gut me. We all saw and heard the same things but we kept the memory—*a memory I want dead*—alive inside us in our own ways. Memories live as long as we let them. You're the only one left keeping this one alive."

In Robert's face, the memory lashes like the tail of a whirlpool, desperate to flee the boundaries of his expression, which cracks as panic forces fresh tears from his eyes. His lips tremble.

"You… *killed* them?" he says.

"To kill a memory," you say, "no one else can be allowed to

remember what you want to forget. As long as someone else remembers a thing, it happened. If no one remembers, the memory dies. Everything bad in my life is your fault—yours and everyone else's for not letting me forget the things I want to. It'll get easier now I've worked out how to kill those memories. What Mary did to me isn't the worst of what I need to get out of my head."

You stand and press the gun barrel to the top of Robert's skull.

The memory squirms in his face.

"Wait... *wait*," Robert says. "What if I forget too? Wouldn't that... get rid of it?"

You shake your head. "How could you ever forget it? Especially after all this."

"No..." Robert's voice strains, chest heaves. "Don't... kill... me... *please*."

"I'm not," you say. "I'm killing a memory. I'd spare you, if I could, but it doesn't work like that."

The memory writhes. It wants to lash out at you, cut your throat, punch a hole in your heart, or rip open your scars from that night and wither you with sadness. Its shadow twists in Robert's face like a cornered, wild animal. Robert is barely there anymore—suppressed by the memory. It saddens you they have to die together, but there's no other way. A bad memory is like an invasive tumor. That's how you describe it. After this, though, the cancer will be gone. You'll never feel this memory's humiliation again, never shiver from the crippling, cold, lonely sensation that wells up inside you whenever you remember it.

"Angie?" you say.

"Got your back," she says. "I'll remember for you. I'll be your final memory."

Remember why you have to pull the trigger, I say.

Do it this time. Please.

"Thank you," you say.

A squeeze of the trigger. The report of the gun and a spray of hot blood remake the world in a flash of acrid heat and raw violence. The dying memory bleeds from Robert, screaming as it flickers in the air like ball lightning, struggling to survive, then gives out while the echoes of its cries fade away. Robert's ruined face becomes his own again. You thrust the gun into Angie's hand then rush to a corner, double over, and heave, ejecting more than bile, coughing up the last, red remnants of something dead inside you that you once shared with Robert and four others. The pieces twitch on the ground before they dissolve, leaving behind a dark, foamy stain. When your guts settle down, you take another look at Robert. Angie stands beside him, her face and shirt spotted red, gun in her hand.

"I killed him?" you ask.

"Yes," Angie tells you.

"Who was he?"

"A memory to be forgotten."

"I had to kill him."

You killed a memory.

"Yes."

"Why? I don't remember."

Because you're weak.

"That's right. That's very good," Angie says. "I'll remember for you."

Angie sips the Cure from a green glass bottle. You've given up riding her about how much of it she drinks, but you still don't like it. You lay on the lumpy hotel bed, drying from the shower, the TV news humming like a distant beehive. You tell Angie the gaping space the bad memory once filled in your head itches like the edges of a healing wound. It feels good, feels right. Angie nods then drains the bottle. She switches off the lamp because the Cure widens her pupils to twin eclipses blotting out her irises.

She stands, sways.

You say, "You look like a cat when you're high. All the harshness leaves you."

You follow her into the bathroom, watch her undress and run the shower. Steam appears in the tub, fogs the edges of the mirror above the sink. Angie slips under the spray. Water strikes her body and races off her skin in frantic zigzag streams made by her scars. Their tough surfaces shine in the water. Her thighs and torso glisten. Keloids form a constellation on her belly. Whorls of thick tissue clutch her right breast tight to her chest. Lines of it stretch up the right side of her neck. Pink webs. Cracks in red leather. The signature of torn metal and shattered windshields, broken pavement and fire, the odor of gasoline. And screams. Of children, of a man. Angie says she drinks the Cure because it all still hurts, inside and out. She can never forget what's etched into her flesh and bone. There's no killing a memory like that. She remembers—keeping them alive in an instant of terror and pain—like she remembers for you.

This is what happened, I say. I remember. I remember for you all.

"My father beat the shit out of me once in front of my cousins. He usually didn't hit me when other people were around, but that time was different," you say while she washes her hair. "He bloodied my lip, broke my nose, almost broke my arm, all because he thought I lied to him."

Angie arches her back, rinsing away shampoo. "Did you?"

"No."

"Why didn't he believe you?"

"That's how he was," you say. "Couldn't find his wallet so he found someone to blame. My cousins were with us for the weekend. One of them said he'd seen me hide it from him for a joke. I had no idea where it was, but Dad was paranoid about things like that. He wanted to beat the truth out of me. My cousins even joined in, kicking me when I fell down. Then Dad's wallet dropped out of Nick's coat pocket. *He'd* taken it and then lied. Dad didn't lay a finger on him or his brothers. They weren't his kids. Dimmi, Marco, and Nick teased me about that for years."

"Did you hit your father back? Or your cousins?"

You shake your head. "I was only a kid. I was too weak."

"Shall we kill that memory next?"

You expel a long sigh. "I think so."

"How many?"

"Dad died years ago. Cancer took Dimmi last summer."

"Two, then."

"Nick and Marco."

Soapsuds running off her body, Angie's dark eyes seek yours, but you only stare at her scars shimmering in the water, at your final memory gestating in her face, driving her own horrible memories down deep so she can escape them for a little while. She spreads her arms, invites you into the shower, opening her body to you like she did her soul the night you met in the shelter and she agreed to be your final memory.

"One or two good memories between us wouldn't hurt things, would it?" she asks.

"It would ruin everything," you whisper.

You retreat from the bathroom to peeling wallpaper and a television ten years out of date, to a worn-out mattress with yellowed sheets and walls so thin you hear snoring from the room on one side and lazy moans of pleasure from the other. Angie leaves the shower, dries off, watching you as your legs bump the edge of the bed, and you fall backward onto it and into sleep.

You surprise visit Marco, introduce Angie as your girlfriend, get him drunk on wine, then leave him in his car in the garage with the motor running and the door closed. His ex-wife finds him five days later after he misses a court date over their child custody dispute. The police rule it suicide because the divorce depressed him. You wonder if the memory of your father beating you that lived inside him knew it had been tricked before it died.

The presence of your mother, in a black dress and a small, black hat with a veil, keeps you away from Marco's funeral. You watch from the shadows of trees across the cemetery then after almost everyone leaves, catch up to Nick, and explain how you didn't want the family to see you since you've been out of touch so long, but you're so sorry about Marco. He takes in your threadbare clothes, dirty shoes, and hungry face, and then invites you to his apartment in the old neighborhood. You get together late one night, making sure no one sees you and Angie come or go or the two of you together with Nick, and Nick breaks down, crying over his dead brothers. Behind his tears, though, his face is boyhood Nick's face, thirty years younger, and it wears a mask of scorn where your father's shadow still lives, kicking your small, child's body curled up on the ground. A pulsing vein in Nick's forehead matches the *thump thump thump* of your father's foot striking your stomach. Nick drinks until his face becomes a window to that day. Stealing your father's wallet. Telling the lie. The memory burns in him. A serpentine coil of fire taunting you with a hissing laugh, stoking its reflection inside you.

Nick follows you and Angie out, "for a walk, for some fresh air to sober up," so drunk he doesn't realize it when you lead him onto the East Side railroad tracks. The memory surges in his eyes, though, livid to escape, wanting to hurt you like it has so often before. You watch its angry, panicked throes in the light of the approaching freight train as it realizes Nick is far too drunk to make his way off the tracks, and its fury explodes from his face.

Nick disappears into a black streak of motion and dark metal.

Horrible sounds of metal striking flesh.

Scent and spray of blood in the air.

His memory of the day your father beat you lingers like a toxic cloud before it disperses into the wind and nothingness.

You clutch your stomach, double over, and vomit crimson chunks into the weeds.

Brakes squeal as the train slows. Angie leads you into the shadows of a run-down shed then away into the night. You don't remember why you're in the old neighborhood—but Angie does. She knows why; she knows your way home.

She's your final memory.

"Your cousins are gone," she says.

"I never had any cousins," you say.

Angie smiles and leads you to the motel room, to the next town, to the next memory.

Your third-grade best friend, Archie, who knows you wet yourself on the second day of school and reminded you of it almost daily until after high school.

Jeff and Lance, bullies, who made your life hell all through middle school; the teacher, Mrs. Carter, who blamed you for it.

Mr. Williams, down the street, who asked you to help him carry bags of leaves to the curb then groped you in his backyard and lied about it when you told your parents.

Your high school homeroom teacher, Mr. Connolly, who mocked how you dressed, or talked, or combed your hair every day; Andrea and Tomas, classmates who piled on with him.

Your pothead roommate, Fallon, and his brother, Nestor, who beat you up and sent you to the hospital freshman year because he thought you hit on his girlfriend.

Helena, who laughed when you asked her to marry you.

The waiter, who snickered as he overheard Helena say no. He proves hard to track down, but you find him, Carlos Ruiz, living in a crumbling tenement on the edge of the meat-packing district. It's frightening how vibrant the memory remains in him. It twists his face, makes him into a monster as it struggles. But it's only a memory. Its power dies when you tighten the noose around Carlos's neck. The memory leaves a rank taste in your mouth as it rises and spills past your lips. Afterward the man hanging from a hook in his closet puzzles you.

Angie remembers. "You put him there," she says, "to kill a memory."

She gathers your dead memories and holds them in her ossuary soul.

You feel lighter and freer after erasing each one, while her burden grows, but she only leads you further along the barbed line of your past.

The job interviewer, Forbes MacNeil, who cut you down question after question, made you feel worthless, called you "ridiculous," before you walked out of his office into a depression that lasted a month. Your co-workers, Rita, Sandra, and Sam, who stole your work, badmouthed you behind your back, and screwed your promotion. Your boss, Mr. Eisenstein, who fired you to cover his mistakes. Your friend Kevin, who stole a box of valuable old records from you. The landlord, Mr. Lopez, who evicted you. Kristin, your ex-girlfriend who dumped you while you stood in her doorway with all your clothes and belongings shoved into two suitcases and a backpack, asking to crash with her for a few days. She told you to "start over and get a new life without her" then slammed the door in your face. One more boot pushing you back down into a hole you could never figure out how to climb out of, a darkness that kept you lost.

"I wanted to start over," you say the night before you kill the Kristin-memory. "My old life got in my way. My memories made me sick."

You tell Angie you surrendered to the streets then, ashamed to let your family remember you that way. You wound up in a shelter full of people like you—poisoned by memories, and saw only one way to ever exterminate them.

"I realized it the night I met you," you say. "You were high on the Cure, but I knew you were right. The only thing you said would ever free you from your own bad memories could free me as well, but I could still live."

Do it this time, I say. Please, do it.

I still remember.

Time and again, the police question you, but you know nothing of the deaths of people you don't remember. You show genuine confusion about their suspicion. You cooperate, pass polygraph tests. Angie coaches you how to talk to them. She knows their techniques. She's made sure neither of you left behind any evidence where you killed your memories and few clues to connect any of them other than that they all happened to know you at some point in your life. Before Angie found the Cure and followed it to the highway where she destroyed her life, she was a good cop—good person too. Some people—weak, helpless people—let that slip through their fingers. Others have that ripped away from them. Their old lives, their good days. Until only bad memories remain. Angie knows how to make deaths look like accidents or suicides, how to make the police see things to make them turn elsewhere for answers. After a while they stop talking to you, stop tracking you.

Still, you're careful no one ever sees you with Angie.

It's not hard. No one misses her.

You left the shelter together after the first night you met.

No one connects you two.

Months pass while you wipe clean your past's dark geography piece by piece. Existence becomes a patchwork of motels, stolen cars, and sleeping parked in alleys and abandoned places around the city. Vacant lots. Shuttered factories. Neglected parks. You drift along the life-flow of the streets. Steal food when you can. Rely on library computers to track down your memories. As your mind empties, Angie's bloats. She never again opens her arms to you, but she takes the Cure more often, except when you hunt. As each memory falls, the space it held opens in you, revealing an end to the shadows though the darkest ones still wait.

The last memories prove the hardest for Angie. Memories of your own mistakes. She never cried when you killed memories of people hurting you, never hesitated over recollections of others mistreating you, victimizing you, humiliating you—but she cries for those you wronged and betrayed.

Those memories have to die too, though, because their shame weighs the strongest.

Your high school girlfriend, Lisa. You lied to her, said you loved her to take her virginity then broke up with her. Your sophomore year roommate, Len, whose money you stole, and Tara, his friend, whom you convinced him had taken it. Your co-worker, Parnell, who you envied so much you spread nasty rumors about him and got him fired. Half a dozen others you deceived or screwed or hurt. The hardest is your mother, the last of your family. She remembers more about you than anyone else and will never forget any of it, never let it go. Mothers never do, because as mundane and painful as some of those memories are, mothers keep their children alive inside them at any cost, any pain, any suffering.

Angie refuses to remember this for you.

She disappears for several days until you think she'll never come back, but she does because all your shared plans fall apart if your final memory is incomplete, and only Angie can be your final memory now because only she remembers. She finds you sleeping in the car behind an abandoned hospital, knocks on the window, and tells you how you'll kill the last memories on your list.

The next day, you clean yourselves, buy cheap, new clothes, and then go to your mother's house. She's aged much in the years since you last saw her, and she stares at you like she's seeing a ghost when she opens the door. Her joy beats out her uncertainty, though, and she welcomes you into her house—your childhood home. Memories live in every wall, door, and piece of furniture, but they'll all fade and die with the memories in your mother.

You introduce Angie as your fiancé, and tell your mother you're starting a new job soon, getting your life back on track, starting a family. All she could ever want for her son, you tell her it's happening. She's overjoyed. She makes you coffee, puts out cakes and cookies, tells you to visit more often because she wants to be close to you again. The memories swarm in her face, her eyes, her lips, her touch, so many things from your past, good, bad, light, and dark, things you might cherish if they weren't interwoven with the rot that has weighed you down for so long.

After a second cup of coffee, you excuse yourself for the bathroom, and then, while your mother talks with Angie about future
grandchildren, you slip down to the basement and rig the furnace
how Angie told you. Half an hour later, you give your mother a last
kiss, the warmest hug you've ever managed for her, and wish her
goodbye. You and Angie drive away, circle back, then park down
the block, and watch the lights go off on the first floor of your
mother's house. The single light on the second floor soon follows.
You watch the darkened house for two hours before you drive
away. Sometime in the night, you wake in the back seat, no idea
where you are, Angie watching you from the passenger seat.

She says, "Tell me about your mother."

"I... I don't remember my mother," you say.

Snapping open the door, you jump out of the car and throw up
into sand and gravel. Your body quakes; pain rips you, trying to
tear you apart. A flood of glistening, red blobs pours from your
throat, heaves and flows, pools on the ground, until you fall back
against the car exhausted. Angie helps you crawl back inside.

"Angie," you say.

I got your back, I say.

I remember for you.

Because you're too weak.

"Yes?" she says.

"Do you remember?"

"Yes."

"Okay," you say, then fall asleep.

The next morning Angie makes an anonymous phone call; the
police find your mother in her bed, dead from carbon monoxide
poisoning.

Your final memory sits across from you on a bed in a dingy motel
room off the highway, where the walls reek of cigarette smoke, and
the rumble of traffic vibrates through the building. Tears streak
down her face. All your shame and hurt swell inside her.

Your final memory speaks all the things you've done, all the memories you've killed, and how, and why. She remembers for you. All your dead memories gathered in her. Angie speaks your past. The shadows of your memories curl and twine across her face. She sips from a green bottle. She moans. Her eyes darken. Your memories swim inside them. She peels away her clothes and sits naked on the bed, her tortured flesh exposed.

"See my scars," she says. "Understand everything you're going to kill. Not only your memories, but mine too. You'll be free to live, and I'll be free from the hell I made of my life."

She hands you a gun, presses your finger around its trigger.

"I'm your final memory. You won't remember when you're done. You'll walk out of here, and the memories I've held for you will never grow back. I give you my life because it's worthless to me, and because you're a pathetic, pitiful excuse for a man who couldn't pull his shit together. People get over all the petty crap in their lives and move on, but you wallowed in self-pity. Defined yourself by your failures. Clung to your depression. Blamed everyone else for your weakness. I saw it all in you the night we met. I've hated you our whole time together, but I don't deserve to die for any better reason than to give a piece of shit like you a chance to live better. Perfect punishment for the lives I ruined. Maybe you'll find some good in all this. I hope so."

Don't be confused, I say.

I remember for you.

I got your back.

Please, do it now. Don't make me wait any longer. Don't make either of us wait.

I am your final memory.

All your darkness, sadness, hate, shame, regret, failure, loss, pain, all of it is inside me, collected and tended, nested beside my own pain and horror, for you to kill once and for all.

Writhing, squirming in my face.

Do it. This time, please.

Kill my memories too.

Squeeze the trigger.

You shudder as Angie sighs. She opens a fresh green bottle and sips.

She grips your tired hand and raises it, re-aiming the gun toward her.

"I am your final memory," she says, resigned, repeating. "You tie a humiliating old memory to a chair. You bind his hands behind the wooden back, fasten his ankles to the chair legs, the coarse rope scratching your fingers."

You have to squeeze the—

FLOWERS BLOOMING IN THE SEASON OF ATROPHY

MAX BOOTH III

1

I'M STARVING, MOMMA. I am so hungry it hurts. The pain isn't just in my stomach, but all over. It is eating me up inside, chewing me all to pieces. My head never stops hurting. I hate it, Momma. I can't stand it. I want it to go away more than anything.

And I know how to stop it—what I need to do. But I don't really want to do it; you have to believe me, Momma, it isn't my choice. I have tried for a long, long time to make the Need go away, but it's just so strong, I can't fight it anymore.

If I could tell you one thing, face-to-face, before all this happens, it would be how sorry I truly am. I never wanted any of this. I never wanted to hurt you. So you got to believe me, Momma. I'm sorry. I am so, so sorry.

2

Stuart Hardy was in the boy's restroom, napping in one of the bathroom stalls, when he heard something that sounded like thunder. Only it was sunny outside, and that noise—it had come from the hallway. Then there was another sound that followed—again, like thunder—and everyone in the high school began screaming.

Stuart did not leave the stall until much later, when the police had finally burst in searching for survivors.

3

Conrad Hillstrum was on the football team. At the rate he was going, a scholarship would be inevitable. He was dating Cindy Johnson; he believed he loved her. He was even watching her in Math, smiling to himself at how beautiful she was and how lucky *he* was, when the first bullet ended his life. He never even heard the gunshot.

4

Later, during the investigation, Henry Codwell, close friend to Conrad Hillstrum, was asked why the shooter would have targeted Conrad first.

"Look, Connie and me, we were tight, you know? We were cool. But he wasn't always cool to everyone else. Neither of us were. That boy with the gun... Connie was an asshole to him. Had been for years. Why? The boy was a freak, simple as that. Always did weird shit, ya know? If you had asked Connie about it upfront, he'd have told you he was trying to set the boy straight, make him act normal, you know, like the rest of us. But the truth was, Connie just enjoyed being an asshole. But me and him, we were cool. We were okay. God, I miss him."

5

Before Cindy Johnson passed away in her hospital room, she had been asked the same question.

"Connie never did anything to that monster. He was the love of my life. I had never met a kinder man. He did not deserve to die. He didn't deserve any of this."

6

I know, after this is all over, people are going to say a lot of mean things about me. Believe me, Momma, they are all true.

I am weird. I am sick. I am insane. I am hungry. I am me.

FLOWERS BLOOMING IN THE SEASON OF ATROPHY

7

Lisa Roberts had only been a teacher for three years. She heard horror stories like this all the time on the news, but not once had she ever considered the possibility that it could happen to her.

She even knew the shooter, the boy who had done this. She was his English teacher. Some of the papers the boy had written, they hadn't always been the most by-the-book writings. In fact, some of them had been downright strange. Especially the creative writing assignments.

Like the story he had once written about the dog who, when every time he attempted to eat, his master would kick him. Finally, it came to a point where the dog refused to eat altogether, even after he'd been taken to a new house and owner. The dog eventually died of starvation.

She thought about that story a lot these days.

8

It was the first time the President had cried on public television.

It was not a clever ploy to sympathize with the viewers. It was a real, honest to God sobbing. He was not thinking about gun control or any other future laws he would have to consider. He was not thinking about the future at all.

All he could see were the faces of those who had died. Of the one who had done the horrible shooting. Even though no names had been officially released, he had already been briefed on everyone's identity.

He did not understand how something like this could have happened. These were *his* people. His people, who today were dead. His people, who today were mourned. He had let them down. He had let the whole country down.

So he cried.

Cried not for what people would think of him, but for what he thought of them. For the first time since he began his term of office, he wondered if maybe he had chosen the wrong career.

9

Sitting offstage, out of the camera's view, the President's political advisors tried not to smile, but it was hard. They had not expected him to cry so much. Some might view it as a sign of weakness, but most would be crying right alongside him. His ratings were about to go through the roof. The hunger in their stomachs growled for victory. This was a career making moment for all of them.

10

Mary Stephenson had first heard about the shooting on the news. She nearly dropped her lunch when it came on the TV. All she could think about was Harry. *Oh, God,* she thought, *please be okay. I don't care about the rest of those kids. Just you. Please be safe. Oh, Harry.*

11

Detective Daniels approached the Stephenson household. Everything in him felt empty. Hollow. Like he was hungry; only the thought of food made him want to be sick. He couldn't do this. No, he could not do this anymore.

He rang the doorbell. Waited.

God help us. God help us all.

A woman answered the door. She looked worse than he did. And when she saw him, she completely lost it. She started screaming, pleading, "*No! Not my Harry! Oh, God, no!*"

Detective Daniels just stood there and watched, hungry for a different time, a different place, anything but this.

"Is he dead?" she asked, grabbing on to his collar. "Is my Harry dead?"

And all he could do was look down at his feet and slowly nod. He knew the agents were getting impatient back in the car. Why was he the one in charge of doing this? Why, dammit?

"Ma'am," Detective Daniels finally said, "I am going to have to ask you to let us come inside and search your son's room."

And she just looked at him, like he wasn't making any sense. "What? But why?"

"Ma'am..." He almost started choking. This was too much. Too goddamn much. "Ma'am, it is my deepest regret to inform you that your son, Harry Stephenson, took his own life this morning, after killing and injuring the majority of his Math class."

And the woman began screaming, and did not stop.

12

Momma, when you find out what I've done, you are going to hate me. And you're going to hate yourself, too, for raising such an awful little psychopath. Know this is not your fault. This is no one's fault but my own.

I am weak, Momma. I have always been weak. That's one thing the kids at school are right about. If I was stronger, I would be able to fight this sickness, this hunger. This parasite of lunacy eating me from the inside out.

I am wasting away under a very hot sun.

I am a deterioration.

I am atrophy.

So please hate me, Momma, for I deserve to be hated. But please— please—don't hate yourself. You are the best momma a boy like me could ever ask for.

13

James Oswalt straightened his tie. Last week he feared that he would lose his job. Today, he was the top reporter at his newspaper. Well, at least he would be, once they found out who he was interviewing.

Sitting across from him was the best friend of the little shit who had shot up that school.

The hunger to succeed was high in James today. He wanted his name to be known. He wanted to be a well-respected writer. This was his chance, his opportunity for fame. He would have kissed that shooter kid right on the lips if he hadn't already blown his brains out.

The interview began.

"You were his friend. Can you tell me a little bit about Harry?"

"I don't know. He was given a lot of shit from some of the bigger guys. But we were all given shit from them. I don't know."

"Did he ever come across as the type of person who would do something like this?"

"Of course not. What kind of question is that? Have you ever looked at one of your friends and thought, 'Gee, I bet underneath, this guy is a raging nutcase who one day might go on a killing spree'?"

"So you admit that you think he was mentally insane."

"Shit, man, you'd *have* to be crazy to do something like that. Harry was my friend. He had always been a little weird, yeah, but so is everyone. We're all weird in our own ways. I loved that kid like a brother. But the boy that came into our school with a gun, that was not Harry. I don't know what happened to Harry but that wasn't him."

"Do you have any idea where Harry could have gotten a firearm, or learned how to use it, for that matter?"

"No. He did not like guns. I've already told the police this. He could have gotten the gun from anywhere. I just... I don't know."

"Do you think a ban on firearms could have prevented this?"

"I don't know. I don't think it matters, there's no point in dwelling on all these 'what-ifs'. All those kids are dead. Kids I personally knew. How dare you attack me with your damn agenda?"

"I am not attacking, and I do not have an agenda. Now is the time to debate this, so we can prevent future tragedies."

"I am seventeen years old and I just lost my best friend and half my Math class. Are you serious?"

"Did Harry play a lot of violent video games?"

"Oh, give me a fucking break."

14

Lilly Stephenson refused to leave her room. The reporters waited outside like vultures circling the land for decaying carcasses. She had tried calling and texting a few friends but no one would answer her. When she logged onto her I.M. account, everyone else logged off. She googled her brother's name. She cried.

Only the reporters wanted to talk to her now. And all they wanted to talk about was the unspeakable.

She just wanted someone to love her again. It was the worst hunger in the world—to be loved.

15

Mary Stephenson sat on the couch looking over old family albums. She wished there were more pictures of her late husband, but he was the one who had always taken the pictures. Up until the cancer consumed him.

At least there were a lot of pictures of Harry as a baby. She couldn't stop looking at him. She wished she could hold him again; wished that he was still that small and innocent.

She felt sick. She always felt sick.

It had come to a point where she could no longer stand it. Her stomach was small and empty and painful. She couldn't eat anymore. She could barely even move. She just sat on the couch looking at these photos as she wasted away. And she *wanted* to waste away, was the thing. This was her punishment for not stopping her son before it was too late. She should have seen the signs. She should have paid better attention to him. Harry had been a fragile boy. He needed to be treated with care.

If only she could have a second chance. She would make things right. She would make her little boy all better and no one would be hurt.

All she wanted was to hold him again. Just one more time. She needed it. Craved it. Hungered for it.

Just to have her arms around him, to tell him everything was going to be okay.

16

Oh, Momma, I wish I had the strength to talk to you. I wish I could tell you about this hunger eating me alive. There is something in me that wants out and I can't fight it anymore, Momma, I'm gonna do bad. Oh, Momma, I am so sorry. You shouldn't have to go through this. No one should.

17

Twelve dead. Six injured.

18

Bryan Larsen was obsessed with the story.

The shooting had happened at a school a little over an hour away from his house. He couldn't stop reading articles and watching videos about it online. It was so crazy. So sad and messed up.

It amazed him how much this kid reminded him of himself. It frightened him. Since he started reading about the story, he hadn't been able to stop crying.

This could have been me...

That's what he kept obsessing over. How easily this could have been him. It *would* have been him, too, if this hadn't happened today on the news. God knew he had been planning it long enough. The hunger had been consuming him.

But now he looked at the faces of the victims from this other shooting, and he couldn't handle it. He just couldn't. All at once the hunger to revenge those who wronged him vanished. How could he have been so goddamn selfish?

Bryan tried to stop crying but couldn't. He didn't want to be another monster, didn't want to ruin anymore lives. He had been close. So, so close. Oh, God.

Bryan reached under his mattress and pulled out the handgun he had been hiding there the past couple of weeks. He walked downstairs. His mother was in the kitchen fixing dinner. He placed the gun down on the table and she stared at it for a long time. He took out the letter from his pocket and laid it out next to the gun. He had written it a week ago, before any of this had happened.

The letter opened with the following:

"I'm starving, Momma. I am so hungry it hurts. The pain isn't just in my stomach, but all over. It is eating me up inside, chewing me all to pieces. My head never stops hurting. I hate it, Momma. I can't stand it. I want it to go away more than anything."

Then Bryan said, "Momma, I think I need help."

THE COUNSELOR
MORT CASTLE

THE COUNSELOR

I am a counselor. I help with problems: stress management, self-esteem, issues related to aging and illness, all the myriad difficulties of mental and emotional health.

My vocation is challenging. I am good at it. I treat it seriously. It is a sacred calling.

In mid-September, Darby Hillison calls me.

Darby Hillison, a former "counselor"—prior to his retirement, he'd been in the academic advising department of Elvera Community College—needs counseling. There's no irony intended in my remarking that. From time to time, all of us need "objective input" presented with "empathic listening," need someone to vent and rant to, need friend, spouse, clergyman, shaman or shrink to provide sympathetic ear or cluck-clucking tongue or "cut the bullshit" or "you're avoiding the issue" or hearty pat on the back or heartier kick in the ass.

I arrive at midnight. That is often the time we visit a client, though it's not a hard and fast rule: Midnight is the balance point between day and night. But counselors are flexible. If you need to meet me at 2:38 P.M. in the lobby of the Red Roof Inn on Butterfield Road in Downer's Grove or by the bank of dryers at Laun-DRYland in Lincoln, Nebraska, that is fine, as long as it will enable us to get the job done.

The house is an older ranch, with aging vinyl siding; a cracked concrete drive leads to the attached garage.

There's the sudden illumination of a yellow bug light and Darby Hillison is at the door.

DARBY HILLISON

I ask him in. I do not *welcome* him. I do not want his company. I need his counseling. I know that.

I still think of this place as "our" house, Anna Belle's and mine. We own it. I don't think anyone actually plans to pay off a mortgage, not nowadays. Perhaps our generation is the last to establish that goal. A ceremony: We even burned the mortgage, but because we had no fireplace, we did it on the Weber kettle.

Our house.

Our generation.

My house. *My* generation.

It is no longer *Anna Belle* and *Darby* though I know that is how friends still think of us. Forgive the melodrama of my loneliness.

I miss her. I think maybe she could have helped me get through this, my Anna Belle...

On her birth certificate, it's only *Anna*. She informally added *Belle* because she liked it two years after we were married in 1966. I liked it, too. She was Anna Belle.

Strange how loss can come upon you: One day Anna Belle awoke not feeling well. This was right after my retirement from Elvera. She felt quite bad and weak and so dizzy that it was almost as though her legs wouldn't hold onto the Earth and that she might float off... All right, she actually said it, said she felt like she was *dying*. Anna Belle had a poetic nature but was not given to hyperbole. She scared me, and I was telling myself it was impossible that she could die. She needed to see a doctor and quickly.

We'd get into the Toyota Camry and I would drive her to Chadbourne County Hospital, to the emergency room. It was only 18 miles. I was in control. I was not panicked. I was a good driver. Goddamn it, I was a good driver. I *am* a good driver.

No, she said she was too *gone*—that is the word she used— even for that, so I dialed 911 and the EMTs came in the firehouse ambulance and as they were getting her into it she said very fluttery

"Oh, my" and they tried to help, they were fine young people and they knew what they were doing—I think I might even have advised one of them at Elvera some years back—but it turned out that the last words of my wife Mrs. Anna Belle Hillison were "Oh, my." It was a burst abdominal aortic aneurysm.

It is the kind of thing that can "just happen." So many things can just happen. If you ever really stop to think about all things that can *just happen*, you would go catatonic or lie whimpering under your blankets. You could go nowhere, do nothing.

The counselor sits down. I sit down. The counselor looks at me. I look around the room. There are pictures of friends' and relatives' children on the wall and the shelves. They are not our children. Anna Belle and I could not have kids.

The woman who has my position in the advising department at Elvera CC has a digital picture frame. An endless slide show like that, on what used to be my desk, it is a little disturbing, you know, like nothing is meant to stay still, nothing meant to stay as it was.

The counselor asks, "How are you?"

"All right," I say.

The counselor says nothing and blinks slowly, as though giving me a signal: *one-two-three.*

"Not so good."

The counselor nods.

"No good."

"I understand," the counselor says.

What he says is not just words. I can hear that.

Anna Belle used to read *Guideposts*, used to subscribe. There was a *Guideposts* poem she used to quote sometimes:

> *I listen not just to your words*
> *but to what makes you say them*
> *and me listen*

The counselor cants forward, hands out, as though taking a measurement. "It is six months."

It is six months and three days.

I tell him, "I need to talk."

"I know."

"About the girls," I say.

"Yes," The Counselor says.

This is the way we are put together, we normal ones. If the toothache of its own accord stops pounding with pain for more than a moment, we have to jab away at it with the tip of our tongue to set it throbbing once more.

"The girls," I say. "We must talk about them again."

THE GIRLS

Once there were four girls, BFF, and now there is one, Jessi Lynn Campbell, and she has a limp, although after two surgeries and three times a week therapy, it is much less pronounced. It is not impossible this disability will eventually vanish, or become perceptible only when she is extremely tired. Jessi Lynn has told her psychologist she is not certain she really wants to lose the limp, because—it's strange, somehow—that would be for her the irrevocable ending of the other three girls or at least the group identity they created and shared.

> *There are some things you have to let go of. You have to move on. That's the bullshit they give you. No, thank you, I don't think so, I do not think so. Utterly bogus. You lose your iPhone, okay, you let go of it, it's just a fucking phone. Your hamster dies and after a while you don't care because all it means is there's no squeaky exercise wheel waking you up at three in the morning.*

But Jessi Lynn has lost...

BFF:

1. Torme Bannings: red headed and six feet one in height, maybe a tad more, and constantly pushed toward basketball (and weren't those coaches hearing "Go, Big Red!" and seeing trophies, but *Uh-uh—no way-es imposible!"* Torme suffered from an overactive klutz gland. Back when they were all in kindergarten, the teacher always made Torme sit on the floor because that way she was "not likely to fall off." Most improper to say something like that, of course, ever so much potential damage to self-esteem. But Torme —no exaggeration—from very early on, got along quite well with herself. She knew she'd always be the tallest and the gawkiest, a spastic flamingo, knew her hair would get attention which she could either choose to accept or try to run from—and given her (non-) coordination she'd probably break both ankles. So she learned to laugh at herself, and, if you can do that, you can handle almost anything.

> *Funny, though, Torme was* good *at riding a bicycle. The rest of us still had training wheels and there she was, zooming all over the place. God, don't you hate irony?*

2. Velma Sheffield: Bold Venture Velma, rock climber and rappeller, snorkeler and skier, surfer and snowboarder. Velma the Extreme. She rode English and even with the helmet, one time when she got tossed on her head—BONK!—she saw double for two weeks, but hey, a life that's not lived is a life you're not *living*, and so as soon as the doctors said "Concussion free and good to go" she was out there jumping. Velma was cute as hell, blondicious cheerleader cute, check out that itty-bitty nose and it's genetic not rhinoplastic, and no call for orthodonture on those pearly whites. And she was smart, smart as hell, 35 on the ACT, and she had boy

friends, but they were more *friends* and she was so vivacious and up and out there—a little overwhelming for high school guys, to tell the truth, so there just weren't any romantic romances.

The Girl Gang... If Velma was there for you, she was 110% *there* for you. Always.

> *Funny, I'm saying it figures it was Velma who came up with a bicycle trip, a "senior rite of passage" (ride of passage?) and that makes sense, because Velma was the one who made stuff happen, but... I've got it in my mind that it was all of us made the decision. It was like group think.* Gestalt.

3. Mary Smith. Most American of us all, and happy to be so, and she was in her church (Methodist) youth group and played piano ("Für Elise" and "Raindrops (Keep Falling on my Head)" her favorites) and liked to bake (cookies with twice the recipe's chocolate chips) and always took Cosmo the Lakeland Terrier for a walk. Mary Smith was adopted as an infant and John and Alice Smith, her adoptive parents, had flown to Ethiopia to get her and when the time came that she could ask why she was so dark and they were nearly transparent, they explained the situation and they must have done a fine job of it because something in her reverberated in affirmation of all that could be offered by the USA. She believed in God. She believed in Obama. She believed in hard work. She earned money babysitting. She supported the troops. She had perfect attendance every year except for seventh grade when she had mono. She and her mother watched *Old Yeller* once a year to cry and *The Christmas Story* to laugh.

> *You know what gets me crying sometimes, I mean, the worst fucking kind of crying?* Mary Smith. *Mary was just so goddamn nice. And I don't mean the horseshit fakey nice that makes you reach for your insulin. She was just the*

nicest goddamn person. She was grateful *for life. She was abundantly grateful.*

These were good kids. Two of them 17, two 18, all seniors at Prairie-Way. They were mature in the right way (not cynical and snottified). If their lives were shaped by privilege, they were also laden with promise. No back story here, no addictions or self-asphyxiations, no bullying or bulimia, no cutting, purging, unprotected sex, no suicide attempts and few thoughts of death beyond the abstract, the metaphysical, the ageless wondering of adolescents (and everyone else): *Where do we go from here?* No gossip grist and gristle for *The View, Larry King, Wolf Blitzer*, the Fox Network.

Not a cliché: Everybody loved them.

Once there were four girls.

Now three are dead.

THE BICYCLE TRIP

A Spring Break trip. New bicycles? Well, a decent bike, a Marin Portofina or a BikeHard LadyCruz, you're looking at 500 to 800 bucks, but it's something they'll take to college, and it will last for years; it's not frivolous or faddish. Southern Illinois. Spring hits earlier down there than the northern part of state. Everything's green. There's rolling land and lakes and Shawnee National Forest and the town of Makanda inhabited by artists and artisans and leathery unreconstructed hippies and site of the annual VultureFest (Groovy! Look it up in your Funk and Wagnall's—that is, Wikipedia).

And they'd planned it carefully. While it's been proven the average American high schooler could not find the Grand Canyon if you dropped him into it with a GPS super-glued to his head and an iPad stuck to his ass, the girls consulted Messrs Rand and McNally, mapped out scenic routes...

But, come on, you're talking kids here—and, say, maybe I'm old fashioned, but girls at that, four girls traveling through, among other places, Williamson County, known for historical reason as "Bloody Williamson," and Nile City, aka the Midwest's Merry Meth Capital. The world is not what it used to be, you know, you hear all kinds of things...

Sure do. You will notice, *s'il vous plaît*, these kids have heads under their bicycle helmets. That's why they asked Jessi Lynn's very own personal *father*, Mr. James D. Campbell, DDS, to chaperone them.

He was flattered. He was due a vacation. He had family in Southern Illinois, had fished and boated in the summer at Lake Benton. So he'd drive along with 'em, cell phone and visual contact, roger that, and he'd try to stay out of their way when they wanted him to...

FROM THE SOUTHERN ILLINOIS HERALD

...according to police, the 68 year old driver, Darby Hillison of Thomsville, veered across a rural stretch of highway in southern Illinois and collided with the four bicyclists, killing...

...maintained that his 2004 Toyota Camry suddenly accelerated, causing him to lose control and cross the center line... no evidence of drug or alcohol impairment... safe driving record... cited for improper lane usage...

...were pronounced dead at the scene... ruptured spleen and sheered socket of the right hip, she is expected to make a full recovery...

THE COUNSELOR

Darby Hillison says, "It is not my fault."

I say nothing.

"So whose fault is it?" Darby Hillison says. "Toyota's? God Himself?"

Is this about assigning blame? The police cited him only for a minor traffic violation; there were no criminal charges filed. The mother of Mary Smith—Dear God, *Mary Smith!*—said at her child's funeral that she knew Mary would have forgiven him because that was what Christ taught and she...

Blame does not have to exist.

There *can* be accountability.

Three children are dead.

Their families can never fully heal, can never be made whole.

That's what matters.

That and what Darby Hillison feels in the depths of his heart, in his lonely house, in the silences of the long nights.

Darby Hillison is utterly still for a heavy, contemplative moment. I am here. He knows he has my support.

Then he tells me what he intends to do.

DARBY HILLISON

Darby Hillison is behind the wheel of the Toyota Camry. He starts the engine. Cars today, oh, they don't make 'em like they used to. Now, cars always start, no matter if it's raining or the temperature hits 20 below. The motor is a soft purr, so smooth and so quiet.

You can count on Toyota.

And he rolls his window down.

And he leans back in the comfortable driver's seat.

And after a while, his eyes close.

And you might think he is drifting off to sleep, there at the wheel of his car inside his garage, but he is drifting away, losing consciousness.

He is dying, is what he is doing.

And then after not very long a time, Darby Hillison is dead.

THE COUNSELOR

I am a counselor.
I help with problems.
I set things right.

DEAR BOY

JOHN BIGGS

I'M REMEMBERING THIS: grownups do not like Dear Boy. They don't like my bent legs that are a little bit too short, or my arms that are a little bit too long, or my extra thick fingers that are perfect for dancing an action figure across the table toward Little Brother's birthday cake.

I kiss the dancing man on his white plastic lips. I tell the birthday-party-people, "His name is Davy," as clear as the evening news so they have to listen.

Davy jumps like a ninja spider. He floats like an astronaut's ghost in orbit around Little Brother's cake. He pulls my hand behind him the way jet planes pull white lines across the sky. All the birthday-party-children want to be Dear Boy—only for a little while, only long enough to fly with Davy.

The birthday-party-parents want Dear Boy to be somewhere far away, some place with locked doors and fences and other boys like me. They read the icing words on Little Brother's cake; they stare at the two smoldering candles so they won't have to look at me; they pretend Davy isn't singing, "Happy birthday to you."

He sings louder and the grownups move further away, as far as they can get from the Davy-voice that bubbles in the back of my throat like phlegm.

I try to tell them, "That's how Davy talks," but the words twist around my tongue and come out backwards.

Little Brother laughs. He reaches for Davy and I pull him back in the nick of time. He takes a candle from his birthday cake as if that's what he wanted all along. He crunches it to mush with his Little Brother teeth, as deadly as a shark in the Atlantic Ocean.

Davy tells me, "Little Brother will hate us when he's older, just like everyone else." Davy knows everything I don't.

But Little Brother doesn't hate me yet. He smiles as I crawl on-to the table. The grownups pull back a little more in case someone has to stop me.

"Quickly, Dear Boy. Before they organize." Davy's phlegmy voice makes the party people clear their throats.

"Nearly there."

"What's he doing?" someone says from the back row of grownups.

"Will he hurt the baby?"

"Why would I hurt Little Brother?" The words come out in grunts and drools.

Before anyone moves my way, I throw my arms around Little Brother and kiss him on the lips. He tastes like candle wax and chocolate icing. Little Brother kisses me back. His kiss is so sweet I forget to breathe.

Davy tells me, "Little Brother steals all the love, Dear Boy. Don't let him take yours."

"Too late," I say with my thinking voice. "He's got most of it already."

"I'm your true and only friend," Davy reminds me. "I'll fix it so you're the best again. Wait and see."

Davy's phlegmy voice worries Mom.

"Get him," she says to everyone and no one.

"Get him, please!"

When she uses the magic word, Da has no choice. He lifts me off the table, holds me away from him, like he does with Kitty when she doesn't want to be picked up. I stretch my neck as far as it will go and kiss Da on the lips. He makes a face but can't pull back—not with the birthday people watching. His mouth tastes like Emily. She used to be Mom's special friend but now she likes Da better.

"Little Brother spoils it for everybody," Davy says.

The Da-kiss goes on and on, even with all the Davy phlegm talk and the sour-milk-taste of Emily. I don't know when to stop a kiss unless Davy tells me, and he's busy telling me bad things about Little Brother.

"Not potty trained, even though he's ready."

"Puts everything in his mouth."

"He's smarter and cuter than Dear Boy and he'll figure that out pretty soon."

Davy tells me Little Brothers last forever unless something happens—something no one expects but everyone watches out for."

"Matches, electric chords, choking hazards, stranger dangers." Davy lists them one by one.

When Da finally pulls away. I look around the circle of grownups who can't quit watching me. I search the circle, one face at a time until my eyes find Emily.

I point at her with one of my too-thick fingers and shout, "Whore!" It comes out perfect. Just the way Mom said it to Da this morning.

Every grownup eye is on me now. Hateful eyes. Disgusted eyes. Eyes that want to see me someplace far away.

"An institution," Davy says. "Where Mom and Da will forget Dear Boy forever."

Forever makes the world spin. A sound starts at the back of my throat, like Kitty getting a hairball ready. For a second I think it's Davy's trying to say something important, then suddenly a protective layer of vomit covers me and Da.

"Saved," Davy says.

Da curses under his breath and carries me to the bathroom to wash away our shame.

I'm remembering this: Davy called to me from a toy box in the hospital on the day I met Little Brother.

"Hey there, Dear Boy, come and get me."

There were Hot Wheels in the box and Fisher Price telephones and an airplane with a broken propeller, but Davy was the only one who talked.

"Underneath the puzzle game," he told me. "The one with shapes that fit into especially made holes."

I didn't like the triangles and circles game. I didn't want to touch it because sometimes I start playing without meaning to.

"You'll need a true and only friend when they bring Little Brother home," Davy said.

"Take me quickly before it's too late."

Da's shadow passed over me like a storm cloud that sends everyone running for the cellar.

"Time to go see Little Brother now." Da was careful not to touch me. Careful not to say my name.

There was Davy underneath the shape game exactly where he said. The whitest white plastic ever. He had a coonskin cap. One hand was at his side and the other was in the air, like he'd been holding something before a bad little boy chewed it off.

I grabbed Davy in the nick of time

"It's not stealing if the plastic man asks you," I told Da.

The words came out jumbled so he pretended not to hear. He looked at his watch to remind me how seconds turn into minutes. Minutes turn into hours. Hours turn into forever.

"Time to go."

He held out one hand so I'd take it. My hand in his, my arm stretched as far as it would go to make up for my too-short legs. He wouldn't pick me up because that would be like telling everyone I was the best he could do when it came to making sons.

He let me push the buttons in the elevator. I asked Davy if that would change when we brought Little Brother home.

He said, "Everything will change, Dear Boy—everything."

I'm remembering this: Kitty has needles in her paws. She chases things across the floor; she pretends they are alive but won't be too much longer.

"Kitty is the best killer ever." Davy shouts from my pocket. Loud, so I can hear him over the television cartoons that Da turns on when it's his turn to watch us. I take Davy out so I can hear him better, which really doesn't change things because his voice comes from the back of my throat.

Kitty likes the phlegmy sound. She stops batting Hot Wheels and bumps her face against mine. She purrs like the refrigerator motor. Warm and friendly, but her breath smells like rotten meat.

Davy says, "Don't let her get me, Dear Boy. She'll chase me under the couch for sure."

That's what kitty does with everything. There are Hot Wheels under there, and Ben Ten action figures, and marbles from the Chinese checkers game Mom put away after Little Brother learned to crawl. Things have been under the couch since forever, all chased there by Kitty.

Little Brother stops chewing on the leg of a plastic cow and bangs it on roof of his Fisher Price barn.

"Ki…" Little Brother reaches a hand in Kitty's direction; he grabs the air with his fingers. "Ki…"

Kitty turns one ear in Little Brother's direction, but the rest of her is pointed at Davy. She nudges him with her paw. She keeps her needle claws safely hidden, because so far it's just a game. When I fly Davy over Kitty's head she stands on her back feet and makes an electric sound, like before she kills a butterfly.

"Ki…" Little Brother pushes a button inside his Fisher Price barn and makes a sheep noise that's not as interesting as Kitty's butterfly killing sound. He throws his plastic cow at me.

"Ki…" Little Brother wobbles as he stands. He falls onto his bottom. He stands again—so interested in Kitty he forgets to cry.

"Dear Boy!" Davy is too nervous to make a plan.

"He wants Kitty, Dear Boy. Stop him!"

What can I do? Little Brother gets everything he wants. My best toys, Da's best smiles.

"Ki…" Little Brother wobbles across the room.

Kitty falls over on her side instead of running. She curls her paws, pretending Little Brother doesn't want her. She tries to keep her needle claws from coming out because the worst thing in the world is hearing Little Brother Scream.

I try to tell him no but the no's get tangled behind my tongue. Finally they break loose at once and come out in a shriek.

"Noooooo!" Not as clear as a television word but it gets Da's attention. It gets Kitty's attention too. Her ears lay back. Her tail twitches like she's getting ready to climb the curtains and doesn't care who's watching.

When Little Brother grabs her, Kitty's needles come out. He screams even louder than I did, but he doesn't let go until she draws scratch lines across his face.

Da moves slow at first, like a train that might not make it to the top of the hill. Then he speeds up, without seeing anything between him and his only perfectly good son.

Da's knee knocks me on my back so hard I drop Davy. Da has Kitty in both hands, shaking her, calling her all the "Goddamned" names Mom doesn't like to hear. He opens the sliding glass patio door and tosses Kitty way too hard into a holly bush. He picks up Little Brother, but he doesn't throw him into the holly. He kisses the scratched places. He runs his fingers through little brother's hair. He tells Little Brother, "That bad old kitty lives outside now. She'll never bother you again."

I'm at the patio door, watching Kitty climb out of the holly bush. Davy calls to her but she's afraid since Da went crazy.

"Little Brother spoiled things for Kitty," Davy says. She won't come close, even when he waves to her with his plastic hand. The reflection of Da's face is big and mean when he looks toward the patio door. Some of the meanness gets through to Kitty but most of it bounces against the glass and falls on me and Davy.

I'm remembering this: Little Brother likes plastic action figures. He sits by the patio door watching Kitty through the glass, tapping on it with a green soldier whose head has been chewed off.

Kitty is killing bugs and watching Little Brother in case he's learned to open doors all by himself. He holds the green plastic man where she can see it, twists the soldier between his fingers so his spit reflects spots of sunlight onto the living room ceiling.

"Da's turn to watch us again, Dear Boy." Davy dives off of the coffee table and bounces on the carpet. I pretend it's the Atlantic Ocean full of sharks that will get Davy if he doesn't swim to shore pretty fast. He hops onto my knee in the nick of time, ready for another adventure.

"You never know what is going to happen with Da around." Davy flips into the carpet-ocean again, ignoring the sharks because they are pretend, paying close attention to Da because he's real.

He pays so much attention to Da that he doesn't notice Little Brother crawling across the floor. Pretending he's a baby. Babies never get punished for anything, no matter how bad. Dear Boys get punished for everything, even things that aren't their fault. Sometimes Dear Boys get a smack if Mom isn't around to see.

Before Davy can swim to safety, Little Brother has him. Faster than a shark, he puts Davy in his mouth.

"Help me, Dear Boy!"

Kitty watches everything through the patio door. Da watches from his Lazy Boy recliner. Kitty can't do anything. Da could help, but he doesn't care if Little Brother chews Davy's head.

I try to shout but the words get stuck. I try to cry, but my tears don't work and Da wouldn't care anyway, so I pretend to be a TV super hero and jump on Little Brother.

Like Super Man. Like the Incredible Hulk. Like the biggest strongest Dear Boy ever. I land on Little Brother and snatch Davy and try to get away before Da knows what's happening.

Not fast enough. Da grabs me by the shoulders and shakes me hard enough to vibrate the world. I make the hairball sound, but my protective layer of super hero vomit won't come fast enough. He pries Davy from my hand and gives him to Little Brother.

"Help me, Dear Boy!"

I don't know what to do and it's hard to think of anything with

Da so close and almost angry enough to smack me.

"Help me!" Davy's head is all the way into Little Brother's mouth, but his voice is still in my throat.

Kitty bats at the glass patio door. She has a spider trapped under her paw, struggling to get away, but it's as hopeless for the spider as it is for Davy.

"It's either me or Little Brother," Davy tells me. "Choose quickly, Dear Boy. Who's your true and only friend?"

Kitty bats the spider off the glass. Knocks it under a lawn chair with a killing blow.

Now I know exactly what to do.

I reach underneath the couch, where Kitty has been batting toys forever. Here is a domino. Here is a plastic Ben Ten action figure. Lots of things that Little Brother wants, but there is something under the couch that Little Brother wants even more than dominoes and plastic men. Something I can trade for Davy.

Marbles! From the Chinese checkers game I never learned to play. Put away by Mom because marbles are dangerous.

"Choking hazard," Mom said. Too dangerous for Little Brother to resist. Once marbles get into a little boy's mouth, they go where nothing is supposed to be.

"Save me, Dear Boy!" Davy's head is already twisting on his neck. In another second it will be too late.

"Look!" The word comes out television clear. I roll the marbles against each other on my palm. The click is perfect. The sparkle is even better. Little brother takes Davy out of his mouth, compares the beauty of the marbles to the white plastic face of a half chewed action figure.

The swap goes so fast, Da doesn't know what's happening. In a second, little brother has the marbles in his mouth. In two seconds they are sliding into the danger zone where they will stop him from spoiling one more thing.

He tries to scream but nothing comes out. He tries to cry but he's already blue. Da turns Little Brother upside down, holds him by his legs, smacks him on the back, trying to shake the marbles loose, but nothing comes out.

I hide Davy in my pocket and wait to see what happens next.

I'm remembering how grownups love Little Brother best of all. They've dressed him in a special suit and laid him in a shiny wooden box that's only big enough for him. Some of them cry. Some of them touch his face. Some of them tell Mom and Da, "You're still young. You can have more children."

"Dear Boy loves you," I tell Mom to remind her of the son she has who isn't *in a better place*. Dear Boy is here. Dear Boy is now. Dear Boy is forever. I try to kiss her but she cries instead of kissing back. Da takes me on his lap and tells me I'll see Little Brother again someday. He combs my hair with his fingers and sings a song so softly I can't understand the words.

"You won't see him again," Davy tells me. "Never, Never, Never." Davy has a plan.

Everybody hears his voice at the back of my throat and they think I'm crying. They've been waiting for my tears since Little Brother choked.

Mom told Da I couldn't cry because I was in shock.

The doctor told them, "He doesn't understand. Too young to comprehend, even if he wasn't developmentally disabled."

Now they think I'm crying just like everybody else. Mom kisses me. Da pats me on the back. Strangers gather around and tell me, "Everything will be all right.

Words like *Heaven* and *Angel* spin around me like water going down the bathtub drain, and before long I really am crying. Even though I don't want to see Little Brother again, and I don't believe he's in a better place.

"Cry louder, Dear Boy," Davy tells me.

I can feel his plastic body pressing on my chest from inside my shirt pocket. I can feel the sharp places on his head left behind by Little Brother's teeth. That makes me cry harder, because those tooth marks are forever and Little Brother isn't.

"Would you like to see him?" Da asks. "Shall I hold you up?"

I try to say no, but Davy answers for me, a deep and phlegmy, "Hold me up!" as clear as Mom sobbing, "Our baby's dead!"

Da flies me over to Little Brother the way I fly Davy over the pretend Atlantic Ocean, the way I fly him over Kitty's head so she can't bat him under the couch.

"Kiss!" Davy calls out from the back of my throat. He's out of my pocket now, in my hand, moving toward Little Brother like a television super hero flying off to save the day.

"Think it'll be OK?" Da asks Mom. "Think I should let him?"

"What harm..." Mom's talking like she's not really sure, but she doesn't want to think about it.

"What harm can it do?" she says as Da lowers me over Little Brother. I kiss him on the lips.

ChapStick, fingernail polish, Black Flag Ant Killer.

"Put me in Little Brother's pocket," Davy tells me. His plan bubbles out of the back of my throat one phlegmy piece at a time.

"You have to do it, Dear Boy."

I want to ask him why, but I'm too full of tears to talk except with Davy's voice.

"Because," Davy answers the question I never asked, "It will break their hearts, Dear Boy. It will make you the best all over again."

"Forever," Davy says as I slip him into Little Brother's jacket pocket.

"Forever and forever." When they close the box, Davy is inside. It's a better box than the one he lived in at the hospital.

Mom and Da wrap their arms around me, crowd me between them so hard I almost disappear.

"You're the best," Mom says in a bubbly voice almost exactly like Davy's.

"The very best," Da says. All according to the plan.

I'm remembering this: Davy knows everything I don't.

INTERFERENCE

ANDREW HOOK

MY PARENTS TOLD ME the first word I read was *ambulance*.

I was three years old. We were driving through Peckham Rye, South London, when the interior of our vehicle was lit by flashing lights and a familiar siren wove its way in and out of our ears. In those days no one wore seatbelts. I used to recline on the back seat of the Ford Cortina and sleep, my head resting on my older sister's legs whilst she stroked my hair. I don't remember the sirens and I don't remember the lights, but my parents said I rose to a kneeling position and looked out of the rear window.

My dad told me to sit down.

Ambulance, I said; and pointed to the vehicle bearing down on us as my dad waited for a few loose pedestrians to move so that he could pull up on the pavement and let it pass.

"That's clever, Rhys," my mother had said.

My sister said, "Duh! He's reading it backwards." She oscillated from believing me very stupid or very clever.

"It's just that he knows it's an ambulance," my dad said, steering the car back to the road as the vehicle passed.

Apparently my mother had nodded. The incident would have been forgotten if I hadn't then said: "E C N A L U B M A. Ambulance."

I never leave the house without a mirror. I've learnt to palm it, a conjuror's trick where I am both magician and spectator. This way I can see both worlds at once. The world that *you* know, where everything is as it should be; and the world that I know where everything is reversed. I tried to explain this to a girlfriend once, who caught me looking at her via a mirror as she lay on her front, naked on my bed.

"It's about perception," I said, "It's about seeing things simultaneously."

Michelle was open to understanding. Her Lydia Lunch record was playing, the cover of *Some Velvet Morning* where Lunch duets with Rowland S. Howard and their voices overlap in a disconnected yet weirdly compelling sequence. Even so, I felt she leant towards my mirror as some kind of perversion. "Tell me about it," she said.

"Next time you're on a train you should stand in the middle of the aisle. Look straight down the centre of the compartment. Everyone is static. Yet in the peripheries of your vision you'll see the outside world on both sides rush past as though sucking you into a vortex. That's how I see the world most of the time."

She buried her face in the pillow, opened her legs wide so that my gaze was directed between those two narrow limbs and channelled towards the tunnel at their apex. "Is it like this?" she asked.

We fell into each other. Those were the good times.

I palm the mirror in my right hand because I am naturally left handed and that way I can still operate within the world without it being awkward. The fingers of my right hand are almost permanently cupped. When I remove the mirror at the end of a journey there is a squared indentation of flesh that remains in my palm. Before she left me, Michelle had warned that I'd have arthritis one day.

Leonardo Da Vinci was left-handed. Many of his notes are in mirror-image cursive. Some believe this was due to secrecy, although as a code it seems suspect to me. Others believe it was through expediency, mirror writing enabled his fingers to keep up with his brain and it would have been easier to write from right to left without smudging. All I know is that Da Vinci was a genius, and sometimes I glimpse a fraction of what he must have known and seen; but I can't focus on it, like *presque vu* those images, those *words*, remain just out of perception and reach.

The sensation of not being in syncopation with the world has dogged me through every relationship, has harnessed me to the whims of others. I imagine this is why each interaction has failed. And whilst that failure buys me freedom, so with freedom comes loneliness.

◇

My parents were punked-up ex-hippies with one toe in the sixties and the other in the seventies.

"Try him with Rhys," my mother said.

I remember these memories. It would have been a month on from the ambulance episode and Sunday afternoons were spent with pen and paper, my pre-school days learning about myself instead of others.

S Y H R, my father wrote on the paper.

"Rhys," I said.

"Damn," said my mother, "he heard me."

"Of course he heard you; you should learn to shut up."

Annoyance simmered on my mother's face. By now I was used to their arguments. They didn't know how to deal with me.

R E H T O M, my father wrote on the paper.

"Mother," I said, and then my father wrote L O O F. And so it went on; word after word after word.

My sister leant against the door jamb. Outside it rained hard, each drop hit the windowpane like a question mark. I remember watching her watching us, realising she had become an outsider because she was normal. There was dislocation there too, with her as well as me. My learning disability had come between us, caused interference.

I use the term *learning disability* lightly. I have not been diagnosed with such. Throughout my childhood years the system was patient with me. My teachers were provided mirrors so they could mark my essays. Unlike many others who naturally write their way out of the conundrum and reverse their behaviour, or who are forced into learning to write *proper*, I was not coerced into being someone I wasn't. It is those progressive teachers who I blame for my capacity now.

They should have fixed me.

I duck down into the crawlspace which serves as a storage area that runs behind my bedroom in the flat that I rent. It's an anomaly of the house, an aberration of the builders that was then converted into something useful. You can't stand in it. The door itself is Alice In Wonderland-ish. Whilst I don't have to eat something to become small enough to enter, there's a certainty that if I ate too much then I wouldn't be able to fit inside.

Dark presses around me. The crawlspace is not dissimilar to a coffin. I lay on my back and still my breathing. In here there are no indications of the real world, pulsing on the outside like the chambers of a heart. There are no words, no jumbles of misunderstanding. Its position almost makes it soundproof. It's a cocoon from which I always emerge reborn, if only for a few moments.

It's those few moments that I crave.

Nowadays I'm known as Matt. Rhys is consigned to the past. Although Matt itself isn't specific enough. It has to be MATT. MATT is the only way that I can be.

Two dimensional objects, such as alphabetical letters, are not chiral due to the existence of a horizontal symmetry plane, but many of them do become chiral when written on a piece of paper. So the mirror images of the uppercase letters A H I M O T U V W X Y are virtually identical; except for some line thickness and minor artistic details associated with particular choices of fonts. The lowercase letters are all asymmetric except i m o v w x.

One afternoon I spent some time with those letters, rearranging, attempting to find meaning. But I only found my new name. It didn't matter that it still needed to be written back to front, as TTAM; what was important was that its integrity remained in the mirror.

The expression that the camera never lies has always been a falsehood. We can never see ourselves as others see us. This is also true in respect to mirrors. The face reflected back at you is reversed. Either everyone else sees the real you, or none of them do. You choose.

I have drilled a hole in the back of the crawlspace that emerges within a spiral pattern on the wallpaper on the other side. Into the hole I press a fisheye lens, so that when I put my eye to the hole I can see the curved entirety of my bedroom. Yet this is actually just a reflection. What I'm really looking at is the mirror which dominates the opposite wall.

Later when I look through this hole I wonder if I'll see myself enter the room and lay on the bed.

Michelle left when she realised my weirdness was innate and not affected. She was comfortable in it being an act, but not as reality.

"It's not you," she lied. Then paused. "Well, it *is* you."

I had been cutting a red pepper into tiny slivered strips, ready to be thrown into the wok alongside the carrot, spring onion, and bean sprouts which would make up the rest of the chow mein. The slivers resembled arteries.

Focussing on meals helped me concentrate on the world. There was a clear delineation between cause and effect. I hated interruptions when cooking.

"Does this mean we're eating together or not?"

My teeth were pressed tight. Seeds shot out from the side of the pepper as I sliced into the second half.

"It means I don't know about us, is all."

Michelle was back-peddling. Maybe she'd always thought that way, had been desperate to express it, but then once she had the reality of what she was saying undermined her ability to believe it. All I know is that I turned right then, the tip of the blade pointing towards her stomach, in what I hadn't realised was an aggressive gesture. And because she got scared, she didn't come back. I had given her the excuse that she needed.

On the bus I read the headline of the newspaper of the man sitting opposite. I have to be careful with the mirror. Sometimes it catches the light, reflects it into the eyes of the person I'm observing. There have been a few embarrassing moments. Girls think I'm trying to look up their skirts, but I would never do this. I already know the truth that they think is hidden there.

I get off at my stop. Walk forwards whilst looking backwards into the mirror. The future recedes as the past abates. Or is it the other way around?

I read words on advertisement hoardings, house numbers, the names of shops, all correctly represented in the mirror.

Interestingly, from some of the letters A H I M O T U V W X Y you can spell *mouth*.

At the retirement home my mother's mouth gapes open. I nudge the base of her chin with my forefinger and close it for her. Moments later it hangs again, like a faulty trapdoor.

After her stroke a few years back she developed acquired mirror writing. The neurologists were particularly interested, knowing my background. It appeared the stroke affected various peripheral and deep locations in her left hemisphere, but it was transient, lasted for just a few weeks, and was confined to a few letters, words and sentences. My mother was ambidextrous, but the mirror writing only affected her left hand. With her right hand she continued to write normally.

For me, the interesting factor was that she didn't realise she was doing this. She rode those two pathways simultaneously.

Just as on the train, with the interior static and calm and the outside world forcing itself either side; coming at you in a rush.

The neurologist spoke in detail of the corpus callosum, about transcallosal deactivation of contralateral crossed pathways. All of this went over my head. It was when he brought up Da Vinci that my attention clicked back in.

"Of course, centuries ago some academics viewed mirror writing as the natural script of the left-hander. It's a compelling view. One that retains some credence today."

He repeatedly moved his hand back and forth across his head as he spoke. A nervous tic manifested and heightened by my presence. He continued:

"The evidence that mirror writing is the natural script of the left hander arises from everyday observations that abductive movements are generally more natural, and also more accurate, than adductive movements. Writing with a pen held in the left hand will therefore be more readily undertaken leftwards; the script, too, would then be reversed compared with the conventional rightward directed script—that is, mirrored.

"So, mirror writing with the left hand is not a bizarre form of writing at all, but predictable, and presumably a form of writing that is normally suppressed or superseded by conventional writing in order to be read."

I saw then how conventional writing *interfered* with my natural ability. How the real world tried to impose—to superimpose— itself over the world that I saw.

Or, to put it my way, how the world tried to superimpose itself over the *real* world that I saw.

I jiggle my mother's jaw. The second stroke slackened everything in her body and mind. Forwards or backwards, she wouldn't be writing again.

My sister enters as I leave. Dad doesn't come, of course; that relationship is long gone. Neither of us sees much of him, but then we probably wouldn't have done anyway. I don't even see much of my sister, but I always remember lying on the back seat of the car with the sun burning the rectangle of the back window, and one of her hands in my hair with the other holding a book that occasionally would slip and drop onto my face.

"How's it going?" she always says.

I always reply *fine*.

Then she continues into my mother's room and I re-emerge from the crawlspace that is her confinement and have to find my place within the world again.

Integrity remains in the mirror.

There's a fascination with mirrors in everyone. Mirrors are a cliché of horror movies: the glimpse of something standing behind you which wasn't there a moment ago. The specialists who examined me when I was a child used to impress on me that my writing could only be read when viewed in a mirror. What they failed to perceive was that my writing could only be understood by *them* that way. For me, it was perfect already.

I don't need the mirrors to see the world as I see it, but to see the world as you see it.

And I need to do that to exist in that world, because that world predominates over mine.

But there are things I can do: the modification of the crawl-space, the use of mirrors to confuse and contain, to subtly subvert the expectations of those who don't see things the way I do. To reclaim the world as it should be seen.

After Michelle there was Justina. We were once eating in Soho in a tiny Thai restaurant which had just enough space for diners with the kitchen at the rear and a toilet at the bottom of a perilous set of stairs. Justina descended those steps and turned into the full-length mirror which reflected the doorway on the opposite side.

In bed I kissed the raised skin on her forehead. The restaurant had waived the price of our meal, and from the money saved a large box of individually wrapped Belgian chocolates sat on our nightstand. I took out a chocolate, divested it of the coloured paper, and held it close to the bulb within the bedside lamp until the tips of my fingers hurt and the chocolate began to drip. I wrote the word EROHW across her stomach and she laughed and hit me and I bent my head to lick off the words and we fucked like there was no tomorrow.

Once she was asleep I slipped out of bed and into the crawlspace. I watched her in the dim glow from the streetlight outside the window, through the fisheye, with her body reflected in the mirror.

Sometimes I'm just as normal as everyone else.

If it had been *my* head that had hit the mirror this is what would have happened:

I would have awoken the following day in hospital. Bleary-eyed, I would have looked from left to right, then right to left. There would be no mirror in my hand. A surge of panic would fly through my limbs and into my throat, but then I would pause, allow my breathing to regulate, would remember.

And I would see, quite clearly, the world as everyone else saw it, without reflection. That would be how it would be if I had hit my head in the mirror.

It's no coincidence that when I went for an eye-test the ophthalmologist asked me to look at a chart which read:

A

H I

M O T

U V W X Y

My existence flits between acceptance and anger, shards of my life oscillate against each other with a grinding noise; or—when I feel particularly displaced—the interference manifests itself through the sound of ripping paper. A continual tear.

A few years before Da Vinci died he was commissioned by the King of France to make a mechanical lion which could walk forward, then open its chest to reveal a cluster of lilies.

That was almost five hundred years ago.

Historical records are not clear on the circumstances of his death. My belief is that as he rushed towards the void he would have seen everything and nothing simultaneously: an extension of the life that he led.

The pressure of knowledge, of the unseen world being a reflection of the seen world, is a heavy burden to bear. Lesser folk might be driven mad.

Imagine an old-fashioned printing press. The device applies pressure to a print medium such as paper that rests on an inked surface made of moveable type, and in the process transfers the ink. The letters on the press are individually set by the printer. But they're not set in the conventional way that you could read them, because their shapes have to be mirrored onto the paper. For centuries, therefore, knowledge has been transferred from the format I can already understand to a format that you can understand. Which of us has the learning disability now?

One of these days that pressure will become too great. I'll stand at the junction and watch each car. I'll remain static whilst they pass in a blur of confusions and misunderstandings. The world will press in on me, imprinting all its words that insist in being in the wrong order on my mirror-written brain. That pressure, that insistent inescapable force, will cumulate and persist until I discern a larger than average white vehicle out of the oncoming traffic, until the delineation between pavement and highway, between vehicle and myself, becomes equally blurred.

Maybe there'll be lights—maybe there'll be sirens—but I know the last word I will read will be ECNALUBMA. My left hand will be embedded with glass.

PICTURE-IN-PICTURE

DUSTIN LaVALLEY

HE RUNS...

A boy of ten years old, wearing a faded flannel shirt, dirty blue jeans, sneakers and a wool cap on his head of short dark hair runs along the sidewalk of a street ignored by time. The houses stuck in the golden age between the birth of baby-boomers and the Korean War. The paint on their full porches chipped and the wood splintered. No distinction between the next and the last other than the pattern of decay. Ripping through the air like lightening, feet stomping the ground like thunder, he huffs and puffs and his chest rises and falls with each breath. His adolescent energy pushed to its margin by fear, confusion and horror.

The boy continues to run as he and his world are brought up to the corner in a small box to allow a dirty man in a clean room to appear in full-screen. In that corner the boy runs, never stopping. He runs and he runs and he runs...

The dirty man, his best clothes on his back soiled and tattered, sits slouched in a wooden chair; its legs creak as he adjusts his weight. The room, whitewashed, bland and sterile, is empty and devoid of any and all things living besides this man and his story. A juxtaposition of extremes: the man and the room, the cleanliness of the air and the filthiness of his voice. Side by side they couldn't have less connection...

"Blood is the fuel of life. Women are said to be at their wildest during their menstruation. I've never had a problem with a little blood. Period sex has its ups and downs. Well, no, I guess if you don't mind blood it's all positive. I don't mind. Blood that is, never bothered me. Some people are bothered by only their own blood, others the other way round. But me, nah, neither one. I could bleed or make another bleed; blood is blood to me. Sex though... I've had my share. Oh, have I had my share. I've seen some messed up fetishes and I don't mind, really. You want a donkey, a steamer, another man, another woman, a lady-boy... I don't mind, never been one to pass judgment. Rough, loud, hair-tugging tit-smacking bound and gagged, blind-folded, hands on neck good old assertive, dominative sex. Now that's what fucking is about! A little blood comes by the hand… that's just a sign of good sex. A lot of people don't even know what sex is; they lie on top of each other, that's what they do. That's not sex. It's blood, sweat, bitten collarbones and swollen ass cheeks. That's sex. It's like a drug, good sex that is. And drugs, they only make it even better. Not a damn thing wrong with sex and drugs. Not a damn thing wrong with drugs at that…

The box in the corner fades to black and from within that darkness, a picture comes in clear…

In a quickened pace the young boy weaves through his home, past darkened rooms without doors and doorways standing with a slant… broken and buckled foundation beams giving the stained, discolored walls a feel of unease to any unsuspecting visitor. His feet come to a stop and he fumbles with the door-knob of a bedroom. It opens and he takes a step inside, a room lit neon orange by a sign of a beer logo. He hesitates, ready to go forth but stalling at the sight of his parents. Beautiful is his mother, ugly his father-figure—the house's self-proclaimed ruler—in the nude. She rides him, bare skin glossy in the light. Large, soft breasts sway across a trim stomach as she gyrates against his thrusts. Her long, curly blonde hair tickles the arch of her back as she lets her head loll side to side.

For the boy, the moment between first sight and reaction of the man who claims to be ruler and father plays out like hours. He grabs an empty bottle, yells and tosses it at the child. Though caught aghast, the boy ducks in time for the glass to crash against the hallway wall. He witnesses his mother's face contort into a horrid display of befuddled anger and he shuts the door as she yells, "Get the fuck *out!"*

The boy retreats, searching for an exit; he seems lost in his own home. Slowing for doorways that he does not enter, eyeing the darkness for a way out before continuing on.

He runs and as he runs…

The dirty man in the chair continues his story on the large main screen.

…LSD, Lysergic Acid Diethylamide, acid. Ain't nothing can

top that. Let me trip, leave me there, I'll be fine. Weed, nah, not my top choice but nothing wrong with a bubbling bong, nothing wrong with hash cakes. Too tame. Never did a thing for me. Pity what the hippies did to that wonder drug. Dirty, filthy fucking hippies! It's non-addictive and beneficial for pain, used by all sorts for all sorts of ailments from cancer to headaches, anxiety to depression. Man, those filthy fucking hippies ruined it for everyone. Okay, not all of us, but those of us too scared to find it these days. Of course there are side effects, but nothing compared to the shit kids are injecting and now those synthetic bath salts. Jesus, compared to other drugs today, weed is candy cigarettes…

The picture in the corner, the small box containing the child once again shows him on the sidewalk of his neighborhood. His sneakers meet the crumbling, uneven concrete with urgency as he runs and runs…

…Sticking needles in your arm, now that's fucked. Never been any good reasons so stick a needle in your arm. There's too much risk in that, too much risk. People these days, they're disgusting. The rich, the poor, doesn't matter who, they're filled with all sorts of shit. Aids, HIV, Hep-B, the list goes on and on. List so long it's impossible to know of 'em all. Leave the needles alone or you'll end up with some whore's needle sticking in your arm injecting AIDS into yourself. Boom! Death-warrant signed…

The picture of the boy repeats, it sizzles and pops in a snowfall. Frames climb the screen. The same few milliseconds of images replay like celluloid unraveling from the spool or a bad connection on a local television station during an electrical storm. Then, it clicks and the boy is walking up the stairs of a house similar to his own, similar to all the homes on the street which are similar to all the homes in the neighborhood. The door is ajar, noise spills out of the space and he opens it just enough to sidestep inside.

Music envelopes the boy as do billows of smoke. The house is illuminated with red, green, blue and other various colored lighting. His rush comes to a halt. He stands in the middle of a room surrounded by teenagers and twenty-somethings partying. An orgy of drugs hard and soft and alcohol fruity and straight, men and women between the wisps and behind the strobes, many are melted into one another—hands roaming and tongues prodding—in make-out sessions and future regrets. The fear, the confusion and helplessness remains on his face as he scans the foreign land for a familiar body.

There is technical trouble again as the picture freezes on the boy's expression and the man in the whiteness speaks of demise.

...Death. Now that's something you can't touch on without some self-righteous, religious pecker-head telling you you're wrong no matter what you believe in. Atheist, Christian, Muslim, Jewish, Agnostic, we all die. There's no pearly gates, no hundred virgins, no kingdom in the heavens, no Santa Claus or Easter Bunny. You die and you're dead, nothing more. Worm food, one with the soil, ash off the cliff...

The box in the corner begins to skip. Forward, backward, possibly sideways. It is not known.

The boy sits on the back porch. His hands stuffed in his pockets, his legs dangling and eyes on the ground. He is caught in thought when he flinches and whips his head up and toward the sound of a pop. A few beats pass before he drops to the ground and begins to walk in the direction from where the noise came. Head down, watching his sneakers scuff the ground as he walks, hands deep in those pockets, he takes his time.

As the boy approaches the garage, in what seems to be the same lapping image, the dirty man's story in the talking picture interrupts.

...It's like going to sleep I imagine. Sleeping without dreaming. You ever have a night with no dreams? Then you know what death feels like. The process of dying, that's something else. Dying can be long and drawn out, painful or quick and over with. Not always your choice but if you had the choice, if I had the choice? Shit, I don't know. I figure if I was going slowly in pain, I'd drug myself up like they do those terminal cancer patients. Load 'em up so high they don't give two shits...

The boy in the corner reaches the garage. It takes his whole strength to open one of the large, double-wide doors. They're outdated, more fitting for that of a barn as it once was. Now used as a two car hold and workstation. The light of the fading sun casts a cockeyed shadow across a body slumped against the tool bench and the paved floor. The boy wanders forth and stares at his older brother. Blood pours from his mouth, ears and nose. At the end of an extended arm, a .38 revolver is stuck in his right hand. The index finger curled in the trigger guard. The boy mutters a name and of course there is no response. He makes a small step and, as he does so, gently nudges his brother's sprawled out legs. The dead boy's upper body slides down, following the momentum of his head which meets the floor with a wet thump.

The boy is about to burst into a frantic run when the box freezes. The moving picture paused by an unseen force with access to remote viewing. He is not much unlike a two dimensional stick-figure giving chase or being pursued.

The man, again... the dirty man in the sterile room stays on topic.

...Sometimes I think about death. Not about dying or what happens after or before, but death itself. You know, like what color is death? What's its story? Is death religious, does it believe in a god or gods or is it a secular humanist? Does it like music? If so, what kind? You'd think metal, something heavy and fast, right? Something that might cause you to go out blazing, suicide by cop or depress you enough to overdose on sleeping pills. Is it political? Does death have a seat in the GOP, does it ride a pink elephant? This is the stuff the mind wonders but no one talks about. Masturbation is a thing of the past—we're all open to it now; it's not hush-hush anymore—but this, what death is, this no one talks about. Why not? Fear. We fear and we keep our mouths shut. Otherwise, we might end up like some bumbling, stinky crackpot on the street. Shunned by society and burdened by cultural norms. Beggars and bums...

Pause is removed and in a flash the boy is gone, sprinting from the garage and down the driveway. He is up the back stairs and through the back door as if... as if he has just seen a dead man...

...Sweat-pan money. That's what life is about for some. Bums and beggars, roaches and rats is what we are. We're not people and we're not human beings; we're vermin and we're trash. We're on the street and the street is hard. Street life, ain't nothing harder than a street life. Gotta be shameless. Can't have dignity. If you do, it's taken from you, stripped, skin becomes hard as steel. It's gotta be. If you have too much pride to ask a passerby for a few bucks, some change, a cigarette, then you're done. You can't have pride; it's gone. You're shameless, you're stripped nude and naked...

As if taken from a parallel dimension or a deleted scene, up in the corner box, the slightly altered progression to his parents' room for the boy is in a more ardent manner. The paint has flow and matches the trim, the house stands without a slant, and when he opens the door to the bedroom they are moaning in the dark. No neon lighting, no nude bodies, only darkness and the sounds of lovemaking. He shuts the door, fast, but unnoticed by the two inside. There is no beer bottle flung and no yelling to chase him as he runs through the house the way from which he came. Taking every turn and movement with foreseen recognition, he knows the layout and the route to the front door without a misstep.

...They pass you by. Snub you, cross the street. Hold their breath, press their kids tighter to their sides as if they'll be snatched up, swallowed whole by the street itself. It can happen though. It happens and until it does you never know if this is your last night in a bed, at a dinner table, in a warm shower with shampoo. Those little things: the smell of perfume, steam of a warm bath, taste of fresh fruit. Those little things...

The boy in the box stumbles out the front door and down the steps, almost taking a fall as one foot scuffs the other. Regaining balance, his pace picks up and he runs on that crumbling concrete sidewalk.

And the man rambles on.

...When you're on the street, there's no downtime, no nothing, no de-stressor. It's dropping your pride, forgetting your dignity and holding out that expression, that pitiful yet somewhat scary expression you need to put out for that bit of change you're asking for. You look clean, you speak well, you ask the right people, you can show 'em, let 'em know you're not trash, but even then you're still trash to them, ya know? They may give you a few bucks, but it's for their own peace of mind, not you. They couldn't give two shits. Probably thinking you'll go out and waste it on booze, not that you need a sandwich, not that you're literally dying of dehydration and malnutrition. No, they'd keep that far from their mind and let you die long as it's in the back alleys, behind a dumpster where they can't see. Behind a dumpster, unseen and unheard and in their world, you don't exist...

The tracking shot of the boy smash cuts to him standing in his neighbor's house. He is surrounded by teenagers and twenty-somethings. There is no smoke billowing, no drugs being used and there is neither loud music nor multicolored lighting. The party greets him with stares and slack-jaws, their mouths open but wordless, perhaps caught in curiosity by his sudden appearance during mid-conversation. They're silent, taking in the sight of a child out of place. He stands near the door and scans across the room at the perplexed partygoers before spinning around and running out the door where the box turns black.

From the dirty man in the whitewashed room comes a brief break from his nonsense, a hint of textbook wisdom.

I may not look it, but I'm smart. Believe me. I read books, lots of 'em. Text books, too. From the library, where I'm allowed but looked down on and watched. I know lots, but mostly I know about death. I know death well. You know there are many stages? Death isn't simple. There's sociological death, when your friends, family and others aware of your presence in this place accept that you're about to die. Then there is psychological, when you yourself accept that you're dying. And then there's biological, which is pretty straight forward. The body dies...

From the blackness of the screen inside the corner box, the boy emerges. Running as fast as he can, huffing and puffing as his young lungs work themselves as hard as they can, weary of the ruined concrete of the sidewalk, his legs make short strides yet they are nonetheless hasty in his state of panic.

...There are other stages, you've probably heard of 'em. The five stages. One is denial. Two is anger. Three is fear. Four is bargaining and five is acceptance, and they're all emotions. They say these are the emotional stages someone goes through when given a terminal diagnosis. I don't know, never known anyone that's been through that. I haven't myself. Could all be bullshit, hell, it could all be. Birth, life, death... could all be bullshit...

He is out of his neighborhood on the downtown streets in the night, passing closed shops and open bars when and where a young boy should not be. Passersby, there are none, but beggars and bums sitting in archways and resting on benches, there are plenty. They give no acknowledgement to his presence. He turns down an alleyway and slows as he finds the far side of a dumpster. Tears have begun to streak his face and he sits to hug his knees to his chest and tries to make sense of everything he has witnessed in these fleeting moments.

Sitting in the darkness, cold and numb, he leans against a brick wall in the shadow of a dumpster in an alleyway. He is hidden from the world. He is hiding from his own world.

The dirty man concludes his narrative.

...Everything I told you, everything I tell you, remember it. Forget what you know. The closest to the truth you'll get is right here. No one is honest. Sex is an absurdity, you can't get an honest word, everyone lies. It's ridiculous, they're ridiculous and we're ridiculous. Drugs, they're a part of life and you can't escape it. You can't escape death, either. As for the street, it don't matter what your name is, what your bank account has in it... the street calls your name every night. Like death, it calls to you, waits for you and watches for you, for any little opportunity to come snatch you up from your self-induced immortality and show you what it is you've been living for, what you've been missing, what you'll never get back and never have. Turns you into something you never thought you could be. If it catches you young or you're truly weak, it turns you into a monster. To fight off the others at first, but then it creeps further and you're nothing more than a true, real-life monster doing what you never thought yourself able. Doing the work only a monster would do. Believe me, this I know. This, I know..."

For the first time since the room popped up, the man turns his head to the side and the view opens, expands, and like a camera pushing out slowly, a pool of blood enters the frame. A wrinkled hand, a freckled arm, and then a bald head of a bearded man with chapped lips and brown teeth and jowls is in place on the otherwise clean, sterile white floor.

He is the dirty man's victim.

He was the dirty man's audience for the speech on sex, drugs, homelessness and death. An interpretation, the one-man show a sort of self-justification for the taking of life. As he sits and watches the pool of blood grow wider, thicker, the box in the corner—of the young boy—replays itself in another random sequential order.

A moving picture-in-picture to play along with the narrator's personal account, his self-telling of the events in a way only a shattered mind could share. Two pieces of a puzzle: one piece connected and somewhat cohesive, and the other a jumble of events that skip forward, backward and side to side, freeze and repeat in variations, one no more authentic than the other. A mind's memory susceptible to being dubbed and exaggerated by traumatic events, should they have even happened.

In the small box in the corner, the boy runs...

WHEN I WAS
THOMAS F. MONTELEONE

WHEN I WAS 6...

—was the first time I remember it happening.

My first day of school had been a blur of nuns in dark blue, ringing class bells, clapping erasers, and the smell of chalk-dust. Sister Mary Frances told us about numbers from one to ten and how each of us had our own guardian angel.

I hadn't been all that interested in counting, but having someone watching out for me sounded like a great idea, especially when Dad came home late from the plant. That meant he'd stopped for "a few" and that meant he'd be angry and had to slap something with his big right hand. That something was usually me, even if I was upstairs in my bed pretending to sleep.

So where was *my* guardian angel? And why was he letting this happen?

Here's how I found out.

I went up to my room after that first day of school and the heat of early September was cooking the second floor of our little cape cod like an oven. It made me so drowsy, I didn't even bother to change out of my school uniform—navy blue pants, white shirt, and blue tie. The day had worn me out so much that I just stretched out on the bed for a nap. I stared at the ceiling where a section of plaster had cracked into a pattern like a kind of hand or claw. The humidity and heat in the cramped bedroom settled over me like a blanket and I began to drift off to sleep...

That's when the *buzzing* started.

But it was more of a feeling than a real sound. It seemed like it was coming from inside my head and I felt like I was in this weird place right in the middle of being awake and asleep. The buzzing became a tuning fork *hum* behind my eyes. I got scared and tried to get up… and that's when I realized I couldn't move.

Rigid and paralyzed, I lay on my back, and all I could do was stare up at that cracked ceiling. I wanted to scream for my mom, but muscles in my mouth and throat wouldn't work. I'm not sure she would have heard outside hanging laundry on the line, but I couldn't make a sound anyway.

This is what it's like to die, I remember thinking. This is *it*.

And then I saw him.

My eyes were fixed so that I had to keep looking straight ahead, straight up, and he just kind of leaned forward over my bed so I could see him. But I didn't really see him. He was a blurry shape with no real face. More like a shadow, only made of fog or smoke that swirled with a life of its own. He would have been so scary if I didn't know who he was.

You're my guardian angel, I thought. And he nodded and spoke inside my head. Yes, that's right, that's exactly who I am.

I asked if he could protect me from Dad, and he said no, but he could teach me how to protect myself. He told me I was too soft, too nice, too willing to do what everybody told me. Do what *you* want, he said. It will feel good. But I don't know what I want to do, I said.

Let me give you some ideas, he said.

WHEN I WAS 10…

—I had gotten pretty good at getting what I wanted. Doing good in school—even a strict one like Saint Margaret's—was easy once I learned how to be a cheater. Stealing homework during recess, reading test answers off Teddy Dodge's papers, and crib sheets in my sleeves was so much better than spending all those hours *studying*. I would never be dumb enough to do that kind of stuff— thanks to my guardian angel.

Because every once in a while when I'd fall asleep on my back and that buzzing sound filled my ears, he'd come to me and tell me what I needed to know. Like how to stay out of Dad's way and never let him hurt me again. That time would come soon enough. I learned to be happy with smaller things. Like how easy it was to just *steal* anything I wanted from Reade's Drugstore—an old place with dark, narrow aisles and shelves within easy reach. Candy, baseball cards, toys, even a great pocket knife: all for the taking.

WHEN I WAS 13...

—I was getting bored. I had control over my teachers and my classmates; the former thought I was smart and polite while the latter feared me for the bully I'd become. I didn't have what you'd call real friends, but I didn't need them. Kids in our class did whatever I told 'em. I had grown a lot over the summer and I'd inherited the broad shoulders and big hands of my old man, which made it easier to scare people into doing what I wanted.

The old guy was getting drunk more often than not and when he couldn't hit me, which was all the time because I was never home or anywhere near him, he would beat up on my mom, who was stupid enough to let him.

By then, I'd gotten really good at doing my buzz-sleep thing.

Which was cool... or my guardian angel could've never told me that's the way it was with women. They were mostly stupid and good for one thing—getting your dick hard. And after I'd stolen a magazine from Reade's called *Penthouse*, I knew exactly what he was talking about.

He didn't tell me what to do with the rabbit that escaped from the cage in our neighbor's backyard—that had been my idea.

WHEN I WAS 16...

—was when I stopped going to school. There wasn't a whole lot they could teach me, especially those Sisters of Charity with their wrinkled faces and probably cunts to match. All those years of stuff about heaven and hell and the only thing that had ever been true was the part about my guardian angel. Good thing, too, because I never could've gotten this far without him.

I guess I should explain that even though I had no use for my mom, because she was so stupid and boring, I was tired of seeing her face pulpy red and her saggy arms splotched with bruises. She looked even more pathetic than she was.

Then my G.A. told me something really cool. Anti-freeze is a great poison 'cause it has no taste, especially mixed with whiskey. Guess who started getting a new cocktail every night? Well, at least until his kidneys stopped working.

WHEN I WAS 23...

—it became real obvious that jobs and me just didn't get along. The biggest problem with having a job is also having a boss. And I *hate* those guys.

My G.A. had been telling me that growing up to be a guy with big hands, long arms and a short temper made it way easier for me to solve problems in my life—like bosses. So I always ended up breaking their jaws or knocking loose a few teeth.

It always worked like that until the last one at Jerry's Auto Junk out on Route 230. Jerry thought he could go a few rounds with me until I tire-ironed his skull so hard his left eyeball actually exploded from its socket. They'll probably never find him 'cause I put his body in the trunk of an old Dodge Challenger that went into the crusher the next day.

WHEN I WAS 30...

—I always had money because I'd learned how to take it from people. B&E, purses, and even the occasional mugging if I got really short. And I always had women 'cause they follow the money.

But they're all so predictable, they're starting to bore me. It's getting to the point where I'm going to need more kick.

Last time I fell into a buzz-sleep, my life-long protector told me how to make that happen—I never knew a pair of handcuffs and a Zippo lighter could be so much fun.

WHEN I WAS 44...

—was when I got too smart for my own good. I mean, no matter how bold or crazy I got, I never got nailed for it. And that was weird in itself 'cause suddenly it seemed like security cameras were like *everywhere*. I never had the patience to sit and watch much television—made me jittery—but my G.A. told me to try and watch some of those cheesy real-crime shows. Good idea. They showed me how to avoid most of the fuck-ups people did to get themselves caught.

One of the detectives was describing a certain type of suspect—called him a sociopath. I smiled when I heard that one 'cause it sounded like they were talking about *me*.

So anyway, remember what I was saying about never getting nailed for any of the shit I was doing? Yeah, well even *that* was getting boring. It was like playing poker with a bunch of rubes and you actually got tired of taking their money. It got to the point where I was always figuring out ways to up the stakes, to keep things interesting.

So, like usual, next time my guardian angel comes to me when I'm laying on my back with that soft buzz in my ears, he tells me there's only one place left to go.

Now here's where it gets a little strange, even for me.

Up till then, not counting the guy who called himself my father, I'd never really hit the off-switch on Junk Yard Jerry... and that had kinda been self-defense. Even the women I left tied up in hotel rooms; none of 'em had ever died. For me, it had to be personal—had to be a reason to kill the other guy. But now I'm thinking how hard it is to *do* somebody and get away with it—hard for the average mook who ends up getting to wear an orange jumpsuit—that I just gotta try it.

All I needed was a good reason.

WHEN I WAS 48...

—was when that reason finally arrived.

I was loan sharking in a small town outside of Vegas called Pahrump, and one of my customers—a dentist named Larry—had been acting more strange than usual. Finally, he meets me in bar called Sally's Place off Bash Avenue, and he tells me he's been running through the money with me because he'd been getting blackmailed.

Without boring you with the details, it's a familiar story where the guy keeps ratcheting up the payoffs. Usually when the pump runs dry, he does one of two things: spills the beans or fades into the wind. Larry the dentist was convinced he would do the former, and figured the only solution was to have the guy "removed from the equation" (his words). So I took the rest of the dentist's money and delivered the most final of payments to his blackmailer in the form of one silenced 9mm slug and a trip to the desert for a coyote dinner.

Of course, my guardian angel was on this one, and he told me something important Ben Franklin was supposed to have said: *any two men can keep a secret—as long as one of them is dead.*

Which is why Larry never showed up for that root canal on his calendar the following Monday.

WHEN I WAS 57...

—was when they caught me.

And not because I was a fuck-up, 'cause I was never a fuck-up. I had gotten so smooth and efficient that I'd gotten a reputation with the good guys. Trouble for them was they could never get enough on me, nothing that would ever attach long enough for a conviction. It wasn't until they used an undercover agent, a very fine-looking chick claiming she needed a husband with a big insurance policy suddenly killed.

I was off my game 'cause she was beautiful and she played me.

But you know what?—when the pinch came down, I wasn't all that upset. At my age, things hadn't been all that smokin' for a while. It was like I'd been driving along life's highway at pretty much the same speed for most of my life and just as I hit the fifty mile-marker, it was like the road fell out from under me. Thick dark hair, suddenly thin and gray—then just falling out. Skin under my eyes and jaw heading south. Feet sore all the time. Dick only half-hard. I could go on, but the last line of the contract is always the same. This is what we signed on for—a shitty ride if you make it to the end.

Long story short, they concluded I am a very sick and twisted guy, who, in the words of the D.A., was "like a tumor that needed to be excised from the body of society." They convicted me for some stuff that looks pretty puny when you add up all the bills I've collected on. For sure, Lady Justice got short-changed with me.

Didn't matter. If you've been paying attention, you know I get bored easy, and I guess I'd been running out of things to keep life interesting anyway. There wasn't much out there I hadn't done, and now it didn't look like there was much left for me to do.

Maybe I'd think of something, or maybe I'd get some advice from my old pal.

The notion consoled me as I sat in my cell, feeling drowsy, so I lay back on the cot and stared at the ceiling. It didn't take long before that comforting *buzz* filled my ears with a soft familiarity. Pretty soon I couldn't move my arms or legs, which was okay. It was part of the way things worked.

But then, I realized something was different this time.

Fighting the hypnogogic paralysis, I forced myself to blink, and just like that I wasn't looking up any more. I was looking *down*.

...at a small boy in Catholic school uniform.

Are you my guardian angel? he said.

I told him yes, and suddenly knew what I'd be doing with the rest of my life.

TIGHT PARTNERS

GENE O'NEILL

McCARRON,
3:55 A.M. SUNDAY MORNING

Me and Big O came to a stop at the twelve-foot high chain link fence topped with razor wire. I set down my beat-up guitar case near the gate, which was secured with a thick chain and fastened with a heavy-duty *Master* lock. It wasn't the imposing fence or locked gate that had actually stopped us though. No, it was the bigheaded pit bull glaring back at us through the gate with his malevolent tiger-yellow eyes. Ole Rufus didn't growl or bristle, just peered back coldly at me as I edged a step or two closer. Just daring me: *Come on in, pal... and I'll tear you a new bunghole.*

I shook my head and chuckled wryly, thinking: *No way, not this time, Bad Ass, because I have brought you a tasty little snack.* I unwrapped the small ball of raw hamburger and carefully pushed it through the gate to the guard dog. "There you go, Ole Rufus," I said, watching the hungry pit bull begin wolfing down the raw meat in huge gulps.

The Dancing Man kept the damn dog half starved, probably believed it kept him lean and nasty mean. But I'm sending a telepathic memo to The Dancing Man: *Ole Rufus has gone hungry for his last time, and won't be tearing up any more intruders out here in the future.* That hamburger meat was laced with enough horse tranquillizer, ketamine, to drop a pair of Clydesdales—a dose guaranteed by The Cajun over in the Tenderloin to stop even the biggest Great Dane's heart in under two minutes...

I pulled my black ski cap down around my ears and turned up the collar on my black duster, glanced over my shoulder, and whispered to Big O: "Man, the fog's rolling in and I'm freezing my ass off." He just nodded, making a kind of dismissive shrug and wry face, like he hadn't noticed the icy mist. Dude's tougher than Chinese arithmetic.

And it was true, the fog had come in late from San Francisco Bay about three o'clock this morning, and by now was completely blanketing this whole old industrial area of China Basin. Making it tough to see clearly ahead more than thirty or so yards.

I turned back and looked through the fence at the shuttered up old Victorian standing back maybe twenty-five yards from the road. Looked like an outcast sitting there alone amid the acres and acres of cleared area—nothing but cement rubble and assorted debris around it. It was the last remnant of a once really nice block of the City, a neighborhood that preceded the recently demolished industrial buildings—a whole row of Victorians probably built just after the 1906 earthquake.

Now, this, the last of its kind was just waiting for the demolition crew to finally put it out of its dilapidated misery. Then, this whole area would probably be paved over and turned into another gigantic parking lot serving the new SF Giants ballpark, which was recently opened two blocks back on 3rd Street, just beyond McCovey Cove.

From here, because of the thick mist and the sheets of plywood boarding up the Victorian's windows, I couldn't see any light coming from the gloomy old place. Of course the electricity had been shut off for a long time. But The Dancing Man and his sidekick, Black Angus, had been squatting here for about a year now, turning the back end of the second story of this once elegant old place into a shooting gallery. They used candles up there for light... and maybe flashlights. Didn't really need a lot of illumination for their kinda business.

I'd been inside there two times in the last week, buying a balloon each time, but never staying and fixing in the shooting gallery—a busy place on weekends—actually just casing the place out. Me and Big O weren't using anything heavy-duty like black tar—never had. With all my other problems, I didn't need to be taking on any extra weight. Anyhow, probably wouldn't mix too well with the meds I was getting from the VA Medical Center over in the Presidio. Talking Doc over there warned: "*No* street drugs, *no* booze."

But, of course, me and Big O couldn't resist a little taste of the *pure* now and then... Like late this afternoon, after we were rested up, we'd probably stop in at The Greeks, have a couple of *Black Jacks*, and maybe play some organized grab-ass with the ladies. Along with the taste for good booze, we both dearly appreciated a sweet-smelling woman, preferably one who was also *cooperative*. Be nice to have a few extra bucks in our pockets to spend on them tonight, too. We hadn't been holding much cash lately.

But that'd be much later, after we took care of current business. Right now we needed to get our game faces on, and get ready for our operational launch. We'd learned back in Recon that 4:00 A.M. was the best time for a hit 'n run—enemy bodily functions at their lowest ebbs. Not sure if this really applied to dope dealers and junkies—their bodily functions were about on par with the corpses at the morgue anyhow. But, dope business would've settled down by this time Sunday morning, with probably only a few late stragglers still nodding out for the remainder of the night. And, man, there'd be a ton of presidents stashed away up there—you could bet your sweet ass on that.

Ole Rufus was laying on his side now, his breathing heavily labored, convulsing... and dying. Damn dog hadn't let out even one whimper, though. A canine warrior to the end. I admired that; imagine Big O did, too.

I unlatched the lock, which was broken anyhow and just there for a front. Usually, if you were a known customer and wanted to score, you called ahead and Black Angus would meet you at the gate. He'd escort you safely past Ole Rufus, then up to the second story around in back. We didn't call this time—*full stealth mode.*

Before moving inside the gate though, I bent down, picked up the attaché case and the roll of duct tape from the raggedy-ass guitar case in one hand; and with my free hand, I took out my axe—a 12-gauge Rossi riot gun. I had half a dozen extra shells already in my duster pocket. But I didn't plan on having to reload. I glanced again back at Big O, tossed him the attaché case and duct tape, then said: "Okay, dude, you ready to rock 'n roll?"

He had his game face and asshole screwed on tight, and my man definitely looked badass. He nodded.

"Okay, let's do it!"

We crept up to the front of the house, then stopped again for a moment.

Damned if this darkened, spooky old place didn't remind me kinda like that Halloween *Ghost House* over on Shotwell Street that we visited as kids growing up down in the Mission. But I didn't admit that to Big O. Dude would've just laughed his ass off—stuff never scared him as a kid. I shuddered in the icy fog.

I grabbed my nose tight, blew, cleared my ears, cocked my head slightly, and listened intently. Behind me, Big O probably was doing the same. An old Marine trick used on recon patrol to enhance hearing.

Not picking up anything suspicious, we carefully worked our way around back, and stopped again at the foot of the staircase. At the top, there was a small window near the door. I could just make out the flickering light from down here.

"Hey, I think they might be open for business, Big O," I whispered, giving him my best Jack Nicholson devilish grin. Actually, I was pretty keyed up, ready for action, my heart thumping in my ears, and my pulse racing. I sucked in a deep, settling breath. We both knew without my lame attempt to be funny that an inside dealer with a shooting gallery was *never* closed—junkies always needed to get well 24/7.

I let my breath trickle back out across my dry lips, glanced again at my backup, and whispered: "You ready to do this, dude?"

He nodded.

"Okay, let's hit 'em," I mouthed, tucking the shotgun against my right hip, Big O just two steps behind me, his .45 military issue in hand. We went up those rickety-ass stairs as quietly as possible, trying not to alert anyone inside.

A few moments later, we hesitated at the top of the porch, directly in front of the door, the once ornate leaded glass portion replaced with a piece of cardboard.

I closed my eyes, sucked in another deep breath, resigned now to the imminent action; and as usual during this part of a mission, time abruptly slowed down for me—NFL video replay. I blinked, squared up, *smashed* in the bottom of the flimsy door with my booted foot, ducked down slightly, and quickly slipped in past the dangling splintered remnants.

Man, it was focking spooky inside, shadows slowly dancing around the walls from the flickering light cast by a pair of huge candles on a table in the center of the room.

"Get 'em up!" I ordered, centering the shotgun on The Dancing Man's chest.

An almost *stop frame*: Beside the table, he was standing with a big pizza slice in hand, the opened box near one of the candles; his mouth open, but all movement momentarily frozen.

Then, his surprised expression became slowly animated with a face full of weird twitches and tics, his right shoulder jerking out of control, flinching up repeatedly and banging his right ear—all this accented by being in slow motion. Crashing in the door like that and pointing a shotgun at him had set off some of the symptoms of his Tourette syndrome, *Big Time*. The uneaten slice of pizza floated to the floor, finally making a sloppy *splat* in the suddenly quiet room.

"H-H-H-Hey," The Dancing Man finally stammered, slowly pulling his trembling hands up near his chest with palms out in a defensive mode, "b-b-be cool, now, man. Need be *no* shootin here, ya unnerstan?"

I glided a step closer, still holding the riot gun out threateningly, but turning my head slightly to the right, and saying: "Wrap this dude up like a focking Christmas turkey with your duct tape, man."

I heard Big O eventually take one step forward—

Like a Saturday morning cartoon villain, Black Angus, the giant bodyguard thundered out of the closet in the far corner, where they stashed both their dope and cash, his Beretta 9mm automatic coming up ever so slowly, and finally extending out like a dowsing rod. I'd thought when we hadn't initially found him in the kitchen with The Dancing Man that Black Angus was somewhere back in the shooting gallery, tending to business. Despite being wrong, I still reacted as quickly as possible, everything still happening in video slow motion replay.

BOOM.

I got off a blast from the riot gun, but was a bit high off the mark, some of the blast going over the giant's shoulder; but most of the slugs peppering him high in the chest and in the shoulder... Enough of an impact to make him *grunt* loudly, spin about ninety degrees, and slump to the floor on his side.

I should have cranked off another blast into him. But by then, The Dancing Man was moving toward me with his eyes blinking and mouth opened wide, in pretty agile bounds for a guy his size— looked like a pissed-off hippo. More important from my point of view, a Hi-Tech S9 had magically appeared in his right hand. Nasty ass piece, for sure.

But, I wasn't exactly standing around counting spectators, and had automatically jacked another shell into the chamber of my Rossi after hitting Black Angus. Then, before The Dancing Man could squeeze off a burst from his automatic handgun—

BOOM.

This time the blast was dead center.

A tight pattern square in The Dancing Man's chest, driving him backwards as if he'd been hit by a Mike Tyson right. He landed on his fat ass, a stunned look on his face, his eyes slowly glazing over, and a wet red flower opening up across the chest of his white sweatshirt, beginning to blot out the green USF logo.

For a moment I was flashing back to Helmand Province, a raid on a Taliban stronghold, basking in the glow of a six-pack of right-eousness, after the squad burst into a hut and blasted a trio of im-portant terrorist leaders. I blinked, coming back to the present... And like back then, I felt absolutely *no* guilt, after realizing I'd just shot a sleazy drug dealer and his murderous giant sidekick. Enough daydreaming.

"Grab the presidents in the closet, stuff them in your attaché case," I shouted over my shoulder to Big O, gesturing with my shotgun, as I jacked another shell into the chamber.

Then, still working in slow motion and sweating heavily now under the duster, I threw down on the closed door directly in back of the table, which led to the shooting gallery—a long hallway crowded with maybe half a dozen filthy mattresses. But the door remained shut as a few seconds ticked by. Probably all the junkies back there too stoned to react to gunshots or just not giving a big rat's ass.

But, I should have first checked again on the giant bodyguard.

Because, even though Black Angus was hit, bleeding badly, and down, the badass suddenly sat up... and got off a shot from his Beretta—

Felt like I'd been *slammed* with a sledgehammer right above the solar plexus.

Time sped back up as I was driven back a step, lost balance, and unable to break my fall I went down in a sprawl, my shotgun firing off harmlessly into the air. I was hurting in real time.

Old Marine training prevailed though. Because, even flat on my sorry ass, I managed to hang onto the shotgun stock. And I struggled to jack another shell into the chamber. But I was rapidly losing strength in my hands and arms—like the big hole in my gut was draining away all my steam. Didn't have the strength to arm the damned shotgun. And I realized also at that moment that my legs were now completely numb and useless. Man, I'd taken a seri-ous focking hit.

As the blackness began engulfing me, I heard Black Angus crank off another round from his Beretta. But I didn't feel any impact, so he must've been shooting at Big O...

Dead quiet, no return fire from my main man.

My spirit sank, because the bodyguard had probably nailed Big O, too, taking both of us out of action. Man, we'd focked this operation up, *Big Time.*

Then, I was fading out fast, being sucked down, down, down into the icy void.

HOMICIDE DETECTIVE SERGEANT JONES, LATER SUNDAY MORNING, ICU SF GENERAL

"...And the doc says you can talk about the deceased and other questions for a few minutes before you have to get prepped for surgery," Sergeant Jones said. "Not too groggy from the pre-op drugs, right?"

Propped up, Black Angus sighed and shook his head.

"Where did you two meet?" Sergeant Jones said, notebook out.

Black Angus in a tired, slurred voice said: "We met at San Quentin, about ten years ago."

"He was called The Dancing Man back then?"

"Nah, no one called him that in the joint. Sure he'd been already diagnosed with Tourette syndrome, but those facial tics and twitches and limbs jerking weren't too bad at the time. Everyone at Q just respectively called him Luther, you know what I'm saying."

"His given name?"

"Yeah, that's right, Luther Daniel Delacroix, was his full name. I always called him Luther. That Dancing Man stuff, well, I felt it was kinda... what do you call it? The right word?"

"Demeaning or disrespectful?"

"Yeah, making fun of his disease. That Tourette's some serious shit, man."

"So you met exactly how in the joint?"

"Well, Luther liked to watch me fight in the ring. Bet on me. I was a good prison heavyweight back then. Hit hard and had some solid whiskers. But I tore up a rotator cup, right at the end of my time, pretty much destroyed all the plans for turning pro when I eventually rose up."

The detective glanced at his notes. "But it says here that you went right to work at a straight job when you got out?"

"Yeah, I worked at the car wash over on Divisadero. Man, that is some sorry-ass shit, you know what I'm saying."

"But good *honest* work."

"What...? You ever try that kind of work, man? Eight or more hours a day, six or seven days a week? Feet wet all the time. Running, hustling. And all that for minimum wage. Tips really bad. Yeah, it's *shitty* honest. But I hung tough for six months."

And then?"

"When Luther finally rose up, he offered me a job. He needed a dependable *arm*, you know what I'm saying."

"But you were both still on parole then?"

"Yeah, that's right I was still on the leash. But I'd had enough of your honest bullshit to last a while. I've been Luther's muscle since then. And also we been pretty tight friends, too, you know"

"But you've been dealing dope all this time?"

Black Angus shook his head. "Nah, man, he's only been the bagman for Mexican tar... let's see, maybe last two years at most. Really a serious player in the bidness only bout eighteen months. Small time hustle fore that."

"But Luther has been *using* himself for a long time, right?"

"Yeah. With the Tourette and all, he needs it. Kinda like, oh, what do they call it...?"

"Self-medicating?"

Black Angus nodded, not able to prevent his eyes from drooping closed for a moment.

"You okay?"

The big man lying on the bed blinked, sucked in a breath, and nodded.

"Didn't using stir up his disease?"

"Well, it probably didn't do it no good. But wasn't so bad at first."

"You using, too?"

"Nah, man, I don't do that, you know what I'm saying." Black Angus sighed again, looking really worn out.

Sergeant Jones said: "Heard on the street that Luther couldn't stand the sight of needles. How'd he get straight behind that? Just curious."

"Yeah, he had a thing about needles, you know. So, I'd fix him. No problem at first. But, all his veins in his arms and legs eventually got a little too ropey. Hard to bring up a vein. Last couple of months, Luther had to stick his thumb in his mouth and blow hard. I'd hit a big vein puffing out in his neck."

"Jesus! That's pretty hairy, man. Tough to do."

Black Angus nodded, looking exhausted. Then, with his voice lower and weaker, he said: "Yeah, but we were tight, member."

The detective nodded and pushed on. "How many of these guys hit you tonight?"

"I *think* there were two of them busted in the door. Little white motherfucker step up front and shot Luther in the chest with a scattergun. But the other dude, the big one, kinda hung back in the shadows flickering from the candlelight. Barely could see him in the corner, you know. I *think* he had a handgun. But after I shot the white dude, I got the big guy, too. Both of them solid hits, torso bulls eye... But, I was hurting bad and down, you know, and I *guess* that big dude slipped away while I was out."

"You can identify the one we arrested?"

"Yeah, I can finger the shooter, the white guy. The big motherfucker... *no*. Except dude probably has a new asshole in his back, bleeding bad, and hurting, you know what I'm saying."

"If he does, he hasn't checked into any hospital yet."

9redt, who

DETECTIVE JONES,
EVEN LATER SUNDAY AFTERNOON,
OR RECOVERY SF GENERAL

"...You and Cecil Owens have been friends for quite a long time?" Sergeant Jones asked, right after introducing himself to Roddy McCarron, who was recovering from surgery.

McCarron, in a soft, drifty voice, said: "Yeah, Big O and me have been tight partners since elementary school. You know what I mean, closer even than blood brothers."

"Isn't that unusual for a black guy and a white guy to be so tight?"

McCarron shook his head. "Nah, I don't think so. We grew up same neighborhood, starred together in Peewee Football and Little League Baseball. Eventually played four major sports at Mission High—including running track. Man, Big O could run... three speeds: *Fast, faster, and good morning, officer.* Then, we played football for the *Rams* out at City College. My man was an all-league linebacker both years. Second year we played Saddleback College *Gauchos* for the State junior college championship. We lost by one focking point. I played some pretty decent quarterback in that game. So, we've always been real tight, you see."

"That good, you must've both had some college scholarship offers?" Detective Jones asked.

McCarron, still looking dazed from the post-op painkillers and lack of sleep, sighed and nodded. After a few moments, he continued in a halting voice: "Big O did—Cal, USC, and couple others I forget. We *both* almost went here to State and play for the *Gators*. But after all the 9/11 shit came down and then Afghanistan and Iraq, we decided to go into the Marines together. We went in on the buddy plan, first boot camp at MCRD and then ITR at Camp Pendleton. After that, we both landed in Recon, and went to Afghanistan together. Over there, Big O *always* had my back, just like now."

"And after you finally got out of the Marines…" the detective glanced at his notebook. "About a year ago I have here, you attempted to get work here in the City?"

"Well, we tried that route, hit the veteran's programs here in the city with no luck. Tough times right now to get a decent job."

"But you both got some help? You weren't *forced* to rob someone to eat?" Jones said, unable to suppress an accusatory tone.

McCarron looked a little more unsettled by the question. He sucked in a real long breath and said: "Yeah, we both get some disability, a little SSI, and medical stuff over at the VA in the Presidio. And actually we both worked off and on as counselors at a homeless shelter down in the 'Loin. The damn hours and money were really bad though. And the focking messes we had to clean up. Tried the car wash routine briefly, too. And McDonald's and Taco Bell. All just minimum wage jobs. Man, you can't live in the City on that kinda money. Those are kid's jobs. And that just didn't seem right with what all we'd been through overseas. By the time we were discharged from the *Crotch*, we'd both been decorated. Big O was a corporal and I'd just made sergeant—responsible NCOs. We'd led men through some pretty hairy shit over there… So, McDonalds? Homeless centers? Car washes? Nah, man we finally decided to put our training to work for us. We had the balls to go into business for ourselves."

The detective smiled. "Uh-huh, how'd that work out for you?"

McCarron was looking pretty worn out and more than a little irritated by the cop's snarky attitude by now. He didn't try to hide the angry tone in his voice. "Yeah, hey man, you're focking right. Okay? We screwed up. So, it is what it is…"

Detective Jones was quiet for a while, then sucked in a breath, and also shifted the nature of his questioning: "Black Angus *thinks* he hit Big O, too, maybe in the chest. But your friend got away. He may need immediate medical assistance. But we have to know where to find him. You can help us and *him*."

McCarron still looked disturbed by the questioning and said

flippantly: "Sorry, I ain't giving up my man, Big O, to you."

"He could die…?"

There was a long pause and the homicide detective finally added: "Maybe you can save him. He'd do that for you, his tight partner, right?"

McCarron, didn't answer for another minute or so, obviously thinking everything over, looking like someone struggling with a classic *approach-avoidance conflict*. Finally, he sighed deeply and said in a thoroughly exhausted voice: "We live together over at the Hotel Reo in the Tenderloin. Try there. I just hope he made it that far."

LATER SUNDAY EVENING,
HOTEL REO, TENDERLOIN

After introducing himself, Sergeant Jones asked Ferdy, the desk clerk: "You have a Rod McCarron and Cecil Owens living here?"

The skinny clerk, with a cigarette dangling from his lips, carefully looked over the Homicide Detective's badge like it was something he'd never seen. Then he said: "Yeah, McCarron's been stayin here for bout a year off and on. Hmmm… right now, up in room 203. But he ain't in—"

"And Cecil Owens?"

"Name doan ring a bell, officer."

"You don't have a Cecil Owens registered here, up in 203 with McCarron?"

Ferdie shook his head slowly, not taking the lit cigarette from his mouth the whole time.

"You sure? You don't want to be looking at *accessory* charges? "

"I'm *sure*," the desk clerk said, squinting, as ashes dropped off his cigarette onto the desk in front of him. "Doan recollect ever seein that name… And I been on this desk for bout ten years."

"But Rod McCarron is definitely registered here?"

"Ya got that right, officer."

MONDAY MORNING,
SF VA MEDICAL CENTER

Sergeant Jones introduced himself to Dr. Rakesh Patel and explained the nature of the San Francisco Police Homicide Department interest in a USMC veteran being treated at the Center—their official conversation already cleared through the VA administration.

Then, he asked: "I understand you are Roddy McCarron's psychotherapist, doctor?"

"Yes, I am," Dr. Patel said. He already had a fairly large file in front of him—shiny brown covers, with legal-sized pages held down at the top with a long aluminum clip.

"And I understand he is under current psychiatric treatment. Can you tell me the nature of his problem? His diagnosis?"

"Roddy McCarron is suffering from TBI—traumatic brain injury—a serious injury he suffered about fifteen months ago in Afghanistan. Three tiny RPG shrapnel fragments were removed from his frontal lobe. He is experiencing a number of psychological symptoms associated with TBI. He is beginning to recover… but slowly."

"Symptoms?"

"Delusional and hallucinatory behavior, anxiety attacks, lack of impulse control, occasional aggressive behavior, and a general inability to re-adjust easily to normal civilian life. He's under heavy medication for these symptoms at the moment."

"But he is able to live on his own and has been able to hold down a job?"

"He has been only moderately successful living independently—twice returning for brief readjustment periods to the residential VA psychiatric unit over in Martinez in the North Bay. He's been unable to hold any job for more than a day or two. He aggravates his psychological symptoms by regularly abusing alcohol."

It was quiet for a few moments.

Then, the detective asked: "But in your opinion he knows right from wrong? Capable of understanding the nature of his crime?"

Dr. Patel hesitated momentarily, shuffling through some of the pages in the file. Finally, he said: "I think I'd answer yes *but* with some reservations. He's competent most of the time, but has trouble dealing with reality on occasions. His irrational periods are often set off by dreams of the past, his last firefight in Helmand province. When his Recon squad was ambushed on patrol and outnumbered by a superior Taliban force. They took heavily losses. But Sergeant McCarron apparently led his patrol valiantly in that his last action in country—initially keeping them together and putting up stiff resistance, defending their firebase until support finally arrived. He has been awarded both a Silver Star and Purple Heart for that action. Unfortunately, he relives the horrific aspects during recurring nightmares of his squad members being hit and six of them dying."

Jones glanced at his notebook and asked: "And this was the same action when his friend... Corporal Cecil Owens was also wounded? Are you seeing him here at the Center, too?"

Dr. Patel paused, frowned, looked taken aback for a moment; and then, he thumbed through to the back pages of the file. After finding a particular piece of paper he relaxed and smiled thinly.

"I thought I remembered correctly," the doctor said, his forehead wrinkles deepening slightly. "But your question didn't seem appropriate under the circumstances." He sighed and glanced again at the paper. "Corporal Cecil Owens is of course not under treatment here. And has never been. He was indeed a member of that particular combat patrol that was ambushed. Let's see... Ah, here are the relevant details. Corporal Owens has been recommended for the Medal of Honor for his actions during that Taliban ambush. He actually saved his good friend Sergeant McCarron's life by dragging him out of harm's way, and then defending him and several other wounded Marines—almost all the members left alive in that patrol--until a pair of Apache helicopters finally drove off the

Taliban force…"

Dr. Patel paused, and peered at Detective Jones for moment.

The detective nodded, then shrugged his shoulders and lifted his eyebrows.

Then, the doctor tapped his finger at the bottom of the report page. "If Corporal Cecil Owens wins that Medal of Honor for his courageous action a little over a year ago, I'm afraid it will have to be awarded posthumously."

LATE TUESDAY NIGHT,
ROOM 312, SF GENERAL

Roddy McCarron is sitting up in bed, but looking unsettled, exhausted, his face grim. He says to his friend: "Doc said I'm going to live, but be paralyzed from here down, man." He gestures at his waist. Shakes his head sadly. "Sure, I knew my gourd was focked up when we got discharged, but at least I could feel my dick. Piss for myself, you know." He shakes his head again, his voice choking up. "But they are going to permanently put me away, lock my paralyzed ass in a cage like an animal. I don't want to live and die like that, man…" After a pause, he says hoarsely: " I want to go out like a warrior, on my shield. You need to help me, man. Tight partners are forever."

Big O says nothing. But after a long moment of silence, he nods his head.

A few minutes later, the on-duty nurse finds Roddy McCarron dead, his pillow lying across his face.

APPROACHING LAVENDER

LUCY A. SNYDER

RHETTA'S HUSBAND SCOTT TEASED her for bringing her sketchpad along on their honeymoon: "I thought this was supposed to be just you and me. Not you, me and your hobby."

She felt heat rise in her sunburned face at his ha-ha-only-serious tone. It wasn't a hobby, and he knew that. Or she'd thought he did. He'd never complained about her working on her art when they were dating. He'd praised her paintings and cheerfully accompanied her to gallery hops and art shows. It had even been his idea to stop to see the Van Goghs at the museum when they drove through Cincinnati.

"I wanted to get some details of the ocean and the palm trees," she replied.

He waved a cheap digital camera at her. The lens was smeared with sunscreen. "That's why we have this. Put that down and let's go get some margaritas."

A month after they returned from Cancun, he started complaining about her spending her evenings at the studio.

"I never see you," he said. "A wife should be home with her husband. Not off someplace playing with crayons."

She paused, staring at him. He certainly *looked* like the man she'd dated: the same soulful brown eyes, the same tidy blond beard, the same scar on his cheek from when he fell off his bike as a kid. But that was not a sentence she'd ever expected to come out of his mouth. What had changed? Or had *anything* changed? Had she just been oblivious to what he really thought of her passion?

"People are expecting illustrations from me. I have to work—"

He made a dismissive noise. "All that's just a hobby. Your work is at the insurance company."

She wanted to slap him and shout *What is wrong with you?* but her hand stayed perfectly still at her side. "I have contracts. They're paying me. Some of them have already paid. My *work* is expected, and I need to finish it."

"It's hardly any money, though, is it? Just pocket change. Barely anything compared to what you make at the company. Or *could* make if you'd just apply yourself there for a change."

He sounded just like his own father, who'd given him almost the same dressing-down when they'd visited for Christmas. Apparently, Scott's desire to stay in accounting wasn't good enough for Mr. Bershung. His father demanded to know why Scott wasn't on track to become a company executive and turned brutally scornful when Scott insisted he was happy where he was.

Her head spun. Scott had been miserable and frustrated after his father's lecture; why would he say the same thing to her? She'd spent whole evenings talking about her dreams of being a full-time artist, and how the tech writing job was just something to bring in a little cash until she started landing better commissions. Scott had nodded and said *I'm sure you'll do it* and other such supportive things. He'd never cared about her making money. Or had he, and she didn't remember it?

"I'd make more money at my art if I didn't have the day job," she said. "And I could get everything done during the day. I could spend all evening with you. We could go out on dates—"

"No." He shook his head, frowning like she'd just suggested they move to the bad side of town. "You can't quit your job. We need the money too much."

"But if I had more time to work—"

"It's a pipe dream to think you'd ever make anything close to a respectable living as an artist. And that studio space is too expensive. It's at least as much as the cable bill."

"Why? Why do we need so much money? We're doing fine."

"No, we're *not* fine." He turned on her, his face turned dark red; she was afraid he'd start throwing something. She'd only seen him that angry once before after someone keyed his brand-new BMW, and she didn't want to see him like that again.

He took a breath, and seemed a few degrees calmer. "We need to save as much as we can for the house."

"House?" Her voice was a dry croak. She was sure the apartment floor would give way beneath her feet at any moment. She wracked her memory. He'd never even mentioned wanting a house, much less that they had some plan to get one. "What house?"

"My parents' place." He fiddled with his Rolex impatiently. "They're getting a condo down in Florida next year. I offered to buy their house from them; dad wants market price, $500K, and it needs a lot of work, but it's structurally sound—"

"And when were you going to talk to me about this?" She'd been in his parents' house only once for the uncomfortable Christmas where he and his father argued about Scott's career. The huge place was all dark wood and shrouded windows and furnishings from the 1950s. Lots of space and some lovely views from the porch, but on the whole she found it oppressive. Even more oppressive was Scott's father: Mr. Bershung was a stern relic from an earlier era, and with his thick accent and ramrod-stiff bearing she imagined him as a sword-brandishing Prussian general. Very little about Rhetta appeared to please Scott's father. She got along much better with his mother, but the old lady seemed unable to do much besides mouth friendly platitudes and offer cookies. Conversation was a lost art in that house.

"What's to talk about?" Scott stared down at her. "We're married now and we need a house."

It was a done deal to him, clearly, and her opinion wasn't required. She twisted her wedding ring around on her finger and scanned the room, hoping to see the glint of a hidden camera or some other indication that this was just a sick prank involving secret twins or pod people. *We've secretly replaced this woman's husband with an utter jerk. Let's see if she notices!* She flashed back on the Hollywood marriage of a starlet to a country singer; a month in, the starlet had demanded divorce on the grounds of "fraud." At the time, Rhetta had wondered what could possibly constitute fraud in a marriage. Now she was starting to get the idea.

But she wasn't a starlet who could marshal her lawyers and file papers a mere month after her wedding. She made a commitment, 'til death did they part, and she believed in her vows. There *had* to be a way to make this work the way it was supposed to.

"I think what we need," she replied slowly, "is to see a marriage counselor."

Dr. Gates was a pleasant man in his late 50s and came highly recommended on the insurance company's website. His office was outfitted in plush brown leather couches and expensive silk plants. A bright purple Siamese fighting fish drifted in a glass bowl on his desk. An oil portrait of a woman about his age was on the wall behind his desk; Rhetta guessed it was Mrs. Gates. The woman in the portrait was dressed in a pink cashmere sweater and gazed adoringly at a baby in her arms, the very picture of a perfect grandmother. Rhetta was impressed by the colors and the artist's technique; the painting was more life-like than most photos she'd seen.

Rhetta and Scott took the couch closest to the door and Dr. Gates sat across from them in a brown plastic folding chair, listening intently as they both told their stories. When they were done, he leaned forward sympathetically.

"This is exactly the kind of situation that leads to annulments," the kindly therapist said. "I firmly believe that marriage is not something to be entered into or exited lightly, so I'm extremely glad you two came to see me. I think we can get things back on the right track here."

He turned toward her husband. "Scott, it seems to me that you came into this marriage with very regimented gender role expectations that you failed to convey to your wife, certainly before your wedding, but also after it."

"Anything's possible," Scott replied.

Dr. Gates seemingly ignored his skeptical tone. "I'd like to see you make space for your wife's aspirations and most particularly her art. If you want her at home and don't want to pay for studio space, then you need to make room for her whole life at your home. And you need to fully include her in decisions that involve her. And *everything* involves her now."

Scott slumped in his chair, fiddling with his watch.

"Spouses are life partners," the therapist said. "You need to help her become the best possible person she can be."

It seemed to Rhetta that something clicked behind her husband's eyes. He straightened and smiled. "If you put it that way… of course I want her to be the best wife ever."

"Person," Dr. Gates corrected.

"Sure," replied Scott.

The therapist turned to Rhetta. "And I'd like to see you try to be a genuine partner to your husband."

"I thought I have been," she said. "I work a job I don't especially enjoy for the sake of financial goals that are his, not mine."

"Now, Rhetta," the therapist admonished gently. "Everyone has to make a living, and it's not Scott's fault you've chosen a job that doesn't entirely suit you, is it? I respect your art—clearly you are talented from what I've heard—but that, too, is a choice. And it's a choice that's been causing your husband some discomfort."

She felt a slow crab of panic start to scrabble in the pit of her stomach. She could no more choose to stop painting and drawing than she could choose to stop eating. Her soul would dry up.

"So the problem in your view is that I have choices?"

The therapist smiled in an irritated way. "The problem is that you've been insensitive to your husband's needs for comfort and routine. He's clearly a traditional man, and I find it hard to believe that after two years of dating you were unaware of that."

She crossed her arms.

"I told you already. He hid that part of himself."

Inside, she had to agree with Dr. Gates: it did seem impossible that she hadn't seen that side of him. Sure, Scott's father was a domineering tyrant who wanted his wife to serve him coffee every day in exactly the same mug at seven A.M. sharp, but her boyfriend had never been like that at all. The man she knew from two years of dating had been attentive, kind, sexy, spontaneous, and most important, he talked to her. The most perfect of perfect catches, everyone agreed. He'd had a chivalrous streak she found a little old-fashioned and endearing in a world of oblivious hipsters who were often more interested in their video games than they were in her. Most guys had made her feel like she rated only slightly higher than a Fleshlight, but Scott was never indifferent. He'd never failed to make her feel special. Was that the secret-tip off? He'd held open doors and pulled out chairs and mostly bought dinner; was all that her cue that some strange switch was going to flip after the rings were on and he'd start turning into a clone of the old man? She couldn't believe it.

Dr. Gates broke her from her reverie: "You need to be more sensitive to his needs. If he makes space for you at home, will you stay home to paint?"

"Well, of course."

"And would it kill you to cook?" the therapist asked, his tone joking. *Ha-ha, only serious.*

She had to struggle to keep her hand tucked under her elbow.

"I. Already. Do."

"But only a few times a week, right? Takeout and frozen dinners make him feel unloved."

"It was his idea to get Chinese takeout once a week."

"Now, Rhetta. This is about partnership. He has considerably more job responsibilities than you do, and it's only fair that you take over more of the household duties."

Rhetta thought about asking the therapist to do the math on how much work she did between her day job and the freelance, but she bit back that reply. Apparently her career was a choice, and his was a hero's quest. "Fine. I'll cook."

"Then it's settled." Dr. Gates smiled at her, then at Scott. "Be sure to give your father my best."

"I will," her husband replied.

Scott gave up the walk-in closet. It was just big enough for her chair, an easel, a stand for her laptop and Wacom tablet, plus a few bins of supplies. She replaced the sallow overhead light with a bulb that emitted a natural spectrum. A room with a window would have been better, but at least she finally had her own private space in the apartment. She lined the beige walls with her art and made do. It felt a little too much like a cell, and there wasn't enough air circulation for her to use oils or acrylics without feeling woozy, but she was able to immerse herself in the pencil lines and digital paint strokes and got her commissioned pieces done on time.

But her new schedule got harder and harder to maintain. She had to be up by six to catch the bus to work, and after work she immediately got to work on their dinner and chores. Afterward, Scott would want her to keep him company while he watched his favorite sitcoms. Sometimes it was nine or ten before she got to work in her closet. Most nights she was up until one or two in the morning.

The constant low-grade sleep deprivation started taking its toll. She missed her bus a few times and was late to her job, and on a couple of embarrassing situations she fell asleep in long meetings. One day her boss called her into his office and told her she was on probation for three months and would be fired if her job performance didn't improve.

In her gut, she knew nothing good could come of telling Scott about what happened, but decided it would be fundamentally bad for their relationship if she started keeping secrets.

"You better not lose your job!" His tone was an unpleasant echo of his father's Christmas lecturing. "I can't have you unemployed and lounging around the house all day. We need the money for the house."

"I wouldn't be lounging; I made $1,000 on commissions just last month—" she began, but he'd already turned on his heel and marched off to the living room.

The next day, he surprised her with a wrapped box when she got home.

"I realized I acted like a real jerk yesterday, and I'm sorry," he said. "Your happiness is important to me, so I got you this."

She opened the box, and inside she found a new set of red-shellacked brushes and shiny tin tubes of paint. The mink, hog, and badger hair brushes were handmade, and the paints bore hand-inked German labels. She didn't recognize the maker's mark. The whole set had the aura of an expensive boutique.

"Wow. Thank you, honey." She blinked down at the set in pleased confusion. "They're lovely. Where did you find them?"

"My father told me where to get them. A special order from Europe. He commissioned a portrait of my mother a few months after they married, and the artist he hired used the same kind of brushes and paints. They were going through a kind of a rough patch at first, and he said the painting helped her perspective."

Rhetta was pretty sure there hadn't been any paintings in his parents' house at all aside from a couple of art fair landscapes. "Have I seen that one?"

"Oh, no. My father keeps it in his study behind little curtains. Even I haven't seen it; I think he had her pose nude." He cleared his throat, clearly a bit uncomfortable at the thought of seeing the artwork. "But these paints have the best colors in the world."

"If you haven't seen your mom's portrait, how do you know?"

"He got an artist to do a picture of me—I saw it when I went up there a couple of weekends ago. My dad originally planned to have both of us painted for a wedding present, but they couldn't find a good photo of you for the artist without asking me and ruining the surprise, so they decided to just do me. And then my parents decided they liked it so much they wanted to keep it. It's in the foyer; you'll see it next time we visit. It's an amazing portrait; the artist did me as a big-shot CEO. It's like I look at it and I can see my future." He paused, his eyes shining. "I know you can't paint in the closet because of the fumes, so I thought you could set your easel up in the living room."

She blinked at him. "Really?"

He smiled. "Just one condition."

The panic crab shuddered in her stomach. "What?"

"I want you to make *me* a painting for a change. I want you to put aside all that stuff you're doing for strangers and create a portrait of yourself that I'll feel proud to hang in my office. I want to show the world what a beautiful, talented wife I have. Can you do that for me?"

She was touched at his interest, and she couldn't think of a single reason to object. "Sure, honey, I can do that."

He drove her down to Dick Blick's and together they picked out an oil-primed stretched linen canvas.

"Oh, this will be just the right size to go between my bookshelves!" he exclaimed, holding the 30" x 30" canvas up against an imaginary wall in the middle of the aisle.

His enthusiasm was contagious. She smiled. "I'll try to get it done as soon as possible."

"No." He set down the canvas and took both her hands in his, gazing down at her intently. "I want you to take your time with this. I want your very best. I want to be the envy of the entire accounting firm."

The crab stirred inside her, but she didn't know why. She set her fear aside as unreasonable, maybe hormones or the weather. And she made herself smile.

"Absolutely, honey. I'll give you my very best."

"That's my girl." He planted a kiss on her forehead.

◇

When they got home, she emailed her clients to get a few weeks extension on her projects, and then she put down a drop cloth and set the easel atop it in the living room beside the sofa. She started lightly sketching in details with a soft graphite pencil.

"What's that in your hands?" Scott squinted at the sketch.

"Brushes and pastel pencils," she replied.

"I don't like those. Why don't you put in some lavender?"

She paused. "I'm allergic to lavender."

"So? You don't actually have to hold it to paint it, do you? Lavender's pretty. I like it."

Portraying herself holding something she couldn't even be in the same room with violated the fundamental truth of the art, but it also didn't seem worth arguing about. She decided she'd treat her husband like any other client and give him what he wanted. This wouldn't be a self-portrait; it would be a painting of an idealized woman who happened to look a lot like her.

"Okay, lavender it is."

With Scott looking over her shoulder during the sketching, the planned color scheme ended up with more pinks and purples than would have been her choice. She wanted to show herself in her favorite gray sweater; he wanted her in a pale pink suit jacket and cream-colored blouse. Rhetta was able to find some reference photos on the Ann Taylor website. She wanted to leave her lips natural; he asked for ruby red lipstick. Most everything ended up being a shade or two different than she would have chosen for herself.

The next evening, she peeled off the thin foils sealing the paint tubes. The paints had an odd organic smell unlike any other oil paints she'd used. It had a strongly spicy odor; she smelled cloves and lemongrass, and maybe catnip? A touch of licorice or absinthe? Beneath the spice, there was a slight stench of rot. Maybe the paint maker had used animal fats that had started to turn? But who would use an oil that could go rancid?

Rhetta squeezed paints into the wells on her palette and began to mix them. The thick colors flowed together wonderfully. There was no sign the paints had spoiled. She picked out a badger filbert brush and began work on her jacket.

The shaft of the wooden brush was surprisingly cold in her hand; she could almost imagine it was a chilled steel rod except it wasn't nearly heavy enough. As she worked, the cold seemed to seep into the bones of her hand and up into her wrist.

"Everything all right, honey?" Scott asked.

"It's... yes." She rubbed her wrist. "Is it cold in here?"

"Maybe a little; I'll go get you a wrap."

The afghan he brought down did little to keep her warm, and when she was done with her work for the evening, she felt exhausted and shuddered with chills. She knew she couldn't afford to call in sick now that she was on probation, so she took Echinacea and put herself to bed. At least she'd made pretty good progress on the painting; all the shapes and colors were roughed in, and she could start work on the details the next night.

The next morning, she woke in a groggy panic, realizing she'd slept through her alarm. Scott was already gone. She washed up at the sink and dressed as quickly as she could, praying that the second bus would be early for a change and that traffic through downtown would be light. The drive was pure agony; every tick of the clock made her feel like an accused witch being pressed under an enormous stone by inquisitors.

The bus was slow. Traffic was harsh. She got to work fifteen minutes late. Nearly in tears, she hurried up the stairs, thinking of what she could say to her supervisor to save her job—

"Oh, good, you're back." Her supervisor smiled and handed her a thick stack of printouts. "I need these proofed by three P.M."

"Yes, sir." Her hands shook as she took the papers.

He noticed her trembling. "Everything okay?"

"Yes. I... I just got startled on the stairwell."

"All right." He looked her up and down, frowning at her khakis and blue polo. "Were you wearing a different outfit earlier?"

She shook her head, her mouth dry. "No, sir."

"Huh. Must have been a trick of the light. Talk to you later."

Holding the papers to her chest, Rhetta stepped down the cubicle aisle to her gray-walled cell. The keyboard tray was pulled out and her computer was on, the screensaver locked. She set the papers down and unlocked her machine.

A Word document was open, and the cursor bar flashed at the end of a single line:

Finish the portrait.

The sudden smell of lavender crept up her nostrils, and Rhetta sneezed. Dabbing her runny nose with a Kleenex, she looked to the right of her computer. A single stalk of dried lavender lay on her desk. She wrapped it in a plastic bag from her desk drawer and stuck the offending flowers in the trash.

The panic crab squeezed her lungs, and she couldn't seem to get her breath for a moment. Who had broken into her computer and left the lavender? And how did he know about the painting? What was going on?

Rhetta turned to the documentation contractor across the aisle and waved nervously to get his attention.

He pulled out his ear buds. "What's up?"

"Was tech support working on my computer this morning?" Rhetta asked.

"I didn't see them. But you were here before me, so I'm maybe not the person to ask."

It took Rhetta a moment to get more words out. "I... you got here *after* I did?"

"Oh, definitely." He nodded.

"When?"

"Like, I dunno... I cut it pretty close this morning! Like maybe 7:55 or something."

Rhetta thought she might faint. "Okay, thanks."

She turned back to her computer and the cryptic sentence. It didn't make sense. She *knew* she'd just gotten into the office, fifteen minutes late. Was her coworker in on some weird prank people were playing on her? What in the hell was going on?

The building anxiety turned her bowels to liquid, so she got up to go to the ladies' room. When she pushed through the door, she came face-to-face with what she first thought was a newly-installed full-length wall mirror. And then she realized it was a flesh-and-blood woman staring back at her. A woman who looked almost exactly like her, except her double had ruby-red lipstick and wore a stylish pale purple blouse and matching slacks.

Her perfume smelled like lavender.

The woman's eerie face twisted into a scowl. "I told you to go finish the portrait!"

She slapped Rhetta across her cheek, hard, and when her palm connected it felt like she'd been hit with a Taser. The electric shock made her vision go white, and she felt herself drop.

Rhetta came awake in her chair in the living room, a chilly brush in her hand, the afghan draped across her shoulders. The portrait before her was nearly complete; all that was missing were some of the details on her face and in the lavender flowers.

"That is looking *so wonderful*, honey." Scott leaned down and kissed the top of her head. "I'm so proud of you."

"I... think I'm done for the evening." Her voice shook.

"You can finish it tomorrow."

He helped her clean her brushes, then took her upstairs and they went to bed. Once she was sure he was asleep, she crept out of bed, put on her favorite comfy warm-up suit to combat the chill in her core, and went back down to the living room.

Rhetta stopped a yard from the painting and stared at it, afraid to touch it. Whatever was going on, the painting was at the center of it; she could feel it in her bones. She couldn't finish it. She had to make it go away. Cut it up. Bury it. Burn it.

"No," said a voice to her right. Her voice. The lavender double's voice.

Rhetta ducked and raised a hand to ward off another stunning blow, but the doppelganger tackled her instead. They landed on the couch, the double pressing her down into the cushions with its surprising strength. The smell of lavender was nearly overpowering; it was hard to breathe through the flowery stench. How much had the creature already drained from her?

"You'll finish it," growled the doppelganger. Its breath smelled rancid like the undertones in the paints. Rhetta felt an electric prickling where its bare flesh touched hers.

"No, I won't!"

"You're nothing but a left-handed version of me. You'll do as I say." The doppelganger pried Rhetta's mouth open with hard fingers and pressed its lips to hers. The shock was intense but not enough to completely stupefy her.

The doppelganger's fingers stayed vises but the rest of its flesh turned to a foul gel. It started vomiting itself into the artist. The fluid was greasy and bitter with turpentine, poisonous herbs and heavy metals. Rhetta fought, to no avail; the doppelganger flowed into her, filling her throat and stomach and guts, seeping out into her veins and muscles.

Rhetta felt as though she was being worn like a tight suit. She felt her legs lift her body and walk her to the painting; she saw her hands uncover the palette and pick up the damp, cold brushes.

She shut her eyes, hoping that would confound the doppelganger. It did not. She felt the friction of the bristles on the canvas through the frigid shaft.

"It is finished," the doppelganger announced with her own throat. "And so are you."

It marched her out into the dark back yard, knelt beside a pile of autumn leaves, and stuck a finger down her throat.

This time, it was Rhetta's essence carried on the bitter purge. She found herself vomited from her own body, melting helplessly into the parched rakings.

"There." The doppelganger straightened up. It frowned down

at the old warm-up suit it wore, then stripped it off and unceremoniously dumped it beside the leaves. "An important man's wife would never wear something as frumpy as this!"

The doppelganger strode back to the house and shut the door.

Rhetta dried up in the leaves in the moonlight, blind, voiceless, bodiless, but she could still feel everything.

A little after midnight, a wind rose, stirred the leaves, and carried her away into the forgotten places in the night.

ORANGE IS FOR ANGUISH, BLUE FOR INSANITY

DAVID MORRELL

VON DORN'S WORK WAS CONTROVERSIAL, of course. The scandal his paintings caused among Parisian artists in the late 1800s provided the stuff of legend. Disdaining conventions, thrusting beyond accepted theories, Van Dorn seized upon the essentials of the craft to which he'd devoted his soul. Color, design, and texture. With those principles in mind, he created portraits and landscapes so different, so innovative, that their subjects seemed merely an excuse for Van Dorn to put paint onto canvas. His brilliant colors, applied in passionate splotches and swirls, often so thick that they projected an eighth of an inch from the canvas in the manner of a bas-relief, so dominated the viewer's perception that the person or scene depicted seemed secondary to technique.

Impressionism, the prevailing avant-garde theory of the late 1800s, imitated the eye's tendency to perceive the edges of peripheral objects as blurs. Van Dorn went one step farther and so emphasized the lack of distinction among objects that they seemed to melt together, to merge into an interconnected, pantheistic universe of color. The branches of a Van Dorn tree became ectoplasmic tentacles, thrusting toward the sky and the grass, just as tentacles from the sky and grass thrust toward the tree, all melding into a radiant swirl. He seemed to address himself not to the illusions of light but to reality itself, or at least to his theory of it. The tree *is* the sky, his technique asserted. The grass is the tree, and the sky the grass. All is one.

Van Dorn's approach proved so unpopular among theorists of his time that he frequently couldn't buy a meal in exchange for a canvas upon which he'd labored for months. His frustration produced a nervous breakdown. His self-mutilation shocked and alienated such onetime friends as Cézanne and Gauguin. He died in squalor and obscurity. Not until the 1920s, thirty years after his death, were his paintings recognized for the genius they displayed. In the 1940s, his soul-tortured character became the subject of a best-selling novel, and in the 1950s a Hollywood spectacular. These days, of course, even the least of his efforts can't be purchased for less than three million dollars.

Ah, art.

It started with Myers and his meeting with Professor Stuyvesant. "He agreed... reluctantly."

"I'm surprised he agreed at all," I said. "Stuyvesant hates Post-impressionism and Van Dorn in particular. Why didn't you ask someone easy, like Old Man Branford?

"Because Bradford's academic reputation sucks. I can't see writing a dissertation if it won't be published, and a respected dissertation director can make an editor pay attention. Besides, if I can convince Stuyvesant, I can convince anyone."

"Convince him of...?"

"That's what Stuyvesant wants to know," Myers said.

I remember that moment vividly, the way Myers straightened his lanky body, pushed his glasses close to his eyes, and frowned so hard that his curly red hair scrunched forward on his brow.

"Stuyvesant asked, even disallowing his own disinclination toward Van Dorn—God, the way that pompous asshole talks—why would I want to spend a year of my life writing about an artist who'd been the subject of countless books and articles, whose ramifications had been exhausted? Why not choose an obscure but promising Neo-Expressionist and gamble that *my* reputation would rise with his? Naturally the artist he recommended was one of Stuyvesant's favorites."

"Naturally," I said. "If he named the artist I think he did..."

Myers mentioned the name.

I nodded. "Stuyvesant's been collecting him for the past five years. He hopes the resale value of the paintings will buy him a town house in London when he retires. So what did you tell him?"

Myers opened his mouth to answer, then hesitated. With a brooding look, he turned toward a print of Van Dorn's swirling *Cypresses in a Hollow*, which hung beside a ceiling-high bookshelf crammed with Van Dorn biographies, analyses, and bound collections of reproductions. He didn't speak for a moment, as if the sight of the familiar print—its facsimile colors incapable of matching the brilliant tones of the original, its manufacturing process unable to recreate the exquisite texture of raised, swirled layers of paint on canvas—still took his breath away.

"So what did you tell him?" I asked again.

Myers exhaled with a mixture of frustration and admiration. "I said, what the critics wrote about Van Dorn was mostly junk. He agreed, with the implication that the paintings invited no less. I said, even the gifted critics hadn't probed to Van Dorn's essence. They were missing something crucial."

"Which is?"

"Exactly Stuyvesant's next question. You know how he keeps relighting his pipe when he gets impatient. I had to talk fast. I told him I didn't know what I was looking for, but there's something" —Myers gestured toward the print—"something there. Something nobody's noticed. Van Dorn hinted as much in his diary. I don't know what it is, but I'm convinced his paintings hide a secret." Myers glanced at me.

I raised my eyebrows.

"If nobody's noticed," Myers said, "it *must* be a secret, right?"

"But if *you* haven't noticed…"

Compelled, Myers turned toward the print again, his tone filled with wonder. "How do I know it's there? Because when I look at Van Dorn's paintings, I *sense* it. I *feel* it."

I shook my head. "I can imagine what Stuyvesant said to that. The man deals with art as if it's geometry, and there aren't any secrets in—"

"What he said was, if I'm becoming a mystic, I ought to be in the School of Religion, not Art. But if I wanted enough rope to hang myself and strangle my career, he'd give it to me. He liked to believe he had an open mind, he said."

"That's a laugh."

"Believe me, he wasn't joking. He had a fondness for Sherlock Holmes, he said. If I thought I'd found a mystery and could solve it, by all means do so. And at that, he gave me his most condescending smile and said he would mention it at today's faculty meeting."

"So what's the problem? You got what you wanted. He agreed to direct your dissertation. Why do you sound so—?"

"Today there *wasn't* any faculty meeting."

"Oh," I said. "You're fucked."

Myers and I had started graduate school at the University of Iowa together. That had been three years earlier, and we'd formed a strong enough friendship to rent adjacent rooms in an old apartment building near campus. The spinster who owned it had a hobby of doing watercolors—she had no talent, I might add—and rented only to art students so they would give her lessons. In Myer's case, she'd made an exception. He wasn't a painter, as I was. He was an art historian. Most painters work instinctively. They're not skilled at verbalizing what they want to accomplish. But words and not pigment were Myer's specialty. His impromptu lectures had quickly made him the old lady's favorite tenant.

After that day, however, she didn't see much of him. Nor did I. He wasn't at the classes we took together. I assumed he spent most of his time at the library. Late at night, when I noticed a light beneath his door and knocked, I didn't get an answer. I phoned him. Through the wall I heard the persistent, muffled ringing.

One evening I let the phone ring eleven times and was just about to hang up when he answered. He sounded exhausted.

"You're getting to be a stranger," I said.

His voice was puzzled. "Stranger? But I just saw you a couple of days ago."

"You mean, two weeks ago."

"Oh, shit," he said.

"I've got a six-pack. You want to—?"

"Yeah, I'd like that." He sighed. "Come over."

When he opened his door, I don't know what startled me more, the way Myers looked or what he'd done to his apartment.

I'll start with Myers. He'd always been thin, but now he looked gaunt, emaciated. His shirt and jeans were rumpled. His red hair was matted. Behind his glasses, his eyes looked bloodshot. He hadn't shaved. When he closed the door and reached for a beer, his hand shook.

His apartment was filled with, covered with—I'm not sure how to convey the dismaying effect of so much brilliant clutter—Van Dorn prints. On every inch of the walls. The sofa, the chairs, the desk, the TV, the bookshelves. And the drapes, and the ceiling, and except for a narrow path, the floor. Swirling sunflowers, olive trees, meadows, skies, and streams surrounded me, encompassed me, seemed to reach out for me. At the same time I felt swallowed. Just as the blurred edges of objects within each print seemed to melt into one another, so each print melted into the next. I was speechless amid the chaos of color.

Myers took several deep gulps of beer. Embarrassed by my stunned reaction to the room, he gestured toward the vortex of prints. "I guess you could say I'm immersing myself in my work."

"When did you eat last?"

He looked confused.

"That's what I thought." I walked along the narrow path among the prints on the floor and picked up the phone. "The pizza's on me." I ordered the largest supreme the nearest Pepi's had to offer. They didn't deliver beer, but I had another six-pack in my fridge, and I had the feeling we'd be needing it.

I set down the phone. "Myers, what the hell are you doing?"

"I told you…"

"Immersing yourself? Give me a break. You're cutting classes. You haven't showered in God knows how long. You look like shit. Your deal with Stuyvesant isn't worth destroying your health. Tell him you've changed your mind. Get another, an *easier*, dissertation director."

"Stuyvesant's got nothing to do with this."

"Damnit, what *does* it have to do with? The end of comprehensive exams, the start of dissertation blues?"

Myers gulped the rest of his beer and reached for another can. "No, blue is for insanity."

"*What?*"

"That's the pattern." Myers turned toward the swirling prints. "I studied them chronologically. The more Van Dorn became insane, the more he used blue. And orange is his color of anguish. If you match the paintings with the personal crises described in his biographies, you see a correspondent use of orange."

"Myers, you're the best friend I've got. So forgive me for saying I think you're off the deep end."

He swallowed more beer and shrugged as if to say he didn't expect me to understand.

"Listen," I said. "A personal color code, a connection between emotion and pigment, that's bullshit. I should know. You're the historian, but I'm the painter. I'm telling you, different people react to colors in different ways. Never mind the advertising agencies and their theories that some colors sell products more than others. It all depends on context. It depends on fashion. This year's 'in' color is next year's 'out.' But an honest-to-God great painter uses whatever color will give him the greatest effect. He's interested in creating, not selling."

"Van Dorn could have used a few sales."

"No question. The poor bastard didn't live long enough to come into fashion. But orange is for anguish and blue means insanity? Tell that to Stuyvesant and he'll throw you out of his office."

Myers took off his glasses and rubbed the bridge of his nose. "I feel so... maybe you're right."

"There's no maybe about it. I *am* right. You need food, a shower, and sleep. A painting's a combination of color and shape that people either like or they don't. The artist follows his instincts, uses whatever techniques he can master, and does his best. But if there's a secret in Van Dorn's work, it isn't a color code."

Myers finished his second beer and blinked in distress. "You know what I found out yesterday?"

I shook my head.

"The critics who devoted themselves to analyzing Van Dorn..."

"What about them?"

"They went insane, the same as he did."

"*What?* No way. I've studied Van Dorn's critics. They're as conventional and boring as Stuyvesant."

"You mean, the mainstream scholars. The safe ones. I'm talking about the truly brilliant ones. The ones who haven't been recognized for their genius, just as Van Dorn wasn't recognized."

"What happened to them?"

"They suffered. The same as Van Dorn."

"They were put in an asylum?"

"Worse than that."

"Myers, don't make me ask."

"The parallels are amazing. They each tried to paint. In Van Dorn's style. And just like Van Dorn, they stabbed out their eyes."

I guess it's obvious by now—Myers was what you might call "high-strung." No negative judgment intended. In fact, his excitability was one of the reasons I liked him. That and his imagination. Hanging around with him was never dull. He loved ideas. Learning was his passion. And he passed his excitement on to me.

The truth is, I needed all the inspiration I could get. I wasn't a bad artist. Not at all. On the other hand, I wasn't a great one, either. As I neared the end of grad school, I'd painfully come to realize that my work never would be more than "interesting." I didn't want to admit it, but I'd probably end up as a commercial artist in an advertising agency.

That night, however, Myers's imagination wasn't inspiring. It was scary. He was always going through phases of enthusiasm. El Greco, Picasso, Pollock. Each had preoccupied him to the point of obsession, only to be abandoned for another favorite and another. When he'd fixated on Van Dorn, I'd assumed it was merely one more infatuation.

But the chaos of Van Dorn prints in his room made clear he'd reached a greater excess of compulsion. I was skeptical about his insistence that there was a secret in Van Dorn's work. After all, great art can't be explained. You can analyze its technique, you can diagram its symmetry, but ultimately there's a mystery words can't communicate. Genius can't be summarized. As far as I could tell, Myers had been using the word *secret* as a synonym for indescribable brilliance.

When I realized he literally meant that Van Dorn had a secret, I was appalled. The distress in his eyes was equally appalling. His references to insanity, not only in Van Dorn but in his critics, made me worry that Myers himself was having a breakdown. Stabbed out their eyes, for Christ's sake?

I stayed up with Myers till five A.M., trying to calm him, to convince him he needed a few days' rest. We finished the six-pack I'd brought, the six-pack in my refrigerator, and another six-pack I bought from an art student down the hall. At dawn, just before Myers dozed off and I staggered back to my room, he murmured that I was right. He needed a break, he said. Tomorrow he'd call his folks. He'd ask if they'd pay his plane fare back to Denver.

Hung over, I didn't wake up till late afternoon. Disgusted that I'd missed my classes, I showered and managed to ignore the taste of last night's pizza. I wasn't surprised when I phoned Myers and got no answer. He probably felt as shitty as I did. But after sunset, when I called again, then knocked on his door, I started to worry.

His door was locked, so I went downstairs to get the landlady's key. That's when I saw the note in my mail slot.

> *Meant what I said. Need a break. Went home. Will be in touch. Stay cool. Paint well. I love you, pal. Your friend forever,*
>
> *Myers*

My throat ached. He never came back. I saw him only twice after that. Once in New York, and once in…

Let's talk about New York. I finished my graduate project, a series of landscapes that celebrated Iowa's big-sky rolling, dark-soiled, wooded hills. A local patron paid fifty dollars for one of them. I gave three to the university's hospital. The rest are who knows where.

Too much has happened.

As I predicted, the world wasn't waiting for my good-but-not-great efforts. I ended where I belonged, as a commercial artist for a Madison Avenue advertising agency. My beer cans are the best in the business.

I met a smart, attractive woman who worked in the marketing department of a cosmetics firm. One of my agency's clients. Professional conferences led to personal dinners and intimate evenings that lasted all night. I proposed. She agreed.

We'd live in Connecticut, she said. Of course.

When the time was right, we might have children, she said.

Of course.

Myers phoned me at the office. I don't know how he knew where I was. I remember his breathless voice.

"I found it," he said.

"Myers?" I grinned. "Is it really—? *How are you? Where have—?*"

"I'm telling you. I found it!"

"I don't know what you're—"

"Remember? Van Dorn's secret!"

In a rush, I did remember—the excitement Myers could generate, the wonderful, expectant conversations of my youth—the days and especially the nights when ideas and the future beckoned. "Van Dorn? You're still—?"

"Yes! I was right! There *was* a secret!"

"You crazy bastard, I don't care about Van Dorn. But I care about you! Why did you—? I never forgave you for disappearing."

"I had to. Couldn't let you hold me back. Couldn't let you—"

"For your own good!"

"So *you* thought. But I was right!"

"Where *are* you?"

"Exactly where you'd expect me to be."

"For the sake of old friendship, Myers, don't piss me off. *Where are you?*"

"The Metropolitan Museum of Art."

"Will you stay there, Myers? While I catch a cab? I can't wait to see you."

"I can't wait for you to see what *I* see!"

I postponed a deadline, canceled two appointments, and told my fiancée I couldn't meet her for dinner. She sounded miffed. But Myers was all that mattered.

He stood beyond the pillars at the entrance. His face was haggard, but his eyes were stars. I hugged him. "Myers, it's so good to—"

"I want you to see something. Hurry."

He tugged at my coat, rushing.

"But where have you been?"

"I'll tell you later."

We entered the Postimpressionist gallery. Bewildered, I followed Myers and let him anxiously sit me on a bench before Van Dorn's *Fir Trees at Sunrise*.

I'd never seen the original. Prints couldn't compare. After a year of drawing ads for feminine beauty aids, I was devastated. Van Dorn's power brought me close to…

Tears?

For my visionless skills.

For the youth I'd abandoned a year before.

"Look!" Myers said. He raised his arm and gestured toward the painting.

I frowned. I looked.

It took time—an hour, two hours—and the coaxing vision of Myers. I concentrated. And then, at last, I saw.

Profound admiration changed to…

My heart raced. As Myers traced his hand across the painting one final time, as a guard who had been watching us with increasing wariness stalked forward to stop him from touching the canvas, I felt as if a cloud has dispersed and a lens had focused.

"Jesus," I said.

"You see? The bushes, the trees, the branches?"

"Yes! Oh, God, yes! Why didn't I—?"

"Notice before? Because it doesn't show up in the prints," Myers said. "Only in the originals. And the effect's so deep, you have to study them—"

"Forever."

"It seems that long. But I knew. I was right."

"A secret."

When I was a boy, my father—how I loved him—took me mushroom hunting. We drove from town, climbed a barbed-wire fence, walked through a forest, and reached a slope of dead elms. My father told me to search the top of the slope while he checked the bottom.

An hour later he came back with two large paper sacks filled with mushrooms. I hadn't found even one.

"I guess your spot was lucky," I said.

"But they're all around you," my father said.

"All around me? Where?"

"You didn't look hard enough."

"I crossed this slope five times."

"You searched, but you didn't really see," my father said. He picked up a long stick and pointed it toward the ground. "Focus your eyes toward the end of the stick."

I did…

And I've never forgotten the hot excitement that surged through my stomach. The mushrooms appeared as if by magic. They'd been there all along, of course, so perfectly adapted to their surroundings, their color so much like dead leaves, their shape so much like bits of wood and chunks of rock that they'd been invisible to ignorant eyes. But once my vision adjusted, once my mind reevaluated the visual impressions it received, I saw mushrooms everywhere, seemingly thousands of them. I'd been standing on them, walking over them, staring at them, and hadn't realized.

I felt an infinitely greater shock when I saw the tiny faces Myers made me recognize in Van Dorn's *Fir Trees at Sunrise*. Most were smaller than a quarter of an inch, hints and suggestions, dots and curves, blended perfectly with the landscape. They weren't exactly human, though they did have mouths, noses, and eyes. Each mouth was a black, gaping maw, each nose a jagged gash, the eyes dark sinkholes of despair. The twisted faces seemed to be screaming in total agony. I could almost hear their anguished shrieks, their tortured wails. I thought of damnation. Of hell.

As soon as I noticed the faces, they emerged from the swirling texture of the painting in such abundance that the landscape became an illusion, the grotesque faces reality. The fir trees turned into an obscene cluster of writhing arms and pain-racked torsos.

I stepped back in shock an instant before the guard would have pulled me away.

"Don't touch the—" the guard said.

Myers had already rushed to point at another Van Dorn, the

original *Cypresses in a Hollow*. I followed, and now that my eyes knew what to look for, I saw small, tortured faces in every branch and rock. The canvas swarmed with them.

"Jesus."

"And this!"

Myers hurried to *Sunflowers at Harvest Time*, and again, as if a lens had changed focus, I no longer saw flowers but anguished faces and twisted limbs. I lurched back, felt a bench against my legs, and sat.

"You were right," I said.

The guard stood nearby, scowling.

"Van Dorn did have a secret," I said. I shook my head in astonishment.

"It explains everything," Myers said. "These agonized faces give his work depth. They're hidden, but we *sense* them. We *feel* the anguish beneath the beauty."

"But why would he—?"

"I don't think he had a choice. His genius drove him insane. It's my guess that this is how he literally saw the world. These faces are the demons he wrestled with. The festering products of his insanity. And they're not just an illustrator's gimmick. Only a genius could have painted them for all the world to see and yet have so perfectly imposed them on the landscape that *no one* would see. Because he took them for granted in a terrible way."

"No one? *You* saw, Myers."

He smiled. "Maybe that means I'm crazy."

"I doubt it, friend." I returned the smile. "It does mean you're persistent. This'll make your reputation."

"But I'm not through yet," Myers said.

I frowned.

"So far all I've got is a fascinating case of optical illusion. Tortured souls writhing beneath, perhaps producing, incomparable beauty. I call them 'secondary images.' In your ad work I guess they'd be called 'subliminal.' But this isn't commercialism. This is a genuine artist who had the brilliance to use his madness as an ingredient in his vision. I need to go deeper."

"What are you talking about?"

"The paintings here don't provide enough examples. I've seen his work in Paris and Rome, in Zurich and London. I've borrowed from my parents to the limits of their patience and my conscience. But I've seen, and I know what I have to do. The anguished faces began in 1889, when Van Dorn left Paris in disgrace. His early paintings were abysmal. He settled in La Verge in the south of France. Six months later his genius suddenly exploded. In a frenzy, he painted. He returned to Paris. He showed his work, but no one appreciated it. He kept painting, kept showing. Still no one appreciated it. He returned to La Verge, reached the peak of his genius, and went totally insane. He had to be committed to an asylum, but not before he stabbed out his eyes. That's my dissertation. I intend to parallel his course. To match his paintings with his biography, to show how the faces increased and became more severe as his madness worsened. I want to dramatize the turmoil in his soul as he imposed his twisted vision on each landscape."

It was typical of Myers to take an excessive attitude and make it even more excessive. Don't misunderstand. His discovery was important. But he didn't know when to stop. I'm not an art historian, but I've read enough to know that what's called "psychological criticism," the attempt to analyze great art as a manifestation of neuroses, is considered off-the-wall, to put it mildly. If Myers handed Stuyvesant a psychological dissertation, the pompous bastard would throw Myers out of his office.

That was one misgiving I had about what Myers planned to do with his discovery. Another troubled me more. *I intend to parallel Van Dorn's course*, he'd said, and after we left the museum and walked through Central Park, I realized how literally Myers meant it.

"I'm going to southern France," he said.

I stared in surprise. "You don't mean—"

"La Varge? That's right. I want to write my dissertation there."

"But—"

"What place could be more appropriate? It's the village where Van Dorn suffered his nervous breakdown and eventually went insane. If it's possible, I'll even rent the same room *he* did."

"Myers, this sounds too far out, even for you."

"But it makes perfect sense. I need to immerse myself. I need atmosphere, a sense of history. So I can put myself in the mood to write."

"The last time you immersed yourself, you crammed your room with Van Dorn prints, didn't sleep, didn't eat, didn't bathe. I hope—"

"I admit I got too involved. But last time I didn't know what I was looking for. Now that I've found it, I'm in good shape."

"You look strung out to *me*."

"An optical illusion." Myers grinned.

"Come on, I'll treat you to drinks and dinner."

"Sorry. Can't. I've got a plane to catch."

"You're leaving *tonight*? But I haven't seen you since—"

"You can buy me that dinner when I finish the dissertation."

I never did. I saw him only one more time. Because of the letter he sent two months later. Or asked his nurse to send. She wrote down what he'd said and added an explanation of her own. He'd blinded himself, of course.

You were right. Shouldn't have gone. But when did I ever take advice? I always knew better, didn't I? Now it's too late. What I showed you that day at the Met—God help me, there's so much more. I found the truth, and now I can't bear it. Don't make my mistake. Don't look ever again, I beg you, at Van Dorn's paintings. The headaches. Can't stand the pain. Need a break. Am going home. Stay cool. Paint well. I love you, pal. Your friend forever,

Myers

In her postscript, the nurse apologized for her English. She sometimes took care of aged Americans on the Riviera, she said, and had
to learn the language. But she understood what she heard better
than she could speak it or write it, and hoped that what she'd written made sense. It didn't, but that wasn't her fault. Myers had been
in great pain, sedated with morphine, not thinking clearly, she said.
The miracle was that he'd managed to be coherent at all.

> *Your friend was staying at our only hotel. The manager
> says that he slept little and ate even less. His research was
> obsessive. He filled his room with reproductions of Van
> Dorn's work. He tried to duplicate Van Dorn's daily
> schedule. He demanded paints and canvas, refused all meals,
> and wouldn't answer his door. Three days ago, a scream
> woke the manager. The door was blocked. It took three
> men to break it down. Your friend used the sharp end of a
> paintbrush to stab out his eyes. The clinic here is excellent.
> Physically your friend will recover, although he will never see
> again. But I worry about his mind.*

Myers had said he was going home. It had taken a week for the
letter to reach me. I assumed his parents would have been in-
formed immediately by phone or telegram. He was probably back
in the States by now. I knew his parents lived in Denver, but I
didn't know their first names or address, so I took a cab to the
New York Public Library, checked the Denver phone book, and
went down the list for Myers, using my credit card to call every one
of them till I made contact. Not with his parents but with a family
friend watching their house. Myers hadn't been flown to the States.
His parents had gone to the south of France. I caught the next
available plane. Not that it matters, but I was supposed to be married that weekend.

La Verge is thirty kilometers inland from Nice. I hired a driver. The road curved through olive trees and farmland, crested cypress-covered hills, and often skirted cliffs. Passing an orchard, I had the eerie conviction that I'd seen it before. Entering La Verge, my déjà vu strengthened. The village seemed trapped in the nineteenth century. Except for phone poles and power lines, it looked exactly as Van Dorn had painted it. I recognized the narrow, cobbled streets and rustic shops that Van Dorn had made famous. I asked directions. It wasn't hard to find Myers and his parents.

The last time I saw my friend, the undertaker was putting the lid on his coffin. I had trouble sorting out the details, but despite my burning tears, I gradually came to understand that the local clinic was as good as the nurse had assured me in her note. All things being equal, he'd have lived.

But the damage to his mind had been another matter. He'd complained of headaches. He'd also become increasingly distressed. Even morphine hadn't helped. He'd been left alone only for a minute, appearing to be asleep. In that brief interval he'd managed to stagger from his bed, grope across the room, and find a pair of scissors. Yanking off his bandages, he'd jabbed the scissors into an empty eye socket and tried to ream out his brain. He'd collapsed before accomplishing his purpose, but the damage had been sufficient. Death had taken two days.

His parents were pale, incoherent with shock. I somehow controlled my own shock enough to try to comfort them. Despite the blur of those terrible hours, I remember noticing the kind of irrelevance that signals the mind's attempt to reassert normality. Myers's father wore Gucci loafers and an eighteen-karat Rolex watch. In grad school Myers had lived on as strict a budget as I had. I had no idea he came from wealthy parents.

I helped them make arrangements to fly his body back to the States. I went to Nice with them and stayed by their side as they watched the crate that contained his coffin being loaded onto the baggage compartment of the plane. I shook their hands and hugged them. I waited as they sobbed and trudged down the boarding tunnel. An hour later I was back in La Verge.

I returned because of a promise. I wanted to ease his parents' suffering—and my own. Because I'd been his friend. "You've got too much to take care of," I'd said to his parents. "The long trip home. The arrangements for the funeral." My voice had choked. "Let me help. I'll settle things here, pay whatever bills he owes, pack up his clothes and…" I took a deep breath. "And his books and whatever else he had and send them home to you. Let me do that. I'd consider it a kindness. Please. I need to do *something*."

True to his ambition, Myers had managed to rent the same room taken by Van Dorn at the village's only hotel. Don't be surprised that it was available. The management used it to promote the hotel. A plaque announced the historic value of the room. The furnishings were the same style as when Van Dorn had stayed there. Tourists had paid to peer in and sniff the residue of genius. But business had been slow this season, and Myers had wealthy parents. For a generous sum, coupled with his typical enthusiasm, he'd convinced the hotel's owner to let him have that room.

I rented a different room—more like a closet—two doors down the hall and, my eyes still burning from tears, went into Van Dorn's musty sanctuary to pack my dear dead friend's possessions. Prints of Van Dorn paintings were everywhere, several splattered with dried blood. Heartsick, I made a stack of them.

That's when I found the diary.

During grad school I'd taken a course in Postimpressionism that emphasized Van Dorn, and I'd read a facsimile edition of his diary. The publisher had photocopied the handwritten pages and bound them, adding an introduction and footnotes. The diary had been cryptic from the start, but as Van Dorn became more feverish about his work, as his nervous breakdown became more severe, his statements deteriorated into riddles. His handwriting—hardly neat, even when he was sane—went quickly out of control and finally turned into almost indecipherable slashes and curves as he rushed to unloose his frantic thoughts.

I sat at a small wooden desk and paged through the diary, recognizing phrases I'd read years before. With each passage my stomach turned colder. Because this diary *wasn't* the published photocopy. Instead, it was a notebook, and though I wanted to believe that Myers had somehow, impossibly, gotten his hands on the original diary, I knew I was fooling myself. The pages in this ledger weren't yellow and brittle with age. The ink hadn't faded till it was brown more than blue. The notebook had been purchased and written in recently. It wasn't Van Dorn's diary. It belonged to *Myers*. The ice in my stomach turned to lava.

Glancing sharply away from the ledger, I saw a shelf beyond the desk and a stack of other notebooks. Apprehensive, I grabbed them and in a fearful rush flipped through them. My stomach threatened to erupt. Each notebook was the same, the words identical.

My hands shook as I looked again to the shelf, found the facsimile edition of the original, and compared it with the notebooks. I moaned, imagining Myers at this desk, his expression intense and insane as he reproduced the diary word for word, slash for slash, curve for curve. Eight times.

Myers had indeed immersed himself, straining to put himself into Van Dorn's disintegrating frame of mind. And in the end he'd succeeded. The weapon Van Dorn had used to stab out his eyes had been the sharp end of a paintbrush. In the mental hospital, Van Dorn had finished the job by skewering his brain with a pair of scissors. Like Myers. Or vice versa. When Myers had finally broken, had he and Van Dorn been horribly indistinguishable?

I pressed my hands to my face. Whimpers squeezed from my convulsing throat. It seemed forever before I stopped sobbing. My consciousness strained to control my anguish. ("Orange is for anguish," Myers had said.) Rationality fought to subdue my distress. ("The critics who devoted themselves to analyzing Van Dorn,"

Myers had said. "The ones who haven't been recognized for their genius, just as Van Dorn wasn't recognized. They suffered... And just like Van Dorn, they stabbed out their eyes.") Had they done it with a paintbrush? I wondered. Were the parallels that exact? And in the end, had they, too, used scissors to skewer their brains?

I scowled at the prints I'd been stacking. Many still surrounded me—on the walls, the floor, the bed, the windows, even the ceiling. A swirl of colors. A vortex of brilliance.

Or at least I once had thought of them as brilliant. But now, with the insight Myers had given me, with the vision I'd gained in the Metropolitan Museum, I saw behind the sun-drenched cypresses and hayfields, the orchards and meadows, toward their secret darkness, toward the minuscule, twisted arms and gaping mouths, the black dots of tortured eyes, the blue knots of writhing bodies. ("Blue is for insanity," Myers had said.)

All it took was a slight shift of perception, and there *weren't* any orchards and hayfields, only a terrifying gestalt of souls in hell. Van Dorn had indeed invented a new stage of Impressionism. He'd impressed upon the splendor of God's creation the teeming images of his own disgust. His paintings didn't glorify. They abhorred. Everywhere Van Dorn had looked, he'd seen his own private nightmare. Blue was for insanity, indeed, and if you fixated on Van Dorn's insanity long enough, you, too, became insane. ("Don't look ever again, I beg you, at Van Dorn's paintings," Myers had said in his letter.) In the last stages of his breakdown, had Myers somehow become lucid enough to try to warn me? ("Can't stand the headaches. Need a break. Am going home.") In a way I'd never suspected, he'd indeed gone home.

Another startling thought occurred to me. ("The critics who devoted themselves to analyzing Van Dorn. They each tried to paint in Van Dorn's style," Myers had said a year ago.) As if attracted by a magnet, my gaze swung across the welter of prints and focused on the corner across from me, where two canvas originals leaned against the wall. I shivered, stood, and haltingly approached them.

They'd been painted by an amateur. Myers was an art *historian*, after all. The colors were clumsily applied, especially the splotches of orange and blue. The cypresses were crude. At their bases, the rocks looked like cartoons. The sky needed texture. But I knew what the black dots among them were meant to suggest. I understood the purpose of the tiny blue gashes. The miniature, anguished faces and twisted limbs were implied, even if Myers had lacked the talent to depict them. He'd contracted Van Dorn's madness. All that had remained were the terminal stages.

I sighed from the pit of my soul. As the village's church bell rang, I prayed that my friend had found piece.

It was dark when I left the hotel. I needed to walk, to escape the greater darkness of that room, to feel at liberty, to think. But my footsteps and inquiries led me down a narrow cobbled street toward the village's clinic, where Myers had finished what he'd started in Van Dorn's room. I asked at the desk and five minutes later introduced myself to an attractive, dark-haired, thirtyish woman.

The nurse's English was more than adequate. She said her name was Clarisse.

"You took care of my friend," I said. "You sent me the letter he dictated and added a note of your own."

She nodded. "He worried me. He was so distressed."

The fluorescent lights in the vestibule hummed. We sat on a bench.

I'm trying to understand why he killed himself," I said. "I think I know, but I'd like your opinion."

Her eyes, a bright, intelligent hazel, suddenly were guarded. "He stayed too long in his room. He studied too much." She shook her head and stared toward the floor. "The mind can be a trap. It can be a torture."

"But he was excited when he came here?"

"Yes."

"Despite his studies, he behaved as if he'd come on vacation?"

"Very much."

"Then what made him change? My friend was unusual, I agree. What we call high-strung. But he *enjoyed* doing research. He might have looked sick from too much work, but he thrived on learning. His body was nothing, but his mind was brilliant. What tipped the balance, Clarisse?"

"Tipped the—"

"Made him depressed instead of excited. What did he learn that made him—?"

She stood and looked at her watch. "Forgive me. I stopped work twenty minutes ago. I'm expected at a friend's."

My voice hardened. "Of course. I wouldn't want to keep you."

Outside the clinic, beneath the light at its entrance, I stared at my own watch, surprised to see that it was almost eleven-thirty. Fatigue made my knees ache. The trauma of the day had taken away my appetite, but I knew I should try to eat, and after walking back to the hotel's dining room, I ordered a chicken sandwich and a glass of Chablis. I meant to eat in my room but never got that far. Van Dorn's room and the diary beckoned.

The sandwich and wine went untasted. Sitting at the desk, surrounded by the swirling colors and hidden horrors of Van Dorn prints, I opened a notebook and tried to understand.

A knock at the door made me turn.

Again I glanced at my watch, astonished to find that hours had passed like minutes. It was almost two A.M.

The knock was repeated, gentle but insistent. The manager?

"Come in," I said in French. "The door isn't locked."

The knob turned. The door swung open.

Clarisse stepped in. Instead of her nurse's uniform, she now wore sneakers, jeans, and a sweater whose tight-fitting yellow accentuated the hazel in her eyes.

"I apologize," she said in English. "I must have seemed rude at the clinic.

"Not at all. You had an appointment. I was keeping you."

She shrugged self-consciously. "I sometimes leave the clinic so late, I don't have a chance to see my friend."

"I understand perfectly."

She drew a hand through her lush, long hair. "My friend got tired. As I walked home, passing the hotel, I saw a light up here. On the chance it might be you..."

I nodded, waiting.

I had the sense she'd been avoiding it, but now she turned toward the room. Toward where I'd found the dried blood on the prints. "The doctor and I came as fast as we could when the manager phoned us that afternoon." She stared at the prints. "How could so much beauty cause so much pain?"

"Beauty?" I glanced toward the tiny, gaping mouths.

"You mustn't stay here. Don't make the mistake your friend did."

"Mistake?"

"You've had a long journey. You've suffered a shock. You need to rest. You'll wear yourself out as your friend did."

"I was just looking through some things of his. I'll be packing them to send them back to America."

"Do it quickly. You mustn't torture yourself by thinking about what happened here. It isn't good to surround yourself with the things that disturbed your friend. Don't intensify your grief."

"'Surround myself?'" My friend would have said 'immerse.'"

"You look exhausted. Come." She held out her hand. "I'll take you to your room. Sleep will ease your pain. If you need some pills to help you..."

"Thanks. But a sedative won't be necessary."

She continued to offer her hand. I took it and went to the hallway.

For a moment I stared back toward the prints and the horror within the beauty. I said a silent prayer for Myers, shut off the lights, and locked the door.

We went down the hall. In my room, I sat on the bed.

"Sleep long and well," she said.

"I hope."

"You have my sympathy." She kissed my cheek.

I touched her shoulder. Her lips shifted toward my own. She leaned against me.

We sank toward the bed. In silence, we made love.

Sleep came like her kisses, softly smothering.

But in my nightmares there were tiny, gaping mouths.

Sunlight glowed through my window. With aching eyes I looked at my watch. Half past ten. My head hurt.

Clarisse had left a note on my bureau.

> *Last night was sympathy. To share and ease your grief. Do what you intended. Pack your friend's belongings. Send them to America. Go with them. Don't make your friend's mistake. Don't, as you said he said, "immerse" yourself. Don't let beauty give you pain.*

I meant to leave. I truly believe that. I phoned the front desk and asked the concierge to send up some boxes. After I showered and shaved, I went to Myers's room, where I finished stacking the prints. I made another stack of books and another of clothes. I packed everything into the boxes and looked around to make sure I hadn't forgotten anything.

The two canvases that Myers had painted still leaned against a corner. I decided not to take them. No one needed to be reminded of the delusions that had overcome him.

All that remained was to seal the boxes, to address and mail them. But as I started to close the flap on a box, I saw the note-books inside.

So much suffering, I thought. So much waste.

Once more I leafed through a notebook. Myers had translated

various passages. Van Dorn's discouragement about his failed career. His reasons for leaving Paris to come to La Verge—the stifling, backbiting artists' community, the snobbish critics and their sneering responses to his early efforts. *Need to free myself of convention. Need to void myself of aesthete politics, to shit it out of me. To find what's never been painted. To feel instead of being told what to feel. To see instead of imitating what others have seen.*

I knew from the biographies how impoverished Van Dorn's ambition had made him. In Paris he'd literally eaten slops thrown into alleys behind restaurants. He'd been able to afford his quest to La Verge only because a successful but very conventional (and now ridiculed) painter friend had loaned him a small sum of money. Eager to conserve his endowment, Van Dorn had walked all the way from Paris to the south of France.

In those days, you have to remember, the Riviera was an unfashionable area of hills, rocks, farms, and villages. Limping into La Verge, Van Dorn must have been a pathetic sight. He'd chosen this provincial town precisely because it *was* unconventional, because it offered mundane scenes so in contrast with the salons of Paris that no other artist would dare to paint them.

Need to create what's never been imagined, he'd written. For six despairing months he tried and failed. He finally self-doubted, then suddenly reversed himself and, in a year of unbelievably brilliant productivity, gave the world thirty-eight masterpieces. At the time, of course, he couldn't trade any canvas for a meal. But the world knows better now.

He must have painted in a frenzy. His sudden-found energy must have been enormous. To me, a would-be artist with technical facility but only conventional eyes, he achieved the ultimate. Despite his suffering, I envied him. When I compared my maudlin, Wyeth-like depictions of Iowa landscapes to Van Dorn's trendsetting genius, I despaired. The task awaiting me back in the States was to imitate beer cans and cigarettes for magazine ads.

I continued flipping through the notebook, tracking the course of Van Dorn's despair and epiphany. His victory had a price, to be sure. Insanity. Self-blinding. Suicide. But I had to wonder if perhaps, as he died, he'd have chosen to reverse his life if he'd been able. He must have known how remarkable, how truly astonishing, his work had become.

Or perhaps he didn't. The last canvas he'd painted before stabbing his eyes had been of himself. A lean-faced, brooding man with short, thinning hair, sunken features, pallid skin, and a scraggly beard. The famous portrait reminded me of how I always thought Christ would have looked just before he was crucified. All that was missing was the crown of thorns. But Van Dorn had a different crown of thorns. Not around but *within* him. Disguised among his scraggly beard and sunken features, the tiny, gaping mouths and writhing bodies told it all. His suddenly acquired vision had stung him too much.

As I read the notebook, again distressed by Myers's effort to reproduce Van Dorn's agonized words and handwriting exactly, I reached the section where Van Dorn described his epiphany: *La Verge! I walked! I saw! I feel! Canvas! Paint! Creation and damnation!*

After that cryptic passage, the notebook—and Van Dorn's diary—became totally incoherent. Except for the persistent refrain of severe and increasing headaches.

I was waiting outside the clinic when Clarisse arrived to start her shift at three o'clock. The sun was brilliant, glinting off her eyes. She wore a burgundy skirt and a turquoise blouse. Mentally I stroked their cottony texture.

When she saw me, her footsteps faltered. Forcing a smile, she approached.

"You came to say good-bye?" She sounded hopeful.

"No. To ask you some questions."

Her smile disintegrated. "I mustn't be late for work."

"This'll take just a minute. My French vocabulary needs improvement. I didn't bring a dictionary. The name of this village. La

Verge. What does it mean?"

She hunched her shoulders as if to say the question was unimportant. "It's not very colorful. The literal translation is 'the stick.'"

"That's all?"

She reacted to my frown. "There are rough equivalents. 'The branch.' 'The switch.' A willow, for example, that a father might use to discipline a child."

"And it doesn't mean anything else?"

"Indirectly. The synonyms keep getting farther from the literal sense. A wand, perhaps. Or a rod. The kind of forked stick that people who claim they can find water hold ahead of them when they walk across a field. The stick is supposed to bend down if there's water."

"We call it a divining rod. My father once told me he'd seen a man who could actually make one work. I always suspected the man just tilted the stick with his hands. Do you suppose this village got its name because long ago someone found water here with a divining rod?"

"Why would anyone have bothered when these hills have so many streams and springs? What makes you interested in the name?"

"Something I read in Van Dorn's diary. The village's name excited him for some reason."

"But *anything* could have excited him. He was insane."

"Eccentric. But he didn't become insane until after that passage in his diary."

"You mean, his *symptoms* didn't show themselves until after that. You're not a psychiatrist."

I had to agree.

"Again, I'm afraid I'll seem rude. I really must go to work." She hesitated. "Last night..."

"Was exactly what you described in the note. A gesture of sympathy. An attempt to ease my grief. You didn't mean it to be the start of anything."

"Please do what I asked. Please leave. Don't destroy yourself like the others."

"*Others?*"

"Like your friend."

"No, you said, 'others.'" My words were rushed. "Clarisse, tell me."

She glanced up, squinted as if she'd been cornered. "After your friend stabbed out his eyes, I heard talk around the village. Older people. It could be merely gossip that became exaggerated with the passage of time."

"What did they say?"

She squinted harder. "Twenty years ago a man came here to do research on Van Dorn. He stayed three months and had a breakdown."

"He stabbed out his eyes?"

"Rumors drifted back that he blinded himself in a mental hospital in England. Ten years before, another man came. He jabbed scissors through an eye, all the way into his brain."

I stared, unable to control the spasms that racked my shoulder blades. "What the hell is going on?"

I asked around the village. No one would talk to me. At the hotel the manager told me he'd decided to stop renting Van Dorn's room. I had to remove Myers's belongings at once.

"But I can still stay in *my* room?"

"If that's what you wish. I don't recommend it, but even France is still a free country."

I paid the bill, went upstairs, moved the packed boxes from Van Dorn's room into mine, and turned in surprise as the phone rang.

The call was from my fiancée.

When was I coming home?

I didn't know.

What about the wedding this weekend?

The wedding would have to be postponed.

I winced as she slammed down the phone.

I sat on the bed and couldn't help recalling the last time I'd sat there, with Clarisse standing over me, just before we'd made love. I was throwing away the life I'd tried to build.

For a moment I came close to calling back my fiancée, but a different sort of compulsion made me scowl toward the boxes, toward Van Dorn's diary. In the note Clarisse had added to Myers's letter, she'd said that his research had become so obsessive that he'd tried to recreate Van Dorn's daily habits. Again it occurred to me—at the end, had Myers and Van Dorn become indistinguishable? Was the secret to what had happened to Myers hidden in the diary, just as the suffering faces were hidden in Van Dorn's paintings? I grabbed one of the ledgers. Scanning the pages, I looked for references to Van Dorn's daily routine. And so it began.

I've said that except for telephone poles and electrical lines, La Verge seemed caught in the previous century. Not only was the hotel still in existence, but so were Van Dorn's favorite tavern, and the bakery where he'd bought his morning croissant. A small restaurant he favored remained in business. On the edge of the village, a trout stream where he sometimes sat with a mid-afternoon glass of wine still bubbled along, though pollution had long since killed the trout. I went to all of them, in the order and at the time he recorded in his diary.

After a week—breakfast at eight, lunch at two, a glass of wine at the trout stream, a stroll to the countryside, then back to the room—I knew the diary so well, I didn't need to refer to it. Mornings had been Van Dorn's time to paint. The light was best then, he'd written. And evenings were a time for remembering and sketching.

It finally came to me that I wouldn't be following the schedule exactly if I didn't paint and sketch when Van Dorn had done so. I bought a notepad, canvas, pigments, a palette, whatever I needed, and, for the first time since leaving grad school, I tried to *create*. I used local scenes that Van Dorn had favored and produced what you'd expect: uninspired versions of Van Dorn's paintings. With no discoveries, no understanding of what had ultimately undermined Myers's sanity, tedium set in. My finances were almost gone. I prepared to give up.

Except...

I had the disturbing sense that I'd missed something. A part of Van Dorn's routine that wasn't explicit in the diary. Or something about the locales themselves that I hadn't noticed.

Clarisse found me sipping wine on the sunlit bank of the no longer trout-filled stream. I felt her shadow and turned toward her silhouette against the sun.

I hadn't seen her for two weeks, since our uneasy conversation outside the clinic. Even with the sun in my eyes, she looked more beautiful than I remembered.

"When was the last time you changed your clothes?" she asked.

A year ago I'd said the same to Myers.

"You need a shave. You've been drinking too much. You look awful."

I sipped my wine and shrugged. "Well, you know what the drunk said about his bloodshot eyes. You think they look bad to you? You should see them from *my* side."

"At least you can joke."

"I'm beginning to think that I'*m* the joke."

"You're definitely not a joke." She sat beside me. "You're becoming your friend. Why don't you leave?"

"I'm tempted."

"Good." She touched my hand.

"Clarisse?"

"Yes?"

"Answer some questions one more time?"

She studied me. "Why?"

"Because if I get the right answers, I might leave."

She nodded slowly.

Back in town, in my room, I showed her the stack of prints. I almost told her about the faces they contained, but her brooding features stopped me. She thought I was disturbed enough as it was.

"When I walk in the afternoons, I go to the settings Van Dorn chose for his paintings." I sorted through the prints. "This orchard. This farm. This pond. This cliff. And so on."

"Yes, I recognize these places. I've seen them all."

"I hoped if I saw them, maybe I'd understand what happened to my friend. You told me he went to them as well. Each of them is within a five-mile radius of the village. Many are close together. It wasn't difficult to find each site. Except for one."

She didn't ask the obvious question. Instead, she tensely rubbed her arm.

When I'd taken the boxes from Van Dorn's room, I'd also removed the two paintings Myers had attempted. Now I pulled them from where I'd tucked them under the bed.

"My friend did these. It's obvious he wasn't an artist. But as crude as they are, you can see they both depict the same area."

I slid a Van Dorn print from the bottom of the stack.

"*This* area," I said. "A grove of cypresses in a hollow, surrounded by rocks. It's the only site I haven't been able to find. I've asked the villagers. They claim they don't know where it is. Do *you* know, Clarisse? Can you tell me? It must have some significance if my friend was fixated on it enough to try to paint it *twice*."

Clarisse scratched a fingernail across her wrist. "I'm sorry."

"What?"

"I can't help you."

"Can't or won't? Do you mean you don't know where to find it, or you know but you won't tell me?"

"I said I can't help."

"What's wrong with this village, Clarisse? What's everybody trying to hide?"

"I've done my best." She shook her head, stood, and walked to the door. She glanced back sadly. "Sometimes it's better to leave well enough alone. Sometimes there are reasons for secrets."

I watched her go down the hall. "Clarisse…"

She turned and spoke a single word: "North." She was crying. "God help you," she added. "I'll pray for your soul." Then she disappeared down the stairs.

For the first time I felt afraid.

Five minutes later I left the hotel. In my walks to the sites of Van Dorn's paintings, I'd always chosen the easiest routes—east, west, and south. Whenever I'd asked about the distant, tree-lined hills to the north, the villagers had told me there was nothing of interest there, nothing at all to do with Van Dorn. What about cypresses in a hollow? I'd asked. There weren't any cypresses in those hills, only olive trees, they'd answered. But now I knew.

La Verge was in the southern end of an oblong valley, squeezed by cliffs to the east and west. To reach the northern hills, I'd have to walk twenty miles at least.

I rented a car. Leaving a dust cloud, I pressed my foot on the accelerator and stared toward the rapidly enlarging hills. The trees I'd seen from the village were indeed olive trees. But the lead-colored rocks among them were the same as in Van Dorn's painting. I skidded along the road, veering up through the hills. Near the top I found a narrow space to park and rushed from the car. But which direction to take? On impulse, I chose left and hurried among the rocks and trees. My decision seems less arbitrary now. Something about the slopes to the left was more dramatic, more aesthetically compelling. A greater wilderness in the landscape. A sense of depth, of substance.

My instincts urged me forward. I'd reached the hills at quarter after five. Time compressed eerily. At once, my watch showed ten past seven. The sun blazed, crimson, over the bluffs. I kept searching, letting the grotesque landscape guide me. The ridges and ravines were like a maze, every turn of which either blocked or gave access, controlling my direction. I rounded a crag, scurried down a slope of thorns, ignored the rips in my shirt and the blood streaming from my hands, and stopped on the precipice of a hollow. Cypresses, not olive trees, filled the basin. Boulders jutted among them and formed a grotto.

The basin was steep. I skirted its brambles, ignoring their scalding sting. Boulders led me down. I stifled my misgivings, frantic to reach the bottom.

This hollow, this basin of cypresses and boulders, this thorn-rimmed funnel, was the image not only of Van Dorn's painting but of the canvases Myers had attempted. But why had this place so affected them?

The answer came as quickly as the question. I heard before I saw, though hearing doesn't accurately describe my sensation. The sound was so faint and high-pitched, it was almost beyond the range of detection. At first I thought I was near a hornet's nest. I sensed a subtle vibration in the otherwise still air of the hollow. I felt an itch behind my eardrums, a tingle on my skin. The sound was actually many sounds, each identical, merging, like the collective buzz of a swarm of insects. But this was high-pitched. Not a buzz but more like a distant chorus of shrieks and wails.

Frowning, I took another step toward the cypresses. The tingle on my skin intensified. The itch behind my eardrums became so irritating, I raised my hands to the sides of my head. I came close enough to see within the trees, and what I noticed with terrible clarity made me panic. Gasping, I stumbled back. But not in time. What shot from the trees was too small and fast for me to identify.

It struck my right eye. The pain was excruciating, as if the white-hot tip of a needle had pierced my retina and lanced my brain. I clamped my right hand across that eye and screamed.

I continued stumbling back, agony spurring my panic. But the sharp, hot pain intensified, surging through my skull. My knees bent. My consciousness dimmed. I fell against the slope.

◇

It was after midnight when I managed to drive back to the village. Though my eye no longer burned, my panic was more extreme. Still dizzy from having passed out, I tried to keep control when I entered the clinic and asked where Clarisse lived. She'd invited me to visit, I claimed. A sleepy attendant frowned but told me. I drove desperately toward her cottage, five blocks away.

Lights were on. I knocked. She didn't answer. I pounded harder, faster. At last I saw a shadow. When the door swung open, I lurched into the living room. I barely noticed the negligee Clarisse clutched around her, or the open door to her bedroom, where a startled woman sat up in bed, held a sheet to her breasts, and stood quickly to shut the bedroom door.

"What the hell do you think you're doing?" Clarisse yelled. "I didn't invite you in! I didn't—!"

I managed the strength to talk: "I don't have time to explain. I'm terrified. I need your help."

She clutched her negligee tighter.

"I've been stung. I think I've caught a disease. Help me stop whatever's inside me. Antibiotics. An antidote. Anything you can think of. Maybe it's a virus, maybe a fungus. Maybe it acts like bacteria."

"*What happened?*"

"I told you, no time. I'd have asked for help at the clinic, but they wouldn't have understood. They'd have thought I'd had a breakdown, the same as Myers. You've got to take me there. You've got to make sure I'm injected with as much of any and every drug that might possibly kill this thing."

"I'll dress as fast as I can."

As we rushed to the clinic, I described what had happened. She phoned the doctor the moment we arrived. While we waited, she disinfected my eye and gave me something for my rapidly developing headache. The doctor showed up, his sleepy features becoming alert when he saw how distressed I was. True to my prediction, he reacted as if I'd had a breakdown. I shouted at him to humor me and saturate me with antibiotics. Clarisse made sure it wasn't just a sedative he gave me. He used every compatible combination. If I thought it would have worked, I'd have swallowed Drāno.

What I'd seen within the cypresses were tiny, gaping mouths and miniscule, writhing bodies, as small and camouflaged as those in Van Dorn's paintings. I know now that Van Dorn wasn't imposing his insane vision on reality. He wasn't an Impressionist. At least not in his *Cypresses in a Hollow*. I'm convinced that this painting was his first after his brain became infected. He was literally depicting what he'd seen on one of his walks. Later, as the infection progressed, he saw the gaping mouths and writhing bodies like an overlay on everything else he looked at. In that sense, too, he wasn't an Impressionist. To him, the gaping mouths and writhing bodies *were* in all those later scenes. To the limit of his infected brain, he painted what to him *was* reality. His art was representational.

I know, believe me. Because the drugs didn't work. My brain is as diseased as Van Dorn's... or Myers's. I've tried to understand why they didn't panic when they were stung, why they didn't rush to a hospital. My conclusion is that Van Dorn had been so desperate for a vision to enliven his paintings that he gladly endured the suffering. And Myers had been so desperate to understand Van Dorn that when stung, he'd willingly taken the risk to identify even more with his subject until, too late, he'd realized his mistake.

Orange is for anguish, blue for insanity. How true. Whatever infects my brain has affected my color sense. More and more, orange and blue overpower the other colors I know are there. I have no choice. I see little else. My paintings are *rife* with orange and blue.

My paintings. Because I've solved another mystery. It always puzzled me how Van Dorn could have suddenly been seized by such energetic genius that he painted thirty-eight masterpieces in one year. I know the answer now. What's in my head, the gaping mouths and writhing bodies, the orange of anguish and the blue of insanity, cause such pressure, such headaches that I've tried everything to subdue them, to get them out. I went from codeine to Demerol to morphine. Each helped for a time but not enough. Then I learned what Van Dorn understood and Myers attempted. Painting the disease somehow gets it out of you. For a time. And then you paint harder, faster. Anything to relieve the pain. But Myers wasn't an artist. The disease had no release and reached its terminal stage in weeks instead of Van Dorn's year.

But *I'm* an artist—or used to hope I was. I had skill without a vision. Now, God help me, I've got a vision. At first I painted the cypresses and their secret. I accomplished what you'd expect. An imitation of Van Dorn's original. But I refuse to suffer pointlessly. I vividly recall the portraits of Midwestern landscapes I produced in grad school. The dark-earthed Iowa landscape. The attempt to make an observer feel the fecundity of the soil. The results were ersatz Wyeth. But not anymore. The twenty paintings I've so far stored away aren't versions of Van Dorn, either. They're my own creations. Unique. A combination of the disease and my experience. Aided by powerful memory, I paint the river that flows through Iowa City. Blue. I paint the cornfields that cram the big-sky rolling country outside of town. Orange. I paint my innocence. My youth. With my ultimate discovery hidden within them. Ugliness lurks within the beauty. Horror festers in my brain.

Clarisse at last told me about the local legend. When La Verge was founded, she said, a meteor streaked from the sky. It lit the night. It burst upon the hills north of here. Flames erupted. Trees were consumed. The hour was late. Few villagers saw it. The site of the impact was too far away for those few witnesses to rush that night to see the crater. In the morning the smoke had dispersed. The embers had died. Though the witnesses tried to find the meteor, the lack of the roads that now exist hampered their search through the tangled hills to the point of discouragement. A few among the few witnesses persisted. The few of the few of the few who had accomplished their quest staggered back to the village, babbling about headaches and tiny, gaping mouths. Using sticks, they scraped disturbing images in the dirt and eventually stabbed out their eyes. Over the centuries, legend has it, similar self-mutilations occurred whenever someone returned from seeking the crater in those hills. The unknown had power then. The hills acquired the negative force of taboo. No villager, then or now, intruded on what came to be called the place where God's wand touched the earth. A poetic description of a blazing meteor's impact. La Verge.

I don't conclude the obvious: that the meteor carried spores that multiplied in the crater, which became a hollow eventually filled with cypresses. No—to me, the meteor was a cause but not an effect. I saw a pit among the cypresses, and from the pit, tiny mouths and writhing bodies resembling insects—how they wailed!—spewed. They clung to the leaves of the cypresses, flailed in anguish as they fell back, and instantly were replaced by other spewing, anguished souls.

Yes. Souls. For the meteor, I insist, was just the cause. The effect was the opening of hell. The tiny, wailing mouths are the damned. As *I* am damned. Desperate to survive, to escape from the ultimate prison we call hell, a frantic sinner lunged. He caught my eye and stabbed my brain, the gateway to my soul. My soul. It festers. I paint to remove the pus.

I talk. That helps somehow. Clarisse writes it down while her female lover rubs my shoulders.

My paintings are brilliant. I'll be recognized, as I'd always dreamed. As a genius, of course.

At such a cost.

The headaches grow worse. The orange is more brilliant. The blue more disturbing.

I try my best. I urge myself to be stronger than Myers, whose endurance lasted only weeks. Van Dorn persisted for a year. Maybe genius is strength.

My brain swells. How it threatens to split my skull. The gaping mouths blossom.

The headaches! I tell myself to be strong. Another day. Another rush to complete another painting.

The sharp end of my paintbrush invites. Anything to lance my seething mental boil, to jab my eyes for the ecstasy of relief. But I have to endure.

On a table near my left hand, the scissors wait.

But not today. Or tomorrow.

I'll outlast Van Dorn.

IN THE EYES OF THE BEHOLDER

ANN K. BOYER

IT WAS THE EYES. ~~At first.~~ They tormented me.

I'm not exactly sure when their love/caring/approval turned to contempt.

Yes, you do.   *Stop lying.*

                             You're not blind.

             Don't play dumb.

I just ~~know~~ felt that once they did, I couldn't escape their ridicule. I tried to please them. I painted my ~~mask~~ face in rouges and porcelain powders, and dressed in ~~tight~~ form-fitting, imported fabrics to make my body more appealing. I noticed the hungry looks that accompanied the heavy breath and thirsty palate. No matter the attention I received, *those* eyes were unimpressed by it, criticizing my portrait and frame, targeting every flaw and imperfection.

Maybe they're jealous, I thought.

                   He wants you...

                       ...to taste you...

                           ...feel you.

I didn't like the way he drooled after me, ~~eye-fucked~~ gawked at me whenever I was near—

You're such a pretty kitty, come drink daddy's milk.

—just like the rest of them.

You know you like it.

                   That's right, come get some.

             You loved it.

Soon those scornful eyes multiplied, infecting the next pair of eyes with the same cancerous glare. Eyes of every color and shape crucified me. At the grocery store, gas station. No matter where I went, they were there. Looks blasted me while hands shielded the curious children. Heads twisted away as lips curled in disgust. My skin crawled beneath goose-pimpled skin every time I attempted to leave my home.

Whore!

My breathing would become labored and my chest would grow heavy with keen pain.

Skank!

~~The world~~ Invisible walls closed in on me.

Trash!

I hoped that maybe if I'd change my look completely, those eyes would accept me. I maxed my credit on formaldehyde-based straighteners and ceramic flatirons that burned away the flowing waves that once edged my face. A rainbow of bleaches and dyes stripped each strand from its original chocolate color, leaving the follicles brittle and forked, fried. I was helpless to prevent the wiry clumps from abandoning my head, clogging the drain, and carpeting the tiles. When that didn't work, I emptied my savings account on a new nose and veneers.

Look at you now.

You're still filthy.

Fake.

~~My~~ Their attention eventually shifted to my body. I fed myself a multitude of pills to starve the hunger, to vomit up the obscenities that haunted the darkest corners of my mind. When tooth-trimmed nails failed to ~~scratch~~ dig out the horrific ~~memories~~ nightmares that squirmed like worms/maggots/disease beneath, I found brief comfort with ~~alcohol/drugs~~/the razor. I carved a roadmap into my skin, dived into crimson waves, releasing my bloodsoulpain. It was only a temporary escape. My desperation was broadcasted in cherry scars and those eyes zeroed in on my ~~obsession~~ infliction. Even when I covered myself in layers of cotton, a blanket of shame, those eyes saw right through.

What's wrong with you?   *Cut deeper…*

Pathetic little lamb, do yourself the favor.

Freak!

Every morning I'd wake, hoping to be freed from their disapproving sight. But days turned to weeks, which turned to months, and then years, and I remained trapped within constant paranoia that I might catch a glimpse of those evil eyes—their silent insults lodging in my throat and choking-strangling-killing my breath.

Boo-fucking-hoo!

I was left with no other choice. I had to—

Whine some more?

—**cut them out**.

Taking my time, I drew a dotted line with a Sharpie around each socket to use as a reference when making my incisions ~~like the surgeons on YouTube~~. Being right-handed, I naturally started with the left eye. It was difficult at first. No matter how I gripped the brow or tilted my head, the eyelid kept blinking, flinging its lashes in the way of the guide. Then I paused, looking over the trembling razor pinched between my fingers, and peer into those eyes for a moment, taking them all in. The malevolency directed at me, ~~hurt me~~ ~~frightened me~~ ~~ANGERED ME~~ amused me.

Inflicted with mixed/all emotions, I felt my warm, salty tears flow down my cheeks and into my mouth, blurring my sight and breaking my gaze.

Pussy.

"You're weak," they seemed to say to me. "You won't do it."
Chicken shit.

I wasn't scared. I didn't *want* to do it! Please understand. At one time, I had actually adored/loved/admired those big, emerald eyes and the way they're surrounded by a thick forest of black lashes. They're mysterious(sexy). They're my favorite.

But, *they* changed! *They* became cold and callus!

"Can't you see? You made me do this!"

With a loud growling breath/grunt, I hooked my nubby nails into the scalp while the edge of the razor pressed through the fine skin and sank into the red flows concealed beneath. The incision was jagged. Messy. And that was all right. Those thick eyelashes and the pelt they were attached to were no longer ~~a nuisance~~ in my way, laying in a folded mess in the sink.

I grew more comfortable with each cut that followed.

Or maybe I grew numb to it.

It wasn't long before the sharp jerking of my movements calmed to smooth, surgical skill ~~just like those surgeons~~. My tight grip on the razor loosened as it sliced through fleshy pink muscles: orbital and rectus muscles, if my memory of high school AP Anatomy & Physiology was correct. The salmon tissue was slippery/gelatinous/gross, and it took several slices for the blade to sever the tough fibers.

I was careful though.

I couldn't risk any slips by mistakenly cutting through into the sclera. I didn't want to damage those perfect orbs. I had a special place in mind to keep them: a small music box given to me by my mother—*before the pull of her finger ruined her face*. I decorated it myself, with tiny seashells I'd collected, because I loved the way they ~~looked~~ felt, some pearlescent and smooth and others rippled like my favorite potato chips. It was filled with a pillow made from cotton balls and a scrap of silk. I wanted the eyes to be comfortable within the black static of the box. Because I had loved them, but...

But?

Uh oh...   *You fucked up!*

Although my world is filled with darkness, I can still ~~see~~ feel HEAR those horrible eyes, mocking me. They were supposed to be in the same blackness that would fill my world, finally freed from their discontent.

But, I...

...am stupid.
...can't get anything right.

...screwed up.

I couldn't catch it. As I severed the second optic nerve, it fell from its socket, slipping through my fingers and landing with a wet slap somewhere on the floor. It had rolled to some hidden place I might never find.

And…?

Go on…

And in my search, I somehow knocked over the music box, sending the first eyeball ~~rolling~~ escaping to join the other.

You're such a fuck up.

"I'm not a fuck up!"

Oh really? Whose fault was it?

Not mine.

Me neither.   *Yours.*

I didn't do it.

"I know it's my fault! I don't need all of you reminding me!"

What're you going to do about it?

Cry some more?

You're such a crybaby!

"Leave me alone!"

I can't.

I won't.

Stop me.

"Stop it! Stop staring at me!"

Find me, first.

"Shut up! I'm not talking to you!"

I'm talking to you.

Do you think I couldn't feel you cringe at the sight of me?

You think you're a safe distance away—that I

couldn't feel you reading me,

judging me,

disgusted by me?

STOP.

LOOKING.

AT ME!

Or you'll be next…

EMPATHY

JOHN SKIPP

YES, YOU'RE BAD. You've done a horrible thing. And you'll do it again. I know.

If there's one thing I understand, it's that you will do it again.

You are laying there, drenched in a spackle of sweat that is equal parts shame and relentless heat. 98 degrees in Hollywood. At least 110 in the Valley. There exists, at this point, no meter to gauge the level of shame you feel. A fan is blowing, its oscillation locked, riveted by a pin to blast its blades straight at your head. It doesn't matter. You have fallen, and you can't get up: paralyzed with self-loathing, and the perfect understanding that you're right. It's all wrong. You. Me. God. Everything. Wrong.

At this point, I am just awakening. You feel the ripple as the veil of sleep parts, and choose that moment to enter me.

I slide into wakefulness, and know you are there. Get up off the bed. Go down the hall. Take a long, exultant pee. Today is gonna be an extra-fine day, whether you wanna just fucking lay there or not. I am going to have fun.

I am going to be fun.

I go into the living room, slap on the yoga tape. Dixie Carter is just so sweet, and the exercises really help. I hear the growling in my tummy, and totally don't care. I will eat when I'm done. Then I'll go out and run. In the meantime, I stretch, feel my muscles spring to life. I am alive. I'm so alive it's almost stupid.

Already, I am projecting ahead. My immediate future has been carefully planned. I prepare to inhabit it, one speck at a time.

I just wish you would fucking get over it.

My breakfast is lean; I am down to 118 again. I would say that that's a good look for me. I can wear a bikini, or even less, without cringing. If I have a complaint, it would have to be that I've lost so much in the cleavage department. At this weight, I really miss my titties. But at least my ass is contained.

I go back into the bedroom, peel off my sleepy workout garb. Of course, you are awake.

"I can't get up," you say.

"Uh-huh." I nod, walk into the closet.

"I must be getting old," you say. "Three drinks, and I'm gone. Three glasses of wine. It's fucking absurd. I'm twenty-seven years old. Used to be I could drink all night."

"You also drank rum," I remind you. "And a margarita."

I feel you shrug. "Whatever. I could puke up a single lite beer. Doesn't matter what I do. I get sick. I can't deal."

"Has it occurred to you," I say, "that you might have developed an allergy?"

"Oh, yeah," you say. "I'm allergic to alcohol. I break out in handcuffs."

I start to laugh.

"It's like Joe Bob said," you continue. "Just because a woman sleeps with every man she meets, that doesn't mean she's cheap."

"Oh, that's priceless," I tell you. "'Break out in handcuffs.' You really need to write that down."

"You write it down," you say. "I can't get up."

"Oh, yeah." At this point, a flicker of annoyance runs through me. I think, *so much self-pity, so early in the morning. No wonder you puke.*

But I don't say that. Instead, I say, "Sure, I'll write it down. In fact, I'll tell you what. I'll get you up. Put you in the shower. Make your breakfast. Eat your breakfast. Drive you to work. Do all your work. Digest your food, and bring you home. Hell, I'll even shit it out for you."

"That's nice," you say, and roll over in bed. So much for conversation.

Whatever.

That's fine with me. I throw on shorts, socks, sneakers, and the t-shirt that says JESUS IS COMING. LOOK BUSY. Then I'm out the door, walking briskly up the hill toward the dog park. And away from you.

It is now 8:45. The heat is almost stunning. It bakes the urine of a trillion dogs into a crispy nose soufflé. I wish I had time to drive to the reservoir instead, do three miles, stare at Madonna's old house. But no. My first meeting's at ten. Never make it. No way.

By 9:15, I am hosing down in the shower. Every toxin my body has ever known has been caught up in sweat beads, now sluicing down the drain. I feel more than clean. I feel Zestfully clean.

When I come back out, it's like you are not even there.

Which is totally fine with me. I don't even want to think about you. No offense—you know I love you to death—but you're a total fucking loser, and you're making me sick. You're letting yourself get fat and ugly and, yes, even stupid. Laying there like a lump. Scintillating as mud, and sexy as a tumor.

In my closet, there are clothes that I can finally wear again. One of life's crowning glories: I can wear my own clothes. Which, of course, is more than you can say, oh Queen of Lard and Mopiness. I almost start to feel sorry for you, but then the thought just pisses me off.

I dress and put on makeup in silence, sculpt a little 40s flip into my hair. I love the glamour of the old Hollywood, feel entitled to a bit of it now. There's a whole town out there that is crawling with money, with the privilege that comes from dedicated hard work. And I am working my ass off, not working my ass.

Which is more than I can say for you.

I show up for my meeting with five minutes to spare, spend them happily schmoozing with the receptionist. Her name is Allison, and she is a hoot. Very pretty. Just a little bit overweight.

This town can be ruthless—in fact, it just *is*—and though I hate to be a party to it, I can no more shut it off than I can stop my own heart. While we talk, I can feel her measuring me, sensors gauging my anatomical stats. It's subtle, but it's sad, because I know she can't help it. None of us can help it. It's in the fucking air, a particulate component of the smog: five parts carbon monoxide, two parts bitchiness, with a lingering afterwaft of decay.

I am here for a callback on a very nice part in a low-budget action thriller. Not another hooker with a heart of gold. Not another understanding girlfriend or wife. And not another teenage bed wench who gets to scream just before the knife goes in.

The character's name is Verona Gabor, and she's a full-on psychopathic contract killer. Shades of *Romeo is Bleeding*, but one could do worse. I think of Lena Olin, how empowered she was. How frightening and gorgeous, free of inhibition or remorse.

I want to do that. Oh yes indeed. I want to go wallow in untrammeled ferocity. Show my teeth. Show my tits. Show my victims their spleens.

I joke with Allison about that very thing, and she is right there with me. I can tell that she'd love to play that part, too. If only she lost ten pounds.

The meeting goes well. I get to read; but more than that, I get to pace and stalk, to glower and grin and stake my claim on the turf that is Verona Gabor. The casting director and producer are impassive; but, of course, that's their jobs. On the other hand, the director is cupping his nuts. Not only does he keenly appreciate my talent, he wants to fuck me so bad it's coming out of his ears.

I would never do that, of course. Better to keep him steamed up than to get intimate, let him dissipate the heat. On top of that, the fucker looks like Gary Shandling, who I love but wouldn't bed if he came with four posters and a canopy.

I leave with a really good feeling. I feel like I have rocked the house. The meeting went over by almost forty minutes; the next girl in line looks severely pissed. I check her out, as she does me. *Fat chance*, I think, though she is scrawny as a pole.

I grab a bite at noon: broiled chicken, a little cottage cheese. It's not nearly enough, but it will have to do. My next audition is at

1:45, in Venice. Corman film. Hooker with a heart of chintz, who befriends a psychic frog. He becomes a prince, of course, and marries me or whoever gets the part.

There are roughly 87,000 girls in the office, the parking lot, the road leading in. If I didn't need the money, I would blow this hot dog stand. You've never smelled so much Victoria's Secret and bitter cooze. At least not since the last cattle call.

Funny, how I find myself thinking of you.

It's the comparison test. The one-against-all. The pitting of beauty against beauty against beauty. I realize how many of me there are. How many diligent, arrogant dreamers, daring to think that they could ever possibly stand out. I hear the catty whispers as I stride to the desk.

It makes me want a fucking drink.

An hour and a half later, I get to read. It goes fairly well, but these people are numb, and getting number by the second. I try to imagine what criteria they're going to judge on. Looks? Talent? Character? What difference does it make? This mecca for models who think they can act will go straight down to video and sink like a stone. Everybody knows it. And nobody cares.

It's almost five by the time I get home, what with traffic and bullshit and a stop at the store. Jason will be here at seven, which gives me just enough time to catch up on my messages and make some calls, keep the boulder rolling uphill.

Of course, you are sprawled on the couch, watching TV.

I don't even want to talk to you. You are fucking depression incarnate. On the screen, spineless women get up in front of millions, defend their utter servitude to ugly, stupid men. It is God's will for them, they heartwarmingly insist, to serve their Bombo's every need. Make his food. Scrub his hairy back. Chew the corns off his reeking feet, the second he gets home from the insecticide plant.

I guess it makes you feel better, but it makes me want to scream.

Where is your self-respect? I wonder.

Then I go *oh, yeah. It's in the toilet, with your lunch.*

I say nothing, stripping down and showering again. I am careful not to get my hair wet this time. Twenty-seven years old, and already the gray hairs are showing up. What the fuck is that? What is the matter with me?

I can't allow that kind of thought inside. It's the kind of thing that you would say. I choke it back like day-old bile, think pretty thoughts exclusively.

But that is my hell. I think too much. I live inside my head. Planning things out. Sculpting trajectories. Maintaining the fortress that is my flesh. I take a lot of maintenance, attention to detail, constant care. And above all, forward momentum.

Because if I stop, for even a second, I start to turn out like you.

And I would honestly rather die.

Jason is fifteen minutes early, but that's cool. I am ready freddy, and looking hot. Jason is duly appreciative, which is not a surprise. Jason loves me so much it is almost retarded.

Jason is a screenwriter. A very very good one. He is also a fairly cute boy. Not drop-dead like Damian, gorgeous like Gary, breathtaking like Armando Bane (big sigh). But I am done with actorboys, their vanities on parade. Actor-boys—celebrities, especially always have to be the center, the pivot on which the whole universe spins. That doesn't leave much room for me. God knows, I need some, too.

Which is what Jason wants to talk with me about. He is writing a new script, he says. And he's tailoring it for me. It's a perfect part. Lots of depth. Lots of courage. Lots of wit. A little bit of pathos, but nothing you could drown in. Just enough to let the inner strength and beauty shine through.

Naturally, I'm interested. He has placed three scripts in the last ten months, and his career is heating nicely. There is talk of letting him direct one soon, which is where this script comes in. If he can actually hang on to control, he could in fact cast me, which would be really sweet.

I am determined not to fuck him.

He smokes a joint before we leave. I do not join in. I tell him dope makes me feel hungry and stupid, and I can do that by myself. He laughs very hard; he always gets my jokes. I really admire that in a man.

He asks me where I would like to eat; and for some perverse reason, I think of Acapulco's. It's Dollar Margarita Night. And I would really like a drink.

So away we go, amidst much glittering conversation. I love the way Jason expresses himself, the strange twists and turns his logic takes.

And he's fun. I think I like that most. He's smart, and he's fun, and he gets my jokes. He is also refreshingly honest: about the biz, about himself.

About his feelings toward me.

This is the part I'm least itchy to hear. I order a margarita. Jason sticks with red wine. I send him off to scarf up goodies from the happy hour buffet. Meanwhile, I head for the Ladies'. Pee. Then stare at myself in the mirror.

I wish I could just stop thinking so much.

I wish I could just stop thinking.

A margarita later, it's a little bit easier. I promptly order another. There are more calories at the table right now than I have consumed all week. I joke about it, and Jason laughs, but I watch him appraise me in a surreptitious second.

His conclusion is *but she's not fat.*

And I find myself thinking *if you only knew...*

More food. More drink. More hilarious distraction. We talk about movies that we both love. Quote Monty Python, chapter and verse. Quote *Waiting for Guffman*, which Jason insists was the best horror film of last year. Quote *Fargo* and *Sling Blade* and *Dead Alive.* Quote *Who's Afraid of Virginia Woolf,* which Jason insists is the best horror film ever.

Jason launches into a hilarious story, and I feel myself ballooning underneath my dress: fat cells long dormant, reawakening with fervor, like a cancer of insulation between myself and the world. I catch a stray clever line, and it makes me laugh my ass off. I say it over and over, then can't remember what it was.

Life, at this point, becomes a dull blur, punctuated by moments of obscene clarity. His eyes are aglow in the candlelight. He has beautiful eyes. They are aglow with love.

Oh God, I think. I don't need love. I'm sick of love. I believe in love. I believe that love is the firmament, the thing both above and between all things. I believe that love is the soul of forgiveness, the heart of charity, the essence of faith. I believe, in fact, that God is love; and that God loves me, no matter how stupid I get. How stupid or selfish or grasping or vain.

I believe these things, and I want to cry, because now I am thinking of you. Thinking of you, on the bed or the couch: the only two places you live. I am thinking of a God that could possibly love you. You mattress tramp. You fucking whore. You blimp. You slug. You feeding machine. You worthless deluded heartbreaking blob of bullshit masquerading as a human being.

I try to imagine a God that could love you. It's beyond my power.

I am really fucking high.

Then I look in the general direction of Jason, say some things I will never remember in a million fucking years.

At some point, we wind up back at my apartment. Jason has purchased a bottle of wine. He kisses me, and I guess I let him.

We do some things that I forgot before they happened.

And the next thing I know, I am awake in the bed. Jason is gone, but you are there. So are the handcuffs. Did we use them? Did we not? Did I want to be pinned to that fucking headboard, as if to say *it's not my fault? I didn't do it? I wasn't there?* And did he say *no, I want your hands?* Or did he say *hey, I got you now?*

I'll never know. I will never know. Even if he tells me, I will not know for sure. Because I was gone, and all my painfully painstaking maintenance of the fortress went right along with it. Right out the fucking window. Out the window that probably echoed with my cries, although the odds are equally good, I never made a sound. Not wanting anyone to know. Anyone to know I feel.

But I feel. Oh God, I feel. I feel for poor stupid love-struck Jason. I feel for poor stupid hungry me. I feel for you, who has laid here so long, and never once gotten up long enough to live. Or if you do, you wind up here.

You wind up here like me.

And I cannot move. I cannot move. The heat is astonishing. It pins me to the mattress, as surely as my mind. As surely as the pin in the oscillating fan, which locks the force of the whirling blades upon me.

I have fallen, and I can't get up. But you are there beside me.

I somehow find my arm, make it find your ass, make a finger probe its crease.

You awaken as I enter you. Get up. Find the bathroom. Pee.

And I lay there, listening to you live. Approach the new day with confidence. You move to the living room and put on the tape. Fucking Dixie Carter. I hate her ass.

Everything drones into everything else, as I lay here. Thinking and thinking and thinking. After a while, you come back in. I hate you. I hate myself.

"I can't get up," I say.

You say, "Uh-huh," and go into the closet.

Yes, I'm bad. I've done a horrible thing. And I'll do it again, you know.

If there's one thing you understand, it's that I will do it again.

VERSIONS

E. L. KEMPER

THE BRIGHT SPOT of the penlight trailed a neon afterimage as the doctor moved through the dark.

"Tell me about this blurred vision you're experiencing." Doctor Wilson snapped the overhead lights back on and he and Connie squinted at each other across the room.

"It's not blurry. Just a dark area behind things, like a shadow." Connie blinked a few times, trying to clear away the wavering blob that followed Doctor Wilson as he came towards her. "I noticed it in the recovery room."

"Not at all uncommon. People often see a kind of halo around objects post-surgery. It's called a ghost image. Not a cause for concern, but we'll schedule a follow-up for a few days from now just to make sure." He moved his finger from side to side, watching her track it. "Everything else looks good."

"Maybe I can get work reading auras?" Connie said, wiping at the wetness collecting on her cheek.

"I wouldn't quit your day job. It should clear up on its own." Darkness fell over her eye as the doctor taped down a fresh gauze patch. "Wear this for another day or so. Don't forget to put it back on when you go to bed so you don't rub it in your sleep. No bending, try not to sneeze, nothing strenuous. Yes, you'll heal faster than most considering your age, but you still need to take it easy. Once you're all healed up we'll get you in to do the other one."

Her eye itched and watered from behind its gauze shield.

The shadows didn't go away.

At first they became more defined, no longer a dull smog-blur. Everywhere she looked dark shapes followed, not cast on the ground in relation to the sun, but lurking behind each person. Only people. Not objects, not animals. It went on like that for a day, then colors began seeping in. A woman in a fuchsia scarf bustled down the street, trailing a smoke-figure ringed in the same bright pink. Connie tried to focus, but the aura faded back. When she let her eyes relax the image sharpened. Above the strip of bright pink she could see the rise of a nose, the dark recesses of eyes.

It was the afternoon of the third day after her surgery that she saw the first 'version' fully resolved.

She had just flipped the 'open' sign and was heading to the sales counter, turning on lights and straightening lamp shades as she went. The gritty feeling of sand in her eye was still there, and she resisted the urge to dig in with a knuckle and give it a good rub. Drops at lunch time, doctor's orders. She was almost to the back of her shop when the bell over the door pinged. She turned with a smile, hoping for a customer.

A bright haze of sun backlit the darkened form of a man. She blinked and he came into focus. She blinked again and the thing behind him came into focus too.

"Oh, hi Peter." Connie forced a smile. "Welcome back."

Peter paused on his way toward her, running an open palm under the black tassels of a red satin shade, sending the dangling threads swinging. "Is this one new?"

It was all she could do to keep her attention on Peter's cautiously smiling face. Connie's gaze kept getting pulled to the Other Peter, smiling behind him.

"Yes. Janice just finished the gold leaf on the base yesterday."

"It's gorgeous." Peter brushed a stray thread from the shade.

Other Peter did the same, his hand moving in a perfect echo, like their arms were attached by a string.

"Hold on a second. I'll get your keys."

Connie hustled into the back room blinking against the sandpaper dryness, pressing her eye with the back of her hand. What the hell was going on? Some kind of hallucination? Her hands were so slick with sweat she dropped her purse.

"Hey, are you okay?"

Connie looked over to the work table where Janice—and Other Janice—were bent over a pile of recently salvaged lamp bases. Janice was pulling out worn, corroded wires, stripping the copper out of its plastic housing and chucking it on top of the tangled mass in the recycle bin. All four arms operated in unison, two upturned faces wore the same concerned expressions.

"I'm fine. Can you tell Peter his keys are at my place? I'll return them later."

Connie didn't wait for a response, just dropped her purse on the table and walked into the parts closet, closing the door behind her. She stood there in the dark with her eyes closed, listening as Peter's voice rose from the fog of murmured conversation with stories of wheels and deals, waiting for her heart to stop racing and her body to cool.

"What's going on?" Janice stood close enough that her version was hidden behind her.

"I don't know. It's like I'm seeing double. I called the doctor and I can go in tomorrow. Apparently it's fairly normal, he called it a ghost image. Takes the brain a bit to adjust."

Janice ran a towel under cold water. The other version replicated her movements, but there were subtle differences. When she straightened, Janice tugged her work smock down, as did her other, but over a looser and more prominent stomach. Other Janice's nose was wider and her chin sat closer to her neck, resulting in a cascade of extra chins that wagged when Janice talked.

"Why don't you go home. I can work the front today." Janice moved her head over, in line with where Connie was watching the version in horrified fascination.

The walk home was both terrifying and amazing.

The downtown sidewalk swarmed with people and their other versions. For a moment, when she left the safety of her shop, she was paralyzed. There were just too many. What Connie had noticed with Janice became more and more clear. One suit-wearing man, lugging a briefcase and slurping mechanically from a to-go cup, quick-stepped along, a haggard-looking duplicate strode behind in a suit that hung rumpled and loose.

A couple of adolescent girls in tight jeans stood in front of a convenience store oh-my-god-ing and chewing gum. Their versions had volcanic blemishes on their fleshy cheeks and butts that ballooned up over their waistbands.

Then a little girl walked by. She skipped along, holding tight to her mom, wearing clothes that only a little girl would have chosen to wear: stripy socks, tutu, tiara and strapped on wings. Her other version had the same satisfied grin, her hair kinked by yesterday's braids. But the version's hair writhed and danced in the wind and those wings, they fluttered with a life of their own. Connie watched until the little girl dropped out of sight, tugged down to the subway station by her mom and her mom's worn-out other.

When Connie got to the food bank near her building she had to cover her eye to block them out.

It wasn't the ones with the long beards and winter clothes that were so frightening. They were a wonder. Their other versions were cloaked in shadow and smoke, they breathed flame, their words took form, snaking from mouths that housed sharp teeth and tongues scaled with gold. They were wreathed in power and their skin was painted with inked runes and glowing data streams.

It wasn't them. It was the sick, the wounded, those consumed by addiction. Their versions were grey, skin sagging, falling off, dripping from their bodies, rotting in chunks, dissolving into ash and drifting in a trail of filth. The bodies were bad, but the eyes were worse: glassed over by pain, wide and unblinking, sagging from their sockets and flowing with endless tears.

She almost started running as she passed this line that gathered every day, hungry, waiting. She imagined them turning their eyes on her, mouths opening, closing like beached fish, wordlessly pleading.

But they didn't. The other versions stood behind, lifting a rotting arm in obedience to their master, shuffling forward, gazing down.

When she covered her eye, overwhelmed by the suffering, relief was immediate. The number of people before her halved and the world returned to normal. She gave the woman coming out of her building extra birth, not wanting to walk through the other version she knew was straggling after. Only when she was safe behind her apartment door did she drop her hand.

She made tea and watched TV. She was relieved when the soap opera actors walked through the dramas of their well-dressed lives un-shadowed by their lesser selves. Snug under her lap blanket, legs tucked up despite the doctors warnings about blood clots. Tea steamed her face and she managed to calm down for a moment, to embrace the hope that this was merely a physiological thing and a few tests would sort it all out. It wasn't her mind.

She held her hand up in front of her face. Her hands had been the first thing to go, she recalled. Her hair had started to grey, but that was easily remedied. Reading glasses came next, but she looked good in glasses. Then one day as she was doing some mundane task, ironing a shirt or making the bed, and she had looked down at her hands. Age spots, arm hair longer and darker than it had been before, ridges of vein coursing over her lined flesh, the end of one finger hooked with the promise of arthritis. Her mother's hands.

Now she looked at her close-clipped nails, painted a soft pearl pink, she made a fist and watched as the hand that hovered behind clenched shut and opened, looking no older or more unappealing than its counterpart. Her version was just that, no changes. She saw what she saw. When the doorbell rang, she almost dropped her tea.

It was Peter. He stood sweating in the hallway, short of breath from the three-flight hike to her door. With the extra weight that rode around his middle, he was always sweating and straining. It was new weight most likely, not yet spread to his arms and legs. With a little care, someone making sure he ate a little better, walked a little more, he'd be fit in no time. But Connie wasn't looking for another project.

"Thanks so much for looking after the girls." Peter smoothed back his well-oiled hair. "They barely gave me the time of day when I got home. Walked around with their tails up and pretended they couldn't see me."

He shifted to the side, and his other came into focus in the dim hallway. Connie almost gasped. The other version of Peter stood tall and slim in the shadows. His clothes were tucked smooth and well-fitted, his hair thick and slightly tousled, one lock straying onto his forehead, inviting her touch. All four eyes tracked her as she stepped back to let Peter in, but the version's were clearer, more intelligent, more aware.

"Would you like some tea?" Connie smiled, trying to keep her gaze on her neighbor, who stood hesitant and confused in the hall, unsure if he should accept this unprecedented invitation.

"Um. Well, I'm actually on my way out to work. I'm playing golf with a new client this afternoon. Just wanted to check in and see if you need anything." Peter started backing away.

"I'm fine. Thank you," she said. "You can play golf in that?"

Peter looked down at his long-sleeved dress shirt, wool slacks and loafers. "Oh, I have my golf clothes in my locker at the club. With my clubs." His other's teeth gleamed large and white.

Connie closed the door before she realized she still hadn't returned his keys.

The eye patch she purchased at a nearby dollar store gave her relief.

Her visit to the surgeon had been pointless. Doctor Wilson was distracted during her appointment, tutting at the proper moments, but offering no answers. He told her to be patient. Sometimes it takes the eye and the brain some time to get reacquainted. After the cataract was removed from the other eye she'd be able to see perfectly, the shadows would vanish. But they were not shadows, she wanted to say. She couldn't tell him about the ferret-looking man that stood behind him with swollen bags under his eyes and a sagging chest that his loud tie and pressed lab coat failed to camouflage. She knew what would happen if she did. She remembered the distant sympathy and vague smiles of her mother's doctors as they prescribed more anti-anxiety drugs and sedatives to keep her mother calm and malleable for her caregivers. Connie didn't want to see that expression on Doctor Wilson's face as he handed her a referral for another specialist. It wasn't her mind.

So she bought a pirate costume from a discount bin at the dollar store. For the grandkids, the clerk guessed, using that slow, loud, baby voice people reserved for children, the challenged and the old. Connie felt like pointing out the large birthmark on the woman's chin, asking her if she knew she had something on her face. Would her version change? Would the blot grow and darken before her eyes? At home Connie fished out the black satin eye patch, and chucked the rest. She wore the patch now; even though she was working on her own, to protect her new lens from dust and fumes.

Paint stripper lifted the old varnish from the end table, it bubbled up like plague boils. Then, in her dish gloves with her plastic trowel, she scraped the mucus-like goo from the wood to spill in globs on the plastic-covered work table. Her eyes watered from the fumes. Connie pulled off the respirator and wiped condensation and sweat from her cheeks. With the finest steel wool, she rubbed at the spots where stain had collected in the joints. Finally she took a clean rag and gave the whole thing a good wipe with some mineral spirits. It was beautiful. The oak grain had a nice dark fleck with tiger streaks of gleaming white that popped from the surface like a three dimensional image, catching the light as she walked around her work bench. A good rub with wax was all it needed to make the most of its luster.

As she wiped on the honey-scented paste she thought about Peter and his other version. Peter reminded her of her ex-husband; so desperately in need of renovation, then constant maintenance. When Connie had decided to take her refinishing business out of the basement, her husband left, not right away, but when he did it was with finality. Their friends had assumed it was her constant campaign to change him that had ended their marriage, but they were wrong. It was when her attentions shifted to her business and she no longer had the time to count his calories and make sure his hair was clipped just so. That's when it failed. She'd had no idea their marriage was so fragile.

She tried to imagine picking up with Peter. How strange it would be to share a meal with him, follow his stories of deals and new customers while Other Peter sat behind, drawing her in. How strange to walk hand in hand. Would their others be hand in hand too? How strange to kiss, to make love, Peter heaving and sweating and touching her naked flesh, his other version suspended above them, reaching for her, fingers pressed on flesh that wasn't there, moving restlessly in an echo of lust. Reaching, but never touching.

Connie was grateful she'd sent Janice home early, with her other version bright-eyed and pretty in anticipation of some time with her sweet new guy. There was no one there to see how Connie's hand strayed to her own breast, leaving a warm smudge of beeswax on her blouse. She'd thought she was too old for such fantasies.

She gave the table a vigorous polish, wiping off the excess wax, leaving the wood with a warm glow, blaming the flush of heat she felt on the work.

She hadn't had a chance to return his keys yet. And she needed to understand why he was different, why his version was special, more attractive. Besides, she'd been in his place looking after his cats and watering his plants. Why shouldn't she let herself in and just put his keys on the table, returning them like a good neighbor.

What she'd found in his apartment led her here, to a large rectangular building with the name 'South Broad Park Lodge' in grey institutional font over the automatic doors.

When she'd first entered his apartment she was again confronted with the row of pictures of himself hanging along the hall. In each picture he was shaking hands with a man, both of them grinning wide for the camera. Peter's small eyes squinted into the sun and his forehead shone with sweat.

Connie remembered her dream the night before. Again Peter's naked body strained and flapped above her, and just over his shoulder his other looked down, his eyes hungry, mouth agape with silent grunts of pleasure. And then she was looking down on herself, at her naked body writhing below. But it wasn't her body, it was her mother's, near the end. The old woman's back arched, shriveled breasts lying flat against her bony ribcage, thick gray hairs coiling from dark, leathery nipples. As she jutted her hips up to meet Peter's thrusts, her flaccid buttocks shivered and quaked with each impact. Cloudy eyes gazed up towards the ceiling, and from a pale, flaking scalp, limp strands of grey hair twisted across the pillow. Connie had woken, drenched in sweat, yet unable to shake the vision of Peter's other, his smooth square jaw clenched in anticipation of climax.

She had found a stack of mail in the living room amongst the finance magazines and travel books arranged in neat stacks on side tables purchased from her shop. Each table was topped with one of her restored lamps, tassels swinging with the vibrations of her intrusion across the floor. He'd been a regular customer since she opened; buying so many satin and crystal shaded lamps his place looked like a Bohemian brothel.

His credit card statement was first in the pile. He owed five thousand dollars, his limit. Most of the charges were made in the past week when he said he was on a business trip. All paid to the Bellagio in Las Vegas. Next was a pay stub. The address took her to the edge of the industrial district. South Broad Park Lodge.

The doors gasped open and a hunch-backed little woman with a halo of white hair slid out, pushing a rolling walker. Her other would be there, Connie knew, trailing behind, a painfully hunched ghoul draped in wrinkled flesh, clutching the air with her withered claws. But the eye patch kept that horror from her sight.

No one was at the front desk to question her so Connie went

in, following a teetering old man with bow legs and socks pulled up to his swollen knees.

At the end of the hall was a day room. Grime-coated windows covered one wall, facing out onto a tree-lined side street. A TV hung at one end, a poker table stood at the other. Everywhere in between were the tenants of this gloomy place; the kind of place people without money or family go to die.

She removed the eye patch. It wasn't a conscious decision; her hand just reached up and pulled it off. She had to see them. She had to know. It was worse than she'd thought.

One withered old codger sat in a wheel chair, a blanket thrown over his lap, dumped in the middle of the room to bob his scaly, head and drool into hands that quivered like dying insects on his lap. Behind him sat the other version, suspended in the same posture, keeping time with the restless twitching, his scalp raw, peeling away, with yellowing patches of pus and skull showing through. From the back of the version's neck, his spine rose in swollen knuckles that poked through his drooping hospital gown.

A woman stood near the TV, working her gums together in an endless sucking, with wrinkles radiating out from her mouth where lips had been. Her other wore the same rose-colored sweat suit, inflamed joints stretching the fabric and, as she gummed at the air, her drooping flesh wagged and shuddered. The other's sunken eyes held no spark, mindlessly rolling in a desperate seizure.

There were so many of them. The stench of urine, talc and mint churned her stomach. Connie took a step back, hitting a chair and sending it screeching across the worn linoleum floor. They all turned to look at her with milky, crusted eyes. At once, bewildered and hopeless, that expression repeating over and over on the faces of their others; the brittle, drooling ancients that surrounded her, condemned to this bleached purgatory to moulder and fade, aching and swollen while their senses slowly erode, their world shrinking until all that was left was a shadowy echo of a life; left with only the sound of their own moans to keep them company.

Connie's feet and hands went numb, the room buzzed, then tilted. All those dumb, drooping faces slid towards her, gunk drying in their wrinkles, moles sprouting thick grey antenna, noses and ear lobes stretched and bulbous, crimson with broken blood vessels. And then she heard his voice, cheerful, loud. Peter strode into the room, pushing a wheelchair containing a slug of a man, a little more alert than the rest, with fat lips and a chin that spilled into his collar. Connie hid out of sight behind the swinging door.

"That's right, Mr. Knightly. I'm pretty much guaranteed to double my money on this investment. Everyone has a cellphone these days. Am I right? They're everywhere." Peter paused to set his charge's brakes, positioning the old man in front of the TV, adjusting his slippered feet on the footrests. Peter looked up at Mr. Knightly, lowering his voice to a stage whisper, smiling with all his teeth out. "Last time I got a tip like this I told Arthur Green. You remember Art? Big payout. Huge. Too bad he didn't stick around long enough to enjoy the return. His granddaughter sure was happy, though, with two young kids to look after." Peter stood and smoothed his white uniform. "I'll check on you in a minute, Sir."

Connie wasn't able to focus on what he was saying; all she could do was look at him. She watched as Peter walked through the room, pausing to admire a ring on one pasty finger, retrieve a three of clubs from the floor. This was his domain. And his other wore all the authority and charisma of a politician. He took Connie's breath. So what if Peter had a few extra pounds on him and wore pants with pleated fronts. She could forgive him his little deceptions too. People judged men who held jobs like this. He could learn that he didn't need to impress, he could just be himself. The self she knew he could be, the self he already was. He could be the man that stood behind him now. Knowing the other version was there, even if she stopped being able to see him, could be enough.

Peter moved back to Mr. Knightly, pulled up a chair and sat beside him, slinging his arm companionably around the old man's shoulder. The other version extended his arm into the air. Connie imagined herself under that arm, its touch cool like whispered promises caressing her skin.

Connie sat in the waiting room. She pulled the gauze patch from her eye, blinking against the fluorescents, the grit sensation. Then she looked at the other patients who waited with her.

They were alone. Just one person, no other version lurking behind. Connie sighed and sat back, relieved. Probably just what the doctor said, a communication issue between brain and eye. Even if it had been in her mind, it had been temporary. A glitch. She wasn't going to lose herself like her mother had. At least not yet.

"Do you need a tissue, ma'am?" The receptionist, the one whose shining red curls and smooth milky skin Connie had admired when she arrived, stood over her with a box of tissue. Connie looked up and gasped, clapping her hand over the eye with the new lens, but it didn't change what she saw.

A frizz-haired medusa stood over her with a face splattered by a grotesque profusion of lumpy freckles.

"Are you okay?" When she spoke, the receptionist revealed a mouthful of large, square teeth, gapped and uneven.

Connie mumbled and accepted the tissue, waving the girl back to her desk. Then she took a closer look at the other patients. She didn't know what they'd looked like before. Were these their versions? Connie tried to remember what Doctor Wilson had looked like after the surgery. She remembered just one of him, and how hopeful she had been about what that meant. He had looked more sharp-featured, sly, his eyes wearing those bruise-colored pouches she'd seen on his other version. Was this how it would be until the end? A world full of people's insecurities and self-loathing.

The waiting room door swung open and Peter rushed in, scanning the room before catching sight of Connie. He strode over to her with a sheepish grin, tucking a newspaper into his suit pocket.

"Sorry I'm late. Traffic." Peter laughed, his gaze shifting away for a moment. "There was an accident or something. We can take a different route back."

"That's okay. I appreciate you coming to get me." Connie found herself smiling, despite her worry about this new manifestation, despite the paper folded open to the horse-racing section that poked out of Peter's pocket. He offered his arm, but before she took it she reached up and smoothed back the curl that fell down from the perfect waves of his hair and admired the flex of his smooth, square jaw when he returned her smile.

THE TENDED FIELD OF EIDO YAMATA

JON MICHAEL KELLEY

SOMEWHERE IN THE DISTANCE, *the faint tinkling of a bell...*

In the serenity where he now found himself, Yamata still retained the vista of his previous life.

Sitting meditatively, he could recall every moment of that existence with uncommon clarity. However, he did not recognize from those memories the child standing before him, a girl of obvious Japanese descent, about eight years old, wearing a simple knee-length white dress that seemed remarkably clean and bright, given that her bare legs and feet were black with dirt. A rice hat made of bamboo sat atop her head, and hooked in the bend of an arm was an ikebana basket of similar weave. But there were no flowers.

Except for not having a mouth, she appeared normal in every other way.

But then, Yamata had to look no farther than his own desiccated body to know that, 'here,' 'normal' was not to be the dominant theme. Obviously, the afterlife was amenable to showcasing his wasted form, one achieved in the previous one through self-mummification. But that such a gaunt and withered state had escorted him so authentically into the next realm was rousing some concern, as he could only slightly turn his head, and to a greater degree his right arm.

Am I to remain forever a rigid corpse? he wondered.

As it had for the better part of his life, a yellow robe draped his body, though with much less resolve given his strangled girth.

Interestingly, *he* was able to speak, and had done so upon his relocation; a kindly greeting to the girl. She'd responded only with an unenthusiastic wave of her hand, her brown eyes staring on, mildly curious.

Beyond the girl was a vastness that Yamata was still trying to grasp. And, like the girl, there was nothing he could recall from his previous life to make its comparison; a life spent mostly in the Tōhoku region of Japan's Honshu island, in search of purification. To all points on the horizon, barren furrows radiated outward from where he sat, a lotus posture that was the very hub for those tilled spokes. He was reminded of a naval flag, one belonging to a country that only had his compulsory allegiance: *The land of the Rising Sun*, its red ensign's beams flaring outward in strong allegory. And similar intentions were at work here, he suspected, as neither from the east nor west did *this* sun rise, but instead beat down relentlessly from a perpetual noon.

Although his time here was (in the vaguest sense) relatively new, the tropes for enlightenment were ageless.

The atmosphere was leaden with quietude, as if becalmed eons ago by some great inhalation and had since petrified while waiting for the ensuing release. Once here, Yamata had intuited an acceleration of awareness. Not the *passing* of time (although there were sequential aspects to the construct), but rather a kind of hastened shedding; a sloughing of absolutes, and things now obsolete, receding away like dreams do upon wakening. And very much like dreams, those references slipped no further than the periphery of his erstwhile life, and lingered there, close by and ready should they be called upon to offer up sobering testimonials. Witnesses to a world that was more devoted to the conservation of falsehoods than to their dismantling. That Hell was eternal was just one of those; that death was the end of learning and bettering oneself, another. No fires burned hotter than those of the physical world, the fires of greed, lust, anger, hatred, sickness... Heaven, he believed, was anywhere such conflagrations had been doused.

Not so unlike his previous journey, the one he would begin from here would be chaperoned by contemplation. He would be careful of being too prideful, and remember that it was never about what life had denied him, but rather what he had denied life.

Yamata considered again his permanent seat, his cadaverousness, the hushed girl, the vast field stretching in all directions...

A field unproductive as yet, aside from growing anticipation.

And that fixed ceiling of sunshine. On a profound level, Yamata accepted the unfailing brightness as obligatory to the venue, for the most crucial lessons were often the most evasive, and to achieve their understanding required keeping any and all shadows squarely underfoot.

That, or the enduring sunshine was here to nourish what was clearly an imminent crop of inestimable scope, and aspirations.

In what was without doubt a land of extended metaphor, he considered a myriad interpretations, from the obvious to the abstruse.

Upon those very thoughts, the little girl stepped closer and tipped her basket to allow him to see its contents. Only a few remained of what appeared to be some kind of seed. With much effort he tilted his head and, beyond her, looked again upon the rows, this time focusing on proximity rather than distance. He saw her footprints, deep and purposeful, marching along the soft trenches. Even closer, he saw the tiny indentations where her finger had pushed the seeds into the soil. And he could now see that her impressions weren't just localized but disappeared into the staggering distance; toward a horizon not teetering upon the curvature of a round world, but poised securely upon the blaring infiniteness of a flat one.

A determined girl! Yamata stared at her again and thought she might even be unusually pretty. But the unnatural smoothness below her nose was influencing that illusion. When having first seen the mouthless girl, Yamata thought of her as stage dressing to his soliloquy, a caricature of quiet innocence. A projection, perhaps, of his immaturity in this new place. He now suspected her reason for being here was as much practical as it was chaste metaphor. She was to be, among other things, the assistant to his immobility.

A less liberated person might have called it servitude, but Yamata saw the potential for a collaboration, though he was yet unclear as to what his reciprocal role might be. And that she could read his thoughts wasn't entirely accurate, as he believed her to be, to some degree, the very extension of them; of his mind. In essence, his duality.

Regardless, there was no question that those omitted lips accentuated expression in her eyes. She was smiling in her agrarian achievement.

He smiled back, then impulsively wondered: *Does her white dress suggest virtue? Purity? Or, is it to represent the absence of beguiling color?* After all, beyond the gold tint of his robe there was only a monotonous blend of bucolic hues.

Abruptly, the girl gave a sighing motion with her shoulders, slowly shook her head, then began walking a tight circle, eyes down and focused on her dirty feet.

Watching the demonstration, Yamata was struck with the notion that she was communicating her annoyance with him.

Have I become tedious with my musings? he wondered. *That it is not truth I am chasing but my own tail instead?*

If she agreed with these thoughts, she gave no sign.

Finally, he said to her, "Giving into the assumption that you have no name, even if you could speak it, I shall call you Uekiya."

Upon hearing the word, the girl looked up and nodded to the unfailing field, accepting her new title: Gardner. Then she lowered her eyes and resumed etching a tight circle into the loamy soil.

Again considering the girl's inability at speech, Yamata recalled a quote from Lao Tzu, the founder of Taoism, and wondered if she was the exemplar for such wisdom: *"He who knows, does not speak. He who speaks, does not know."*

Then, to confirm that she either was or was not, in fact, substantial, Yamata reached out his workable hand for her. Stiffly, she stopped going round and round and regarded the gesture with narrow eyes, then slowly shook her head, as if to say that was not appropriate.

Why? he wondered. *Am I being reminded that something's authenticity doesn't necessarily lie in its solidness.* Or, was there still lingering within him a tactile need, one not quite disassociated from his former self?

Then there was sudden growth in the field. Already the girl was bent over and studying the nearest sprout, a thing that vaguely resembled an asparagus spear, no larger than his littlest finger and appearing just as corpselike. A reaffirming sign that this was going to be a harvest most different from any other.

Still bent over, hands on her knees, Uekiya turned her attention to him. Where triumph could not insinuate itself in a smile so it sparkled doubly in her eyes.

From behind him came once again the tinkling of a bell. A declarative echo, perhaps, of his resolve to achieve *Sokushinbutsu*, the practice to reach ultimate austerity and enlightenment through a most ambitious art of physical punishment: self-mummification. For a Shingon Buddhist, it was an enduring commitment. For many years the devoted monk would practice *nyūjō*, adhering to elaborate regimes of meditations, physical activities that stripped the body of fat, and an exclusive diet of salt, pine bark, nuts, seeds, roots, and urushi tea. This tea was especially significant. It was derived from the sap of the urushi tree and highly toxic, and was normally used for the lacquering of pottery. When ingested, vomiting and dehydration followed. Most importantly, it ultimately made the body too poisonous to be eaten by carrion insects and their ilk. If the body absorbed high enough levels, some believed it could even discourage like-minded bacteria.

Finally, when sensing his end drawing near, the monk would have himself locked inside a pinewood box, one barely large enough to accommodate his body, wherein a permanent lotus position was assumed. Some monks would insist on having coal, salt, or even lime heaped around them to stave off the slightest moisture.

Once confined, the practitioner's only connection to the outside world was an air tube, and a bell—one he would dutifully ring every day to let those listening know that he was still alive. When the ringing stopped, the air tube was removed and the makeshift tomb tightly sealed.

After a customary three years had passed, the body was exhumed. Of the many who attempted to achieve such a hallowed state, only a few triumphed. The majority of bodies were found to be in normal states of decay. However, those who accomplished their own mummifications were regarded as true Buddhas. Highly revered, they were placed into the temples for viewing.

For their tremendous spirit and devotion, admiration was still paid those who failed in their endeavors. But for Yamata especially, that was modest esteem—and certainly not the sort he ever hoped to gain through compromise.

Uekiya had dropped her basket and, arms dangling at her sides, was now staring intently at something behind him. And by the tilt of her gaze that something was alleging to be looming from a great height. Her awe was absolute. Had she the proper hinges, Yamata thought, she would have been left slack-jawed. He then became both exhilarated and frightened. What could exist among these rural and most modest trappings to provoke such veneration? If he were prone to such expectations, he might have believed she was beholding a god.

That she was witnessing a massive thunderhead instead was the likelier explanation. After all, from a parched point of view, threatening rain clouds could easily provoke the same respect as any passing deity.

Moisture. Yes, it would be the remaining ingredient needed to placate the construct's agricultural objective. Being unable to turn his head fully to either side, Yamata's visual range was limited, thus leaving the matter most tantalizing. Yet another clue that the lessons here would not be easily learned.

After what may have been a mere moment or the passing of centuries, the girl reached down and retrieved her basket, her wonderment either spent or the spectacle had finally retreated.

Another burst of growth in the rows, now appearing as a more recognizable plant. Although still spindly and emaciated, the stalks were more pronounced and now home to little brown offshoots that were unmistakably leaves, semi-translucent in their infancy. A quality that he found to be strangely reminiscent, but of what he couldn't yet say.

Whatever relevance this germination had to the setting remained unclear. Yamata continued to employ his wisdom, always mindful that this was by its very nature a land of illusion.

Yamata again reached out for the girl, his compulsion growing fierce. This time, Uekiya wheeled and violently slapped his hand away, nearly breaking off the first two fingers. With utter disbelief, Yamata stared at those digits, both dangling now on withered tendons and pointing obliquely, if not forebodingly, to the ground.

The pain was sudden and intense—and disconcerting. He had not anticipated there to be such measurable discomfort beyond physical life. But he did not react instinctively and withdraw his arm. Instead, he left it out there for her to see. A testament to her brashness, to her insolence.

With something akin to compassion, Uekiya's eyes softened. Then she made her way to the closest plant and began plucking its leaves, placing each one carefully into her basket. As Yamata watched, his curiosity grew into trepidation as he realized that those lucent leaves were exactly the same color and texture as his dried, wrinkled skin. After having gathered only a few, Uekiya stepped up to his extended arm and began carefully applying the leaves to his broken fingers, bringing them back together at their fractures then wrapping and gently rubbing the new tissue into place, manipulating and messaging it until it was indistinguishable from his own layering. When she was through, she turned his hand this way and that, regarding her accomplishments with satisfaction.

Yamata flexed his fingers and found them restored to their original, albeit intransigent, state.

Appreciation of Uekiya's handiwork was quickly dissolving, melting into an anxiety unlike any he had ever known, confirming that the most profound realizations were often the most unsettling.

Within the rows there was yet again another acceleration of growth, this time even more telling as a small whitish bulb had become evident at the top of every stalk, each of those now taller by another eight inches, and with heartier girth.

Are they rudiments of a flower? Yamata wondered of the spheres. *A fruit? Or are they the beginnings of something I dare not try to imagine?*

His determined outlook, he realized, was growing dim. A dread had begun building in the thick atmosphere, but there was no beating heart to accompany it to crescendo. Just his quivering essence.

And still the plants grew, now four feet high, their bulbs even whiter and plumper, where within those a restlessness festered. As he stared, they disconcertedly reminded him of caterpillar nests, the larvae inside those silk pouches squirming to break free.

Yamata turned his eyes to Uekiya, as if her own might provide an answer, or at least a concerned recognition to his plight.

He balled his right hand as best he could, and vehemently condemned her speechlessness. *"Are you to remain forever silent, or must I say just the right thing, ask just the right question to elicit a response?"* But her attention had once again been drawn to something behind him. Something gargantuan, was still his impression.

It was then when Yamata noticed that something had gone missing from the construct. He searched his restricted view; frantically so. It was vitally important to remember, he was sure. Everything presented here had dire meaning, and was only expected to change or disappear altogether once its purpose had been understood. Or so he expected.

Then there was movement. Of the nearest plant, its bulb had begun weeping milky rivulets; viscous streams trailing down the stalk with the ambition of warmed honey. Then Yamata realized that the discharge was not comprised of any liquid but was made up of hundreds of pale white worms. And maggots. Upon reaching the ground, the creatures struggled in the loose soil, their frantic undulations less confident but still maintaining a fixed progression toward his still and sitting form.

Bent over once again, hands on knees, Uekiya was watching the bugs' advancement with rapt wonderment.

The first worms to reach Yamata reared up and attached themselves to the lowest parts of his feet, then began burrowing through the brown, shriveled skin. Sparkles of intense pain began dancing behind his eyes, and a shrill, strident noise stung his ears; the pinched squeal, he quickly realized, of his own dry voice.

The pain of them entering his body was memorable, but the kind they ignited once inside was astonishingly bright and bellicose. A feast not had on mere shriveled bone and muscle, he feared, but upon a profound and everlasting food source: his soul. And it too screamed. Sounds not birthed from a decrepit throat, but instead the collected resonances of isolation and grim oblivions, now to be intoned upon an unending existence.

The internal writhing of the worms was equally insufferable, and he cried out for a boyhood god; one he had no occasion to revisit, until now.

Finally, mercifully, the pain slowly receded after the remaining worms had inserted themselves. It was a momentous reprieve. But another look at the burgeoning rows beyond confirmed that such amnesties would be fleeting.

Leisurely filling her basket, Uekiya had set about plucking leaves from the offending plant. Yamata stared out across his field, one that was now growing a perpetual supply of sutures; grafts to outwardly mend the external damage caused by an equally eternal progression of the most vile and ravenous creatures.

But what about the internal *damage?* he desperately wondered. *How will she mend that?*

Uekiya was now kneeling before him, messaging the leaves onto the chewed holes in his feet, restoring the dead tissue.

When finished, she stared at the anomaly behind him.

Yamata prayed that the girl was, in fact, witnessing a storm. Prayed for a deluge to drown the crawling masses. For lightning to scorch them thoroughly. For typhoon winds to scatter them to the endless reaches of this place.

Prayed for any blight that would dissuade his punishment.

Once, his great profundity did not abide the generic concepts of an eternal and torturous perdition. Now, he was being forced to reconsider. Ironically, what remained intact of his fracturing philosophy was the reverberation of his most insightful expression; that it wasn't about what life had denied him, but what he had denied life.

And life, it was being made very clear, was not going to be denied *him*.

Despite his most sincere, consecrated motivations, he had accelerated his own death and thereby corrupted those intentions. To tear away the shiny tinsel of devotion revealed the harsher truth of a prideful suicide. But his biggest sin of all was saturating his body with urushi tea. Having done so, he had denied the carrion eaters their due; had disallowed the natural progression of things, and had done so vainly and with utter disregard for consequence.

The bulb of the second closest plant had opened, releasing its own white undulant stream. Yamata looked beyond the advancing worms and out upon the incalculable vastness, and within that silent horror was revealed the thing that had gone missing. The bell. It was no longer being rung. And on some instinctual level, that awakened in him a fear more primal than the worms themselves.

Uekiya's growing devotion to the unseen behind him was inviting its own species of fear. Her wide brown eyes had assumed a tragically revering expression, and Yamata was now on the brink of admitting that no less than a god could warrant such reverence.

But what sort of god captivates a child while hiding behind an atrocity of infinite proportions?

Yamata one last time contemplated Uekiya's absent mouth, and out of all the convoluted, Byzantine reasons he could think of for it not being there, he finally decided on a most austere one. Once in hell, there is simply nothing left to say.

PLAYING WITH FIRE

RICHARD THOMAS

THE WOLVES don't show themselves when the sun is shining. It's something that took me a long time to figure out. I would hide in the daytime and then cower in the darkness, high up in a massive oak tree as they ran in circles beneath me. How could I get anything done? How would I survive? Before I knew of their existence, and they knew of mine, I wandered the island without a care in the world, my arms filled with seashells and driftwood—and handfuls of fruit from the orchard by the caves. But then they found me. And I was willing to let this be the end. But when the night fell and the owls hooted from the edge of the forest and the fireflies danced at the edge of the field, I remembered that I did care—that I still loved Isabella. Against all that was holy and pure, I wanted to see her again, to hold her in my arms and nuzzle her neck, to feel her lips on mine, her arms around me—our glossy flesh melting into an eternal, liquid enlightenment.

And yet, I lived in fear of her return.

There are things we whisper into a pillow at night, simple requests. Take me, not her. Give me her pain, I can take it. Some prayers are better left unanswered.

The land was still empty then, the rest of the world just down the road, not flooded. There was an endless supply of meat and water, a store for every item I needed, each tool for the job that I wanted at hand. That was then. We are all trapped here now, on this parcel. The hairy beasts, the hooting owls, the google-eyed rats, the shadows in the caves—none of us can escape.

I was not prepared.

The research, my dead wife, the disease that tore down the trees and the fruit, the vanishing that slowly worked its way across the land—it was a lightning bolt from the sky and a slow seeping through a frayed, layered bandage. I went to sleep in a canvas tent, and woke up to an ocean of black reflections. For the work I did, there were wrenches and hammers, spikes and shovels, nets and tape. It was a finite and laughable stock of goods, a treasure chest that I would treat as holy manna.

On the day that I made the saw, the day that I stood on this hill, no roof over my head, no walls to keep the animals away, I asked for many things.

First, I asked for the rain to stop. And it did. And then I prayed for strength.

When it stopped raining and there was nothing in sight, no roads off into the distance, the farmlands and prairies gone for as far as I could see, the lone piece of land that stood up to the on-slaught—that was where I stood.

I couldn't be alone. There must be others—even if I was dead inside.

The tent had been torn apart and sucked up into the wind on the third day after the flood. I huddled against the sheer rock face that lead up to the caves. As the lightening cracked the sky and the moon hung over it all heavy and somber, I stared at the woods that surrounded me and came up with an idea. I had to build a shelter, a cabin, and I had to build it fast.

The wing of the plane. The wing.

I took that wing apart one panel at a time, trying to get to the long strip of sheet metal, one piece about six feet long, in order to build the saw I needed. I spent the first day with a wrench and a hammer, loosening the bolts, unhooking the metal, trying to get at the raw sheet that was no longer going to fly anywhere. I flayed my fingertips and cursed the bloody metal. I slowed down, bandaged my fingers, and went back at it again.

In time I freed the metal, and started to cut in the blades. First I went over it with a black magic marker that I found in the cockpit of the plane. Then I traced over the black line, the jagged teeth as big as my palms, back and forth, tracing over and over, with the tip of a long, silver screwdriver. I didn't have any tin snips, no garden sheers, not even a pair of scissors. I traced this line as the screwdriver gouged into it, slowly curling away strips of the metal.

It was an eternity.

Maybe this was hell.

If I focused on a singular line, back and forth, back and forth, I could see my progress, the line deepening, the indentation pushing through the metal. When it looked like I had gone far enough, I bent the metal back and forth, back and forth until it snapped.

It went on like this for some time. Days. I kept walking back to the caves, resting under the shadow of the oak trees, the open fields unsettling to me. At night I would climb up into its branches.

I stopped keeping track. I knew what lay in front of me, the wood. At some point the last blade popped loose and I had the saw in its rough form. Now, it needed to be sharp.

I scoured the beach for rocks, anything that looked like it could hold up to the blade, the raw metal, and carried them back to the hill. I ran them across the edge and the metal started to shine. The black rocks from down by the waterline, they seemed to hold up the best. But it was tricky. They would dissolve over time, once I got a groove started, leaning just this way and that, waiting for the moment when the metal pushed through and ran its fresh teeth across my flesh. It only had to happen one time, in order for me to understand. Eventually the blades were sharp.

I ate the fruit that I discovered down by the orchard, it looked safe to me, untreated by disease. I thought of Isabelle with every bite, the look on her face when she became swollen with the rotting sickness, trying to forget the way that she expanded.

I set out whatever buckets and tubs I could find.

Then, I prayed for it to rain.

Down on the beach I pull my boat up on the shore and drop it into the hot sand. I am at the south end, searching for driftwood, to add to the fire pit behind the hut. There is plenty today, some of it worn smooth from the water, other pieces fractured on the rocks. I fill up my arms and take it back to the hut, dumping the wood into the pit.

It is a dull indentation in the earth, nothing more than a vessel for fire and ash. And yet, the flames have always flickered hypnotic. Easy to fall into them, their heat and lashing tongues, easy to forget the darkness around me.

Later in the day I stumble across a downed tree at the edge of the small forest that rings the caves. Broken off from the rest of the oak is a massive limb, three or four feet around, and I vow that it will be part of my home. It is not as rotten as the rest of the tree, still solid enough in its six feet of length to resist my every effort to move it. I lift one end and tug at it, pulling it ever so slowly, the hind end gouging out the soft soil, my back straining under the weight.

Each day I walk to the shadow of the caves, staring at the rocky sheer, looking for handholds, eyeing the cracks and imagining the climb. I envision my certain cold plummet, hands slipping, knees barking off of the stone. If only I could be sure that my spine would be severed, my neck snapped, then maybe I would try to climb to the caves. I was not yet desperate enough to feel the sharp teeth of the wolves on my skin, tugging, tearing, as I lay beneath them, paralyzed from the fall, but awake to witness their unchecked hunger.

I have an idea.

I untie the rope that hangs from the front of the boat, and take it with me off to the limb. If I can find a way to distribute the weight, maybe I can pull this log to my home. From the plane wreckage just north of the woods I snag the last of the in-flight blankets.

I lay the small blue blanket at the top of the log, and roll the massive timber on to it with a shove and trembling legs. A tear at the top of the blanket is quickly torn even wider, separating the cloth with a slow and painful rip. I tie the loose ends of the blanket around the thick rope, over once, and then again, in a handmade knot that I am certain will not hold. And then I throw the rope over my shoulder. I dig my heels in and slowly lean forward, the fibers digging into my shoulder, my hands gripping the rope with every ounce of strength I can muster, and I slowly begin to walk forward.

It is slow—my back strains against the weight of the log. It has to be two hundred pounds, if not more, and the way it digs into the earth, clinging to the moss and wild grasses, it protests my thievery of its great heft.

As the sun reaches its zenith and the sweat drips off my face, heat baking into my skin, I finally feel something slip. Not my hands, but in my back. A long rubber band, elastic in its terror, unfurls up my spine as a scream escapes my lips. I collapse into the grass, rolling back and forth, trying to push my hands to my spine to rub the pain away. Stars in my black eyelids implode and turn to dust, the fragility of my simple skeleton revealing itself in throbbing wonder. I can't get up. I can hardly roll over on my back. And then I pass out.

Mosquitoes at my neck, stabbing, piercing, and I slap at my skin and moan into the darkness.

The darkness.

I try to sit up and a sharp pain shoots up my spine. I cut short the yelp that is pushing through my lips and open my eyes to the night. I have to get up—I have to get home. There's no reason I can think of that the wolves haven't found me yet.

I turn over onto my belly and push up with my hands until I'm on all fours. The irony is not lost on me. I bite into my lower lip as my face flushes red, filling my mouth with copper and heat as my vision dances in front of me. Tiny dots, I cannot see—wait, the dots are still moving.

A thin line of tiny yellow spheres extends over the grass, up the hill and ends at the front door to my hut.

Isabelle, my love.

"Thank you," I gasp.

And I start crawling. When the first howl shatters the dark, distorted and filled with echoes, down by the cliff's edge, I stop and consider the distance. The longer I sit here and think, the closer they get. And yet, I still can't move. I am submerged in an ocean of pain.

I lean back onto my knees and my eyes are coated with a thin film, a piercing hot rod running up my spine. I cannot breathe, a stuttering intake, but I know that I have to stand up. I place my hands on my knees and straighten out my back, and the darkness starts to shift at the horizon. I pull one leg forward and bracing my hands on my knee push myself into an upright position, standing tall, wobbling, starting to bend, to hunch over, wondering what it will feel like to walk.

I wonder what it will feel like to run.

I set one foot in front of me and find that if I focus on the trail of yellow lights, if I focus on my breathing, the traveling heat in the small of my back, now the middle of my back, now a knot of tension in my neck? I can assign it to some other man—it is not my pain right now.

I walk as if I am a child. But there is no furniture nearby to balance me—padded and safe—sharp edges hidden from soft flesh. I am chubby legs wobbling, made of rubber, eager to bend at the slightest bit of resistance. I bark a laugh. This is how it will be—alpha to omega, womb to womb—all for a stupid piece of wood.

I don't dare look up, down towards the cliff's edge, across the grass that sighs at my ineptitude. I take the steps I need to get to the door, I count the fireflies and inhale their buttery aroma, and I make it to the stone porch. I paw at the door, grabbing for the handle, sweat running down my neck, tears filling my eyes, and when I turn around to slam the door shut, ignoring the heat that is immolating my back, they swarm across the field and wrap around the house, disappearing into the night without a sound. I am still holding the door open wide—I am barely clinging to consciousness, my mouth filled with cotton and glass.

I close the door and the latch clicks shut. Numb, I ease to the bed, feeling my way in the darkness—and I lie down, glistening, sobbing. I lie down and close my eyes.

In the morning there is no pain.

This is how it goes.

I open the door to sunlight and the distant chirps of angry birds, stepping outside to see what fresh batch of horror awaits me. I walk to the back of the hut to the rain barrel, eager to drink the rainwater. Off into the distance is a long, black, shallow ditch that stretches out over the hill. At my feet sits the log. All up and down the rope are teeth marks buried in the frayed and tormented twine—and in my head, I hear her laughing.

INDIAN SUMMER

PHILIP C. PERRON

THE TUTTLE HOUSE. We in the neighborhood just called it that because that's who used to live there. She was a loner. Mrs. Tuttle. To be honest I don't even know her first name. She was a forty-year-old woman. Divorced. About a year or two ago, her husband just up and left her. No one really knows why. Tommy Castle, who I guess you could call my boyfriend, tried to get her to be one of his customers on his paper route, but she didn't even want a newspaper.

So there she was… a childless divorcee who lived alone. When I practiced cheerleading or worked on my field hockey moves over by the side yard where the moss was short enough, I'd see her occasionally working on her yard. Her house was a good one hundred yards away at the end of the cul-de-sac. From that distance she appeared as this little dot, usually in a pair of fluorescent shorts and a tank top. Nothing about her was exceptional. My father called her a Plain Jane and based off Tommy's opinion, it seemed suitable.

I did meet her once. Last year when I was a freshman I happened to be one of those goodie two-shoes who actually went around knocking on doors when school asked us teenagers to collect for UNICEF. There I was, ringing doorbells with the little orange box in my hand, getting quarters and dimes from all the neighbors. And thinking about it, just like with Mrs. Tuttle, I probably met most of the neighbors face to face only a handful of times.

Our road, appropriately named Ibister Farm Road after the old pumpkin farm that the Ibisters owned before they sold off the land to a builder, was typical. The houses were carbon copy ranch style and all seemed to grow out of the hardy soil like the recently planted willows and catalpas that were barely as high as the roofs. One thing about building on old crop land, the lots were treeless and bare. My father always grumbled how if he had the chance to do it all over, he'd have bought in Wilton, New Hampshire where forests were still thick.

Mrs. Tuttle seemed friendly enough. There was no little dog running to the window to announce my arrival on her doorstep. Only the woman's footsteps greeted me before she appeared behind the screened storm door. I thought it odd, it being late October and a chill already in the air, and yet still she hadn't changed it to a glass pane.

Her demeanor was kind even if a shadow of annoyance passed across her face. That itself wasn't strange since I could count on my ten fingers the same expression from a handful of the other neighbors. Her green eyes had darted to the orange box and before I could explain my intrusion, she had reached over by a small sidebar where a little pink purse lay. Though her fingers somewhat hid her contribution as she dropped the coins within the slot of the box, I saw that it was around eighty cents. I thanked her maybe a little too animatedly, and soon her front door was once more closed with its flat plastic jack-o-lantern grinning at me from its perch upon a small nail.

So that was my only actual meeting of the woman. A few pleasantries between us discussing the weather and my polite gratitude for her donation to an organization I didn't really know all that much about or what it did. But earlier, as I said, Tommy had met her. He had met her a number of times. Once a year he'd go around knocking on the doors of the handful of households that had held out from getting a subscription to the Nashua Telegraph. His success rate wasn't all that fruitful, but he said he had to give it the college try.

His discovery was that folks were already set in their ways with their loyalty to other newspapers and their reading online additions. Tommy used to grumble how next year when he turned eighteen he'd have to go find another job like pumping gas or bagging groceries. He dreaded being told what to do by twenty-year-old bosses who had their soul already sucked up by what he liked to refer to as *the machine*. My father and his generation seemed to call it *the man*. But no matter, whatever one called it, I knew it meant all the same.

Changes did take place in the neighborhood. The day itself had been memorable for a number of reasons. It was six months ago. February. And in New Hampshire it usually was pretty nasty. The Super Bowl was over, so our excitement waiting to watch the Patriots and Tom Brady each Sunday had passed. The weather was usually frigid and a foot and a half of snow blanketed the landscape with its blinding lucidity. And the sun. Oh how it would shine on a clear day and yet no warmth came from it. It teased us with its radiance and tricked us by setting around five o'clock. A cold darkness would replace it until middle morning. Nothing remained but a chilly wind and a quiet that was eerily peaceful.

That February day, six months ago, was different. It was what my mother called an Indian summer. Though her parents were from Vietnam, she herself had grown up in Nashua. I'm not sure if it was just a New England term but it meant an unusually warm day in the middle of winter.

I was over at Tommy's house doing what every parent dreaded their teenage daughter would do. It was just after school and Tommy's parents were still at work. The two of us remained naked in his bed when we heard the first sirens. I was still a bit high both from our intimacy as well as the joint we were smoking. When the second siren passed, we got up. While I pulled my dress over my head, Tommy had opened a window to wave the smoke out.

At that point, a third siren passed, much louder now that the window was open. Tommy mentioned he had seen some sort of fire truck heading down to the end of the street. It was pretty bizarre. A street with fourteen houses that ended in a dead end didn't attract many emergency vehicles.

Even before we walked the length of Tommy's driveway, we could see two police cruisers, a fire department paramedic, and a

Mercedes-Benz parked at the Tuttle house. Neighbors which I knew in passing had congregated out front. When we joined the fray, I went over to Mrs. Gauthier to see what was going on. Her five year old daughter clung to her side, whimpering as the woman bounced the girl against her hip.

She was as clueless as us. Some of the neighbors spoke with the three police officers that came in and out of the house. But they weren't all that forthcoming. The minutes dragged to hours. Most everyone had left but an additional neighbor would come join us every so often asking what was up. February or not, with the oddly warm temperature, Tommy had stripped down to a t-shirt. At one point I wanted to leave, but Tommy held me. I stayed, out of loyalty, as well as the elation of what my mother would call *teen-age infatuation*.

As the third hour rolled out its arrival, the waiting turned into goings-on. The police had locked open the storm door; it still had a screen. Out came one of the blue jacketed firewomen. She walked backwards, almost stumbling down the first of four steps to the shoveled walkway. To my surprise, what followed was a wheeled stretcher covered by a dark blue sheet or blanket. Behind the trailing fireman came a man that looked somewhat like Mrs. Tuttle. I would later find out it was her brother who had come to visit from New Mexico. The Mercedes license plate had plainly showed that. He had driven across country, stopping at various warehouses that he owned before arriving in New Hampshire to check in on his sister. It was he who had found her.

Days passed and no one was really quite sure what had happened. The Nashua Telegraph obituary showed that there was no wake. And if there was any funeral, it was private. My parents had to go to local town news pamphlets to find out what really happened. It appeared Mrs. Tuttle had taken her own life. Details were few, yet the rumor was she had hung herself from a water pipe in the utility section of her cellar.

So the house at the end of the cul-de-sac suddenly went dark when the sun set. One day, a realtor sign was found perched upon a snowbank by the street. During my early morning jogs in March and April while readying for softball, I'd trot past the Tuttle house, stopping to stare at the dark windows of the oversized ranch. The thought of someone taking their own life in a house not but five away from where I lived seemed surreal. A woman I barely knew had lived there and now the house was empty.

As the snow began to melt and the crocuses and tulips started to bloom, the change to that lonely house seemed more appropriate. Spring brought in with it the robins and cardinals, the squirrels and chipmunks, and the flowers and leaves. And though the Tuttle home was lifeless, it had in some ways changed as well. The grass began to grow to a high length. The realtor sent over landscapers to give the house an appearance of living.

Soon spring turned into my summer vacation and the days became longer. One morning, while out jogging in preparation for the field hockey travel team, I saw that the realtor sign had vanished. A handful of weeks went by, but still no change to the house. Tommy's father had told him that he had heard the place was taken off the market. Any prospective buyers were turned away after hearing of the death of the prior owner. Though the house was most assuredly livable, its notoriety was too much for most. Yet somehow Mr. Castle heard this gossip. His understanding was that the house was to be left empty until the following spring, when enough time had passed for Mrs. Tuttle's brother to try once more; and any reputation of the home would be a mere memory.

During these months, Tommy and I discussed our usual topics; the Red Sox season, hitting Hampton Beach on the weekends, driving to Quebec to eat authentic *poutine*, and what new positions to try while in bed. But almost every conversation had mention of the Tuttle house. In the evenings, after eating dinner, we'd get together and take Churchill, his English bulldog, for a walk up and down the street. As the days passed, we watched the lawn of the Tuttle place grow from ankle high to just below my knee. The tops of the grass had fragmented out, giving the appearance of wheat.

Without a realtor providing someone to cut the grass, the house once more changed—from a quiet abode, well-manicured by Mrs. Tuttle, to the house that all the neighbors moaned about. My father one day had driven his John Deer out to the street, only to have my mother run out and stop him. He wondered what harm it was to mow someone's lawn. But my mother protested, saying it wasn't ours to say. Either way, that didn't keep my father from remaining one of the cheerleaders on our street, not too happy about that empty house at the end of the road.

During the middle of July, I began heading over to the high school field to scrimmage with the field hockey traveling team. Fortunately, most practices were in early morning before the humidity was too much. And by the time we were done, it would be no later than noon, giving me the rest of the afternoon to play and screw. The days I didn't have practice, I'd sleep late, having given up my early morning jogs. But the three days a week I played left wing I got a lift from my commuting father as he headed off to work to be told what to do by *the man*. On these mornings, I'd always take a look down the street at the lonely house with its lawn of weeds. Occasionally I'd see Tommy walking his dog, too far away for me to wave.

As the end of July arrived, I'd see Tommy down by the cul-de-sac, alone these early mornings, just standing about near the Tuttle house. By the end of the first week of August, after one of our daily trysts, I finally asked him what he was doing out and about so early. Of course his first response was to say he was giving Churchill his morning walk. But I told him that wasn't so. He hemmed and hawed before finally caving to my questions. For him, I discovered, the Tuttle house in ways had become somewhat of a shrine... a symbol maybe, of change. Of things and dreams that once were and now were gone.

I asked him how so, yet deep within my breast I had felt the same. I could sense a sort of melancholy enveloping my thoughts from some time ago, even prior to hearing about the woman's passing. Generally speaking, there was no reason for me to be blue. I was popular in a way, did well in school and sports, felt I was attractive and smart, and got along with folks. I had a boyfriend like any teenage girl and had a family that loved me. So what was it that made Tommy's very novel view of some house down at the end of the road enlightening?

At first he mumbled on, almost like his mind was spilling out like an overturned beer bottle. None of it really made much sense. But then he said of me, that the way we were... he and I... we were like two artists that had just discovered we were artists. We had the faculty to see the world just a bit skewed. The thought somewhat frightened me since it really did hit home in a way.

He went on explaining how the Tuttle house was a place where a woman once lived. A woman who once was a young girl that had dreams... aspirations... but also maybe insecurities or anxieties that made... maybe just under the surface, that made her existence very painful. Tommy compared it jokingly to how I always complained about the pain of that first walk into the freezing Atlantic on our many trips to the beach. I smiled at that; his levity was much appreciated.

The Tuttle house to Tommy was now not just some house on our street, but a place that represented loss to him. What loss he referred to he never explained, but for me his poignant reflections meant many things. The woman's death had transformed from a thing of mourning to thoughts of neighbors being upset that overgrown grass might lower property values. It was sad, in a way, and made me feel part of that *machine* Tommy always grumbled about. Had a loss of someone's life, and therefore their aspirations, meant nothing more than a yard that wasn't manicured?

So early August turned into the last weeks of the month where everyone was getting ready for school. Those of us who had been starters on the field hockey team the prior season were asked by the coach to meet informally in the afternoons since it was technically... maybe the word was amoral... amoral to have coached practices of presumed players prior to yearly tryouts. So rules and acts to keep things fair had loopholes.

And that leads all to this day; today in late August I skipped a field hockey practice that really wasn't supposed to be a practice. I stayed home. Both of my parents had left for work and I didn't feel like getting laid or high so I didn't bother responding to Tommy's text messages. I happened to be in one of those miserable moods every girl has the right to be in.

I grabbed one of my father's beers from the fridge. Concealing it in my fanny pack, I headed out for a jog. I passed the old Ibister house still owned and lived in by this generation's Ibister; now one wealthy farmer's descendent. When I returned to my street, my jog lead me to our cul-de-sac. My eyes wandered to the Tuttle house. It remained in nice condition, but as expected the bushes needed a trimming and the yard needed a weeding.

I walked up the driveway to the side of the house and circled around back. The last time I had been around back, I was ten years old and used to cut through to get to the convenience store in the next neighborhood. Again, nothing seemed out of the ordinary, except for the condition of the yard. On the other side of the window, set in the back door of the house, was Mrs. Tuttle's kitchen. I don't know what got into me, but I opened the storm door (yes, screen not glass) and tried the doorknob. Surprisingly, it turned and the door popped open.

The kitchen was fairly pedestrian. Unlike my family's house, it still had the original appliances the builder had put in. Nothing fancy, just your utilitarian no-frills kitchen. Besides the handful of additions on a number of the houses on the street, each was either a carbon copy or mirror image of the others. And the Tuttle house was bare essential.

I headed into the next room, an open concept dining and living room arrangement like in my house. Yet I was amazed how huge the rooms appeared. The side bar where Mrs. Tuttle had kept that little pink purse of hers was gone, as was every other piece of furniture, making the place appear massive. I followed the hall to three medium sized bedrooms, all empty and bare of even dust. At this point I opened the beer and drank it while standing in the corner of the master bedroom where sunlight was most bright.

The last room was the common bathroom, the only one in the house. It was empty except for the toilet paper and a bottle of bath wash still sitting in the shower. Whatever came over me must have been the same thing that had me break into the house in the first place. I took off my clothes and showered. The hot water arrived much quicker than the bath at my house.

The mind works in funny ways. While showering, my thoughts travelled from the hot water to the condition of the water heater, and finally settling on the cellar and what Mrs. Tuttle must have felt right before she did what she did. After unsuccessful attempts to use toilet paper to dry off, I went back to the master bedroom and stood once more in the sunlight and its wonderful heat. Though still wet, I threw on my shorts and sports bra, not caring that they were left damp.

The last two doors in the house were the coat closet, which was back in the living room, and the door in the hall across from the bathroom. That one, like in my house, lead to the basement. The stairs were carpeted, reminding me that the Tuttle house, like my family's, had a partially finished basement. The basement windows were few and no larger than a small box.

Paranoid as I was, I left the lights off and slowly made my way down to the landing. The finished section of the cellar was empty but for a small loveseat pushed unceremoniously to the back corner. Mrs. Tuttle's brother had cleaned out the place. Her old furnishings and belongings made no difference to anyone, it appeared.

I turned to the door leading to the utility section of the basement and noticed a white, business-sized envelope stuck to its visage. As I preceded to it, my foot crunched on a roll of Scotch tape. Now, it is impossible to try to explain the surprise I felt when I saw my name written in pen across the face of the envelope. I reached over and opened it.

The single piece of paper within asked if I was ready for… relevance? If not, I should turn back and dial 911.

The note was signed by Tommy.

My eyes watered and I bit the back of my hand as I understood what was to come.

I slowly opened the door and entered the utility basement. And there he was… my Tommy. Hanging from a sewage pipe. A rope around his neck. An upturned stool by his dangling feet.

I walked over to his body. Taking him down felt like it would give back some form of dignity. As I moved forward, I suddenly saw something down the pipe that both horrified and elated me: a second rope in the shape of a noose, waiting for me to join Tommy and Mrs. Tuttle in… relevance.

BLOOD WOMEN

USMAN T. MALIK

YOU COULD SEE the blood women standing under the banyan trees any evening. All you needed was the right *blink*, Haider said.

This is the way we did it: we circled the graveyard three times, for three is the godly number. Haider on his father's bicycle, me on my brother's red and white Made-in-Pakistan tall rider, and ten-year-old Zareen on her three-wheeler clattering over stones, bird bones, and dry branches.

"Ready?" Haider would say, his eyes black as apple seeds.

We nodded, and together we blinked.

The blood women were not there.

"No such thing as blood women," said Zareen the second time it didn't work. "Liar."

"Am not," Haider said.

"Are too."

"Am not."

"Okay, shut up and let's just try to figure out why they didn't show," I said. "Is there a prayer or *mantar* we should've chanted?"

Haider kicked a pebble. "Maybe we should've gone to the grove behind the older graves."

I crossed my arms. "*Mantar* or no?"

He looked sullen. "Don't think so, Asif. No one ever said anything about a *mantar*."

"Let's try again," I said. Cross-linked hands binding us in a circle, we closed our eyes, imagining the shadows that the women must cast: bulbous, yet serpentine from dangling tresses, swollen from lack of any understandable shape...

We blinked rapidly, but they didn't show. They would never show. Not in daytime, when sunlight fell in swatches of fungoid-yellow between the trees, turning Lahore into a bowlful of flesh stewing in tropical sweat. Not in darkness either, when the moon floated like a pale alien ship above the smoggy city landscape.

"They're not real," said Zareen, her eyes bulging, and licked her lips. (She had an iodine-deficient childhood, Mother said, so her neck glands swelled until they pushed her eyes out).

But they were, insisted Haider. On special days, when a suicide bomber hit an intersection, or a missing person was found in a body bag by the roadside, rumors of sightings rippled across our neighborhood. From the tea boys to the garage boys, everyone knew someone who'd seen blood women on the eve of murder.

As if the godly three meant nothing to them. As if the religion of blood was the only religion they believed in.

"How do *you* know?" I said once. "How do you know they're real?"

Standing in the shade of the same banyan trees as the blood women might, Haider looked at me, eyebrows raised. His fingers came together and clutched each other like mating worms.

"Because this is where they found Ali," he said.

In my dreams, sometimes, the blood women stood in a clasped-hands circle that shimmered in the heat haze. Murmurous, murmurous, their chants rang out, calling to passersby.

"A pint of blood for the sons of man, a pint of blood for the sons of martyrs. A pint of blood for the sons of jinns…"

Later we talked about it endlessly, but fact is no one knew what Ali was doing there that night.

Perhaps it was his father, his limping polio-struck father with his beggar's bowl and that awful shisham-wood cane that never stopped swinging when Ali was around. Or perhaps it was the stink of moonshine in his house—the rotten smell of an inescapable future—which made him decide to run away. Either way, Ali ended up under those ghastly trees, where the neighborhood chowkidar found him.

We never learned the details, but some kids whispered Ali had been smothered to death. That it was nearing the end of winter, but his tears were frozen on his cheeks, his fingertips blue, and there were marks all over his chest, back, and buttocks. Underlying the gossip were hints of something far worse, the mere thought of which seemed to make the older kids clam up, look wise, and shake their head.

It was the blood women, Haider told us.

I imagine sometimes what Ali must have seen, our friend, this little boy with bushy eyebrows, which even in pre-puberty were linked like dark hands. Did he see leather-dry tongues forking over lips crusted with blood? Did he go to them in the trance of a siren call, his small fingers reaching out to touch limbs like cold tentacles, allowing the hags full autonomy over his body?

Did he drink his own blood as they must have drunk his?

"They don't drink blood, stupid," Haider said when I put him the question. "They leach it and save it for dark deeds."

"What dark deeds?"

"Dark deeds," Haider said mysteriously, his gaze on the heat-whitened sky, and would say no more.

Those were days of grief in Lahore. The hammer-killers were back; doors and windows of mansions and shanties alike were bolted and checked twice nightly. What we imagined went on outside—we, the children of suicide bombs and drone attacks—we clutched to our chest. It was a secret no one should know, we whispered between the coverlets to each other, as darkness and sweat poured from a sky riddled with heated stars.

Those were days of missing people. Of cellphone-snatching and murder by inept thieves inexperienced in poverty. Of honor-killings and acid-attacks; and Father telling Mother not to let the neighbors know when my brother returned from America with his two-year-old son.

"Why not?" Mother said, dismayed. Not being able to tell acquaintances that her doctor son was back was inconceivable.

Father looked at her, and the fear in his face made my insides churn; a different fear from when he talked about hammer-killers or bombers. Those he *understood*, he said. They were monsters with a *purpose*, he said.

No, what he feared most was mindless chaos. Randomness. A terror of unspeakable things happening through our indifference to the country's collective sins.

"Your *Bhayya* has a little baby, Asif," Father said to me. "Bhayya is a well-to-do doctor. If criminals discovered that, they could take advantage of it, for such is Pakistan these days."

"Why?"

"Because we're not good anymore. Not upright anymore."

"What does that mean, Father?" I said. He wouldn't answer. *No neighbors, Maria,* he told Mother, and the conversation was over.

"What are they?"

We were pitching marbles in the alley behind the cigarette shop owned by Haider's uncle. In a way it was a stupid question, since I knew Haider didn't know any better than I. Regardless of his self-assuredness, Haider lied with a practiced face that was impossible to decipher. It made me distrust everything he said. It made me unsure of my footing in his life.

"Yeah, Haider, what are they?" Zareen stood on the broken horse-cart, pinwheeling her arms, and glared at him. "I asked Baba and he laughed at me. Said no such thing as blood women. Said the older kids made it up to scare little ones."

Haider bounced his marble off the rock in the alley. "What does your stupid Baba know of such things?"

"You take that back." Zareen leapt off the cart and faced him, her dirty brown hands clenched into fists.

"Make me, crybaby." He smiled, and pitched another marble.

Zareen trembled. Her eyes bulged more than ever. She looked like one of those poisonous toads I once saw on TV that can spit venom up to twenty feet. "Your father's stupid. Your whole family's stupid."

Haider laughed. Tears filled Zareen's eyes and she ran sobbing to her house.

"Why'd you say that?" I said.

Haider trudged to the gutter. His spine cracked as he stooped to retrieve the gleaming marbles. "Ali's Ma came to our house last night."

I thrust my hands inside my pockets and listened.

"She said they were getting rid of Ali's clothes. She said some of his shirts might fit me and asked if my mother wanted to buy them." He tried to smile and the rictus of forced unconcern frightened me. "She said they need the money because they might move to Karachi. You know where Karachi is?"

I didn't, but I knew it was very far away. Mother had a sister who lived there. Mother said Khala Abida didn't visit us often because the journey was twelve hours by train.

"Karachi," Haider said to the marbles. "It could've been me or you under that tree. Why, some new family may be living in their house soon. Can you imagine?"

I couldn't.

We had known them forever.

We had known Ali forever.

"Why are they leaving?"

"Ali's father needs another boy to go with him on begging rounds. Ali's Ma won't let him. Says she can't bear to see a stranger replace her son on these streets."

Ali's father still begged on his usual route. I'd seen him shuffle around the neighborhood, and would until they left the city never to come back.

"He's a bastard," Haider said. "Ali's father. Always treated Ali like a dog. A rabid dog more than a son." He leaned against a rotted headboard poking from the trashcan. A shaft of light fell on his arm, revealing webs of fresh bruises. Did he fall off his bike?

Haider saw me looking and yanked his sleeve down. "What?"

He seemed to have a lot of bruises lately. I wanted to ask him about them, but his scowl was feral. "The blood women," I said instead. "What are they?"

His pupils were dark and elongated in the surface of the marble rolling on his palm. "They say they're sati widows."

"Sati widows?"

"Yeah. Like Hindus, you know. When they die and their bodies are burnt, their women jump into the fire after their men. What a waste." He laughed, but his face was pale and humorless. "So anyways, one of the driver-hotel boys told me that once the *Amreekan* drones began blowing up the Taliban, some of their proud women decided to return to their ancient ways. Now they stand on their husband's remains—whatever are collected from the blast site— and slash their own wrists."

"God, that's awful." I stared at him, fascinated.

"Yes, well. So they bleed themselves dry over the wrapped remains until the shroud turns red and they collapse on their men. But before they die they vow not to go to heaven until their men are avenged."

"How will they be avenged?"

Haider shrugged. "Fucked if I know. All I heard is their spirits become these blood women. Angry bitches, you know. You don't wanna see them ever. Unless you're well-prepared to pay the blood ransom." His eyes gleamed. "They say if you're ready, they will show you magic such as you never saw. Power such as you never dreamed. If you can show them that you *respect* them."

"Yeah? Is that why you been wanting to see them?"

Haider grinned. Daylight was fading, and in that grin I saw something that scared me more than the blood women. "They say the Taliban brought their spirits from over the mountains. These are ghost-widows of martyrs, man."

"Martyrs?"

"Yeah, suicide bombers."

The hair on my arm prickled. "You said *martyrs*."

The smile disappeared from his face. Haider flicked the marble off his palm. "Martyrs," he said, and turned away.

The blood women. It was their fault.

They had murdered our gentle Ali. And now they were messing with my friend's head, for we knew that suicide bombers were not martyrs. They were beasts. They were monsters.

But the monsters in my dreams were not the Taliban. Sometimes when the night was moonless, I dreamed of Ali running into the thicket of banyan trees and the figure that chased him, waving a shisham-wood cane, didn't lope, but limped as if it were stricken by disease. Its moonshine breath misted in the winter chill, and the drool from its twisted mouth on my skin was rancid and acidic.

Bhayya came from America with two-year-old Fazl, and my family went nuts over the toddler.

Fazl was the highlight of our year. His shiny eyes goggled at mundane things, and the way he tottered everywhere, his tiny body barely able to keep up with his rubbery legs, was just heartbreaking, Mother said. I myself was more excited about Bhayya being back; he came to Pakistan so rarely. My parents, though, couldn't keep their hands off the toddler.

No one mentioned *Bhabi*, Bhayya's American wife.

"How's *Amreeka*, Bhayya?" I said to him. Bhayya was fifteen years older than I—more a father figure to me than a brother. I was intimidated by his strength and the shaggy mustache and goatee, which framed his mouth like a magic circle. "When can we come visit you?"

Bhayya smiled at me. "It's good, little man, and yeah, you can visit me whenever you like." His Urdu accent had changed. Become softer with a touch of foreignness to it, as if the language in which he spoke surprised him with its cumbersome nature. "Do you watch Disney cartoons?"

I nodded. "Sure. When we have electricity, and when Mother

will let me. She doesn't like the way some of the cartoon girls dress. She says women should always cover their legs."

Bhayya laughed. "Dear old Mother, still stuck in her old world. Never mind her, little man. Mother doesn't quite understand how the world's changing. Even if she did, she wouldn't be equipped to deal with those changes. Either way," Bhayya leaned forward and tipped me a wink, "if you ever come, remember we live within twenty-five minutes of Disney World."

Bhayya flicked a hair out of his eyes. He'd let his hair grow and it fell in straggly bunches over his shoulders and ears. It reminded me of what Prophet Muhammad Peace-Be-Upon-Him's hair must have been like after he migrated from Mecca to Medina.

He's so handsome, I thought, and for some reason the thought made me sad.

"Should we go?" Bhabi was standing behind us, smiling, holding Fazl in the crook of her arms. The electricity was out again and in the candlelight her corn-yellow hair gleamed. Her eyes the blue color of the candle flame focused on Bhayya's face. "You were going to show me Lahore Fort, Zahid?" she said in English. Her cotton shirt was unbuttoned and, when she leaned in to hand Fazl to Bhayya, the swell of her breast emerged, pale and smooth.

Mother doesn't speak English, I thought. My heart was thudding suddenly, and something warm and tremulous throbbed in my belly. *Maybe that's why she never mentions you.*

"You like old places, Bhabi?" I said, trying to distract myself from that strange and wonderful vision.

"Call me Sara." She smiled and straightened. "Of course I do. I like Pakistan. Except when, you know, the bombs and bad stuff are happening."

"Do you want to come?" Bhayya asked me. "It might be boring, but you can if you want to."

Something dark shot across Bhabi's beautiful white face, and disappeared.

"No," I said. "I have schoolwork to do."

"That's a shame," Bhabi said, glancing at her watch. Together they left the room.

I sat for a while, massaging my temples. Yellow floaters ringed in black danced in the corners of my eyes. They smelled like rotten cheese and made me dizzy. I'd had migraines since I was a kid and sometimes I could smell the headache before it happened. I wondered if it was the onset of a migraine making me dizzy. Or the insistent vision of Bhabi's breast in my mind.

Haider began to change.

It was strange and surreptitious. His words changed, his face turned stony when he was around me, and he stopped pitching marbles.

"Are you okay?" I said one evening when he chucked a handful of pebbles at the stray cat nosing through the trash. The mangy creature hissed, unsheathed claws, and leapt away into the night.

"Yes. Why?" Haider scooped up the pebbles and put them in his pocket. He looked tired.

"Well, just the way you yelled at Zareen the other day. The way you've been disappearing every night."

He didn't look at me. "It's nothing. My dad needs me to do some chores, that's all."

"You sure?"

"Back off, man." He looked annoyed. "Yes, I'm sure."

I fell silent. He was lying. His dad was a watchman who spent his nights peddling his bicycle, blowing his shrill banshee-like whistle through dark alleys. Why would he need Haider in the evening? Even if he did, Haider wasn't enthusiastic about going home most days. School was out for the summer, so there was no homework.

I couldn't confront him, though. It would be like prying into Bhabi's room at night when she and Bhayya slept half-naked.

Haider surprised me. "Sorry about yelling at you." He hesitated, then reluctantly: "It's just that I met someone."

"A girl?" I was jealous. We were both twelve and had discovered masturbation the year before. The idea that he was banging a girl terrified and excited me.

He shook his head. "No. I met a Baba."

"What?"

"You know, like one of those saints? A mystic beggar."

"What are you talking about?"

"You won't understand. He's a master of the *way*, you know. The spiritual *way*." Haider pressed a hand to his neck and massaged it. "Great listener too. He says half the secret of the way is in respectful listening."

I stared at him. My head was hot and my scalp itched with feverish intensity. "Who is he, Haider? Tell me. You have to."

"No, I don't." His shoulders lifted. He watched me with eyes black and stern as faith.

"Is he one of the preachers?" Something occurred to me and my jaw dropped open. "Those mullahs from the Lashkar? The ones going door to door, urging folks to join the jihad in Afghanistan? They're terrorists, man. What are you doing talking to them? Are you out of your fucking mind?"

"Fuck you," Haider said. Before I could say anything more, he whirled around and marched off.

I stood in the alley, my stomach heaving. The moon went out in a snuff of monsoon clouds, and in the darkness a vision came to me: Haider lying under starved winter trees and a naked woman with long black hair kneeling beside him. She lifts her slashed wrist above his face: drops of blood big as rupee coins splatter on his lips, and Haider opens his eyes and begins lapping at them. The woman raises her head and howls.

Suddenly terrified, I ran home.

They lynched the cellphone snatcher under the banyan trees.

He was a teenager, fifteen or sixteen. He'd been snatching probably for a couple of years. Part of a back-rider gig: the motorbike driver pulls up next to the car idling at the red light, back rider points a gun and yells at the mark to hand over the cellphone. Usually it takes no more than thirty seconds.

Unfortunately, this time, the man in the plain car they targeted was an SSG commando.

The mark—a six-foot tall, burly man in his early thirties—pretended to tremble when the rider waved the gun in his face. The rider allowed the man to reach into his pocket for the cellphone, and the commando pulled out a handgun and shot him in the face. Before the teenage driver could flee, the commando had dragged him off the bike and thrown him to the ground.

Within minutes, a crowd had gathered.

"Just last week these bastards took my son's cellphone and knocked him down," said an elderly man, his voice shaking with anger.

"My daughter. My fifteen-year-old daughter. They plucked her earrings right through the flesh of her ears! She bled all the way to the hospital."

"My laborer uncle. He waited a whole year to buy his phone, and they..."

As the teenage rider babbled, the crowd began to swell. Rage, summer heat, the pent-up fury—it grew and grew, until someone yelled manically, grabbed the kid by his legs, and dragged him toward the trees. By the time they reached the grove of banyans, the crowd was in the dozens, and chanting loudly.

The Police came. They gathered around the mob and watched. Later, the neighborhood rang with excited rumors: that one of the cops pulled up a chair and ate a kebab-and-roti lunch as the crowd stripped the teenage dacoit, strung him up naked, and stoned him. That the cops smoked cigarettes and laughed, as a bearded man climbed the tree and sliced off the kid's genitals. That the boy shrieked and shrieked as blood spurted from his groin, and the crowd howled and jeered.

We heard of it as did the whole country; the story of the cellphone snatcher who died hanging like a slaughtered goat spread like wildfire, or an unstoppable tide of blood. Many shed tears; some of joyful vindication, some of sorrow.

Later, we heard Haider was amidst the mob. Later, we watched a YouTube video of the incident someone uploaded, and Haider was there, pounding the sky with the others, eyes narrowed in hateful glee. We watched murder on our cellphones and had dinner when it was over.

That night, I went to the banyan grove, hoping that the smell of death might draw the blood women out. I stood there and blinked. Once, twice, a third time.

Nothing.

But, as I left, something skittered in the branches of the trees and whispered to the moon.

Bhabi was screaming.

Where is he, where is my son?

I... I don't know. I thought he was with Mother.

Mother shrieked and shrieked. She'd gone to the kitchen to warm milk for Fazl. When she came back, the toddler was gone.

They took him, didn't they? Kidnapped for ransom. Oh Lord, my baby!

Bhayya didn't reply, but in just a few hours his face had aged. The dappling streetlight showed me lines I'd never seen before.

I never wanted to come here. I never wanted to come to this fucking country. You made me.

We went to the neighborhood mosques. Voices thick with concern made emergency announcements. The Police were called. Someone said a tall man clad in a chador was seen running in the direction of Lahore Railway Station an hour ago. We split up in search teams. Bhayya and Father went to the station. Someone told me to fetch my friends to come and help look.

I went to Haider's house four blocks away. He wasn't home.

"Haven't seen him in two days," his mother said. She didn't seem too worried. "He does that sometimes."

I was halfway down the steps, but I turned. "Really?"

"Usually after his father gives him a thrashing."

"How often is that?"

"Sometimes."

Something snapped inside the house. Maybe knots of wood in a stove. His mother went in, and I bicycled back.

Zareen was waiting outside my house.

"Where have you been? I haven't seen you in weeks."

Her face was pinched and skeletal. "I heard about the baby." Her bug eyes pushed out of her skull. "Asif, I... I'm—" She stepped back, her fingers knotting the loose end of her kameez.

I stared at her. "What?"

A reddish mark glistened along her jawline. Like a rash or a slap. She rubbed her spidery knuckles against it.

"It's Haider," Zareen whispered. "He's not himself. Oh, I'm so scared, Asif." She burst into tears.

I dropped the bike I was pushing and went to her.

"What's wrong?"

She pressed her head against my chest. "I... I think he might have the baby."

My blood ran cold. I gripped her shoulders. "What?"

Her face was miserable. "He said it was the only way to call the blood women. He said they'd had enough of *desi* blood. That... that they wanted *gora* blood."

A strange humming rose in my ears. "American blood." My fingers dug into her and she cried out. "When did you see him?"

"Two nights ago. He came to my house and said he wanted to show me something." Her dusky cheeks glistened with tears. "I was scared. He looked like he was under a spell or something. His eyes were glazed. He had a rosary in his hand and was telling the beads rapidly. So fast it was as if he was trying to crush them. I was so scared. I said no. He said his spiritual Baba was a master. That his Baba knew the secret ways of blood and martyrdom. His Baba—"

Her words drifted away. My head was spinning. A monstrous pain crept out from the base of my neck and roared with laughter.

I shoved Zareen away. She staggered and went down. My fingers were numb when they closed on the bike handles. "Two," I whispered. "Fazl is two years old."

Zareen slumped on the ground. She looked like an old rag doll with chipped, white marbles for eyes. I spun the bike and began to peddle furiously.

Behind me someone wailed, and darkness took the sky.

The grove was silent.

I leapt off the bike, letting it clatter to the ground. Its wheels continued to spin. My head throbbed with each pulse of the migraine. I ran to the spot where I'd heard the skittering the night the teenage thief was lynched. The still, shocked trees prodded the sky as tendrils of mist curled up from the earth, wrapping around their gnarled trunks.

"Haider?" I said to the trees. "Are you here?"

Wisha wisha went the wind between the trees in tune with my ringing headache. Somewhere something gurgled. Rainwater in juddering monsoon puddles? A sick animal?

A baby?

I licked my lips. "Fazl."

A branch snapped. Something dropped from the sky.

I screamed and scrabbled back as Haider came at me galloping on all fours. His face was twisted, his lips drawn back in a snarl, and his face was streaked with fresh blood. He was naked, his skin covered with bruises and cigarette burns like lurid tattoos.

He circled me like a dog, then lifted a leg and pissed. The acrid, bright smell filled the summer air. "Glad you could join me." His voice was the sound of sticks grating against sticks. "Power such as we never dreamed of."

I stepped closer. He growled, a hollow vibrato that raised the hair on the back of my neck.

"Haider, where is he?" I said.

He barked laughter. "The baby." Mist thickened and boiled

from the trees until it blanketed his crouching figure. His voice drifted out from the white: "They wanted a taste of him, you know. Just a touch to fulfill their vow."

The blood women? I began to shake. They were mythic, they were rumors.

Yet, hadn't I looked for them as well in the midst of this terror, a revulsive seeking for a power greater than my own?

The moon sharpened and sliced through the clouds, and a baby began to cry in the trees.

Without thinking, without another word, I rushed forward. Somewhere above me, strung up from the tangled branches, was Bhayya's baby. My poor foreigner Bhayya from a land far away. Where fear was night sweat from an occasional bad dream, not blood running in gutters in daylight. My handsome Bhayya with his beautiful wife who hated our country. Hated us.

Quickly I climbed the hideous banyan tree. Haider snapped at my heels. I kicked him in the face and he tumbled down, crashing through the branches. The mist lunged at me. Shadows danced. The baby cried. I blinked rapidly: once, twice, a third time. Along the foggy edges of consciousness, through the pulsating membrane of my headache, something pale, sticky, and red coalesced. An endless smooth mass like a monstrous breast with eyes like brown nipples, and a jutting mouth that puckered.

A pint of blood for the sons of men.

A pint of blood for the sons of martyrs.

As I wept and climbed, it began to ululate.

Three months later, Bhayya and Bhabi left for America.

Father stood at the front door swaying gently, watching Bhayya load their bags into the taxi, raking the plaster of our barren walls with his fingernails. Bhayya barked orders at the driver and didn't turn to look at us.

It was close to noon, so I brought Bhabi a glass of water and she popped a bright-blue pill in her mouth and drowned it. The violet under her eyes deepened as she raised a trembling hand and waved once at Father. Somewhere inside the house Mother began to chant prayers loudly.

The taxi sputtered. It rolled down the driveway past a red-and-white bicycle with rusted handles lying on the overgrown lawn and turned the corner. It has been years since and that taxi hasn't returned.

After Bhayya left, the newspaper clippings stayed magnetized to the refrigerator door for six months. Policemen came and talked to Father. Our extended family came and gawked. I especially hated a burkah-clad aunty, one of Mother's many cousins, who'd come with a friend to commiserate. She would point at the jagged-toothed baby in blue overalls and a yellow Make-Me-Shine bib grinning at the camera, then elbow her friend and whisper relentlessly, while looking at me with eyes like heated glass.

Eventually, Father yanked the clippings down. He left the baby's picture up for a couple days, then went after it in an after-jummah rage; tore it down, balled it up, and flung it into the garbage-walla's basket.

His anger left me trembling, so Mother took me to see Dr. Wahab who told her to increase the dosage of the Seroquel.

"You still seeing things?" he said. "Any nightmares?"

When I shook my head, he nodded. "Good." He examined the scar on my scalp, pressing around the edges with his stubby fingers. "Looks like it's healing nicely. Boy, your friend did quite a number on you."

"Wasn't him," I said quietly.

"Don't you start with that again. Yes, it was," Mother cried. "It was him. Haider and his nasty terrorist friends. Don't you dare—"

"Wasn't Haider who hit me. He fell." I met her burning eyes, didn't look away. "It was them."

Dr. Wahab tried to help, "Sure. Sure. Anyway…"

He asked me if the migraines had gotten worse. I said no, and we left.

Sometimes, when afternoon shutters into dusk, I sit in the shadow of the peepal tree in our yard (I don't go to the banyans anymore) and stare at its pale, cracked trunk smeared with slug juice. Cicadas sing, fireflies swirl. Swallows and crows flutter home through the checkerwork of its leaves, but I don't see any kind of darkness stir in its branches.

They tell me that Fazl's chador, a four-by-four wool shawl Mother made him, was found wrapped around the banyan's trunk the day after Haider and the baby disappeared.

One moonless night I hid my pills. I slipped out, swung Bhay-ya's bike upright, and pedaled my squeaking way to Haider's house. It was formless in gloom, empty of sound. No one lived there any-more; nothing lingered except the odiferous memory of moonshine and decay on the porch. I gazed at the front door, cobwebbed and weather-browned; at the narrow smoke-stained kitchen window, bolted, glass-cracked; and saw a tall silhouette with shocked tresses step back into the dark and vanish.

I dropped the groaning bike and fled. Past the graveyard with rotten yellow teeth, past the banyan groves where midnight birds still made noise, through the alley behind his uncle's shop, up the steps that led into the neighborhood mosque. I gasped, plunged my face into cold water gushing from the *wudoo* tap, and prayed.

I prayed for a long time that unholy night and for hundreds of nights since, but it still hasn't helped.

WHITECHAPEL

P. GARDNER GOLDSMITH

CAROLINE TAKES ANOTHER DRAG and holds it, tasting the bitterness and ash deep inside. Concentrating, she tries to convince herself that if she can focus on the smoke, luxuriate in the familiar sensations of a habit long-held, she can survive.

Her fingers shake again and she exhales, the blue-grey wisp flowing ghostly into the cold November air. She watches it float away, yet another part of her dissipating soul, lifting high into the somber sky.

"Irresistible forces lead to inescapable ends, everyone," he'd said. *"The world does what it wants. And sometimes there's nothing men can do about it."*

Now she understands.

And wonders why any of them try.

Today's failure lingers in her like a disease. It mixes with the sting of the tobacco, the deeply impregnated essences of bleach and rubbing alcohol, and the burned, sugary sweetness of the tar, and warns of impending collapse. Hers. Her coworkers'. Her superiors'. The entire system. It's going to crash like a condemned building in a gale.

Because the NHS isn't just strained. It's broken, careening out of control. It's a runaway train that nothing can stop, and no one inside knows how it's going to end.

She places a rubber sole against the granite blocks of the building and leans back as she's done so often in the past three weeks, and this time, she feels a chill creep through her jacket that's impossible to deny.

There's nothing but death behind those walls now. Royal London Hospital, the sanctuary created centuries before, is no longer a refuge of hope and resurrection where skilled doctors and nurses use everything they have to save lives and make people better. It's a morgue, and they're just shuffling bodies about.

She chuckles at the idea that another drag will help make anything better, make the fear go away, then pulls the smoke into her lungs anyway, thinking it ironic that she was prepared to quit before this all began. Now, after losing two conjoined adult twins who awoke in the middle of the procedure, she thinks dying of aggressive lung cancer might be preferable to facing patients like those again.

The way they shook and lashed out. The kicks.

The biting and the screams.

Everyone left the surgery exhausted. Dr. Chalmers cried. And she's never seen Rick cry over anything. Not even the Halloween bombing could wring a tear from his handsome Ancalite eyes.

He's still in there. Alone. Drinking from that bottle of scotch he keeps in his office. Who could blame him? Who wouldn't want to be drunk and alone at a time like this? Safety comes in solitude.

A double-decker sweeps by, growling east towards Mile End, or at least that's what it says on the windscreen. Lots of busses don't get to their destinations nowadays. And if they do, it's often not a pleasant sight.

She tosses the butt to the concrete and stamps it out. The double-decker has reminded her that it's time to move on. Much better to walk and take the tube when it's still light. She's thought about staying in one of the spare beds at the hospital, like so many others have done. Easy option. It's safe among the staff now, because the Phenomenon's already swept through. But she's got Gramps to care for, and it's not like he can move into Royal London with her.

Even if they could accommodate a man with encroaching dementia, a good soul who sometimes forgets what happened to his wife, who calls Caroline by the wrong names, and doesn't understand why he can't go for walks, she'd probably try to sleep with Rick in his office. And they promised each other they'd never do that again.

With everything collapsing around them, at least she can choose *not* to break up a fifteen-year marriage and a family with two wonderful girls.

Caroline hefts her backpack, adjusts her reflective green armband, fingers the ceramic knife in her goatskin coat pocket, and starts across the street to Whitechapel Station. Despite her resolve, she can still feel the emotional, sexual pull of that man inside, and it's only heightened by the shared tragedy and horror they keep fighting, day after day.

A few people join her in the crossing, all keeping their distance—self-imposed prisoners in their own isolation wards. Their green armbands flash as they hurry across the tarmac, suspicious eyes darting as if they're animals in flight.

How many of them know? she wonders.

Not everyone. She feels awful being complicit in the cover-up. But what else can the Home Office do? They've got to keep people off the streets, stop public assembly and dissent. The terror alerts and manufactured attacks have been assiduously planned and precisely executed. They serve their purpose.

And she hates to think it, but that first bombing on Halloween might have been a blessing. It gave them cover to fight the real trouble.

A newspaper page flutters by like a low-flying gull, alighting on the meridian and moving west. There aren't too many papers left now, and not many newsagents around to sell them. Not that it would matter. Teenage boys and horny dads get their Page Three jollies from the web, and the "news"—via broadcast, internet, or print—is controlled by the Media Review Board, thank God.

Everything's under strict lock and key. Access to the streets is split into day-parts, with population segments given color codes for their allotted times in the dwindling sunlit hours. The same goes for vendors and businesses. All shops, all professional agencies, are allowed to open their doors for brief periods, to serve only those with certain colors on their sleeves, and to report anyone who disobeys. Needless to say, London is now a ghost town, and business isn't good.

She spies the Indian kebab spot a few doors to the left of the Underground, and sees a young man in a white hoodie—which he had better keep down if he wants to avoid arrest—head inside.

"They'll think they're lucky," Rick had said. *"They'll believe their freedom of movement is based on chance."*

Rick sat them down when the team first met, explaining the system the bureaucrats had penned. Everyone outside would be told the colors were generated by random lottery. The selections might cause a small amount of dissatisfaction and discord—even some protests here and there. But a fiction, a grand façade of randomness, would be worlds better than the truth. If people were to understand the term Haplotype, and know that they were being segregated by genetics? All hell would break loose.

It was the best they could do, given the science they had to go on, and, dammit, if the government needed to stage more terror attacks, catch a few more women and children in their bombings to divert attention and shore up control? It would be worth the sacrifice. Otherwise, the colors could mix, bringing the variant Haplotypes with them, and the Phenomenon would spread faster than the Black Death.

She holds onto the thought like a lifesaver as she hits the sidewalk a few paces behind the hoodie kid, veers right, and joins the weak trickle of people heading toward the Underground entrance.

"Oi!" One of the five large SCO19 officers stationed at the doorways raises his hand. "IDs ready!"

Strange, non-linear queues start to form as her fellow travelers wait to show their badges, each evidently making certain he or she stays a few paces away from the other. There's frustration in their movements, but also defeat. A woman to her right wipes a strand of greasy grey hair out of her cadaverous features and mutters something profane. She stoops, puts her pocketbook on the cement and starts rifling through it, her olive skirt draping, tent-like, over army boots that have seen better days.

After a moment, she glances up, bites her crusty bottom lip, stands, and walks away, disappearing in the gathering gloom.

Caroline lets her backpack hang on her shoulder and fishes the card from her pants pocket, making sure she keeps her other hand ready on the knife.

"Why do we need to show our cards?" she asks.

The big Trinidadian she's gotten to know is studying the ID of a pregnant teenage girl in an oversized anorak.

"New protocols, Caroline," he says, flashing a hand-held laser at the barcode on the card. "Folks've started to sell and trade their armbands on the black market."

He nods the other girl through and waves Caroline forward. "C'mon, kiddo."

She steps up at the same time a nervous-looking man in a too-small business suit and mismatched socks emerges from beyond her field of view. He's in his twenties. No wedding band on the hand that holds his heirloom briefcase.

"Sorry, mate." The officer raises a meaty palm. "Ladies first."

"Right." The other man looks recklessly contrite, stops immediately as if told off by his mum, then steps back, giving Caroline plenty of room. Everyone offers plenty of room nowadays if they really know what's happening.

"How're things inside, hon?" the cop asks, and she feels a flush of embarrassment at his use of the term of endearment.

"No change, Officer Bestwick."

He nods, and a look of sad disbelief seems to work at his dark features. He shakes his shaven head.

"You must be getting tired," he says.

Something in the tenderness of his words, in the simple expression of understanding, is so fresh and unexpected that it catches her off guard. For a moment, she feels a lump in her throat. It's crazy, but she wants to grip his hand, touch his arm; to reach out and make real contact with another human outside the goddamn walls of The Royal for the first time in weeks.

She's amazed that such a moment could mean so much. But the loneliness is gouging away. With each heartbeat that shakes her little chest, she feels the terrible, growing need for some kind of human contact, some kind of touch. A smile, a word, a friendly glance. Anything to fill that expanding sink-hole of her life and make her forget what's happening. She's suddenly glad she has a bond with this man Bestwick. He knows the score about what she's fighting. He knows because, contrary to their orders, she's tipped him off, and he's tipped her off as well.

"You still have what I told you to get?" he asks.

She fingers the blade of the knife and nods, then watches his wan smile fade and his right hand tap the .45 strapped to his belt.

"Good." He scans her card. "Don't hesitate to use it." He raises his eyes to glance at the old hospital and leans towards her, whispering as he hands the card back. "Any more procedures?"

"We lost another pair," she says back, no louder than he. "Same as before…"

His watery gaze moves from her to the people shuffling around them, nervous and taut.

"A lot of 'em know, Caroline. I can see it in their eyes."

They do seem more aware. She can sense it in the distance between them. The stares. Caroline could attribute it to fears of suicide bombers. But her instincts say otherwise. People are beginning to realize that suicide bombers would be blessings compared to this.

"The launch shift had to take down a bloke with a fiberglass machete today. Started indiscriminately chopping at people."

"What? I didn't hear about that… We received no casualties—"

"We've developed a new procedure for removal of the dead."

That stops her for a moment, keeps her silent.

"Things are changing, hon. And I'm afraid even you folks at Royal won't be told."

"But—"

He sighs, nods to the man who's been waiting, an indication that he should approach.

"I dunno, Caroline. What's that line by Voltaire? 'All things are for the best, in this, the best of all possible worlds'?"

"But, you'd tell me, right, Officer Bestwick? Of *changes*?"

He offers her a rueful smile and pats her on her free shoulder. "I just have, hon."

Then he turns to the man with the mismatched socks and nervous demeanor, leaving Caroline to hesitantly step into the station entrance and the shadows beyond.

The station has a stale smell to it today, beyond the usual gut-grabbing stenches of dust, dry rot, oil and urine that lend the Underground its perpetually smothering air of decay. This is something new. Like the breathtaking, robust spores of fruiting bodies rising feral and untamed somewhere deep in the earthen tunnels. Again, she gets the sensation of impending collapse, the feeling that, as Rick said, man cannot stand against nature's plans.

She wonders if the place was always like this and she just never noticed, or if there was once a time—maybe when the government first opened its doors—when everything was fresh, the tiles shone white and new to excited passers-by, and the system didn't seem like an unkempt old man, tottering near oblivion, a mere shadow of what he once was.

Caroline makes her way to the ticket kiosks and fishes for change, dreading the cold wait on the exposed lower platform and vertiginous disorientation of the long, rubberized stairs. From this vantage point, the geometry of Whitechapel has all the nauseating charm of a nightmarish Escher sketch, its dominant characteristic the platforms to the Overground that have been recklessly located below those for the Underground. The District, Hammersmith and City Lines arrive on street level, while trains to West Croydon and Highbury/Islington arrive below. As a result, in order to get home, she has to take those three endless flights of stairs, or descend the broken escalator with its paranoia-inducing sense of confinement.

One side of the stairway is blocked by yellow crime scene tape that's been tied into what looks like big Christmas bows on each rail. Where they don't create garish counterpoints to the steely backdrop, their ends vibrate in the breeze like palsied hands, like her Gramps' when he tries to lift a cup of his favorite Earl Grey. She can still hear the clattering weakness, tapping against the stained saucer that used to be his wife's, and she wonders if it's a form of secret communication between him and his dear departed, as he prepares to make his way.

For a moment, her own weakness overcomes her, standing there atomized, thinking about the love and tenderness the two elders shared for so long. During his lucid years, Gramps had always told her there would be someone for her, her perfect match in the whole entire world. He said Aristophanes had written that men had four legs, four arms and two faces, but Zeus split them apart, so the goal in life was to find one's soul mate. She's spent a lifetime searching, had her heart broken, and left more than her share of detritus and debris along the way. And yet here she stands. Twenty-nine. Cold. Frightened. Alone.

The other passage is dimly lit, barely used. People on it keep to themselves, and stay close to either handrail as they traverse.

Are they lonely? She wonders.

Then she realizes with a shiver that today could be the day.

Her other half could be right here.

She receives her ticket from the impassive machine and moves towards the stairs a few paces behind a skinny, dreadlocked Rasta carrying a guitar case, and the man with the mismatched socks. They hit the left side of the stairs silently, the Rasta first, his tan eyes glancing all around, and the young businessman about twelve feet behind, keeping his head down, briefcase tightly held. The two seem to glide, spectre-like. As if they don't exist. Caroline waits a few seconds, sneaks a peak behind her where Officer Bestwick checks a fat man's card, lets her gaze linger on the incongruous trainers the man wears with his suit, and then heads down.

Her stomach clenches. This is the worst part. Going below to get on that metal tube. It's enclosed and inescapable. It could happen at any time and where would she go? Can she run fast enough? Race back up these steps from Platform 4? Could she dive next to the tracks and avoid getting hit by a train?

She's got to be ready to use the knife. She's got to be ready to kill, because if she doesn't...

Beside her, slipping by like an apparition, she sees the ghoulish ochre stain of the morning's carnage. It's still there, spread over ten steps like some kind of enormous Rorschach test for the depraved, splattered on one side of the escalator exterior, falling over the steps in a Daliesque display. Someone's tried to clean up the mess. She can smell the caustic fluids. But it hasn't done much to help.

Rasta-man pauses at the first landing. Briefcase-man stops in mid-step. Caroline follows suit as if they're playing a game of Red Light-Green Light, her heart pounding, her left hand sweaty around the metal rail. She doesn't want to show fear, but they've already stopped. They must know about the Phenomenon.

The Rasta picks up something from the floor—his ID, it appears—and continues. Both the briefcase-man and Caroline follow.

She fingers the knife. And she wonders if those cases hold other things, sharp plastic and porcelain things—and how prepared those men are to use them. She knows it wouldn't take much for her to pull out the blade. The Attraction could happen at any time. Even when they're not within sight of each other, the Phenomenon slowly draws people together, or one to another innocent victim. It's like a magnet. Like some kind of bizarre gravitational pull. Irresistible and vast. Without knowing it, some folks have spent thousands of Pounds to get flights, trains, and boats, to relocate in new areas, all because of some subconscious, subversive itch. A need.

To find the other half.

Please, not today.

Rasta-man completes the second and third flights, hits the cement of the open-air platform and walks right. Briefcase-man lands just behind, turns left. The orange letters on the scrolling time-table sign between them read:

SHOREDITCH HIGH STREET: CANCELED
HIGHBURY/ISLINGTON: 18:10

Caroline has a ten minute wait.

She sees the pregnant girl now, shaking her head, her pink cheeks flashing over the fuzzy lining of her anorak as she walks towards an armed guard standing beneath the sign.

"How'm I s'posed to get to Shoreditch, then?" she asks, an accent that tells Caroline the girl's an Eastender through and through. She probably won't leave this portion of the city unless forced out.

The middle-aged cop is thick, with pale skin and a five o' clock shadow like charcoal on his upper lip and chin. From the looks of it, he doesn't want to be here.

He wears a green arm band, just like the rest of them.

"Didn't ya see the signs?"

She looks around her, evidently confused.

"No. No. The *signs*, up top! There's been a threat made to Shoreditch, so no access in or out until it's cleared up."

"So?"

"So. You take the bus. They wrote a sign up top. It's not easy to miss."

Caroline missed it.

"Fuckin' 'ell. You mean I gotta walk all the way back up those bloody steps?" The girl opens her jacket wider, more fully exposing her distended belly.

"Fraid so, girl." With one index finger, he pushes his wool cap back a bit, then assesses her. "How far along are you?"

She seems contrite. Lowering her chin, she softly replies. "I'm due in two weeks."

For a moment, the man looks ready to roll his eyes or say something cruel. To Caroline, it looks like he's holding back some harsh thought. But he purses his lips and nods a few quick times, glances around them, then inclines his head towards a shadowy alcove, just beyond the briefcase-man.

"C'mon, girl. I'll take ya to the service elevator."

She walks close beside him. But they never touch.

Nice of him. Caroline thinks. *After all the government's done to fuck things up, at least that girl can get help from one of its lower functionaries. I wonder what she'd do if she found out about their little experiment in eugenics.*

The EU thought the Gene Map should be made a little "cleaner," Rich had said. So the geniuses at the highest levels of government hired a bunch of international whiz kids to figure out ways to insure only certain *kinds* of people could mate. The brightest people. The select few. He'd been told they never proceeded with the plan to introduce the virus, but...

Given what they face now, it seems like this could be connected. Or could it be possible that some *force*, some faceless, shapeless, invisible *power* has just... arisen, to impose its unfathomable will on them all?

Genetic? Pheromonal? A new universal law? Supernatural vengeance?

Her stomach tumbles. The spaces between the waiting passengers are wide. But if any of them have switched armbands, or if their own medical theories need to change, at any moment, one of them could come for her.

Or *she* could begin to feel the Attraction. To her other half.

And it could take just one touch.

The flesh would *meld.* Creep. Mesh. Skin combining with skin. Veins connecting. Locking. Pumping. Nerves rewiring. Fast. Rapidly. So, so fast.

Then. Bone.

Brain.

Fusion.

God. Not today. Let me get back to Gramps. One more safe night. Let me take care of him and start it all again tomorrow. With my knife.

18:07:50.

More travelers arrive.

It's getting crowded. Caroline wants to pace a little, but she knows it's best not to. Some people stake out spots along the wall, so they don't have to look behind their backs. But she doesn't like that approach. It makes her nervous, because she's shut off one dimension of escape. She always stands about fifteen feet away from the wall and makes a slow, steady turn. The habit is defensive and smart, but it doesn't help keep her warm.

A young lady almost bumps into Rasta-man. He steps back rapidly, swinging the case in front of him.

"I'm sorry!" she says, her voice high and tremulous, the sound of a frightened bird. "I'm really sorry!"

He mumbles something like, "That's okay" and lowers the case, glancing at the clock.

And then Caroline sees him.

The briefcase man's eyes are different.

And staring at her.

A flutter like a murder of crows erupts inside her. She stands there, feeling her pulse quicken, her hands sweat. He puts the briefcase on the platform and faces her as if possessed.

No.

18:09:43.

He starts walking.

From this distance, his movements seem stiff and ungainly. Like he's sleepwalking.

Towards her.

Caroline looks for the cop.

He should have come back by now—

People see the man. A ripple of movement as they step away from him. Like fluid yielding to stone.

He might as well be radioactive.

Jesus...

It's undeniable. He's targeted her and he's walking, straight, disregarding those around him. The briefcase is forgotten. She's all that exists.

18:10:00. He passes by the sign. She hitches the pack on one shoulder, wraps her fingers around the handle of the knife, tenses her quads, tries to breathe.

His mismatched socks flash beneath his short pant legs.

A rumble. The train. High-pitched squeals and scratches carried on the rails. It's coming. In the distance. A metal slug creeping closer on its path.

Get here NOW, and put people between us!

A voice through the speakers. A generic, innocuous human robot. Cybernetic. Something about the arrival. The train moves fast. The man's eyes are locked and obsessed. She steps back, fear grabbing her and melding like the Phenomenon into every nerve, every sinew, every pore. She faces her other half, her childish dreams of love and romance and princes yielding to cold, stark, horrible reality—to science.

To death.

He is not human now. He is a threat. Her existence will end if he touches—

She stumbles backwards, but he closes. She bumps the fat man behind her.

"Look out! Look out!" someone yells.

Ten feet? Five?

Screaming wheels and brakes and metallic clangs warp along the tracks. And she's near the edge and the man is close and she can't step back any more but he keeps coming and people fall away. And she swings the backpack off her left shoulder and smacks him as she pulls the knife and as he stumbles to her right. She slices, feels the blade catch on flesh almost without resistance and blood flies as she trips, twists, and grabs his jacket. She sees his horrified face, levers his struggling body towards the yawning chasm of the tracks, slides her foot under his to make him fall with her. She feels the touch of his fingers on the back of her hand as she tumbles—

The train.

In a spray of blood and thunder, it blows him apart, shattering his bones, ripping his pale skin to shreds. Caroline hits the cement inches from the edge, feeling the hot blood and pieces of death and the strong blast of wind carried beside the train. For a moment, nothing exists in the world except noise and shock, and then, the noise dissipates and people are rushing to her. People who know it's safe to touch her.

"You alright?"

"Miss!"

Hands on her arms roll her over, sit her upright, let her see the red gore streaming down her jacket and the knife cutting her fingers nearly to the bone. People are on their knees, and she fumbles to push them aside because she's seen her backpack a few inches from her sneakers and...

The man's briefcase beyond. Half-open. Revealing a trio of red lights blinking like little demon eyes.

"*NO!*"

They don't understand. They try to hold her, fumble with her until—

The lights go solid red. And the bomb ignites.

For an instant, its blinding flash seems like the only warmth she has felt in her life.

Caroline hears words like cotton candy. Sweetened, whipped words with no meaning. Like the voices of dressed-up partiers in a surreal singles bar, they flirt, rise, fall, then go silent. They say things like, "Hematoma" and "Ecchymosis" and "Clotting Factor." Her dark world brightens momentarily and she feels movement, like that of a ship at sea. Then she hears the chirp of an electronic bird, and the term "Liverpool Protocol" and knows she had better awaken. Fast.

"Can you hear me, Caroline?"

It's Rick. Such a lovely, manly voice.

Yes, Rick! I can hear you. I love you, Rick.

"Caroline? Can you hear my voice?"

"Y-yes. Rick… I—"

She opens her eyes and blinks the world into resolution. The room is small, softly lit with a window to her left that looks out through bars at rooftops, chimneys, the familiar grey southern sky, and the Thames that must be somewhere below.

"Rick—"

She reaches for him, barely touches the hair on his right arm as he pats her on the shoulder then turns away to speak through the open door. "Isabelle? She's come 'round."

He turns back to her and she feels the warmth, and care, and something else.

"I'll be back, Caroline…"

There's a flash akin to a smile, but sadder, and then he stands straight and leaves. For a moment, Caroline lies in the bed, feeling the pillows behind her throbbing head, smelling the cleanliness, seeing her bandaged right hand, her legs, splayed out beneath the off-white covers, and she tries to remember what happened to her. There were screams and there was blood and there was that man tumbling and the silver blur, unstoppable and uncaring. The machine took him and made her fall back, and then…

She… killed. She killed that man.

Then she remembers the look in his eyes, and feels her fear, raw and intense, as she thinks about having to pull the knife, use the backpack, whatever she could to stop him from—

Touching her.

Did he touch her?

Didn't their skin meet?

Didn't he touch her as she twisted him in front of that train and made him trip and… killed him?

And didn't their flesh stay the same?

Oh, God.

It can't be. He was coming for her.

Wasn't he?

He was the One. He was going to fuse. He was going to touch her and meld with her and they would both be victims, turning into Siamese Twins, blending into one to be euthanized according to the Liverpool Protocol.

She feels an icy, hellish sweat rise from her skin, and grabs the thin cotton blanket above the sheet to get some kind of tactile sensation that can bring her back to the here and now, away from the memories. The blanket is mottled. Not as pristine as she first imagined. It's seen better days.

"Caroline?"

It's Isabelle. A friendly, blonde-haired waif of a girl who's been a nurse here since… Well, since the Halloween bombing.

Caroline can't reply yet. She fumbles with the edge of the blanket in her hands, thinking, remembering.

That man. The flash.

"Caroline?"

"Isabelle?"

She looks up to find her, but the nurse's face is blurred behind tears Caroline didn't realize were in the forecast. Now, they stream down her face.

"There, there, Caroline…"

Isabelle's green arm band is still evident, even though blurry eyes. She reaches out and pats Caroline's hand.

"I think I killed that man!"

"It's alright, Caroline. Don't you remember the blast? He was a terrorist."

"Yes—"

Isabelle nods and pulls a rolling stool over while continuing to hold her hand. Then she sits and offers Caroline a tissue. As Caroline wipes her eyes with her free hand, she can feel the deep, dull pain in her left shoulder, where she hit the floor.

"He's dead. Caroline. A lot of people are dead."

"Oh, God."

"But, you're alive. You made it!"

"He. I thought—"

"You have a concussion, and a subdural hematoma, but we were able to stop the internal bleeding and the baby is going to be alright."

Statis.

The electronic bird chirps more rapidly beside her.

"Baby?"

Isabelle's expression changes. Her light brows purse over her sparkling green eyes. For a moment, her gaze is like a laser.

"You *do* know you're pregnant, don't you?

"I—"

"You're three weeks along. Rick said you volunteered or the in vitro program, and we're all so proud of your sacrifice."

Caroline feels the woman's grip tighten, looks down at her belly. Sees the bars on the windows once more.

"Honey, you're a brave girl," Isabelle says. "And as long as you're alive, you're *never* going to lose this baby."

THE CHUTE

GARY McMAHON

(For Sharon)

IT WAS TO BE HER FIRST night alone in the new apartment.

After a whole week of moving in her stuff after work and still sleeping at her parents' place every night, she was finally moving in properly. She would have preferred to have done it at the weekend, but her parents were having some overbearing friends over for dinner so she'd decided to come back here tonight. Her new bed had been delivered and assembled (by her dad, God bless him). The walls were freshly painted. Her furniture was all in place. She couldn't think of a valid reason not to be here.

Connie arrived home late from work that night. There was a rush on this week: it was all hands to the pump, and her boss was something of a tyrant when it came to making his team work overtime. She needed the money, so she'd agreed to the extra hours, but the bastard wanted to make sure that he got his money's worth.

She stumbled through the main door of the apartment building at 9:15 P.M. Outside, it was just starting to get dark. Most of the automatic lights in the shared spaces had come on, but it was still creepy because there was no one else around.

Connie adjusted her rucksack. It had fallen from her shoulder as she pushed open the door, so she wriggled and manoeuvred it back into a comfortable position as she headed for the lift.

She took out her earphones and flicked the switch to turn off her MP3 player. The silence of the building rushed forward.

"Oh," she said, and then wondered what she'd meant by it.

She pressed the button to summon the lift and waited. Behind her, the main lobby door opened and swung shut. Light footsteps whispered across the tiled floor and a presence drifted to her side.

"Evening."

She turned and looked at the old man standing next to her. He was shorter than Connie by a few inches, and slim to the point of emaciation. When he smiled, his dentures shifted on his gums.

"Hello," she said, trying to smile.

"You're new here." It was a statement, not a question.

Connie nodded, but didn't say anything in reply.

"I've seen you around. We don't get much of a turnover of tenants here. It's a good place, a nice spot. People generally don't want to leave."

"I'm in number ten," she said, simply because there was nothing else to say.

"Yes... Mrs Grant's place. She was a nice woman. Died in hospital. She'd lived in that flat forever."

That much was obvious. The décor was out of date; the few items of furniture left behind were tatty and mismatched. The whole place needed a facelift, and as soon as she could book some time off work, Connie intended to strip the paper from the walls, throw away what she didn't want, and try to impose some of her personality into the rooms.

"Here's the lift," said the old man. The doors slid open. It was almost soundless. The building was fifty years old, but it had been well maintained. Everything worked like a dream.

Connie allowed the old man into the lift first, and then followed him inside.

"Third floor, please," he said, flashing his dentures again.

She pressed the button, then the one for her own floor, and waited. The doors slid shut; what seemed like seconds later, they opened again, and the old man shuffled out. He turned, raised a hand. "G'night. And don't mind—" The doors cut him off.

Connie got off at her floor and trudged along the short corridor to her door. She fumbled in her bag for the key, misplacing it for a few seconds before her fingers finally closed around its cold, hard surface. She glanced back along the corridor, not at the lift this time, but at the door that led to the refuse chute. It was three doors along from her apartment, and from the moment she'd first seen the door it had unnerved her.

The caretaker had shown her how the chute worked—lift the stainless steel hatch by the handle, throw in your rubbish, and then shut it again. Easy. There was nothing to it. But the sound of the rubbish falling down into the bowels of the building, and the echoes it made, were strange and eerie. She'd never lived anywhere before where refuse was disposed of in this way; it was new to her. Yet something about the entire process seemed so archaic.

She twisted the key in the lock, leaned her weight against the door and opened it. Once she was inside, she locked the door. Then she checked that it was really locked, her mind still on the refuse chute and what might be down there, squatting amid the waste generated by Connie and her fellow tenants.

She went into the bedroom and took off her coat, throwing it on the chair by the window. The view was spectacular. The sky still retained enough light to hold back full-dark and the clouds above the town were tinged with pink and gold. She stared at the sky for a little while, then shut the blinds before taking off her work clothes to change into a pair of old jogging pants and a baggy T shirt.

In the kitchen, she rummaged through the cupboards and found a small tin of baked beans. She grabbed a bag of dried pasta from the cupboard under the work bench and filled the kettle with water. Wasn't this what single people were supposed to eat—Crap Cuisine?

While she waited for the water to boil, she thought about her job, her boss, her work mates. She was becoming bored; the whole set-up was tedious. She barely spoke to anyone on a normal day, just kept her head down until lunch and then went out for a jog to clear her head and stretch her muscles. She was getting pretty fit, but her relationships were suffering. She became more and more withdrawn, and she wasn't sure why. Perhaps she was simply bored of the people around her, and needed to meet a new group?

The kettle switched itself off, the water boiled. She poured the contents over the pasta in the pan and lit the hob. The beans were in another, smaller pan, and she turned down the heat under them. Then she sat down in a dining chair and stared at the cooker.

The pipes behind the kitchen wall made gurgling sounds. Something outside brushed lightly against the window—probably a bird flying too close to the glass. She wasn't scared, here on her own, but she was slightly nervous. Living with her parents had been easy: they never expected much from her; as long as they knew she was around if they needed her, they were happy. Then she'd moved in with Dave, and that had all gone wrong after three months. She'd suspected he was cheating on her, but had gone ahead with it all anyway. When the truth came out, she didn't even bother to feign surprise. She just packed up her stuff and left while he was out at work. She moved back in with her parents until she could find somewhere else.

He hadn't even tried to call. Not even a text message from the bastard.

And now... well, she was here, in this old apartment block. It was nothing special, but it was within her budget and situated in a nice part of town. She could have done a lot worse. She could have done a little better, she supposed, but this place would do until something better came along.

And wasn't that just the theme of her life? Making do until something better came along. But nothing ever did: it was all just more of the same. She was beginning to doubt that something better even existed, and maybe she should start planning for the rest of her life with what she had now—which, if she was honest, didn't amount to much at all.

Later that night, she found herself standing before the refuse chute. She had no idea what she was doing there, but she didn't question it too much. Her last sleepwalking episode had been three years ago, but she'd always known that it could start up again without warning. Ever since coming off her medication, she'd feared this moment. She didn't like being out of control; that scared her more than anything else she could think of.

The light was off in the little annexed room that housed the chute, but she could see well enough in the dark. The chute was open and there were sounds from down there, at the centre of the building. It sounded as if something were trying to climb up the steel walls of the chute: a scurrying of nails or claws slipping against the smooth surface, a constant sound like heavy breathing, and the occasional intake of breath.

Connie took a step closer to the chute so that she was standing directly in front of it. She watched as her hands lifted and grabbed hold of each side of the opening. She started to lean forward, towards the chute, and kept on going until her head went inside and she was peering down into the narrow passageway. It was dark down there. Pitch black, so she could see very little beyond a few inches in front of her face. What she could make out, though, was a series of white marks on the stainless steel walls of the chute. Like scratch marks.

The sounds below halted, as if whatever was down there was looking up, waiting. She imagined it hanging there, balanced precariously, its eyes blinking in the darkness and its mouth opening.

She pulled back from the chute and walked away, opening the door and lurching out into the main corridor. She had the sense that something was laughing behind her... no, not laughing. Chuckling. Yes, that was the right word. Something was chuckling quietly in the blackness of the chute.

She returned to her apartment, to her bed, and lay awake for a long time, waiting for sleep to claim her. She wondered if she should make an appointment with the doctor. She was reluctant to go back on the pills, but they'd helped her before. They'd stopped her from roaming in the night and placing herself in potential danger; stopped her from terrifying her parents when they heard her creeping through the house, or found her standing in odd places—like the garden or the pantry or the bath tub—in the dark.

The next morning was Saturday, so there was no work. Connie had planned to do some cleaning, but she felt tired and anxious from the night's unwanted adventure. She needed some supplies, so decided to do a morning walk to the local supermarket. It wasn't far—about a mile away—and the sun was shining. She showered and dressed in some comfy jeans and a sweatshirt, grabbed her purse, and left the apartment.

The old man was in the lift when the doors opened. She wondered where he had been—he lived on the second floor, so what was he doing descending from above? He smelled slightly unpleasant; she detected an odour of neglect, or even decay.

"Morning."

"Hello again." She smiled, pressed the button for the ground floor. "You're up and about early."

He smiled. Those dentures shifted again, almost falling out of his mouth as he opened his lips. "You know what they say. The early bird catches the worm."

"Yes," she said. "They do say that, don't they?" This time the lift seemed to take ages to reach the ground floor. The old man was staring at her, making her feel uncomfortable. "So, have you lived here for long?"

He nodded, slowly. "I've always lived here."

"Really? Ever since it was built?"

"Always."

The lift doors slid open in their usual soundless manner.

"Well, it was nice talking to you." She walked out into the lobby. The old man stayed where he was. The lift doors remained open.

"Did you sleep well?"

Connie stopped walking, turned back to face him, framed like a statue between the open lift doors. "I'm sorry…"

"Last night. Your first night. Did you sleep okay? This building… it can get a bit noisy at night. The pipes. Rats trying to climb the refuse chute." His smile stretched wider.

"I slept okay, thanks." But she had the strong feeling that he knew she was lying. That he knew exactly what she'd done last night. Had he been watching her as she sleepwalked? Was that what he did here, spied on everyone? Just a lonely little old man with nothing better to do than stick his nose in other people's lives. She felt sorry for him. It was pathetic.

He stepped out of the lift. The doors shut behind him.

"Don't worry," he said. "This is a good place. We're all friendly here. Hopefully you'll sleep better tonight."

"But I… I told you, I did sleep well. I was fine."

He was standing right next to her. "There's no need to lie to me. To us. I'm your friend. I can help you settle in. If you need anything, just ask. Anything. I'm always around. I have no family, and all my friends are here. I've always lived here. It's my home."

Whatever kind of fear she'd felt earlier had now dissipated. He was just a lonely old man who didn't know how to make friends, but who tried his hardest anyway.

"Thank you," she said. "That's very kind of you."

"They built this place fifty years ago. I moved in with my mum when it first opened."

He must have been around thirty years old back than. Living with his mother; no girlfriend. Not much of a life, really. A life filled with waste. But who was she to judge? Was her life really any different?

"She was ill. I cared for her. There was no one else, you see. And after… well, after she died, I stayed on here. I'd got used to the place, and it had grown accustomed to me." His smile was tender now; it had no edge. He was just an old man trying to reach out to someone. "Like I said, if you ever need me, I'll be around. Just look for me." he turned and walked away, his steps slow and uneven. Connie felt bad for doubting him, for finding him creepy. She felt pity.

She walked to the small supermarket and grabbed some essentials: bread, milk, sandwich meat, a few frozen meals and some vegetables to keep her going for a few days. She didn't have much appetite lately, but she knew that she needed to eat. She had to keep her strength up, if only to help her get through the working day.

The other shoppers moved through the aisles like ghosts. She knew they were there—she could see them, hear them—but she felt that they were barely there at all. The girl at the checkout never made eye contact. She just fed the products through the scanner, her movements stiff and robotic.

These people… it's like they aren't even alive.

And neither am I.

She was almost back at the apartment building when her phone began to vibrate. Whenever she was out alone, she held the phone in her hand. It meant that if she ran into trouble, she wouldn't have to go looking for it in her bag. She raised her hand and looked at the screen. There was a text message from David.

Why was he contacting her now, after all this time? He could have called her before, or even sent her a message if he didn't want to speak to her. Why wait until now?

She opened the text: *Can I see you?*

That was just like him: short, insensitive, to the point.

She palmed her phone and continued on her way, heading back home. She had no intention of meeting with David. If he really wanted to see her, he could have done so before now.

When she got home she made some tea and toast. She wasn't hungry enough for anything else, and none of the food she'd bought held any appeal. David's text had ruined her mood completely. She would remain inside for the rest of the day. Read a book, watch some television, or listen to some music.

She sat down on the sofa and grabbed the remote control. There wasn't much on TV, just sport, cookery shows, and some kind of documentary about deep-sea fishing. She didn't even realise she'd fallen asleep until she woke up in the dark. The television had gone into sleep mode; none of the lights were on; the windows showed only darkness and streetlights.

"Shit." She stood, unsteady on her feet, and went for the lamp. When it came on, she winced, her eyes hurting from the glare. She switched the television back on and went into the small kitchen. She made a cup of tea, and when she went to put the used teabag in the kitchen bin she saw that it was almost full.

She paused. It could wait another few days, but there was no reason not to empty the bin, was there?

Why not? This was simply another silly fear she had to face. There was nothing to be genuinely scared of.

She took out the bin bag, knotted it at the top, and carried it out into the corridor. At the last minute, she popped back inside and grabbed a torch. She locked her apartment door and then walked to the door of the little room behind which the refuse chute was hidden. She went inside. The chute was closed. She opened it just like the caretaker had shown her. She moved close to the chute, leaned over the stainless steel lip, and peered down into the darkness. There were no sounds. She dropped the bag into the chute and listened to it slide down into the pit below, where it landed with a soft crunch.

She switched on the torch and shone its beam down into the chute. She saw the same white marks from last night. They looked like they might have been caused by nails or claws; scratches where someone or something had tried to scale the chute. She remembered the old man's comments about rats, then his wide smile and his ill-fitting dentures. She switched off the torch and listened. After a short while she heard the sounds. Like someone breathing, then a scrabbling sound as they started to climb.

She waited a few seconds more, and then she shone the torch beam back into the chute.

There was a naked figure there, hanging from the chute wall perhaps ten or fifteen feet below. She could see the wispy grey hair on the top of his head, his narrow shoulders coated with dust, his white hands bent into claws as they gripped the smooth sides of the chute. As she watched, he lifted his grubby face and stared up at her. He wasn't wearing his dentures; his mouth was a white-rimmed hollow, the gums moist and bloated. He had no eyes; there were only dark holes were eyes had once been. His skin was white and lumpy, like that of a maggot.

His mouth yawned wider, those puffy gums pushing forward between the thin lips. His jaws jerked open as if he was convulsing.

She dropped the torch, bent down to pick it up… and heard him scrabbling back down into the pit. She backed away from the chute, too afraid to go back and shut it. Reaching behind her, she opened the door and tumbled out of the small room. She ran back to her apartment. It was a short distance, only a few feet, but by the time she reached her door she was panting for breath.

Once inside, she leaned against the locked door and tried to control her breathing. It took her a while, but finally she felt better. She was beginning to question what she had seen. Perhaps she was ill—that would explain everything. David's text message had unsettled her further. She needed a rest, perhaps some time off work.

Yes, that was it. She'd call in sick on Monday. Take the week off. Get some sleep.

She went into the living room and sat down in front of the television. There was a film showing, but she wasn't watching it. She wasn't watching anything; her vision was turned inward, trying to process what she'd seen inside the chute.

Later, when she went to bed, she sat propped up with pillows, reading a novel. She read the same passage several times, unable to take it in. Finally she quit trying and turned on the radio. There was a late-night phone-in. People were talking about politics. She drifted; she slept; but, mercifully, she did not dream.

In the morning things were easier to rationalise. She refused to believe that she'd seen the old man crawling up the refuse shaft like a lizard on the side of a rock. It wasn't true; couldn't be. Surely it was impossible. She consulted her address book and noted down the number of her old doctor. She felt bad, as if she were taking backward steps. She'd managed things on her own so well for so long, but now she needed some help.

She made breakfast but didn't eat it. She drank four cups of coffee.

When she heard the knocking on her door, she initially thought she was hearing things.

Oh, no... not him. Not the old man.

She put down her coffee and walked to the door. She stood there and placed the fingertips of both hands against the door. "Who is it?"

She'd expected the old man's quiet voice, so when another voice spoke it took her a little while to recognise who it was.

"David? Is that you?"

"Yes. Yes, it's me. Can I come in? I feel like a stalker out here. People will wonder who the hell I am."

Relieved, she opened the door. Then, when she saw his face, she remembered that she shouldn't feel relieved at all—she should be angry.

"Hi." His smile was small; he was testing the water.

"What are you doing here?"

"Your mother gave me the address. I hope you don't mind." He took a step forward, towards the doorway, but she pushed the door forward an inch, leaving only a small gap.

"Please, Connie. I need to see you."

"Why now. Why after so long? You knew where I was—at my parents' place. You could have called round any time."

"Let me in and I'll explain. I'll explain everything."

She wanted to slam the door in his face. She wanted to scream fuck off through the closed door. She wanted to laugh at him as he walked away. But instead, she opened the door and let him inside. Old habits die hard; old loves take a long time to fade; and some scars run deeper than others.

"Thank you." He followed her along the little hallway and into the living room. "It's nice in here."

She ignored his small talk, sat down, folded her arms across her stomach, and waited. He didn't sit, nor did she invite him to. He remained standing, shuffling his weight from one foot to the other. She liked it when he was nervous like this. It made her feel in control. Or at least it gave her the illusion that she was in control.

"I made a mistake—possibly the biggest mistake of my life. I'm sorry. I need you."

She waited some more. Then she spoke: "Is that it. You wait this long, and that's it?"

"I'm sorry."

"Oh, shut up… I don't want to hear that you're sorry. *I'm* sorry, for letting you in. You can go now. Leave me in peace."

When he moved towards her, initially she thought that he was trying to kiss her, but when he grabbed her by the arm and swung her off the sofa, she realised that this was developing into something far more serious. She was still wearing her nightdress; it rode up her legs, exposing her thighs. That was when she knew. That was when it all made sense. This violence had been inside him all along, just waiting to come out.

"No!" She struggled against him, but he was strong. He lay down across her, pinning her there, on the floor. She writhed, her arms and her legs pistoning, her body bucking like a tied horse. She screamed. Then, during the commotion, she managed to get her arms under her torso and push… he tipped off sideways, and she took the opportunity to scramble out from under him and crawl across the floor on her knees, climbing to her feet. She could hear him pursuing her, but she kept on going. She reached the kitchen, on her feet by now, and went straight for the knife rack.

She grabbed the biggest one by the handle, turned, and slashed at the air. The blade was less than an inch from his face; any closer, and she would have cut him. Part of her wished that she had. He reeled backwards, tripping over his own feet and falling to the floor. His hands came up, his mouth opened, his eyes were bright and moist and alive.

"I'm sorry," he said again, but this time in a whisper.

"What the hell were you thinking?"

He shook his head. "I don't know. Nothing. I *wasn't* thinking. I miss you."

She wasn't sure if he'd been trying to rape her or beat her or just pin her down so she wouldn't leave him again. It didn't matter; only the violation made any sense.

"Get out of here."

He shuffled backwards, standing clumsily, and made his way to the door. She followed him at a slight distance, still brandishing the knife. She felt strong. She was the winner here, in this moment. If he turned on her now, she'd kill him.

He opened the door and stepped outside. He turned towards her, his mouth opening. She slammed the door in his face and slid the bolt. Her hands dropped to her sides but she didn't relinquish her grip on the knife. She dropped her head, closed her eyes, and wished for emptiness. *Fuck off*, she mouthed silently, but it didn't feel as good as she thought it might. There was no real closure, just the lingering sense of things being off kilter.

After a long while, she went back into the kitchen and returned the knife to the rack. Then she tidied up the living room. She sat down and put her head in her hands, weeping dryly for things she did not understand. Despite what had happened here today, she missed David. She missed the idea of him in her life. He had made sense of a part of her that she'd never been able to understand.

She stood and walked into the bedroom. She climbed into bed and pulled the covers over her head. She was thirsty but too tired to get up and fetch a drink. She was hungry, but not for food. This hunger was deeper, darker than anything she'd ever known.

Later, she rose in darkness. She was sleepwalking, but she was not asleep. That was the feeling she experienced: of being simultaneously asleep and awake. She was mesmerised.

The room was warm. The pipes in the walls were gurgling, making noises like happy children. She left the apartment and made her way towards the room where the chute was waiting; where it had always been waiting, just for somebody like her. She shut herself in and opened the chute. Air was released from its depths; a sour, stinking breath, held for too long.

This time she didn't have a torch. She did not need one. Her eyes had grown accustomed to the dark. She leaned over the edge of the chute, her head dangling down into the space below. The sounds rose towards her: scrabbling, panting breath, stifled laughter. She watched the figure as it climbed, drawing closer to her. She could see her own hair as it hung loosely around her head, swaying in the stale air. The figure paused directly beneath her. He was wearing a dark suit jacket, white shirt, dark tie, but his bottom half was unclothed. He was dirty; a light layer of grime covered his clothing. His bare legs looked as if he'd been crawling through oil.

When he stared up at her, his dirt-smeared face looked different, but it was still that of David. He had no teeth; his pulpy gums were spilling out between his lips. His jaws worked as if he was chewing on something tough. His eyes were gone. Black holes stared up at her, through her. It was David, but it wasn't him at all. David had gone home ages ago. It was something else, a thing that had taken on his likeness. She wasn't sure how she knew this, but she did. It was a certainty.

It was something better than David, and it was something so much worse.

This wasn't the person with whom she had lived, the man she'd slept with for so long. It wasn't even the man who'd put his hands on her earlier, threatening her. She didn't think it was a man at all. This, she thought, was something different.

A second figure scrabbled up to join him, slipping a little on the surface of the chute walls but then steadying itself as it climbed higher. It was the old man. Or it wasn't the old man. Again, she knew that this was something else entirely. Like a hermit crab, whatever lived down in the pit at the bottom of the chute was somehow inhabiting these imperfect copies and using them for its own purpose: a queen bee sending out drones to do her bidding. She had no idea what was down there, or where it had come from. Was it something that had evolved from human waste, a being created by the things we throw away? Or had it been summoned by the other tenants, a throw-away god they could worship?

These desperate theories made as much sense as anything else in her life.

The two figures hung there like spiders, the palms of their hands and the soles of their bare feet acting like suckers against the slick sides of the chute. Shoulder to bony shoulder in the cramped space. They were both breathing heavily, their chests rising and falling. Their heads twitched; those black holes in their faces did not blink.

Then, finally, one of them—or perhaps both of them—spoke. The voices were the same voice: two mouths, one being; or perhaps a legion of beings acting as one.

"We've always lived here."

"I know," she said.

"We've been waiting for you."

"Have you?"

"We need you."

"Do you really?"

"We're hungry. We're always hungry."

"So am I," she said, letting her legs slide, allowing her body weight to carry the rest of her through the chute, her knees and elbows bashing against the metal. "I'm hungry, too." Her teeth were falling out, the gums swelling and distending. Blackness filled her vision like ink running through the cracks of the world.

She was starting to feel safe here. It felt like a home, somewhere she could rest: a place of refuge. She realised now that she'd sleepwalked through the rest of her life up to this point. But now, for the first time, she was truly awake.

The figures scuttled around on the chute wall so that they faced down into the pit, moving quickly, like insects in their natural habitat. Their long, thin, dirty nails scraped loudly against the stainless steel sides of the chute. Their skin and clothing whispered against it, like distant voices. They began to move hand over hand, foot over foot, heading downwards, returning to the filth and the darkness of their nest.

"Wait for me," she whispered, falling. She said the words without feeling them, but maybe that would come later, once she'd finally found herself. "I'm coming. *I'm coming home.*"

SCAVENGING

KEVIN LUCIA

SOME FOLKS call it "sidewalk shopping" but for me it's "sidewalk scavenging." I suppose at one time I wouldn't have been above taking an old chair or bookshelf off the curb, but I don't need those sorts of things, now.

I'm past that.

And I didn't start scavenging for the used furniture; I started scavenging for the extra cash. I lost my teaching job about year ago, one year short of tenure and in a way guaranteeing I'd never teach again, and while Clifton Heights is large enough for several churches, a small hospital, two high schools and a zoo, it's also small enough that news travels fast, so the only place willing to hire me was the twenty-four hour Mobilmart outside town, and even then only part-time, third shift. I wasn't crazy about that but rent and utilities looming every month provided plenty of motivation.

But I knew working part time for minimum wage at a gas station wasn't going to cut it, so I had to take additional measures. For example, once a month a Food Bank visits Clifton Heights Methodist Church and though it killed me to accept handouts, it helped lower the grocery bill, which helped me pay bills *and* still eat.

I also began collecting cans and bottles along the interstate and side roads, because The Can Man was offering six and half cents for each. And after seeing an ad in the classifieds for Greene's Scrap Metal saying they pay for metal, I decided to start collecting scrap also, because along the roads I often found pieces of steel from underneath cars and trucks, rusted parts of tail pipes, mufflers, the like. Sometimes if fortune favored, whole mufflers, catalytic converters, aluminum hubcaps and on occasion aluminum wheels.

But the real action proved to be in town on Wednesday nights.

Thursday morning Webb County collects trash, so Wednesday night folks leave it on their curbs. The idea struck me on the way to work one night, passing homes and their garbage: here was scrap metal lying around for the taking.

I did some research first, calling Greene's for a breakdown of the scrap metals rates, and believe it or not you can turn a decent buck scrapping. The most valuable metal, copper, garnered almost two-fifty a pound, but I rarely found much of that, maybe because most folks knew they could get decent money for it themselves. I often collected a fair amount of old brass, however—in doorknobs or exterior lighting fixtures—and that went for a buck sixty a pound.

Mostly I found lots of steel—seven cents a pound—and a decent amount of aluminum, forty cents a pound. After a few trial runs I managed to fill my minivan with old metal lawn chairs, filing cabinets, pots and pans and old propane grills, lighting fixtures, aluminum siding, toolboxes, bed frames... you name it. If it was metal, I took it. Depending on how much aluminum and brass I turned up, Thursday morning I'd earn anywhere from fifty to seventy bucks. That may not sound like much, but even at the minimum, two hundred dollars at month's end. That combined with my gas station wages and the cans I collected made life bearable.

And that's all I'd wanted.

To survive. I knew what I'd done. Knew it was stupid, reckless, that it had caused irreparable harm, and I also knew I'd gotten off relatively easy. So at that point, I'd just wanted to numb myself. Pay my bills and eat.

"Sidewalk scavenging" is legal, too, but I'd already known that. Three years prior to losing my job I'd encountered a scavenger looking over *my* garbage, considering either an old nightstand or a cheap wooden bookcase. He declined both but showed up the following week, looking over some pots and pans before moving on empty-handed again. I called Sheriff Baker and he said long as my landlord didn't care and no one made a mess it was legal.

The fellow didn't return and I never saw him again. I remember feeling relieved because something in his disconnected gaze made me feel uneasy, like I'd been offered a haunting glimpse of how anyone could fall out of the human race.

How ironic, then, that I see that gaze now in my minivan's rear-view mirror.

After several false starts—one week finding only a bent section of an old storm gutter, the next a frying pan—I got better acquainted with most of Clifton Heights' streets and avenues and cul-de-sacs and dead ends. I also learned several things I'd never thought about before, things I might've considered vital if I still felt a connection with people.

For example, I found most my scrap in the better sections of town, not in Center Village Apartments or out at the Commons Trailer Park. You need a certain income to buy new stuff often enough to throw old stuff out. Also, folks living in the poorer sections simply can't afford to throw anything away, even if they're broken. Life has taught them to use everything, waste nothing.

And the poorer sections offered more moving portrayals of humanity. Which, again, probably would've meant more to me if I'd still been teaching English, still reading poems and plays and short stories. Sadly I'd quit reading after getting fired. Most of the time, I consumed hours of talk shows.

One night, I pulled past an apartment building that *almost* made me feel. The worst slum, it had gone unpainted for years, its exterior a mottled gray, no shutters on windows out of which hung battered air conditioners. The front steps leaned and the porch sagged in the middle.

But the lawn offered the most striking portrait. No grass at all...but someone had raked the dirt with meticulous care, like they do the sand at the beach, and under what looked like an diseased elm sat an oval picnic table, the kind with benches built into it, and next to that a charcoal grill. In spite of the apathy I'd cultivated since losing my job, I imagined a small patchwork family of a mother and child and boyfriend, stealing whatever enjoyment they could cooking cheap hamburgers and hotdogs and eating them under that sickly old elm.

And in the middle of this raked dirt lawn sat the most lovingly cared-for flower garden I'd ever seen, filled with pansies and black-eyed susans and iris, mulched with black compost, ringed by stones that had obviously been spray-painted white...

But it looked breathtakingly beautiful. Someone was doing the best with what they had, and I couldn't help wondering if a Mayella Ewell lived there, and what her life was like.

Another thing I learned about Clifton Heights I hadn't known before: its roadways were more complicated than I'd ever realized. Seemed like every Wednesday I turned down a road or into cul-de-sac or into a residential complex I'd never seen before, and often I lost my way, driving around in circles, retracing a road I'd just taken. In fact, once or twice after taking a wrong turn the premonition struck me that maybe I'd gotten *really* lost. In short order, though, I'd encounter a familiar landmark—a sign, a distinct garbage can or porch swing—to find my way again and that dull worry would fade, forgotten until the next time it happened.

Turns out, I should've paid closer attention to how easy it was to get lost in your own hometown.

I never ran into anyone I knew, though I'm certain I must have driven by their homes and scavenged metal from their curbs many times. And it didn't dawn upon me right away, but soon enough I couldn't help but think of that scavenger I'd encountered; couldn't help but think of that discarded look in his eyes, realizing then the same thing was happening to me, that I'd been left at the curb like the refuse I scavenged through, with one major difference...

Like the lost soul who'd looked over my bookcase and pots and pans years ago, no one was likely to come scavenging after me.

I'd been scrapping for about six months when I pulled up to a promising pile of junk before a two-story white home with blue trim on Highland Avenue. After a quick once-over, however, I decided to leave because like many other homes this one had boxes of books on its curb for disposal, which always depressed me. Despite not having read anything since losing my job; despite leaving behind the life of an erudite, witty, literate and urbane high school English teacher (all a façade), it still depressed me to encounter discarded books.

And this house had discarded hundreds of books, neatly sorted in cardboard boxes. For the first time since I started scavenging I felt the urge to rescue those books (even though I wasn't planning on reading them), so I wanted out of there.

But as I rounded the boxes a name jumped out from one of the covers, literally halting me in my tracks.

Ray Bradbury.

And above that: *The Illustrated Man*.

But the cover hit me hardest. It was older, featuring a heavily tattooed man sitting with his back to the reader. Against my will I bent over and with numb fingers picked up the well-worn book. Straightening, I opened the cover and turned a few pages to the blank page after the title page.

Except it wasn't blank.

In an all-too familiar looping script, someone had written: 'TO EMILY: LIVE FOREVER!' And, of course, it had been signed. By me.

Because impossibly, this was the short story collection I'd given one of my students for her eighteenth birthday. This wasn't her house or her neighborhood—I'd avoided *both* since my termination—but I felt certain that, as impossible as it seemed, this was the book I'd given Emily Travis about a year and a half ago, shortly before I'd been fired for sleeping with her, before she killed herself when she learned she was pregnant.

◇

I remember the first time I saw Emily Travis, during my third year of teaching, her ninth grade year. I'd just dashed from the school across a rain-pounded parking lot to my car (then a sporty little VW bug) and was throwing my books into the back seat, struggling with my umbrella, when I saw her.

Sitting on a swing in the playground, head hanging, clutching the swing's chains, arms limp, shoulders sagging. Sitting there in the rain, her black hair plastered to her face.

And I froze, unable to tear my gaze away. Nothing untoward reared in my head then (and nothing like that would occur for several more years), but I couldn't shake the heartbreaking poignancy of the moment: this girl sagging on a swing in a downpour, oblivious and uncaring of the cold rain pelting her shoulders and head and arms.

Today, I know what I should've done. I should've shaken the moment off, resolved to learn the girl's name and maybe alert the guidance office to what I'd seen and left well enough alone.

I didn't do that.

I popped the umbrella up and walked over to the playground to see if she was okay.

Then I gave her a ride home.

And as I stood outside that house on Highland Avenue holding that impossible Ray Bradbury collection with its impossible inscription, the memories of Emily and I tumbled through my head, of which I'll never share with anyone.

I'm not going to pretend what happened between Emily and I was "special." I'll not defend nor justify my actions, because even though I never meant any harm I'm an adult, and I *was* a teacher. A figure of authority and responsibility, and I'd failed that responsibility, destroying her life and mine in the process.

When we slept together, I was only twenty-seven and she was

eighteen, bearing the weight of double those years on her shoulders. However, we were first linked after that day on the playground and though it took several years for it to manifest into life-destroying proportions, I should've been more aware, more cautious, and I should've seen it coming and headed it off. If I had, I might still be teaching today, (though at another school far away), and Emily Travis would still be alive.

But she's dead.

And I'll never teach again. There's nothing that can change that, no matter how hard I search for it.

Doesn't mean I can stop looking.

I left *The Illustrated Man* behind, explaining its existence away. Emily's father more than likely donated all her books to The Book Loft, a used book store on Main Street run by Andrew Slater, (where I still have over a hundred dollars trade-in credit I'll never use) and someone who lived in that house on Highland Avenue had purchased it, ignorant of its origins, and when finished, discarded it with the others.

A logical and rational explanation.

So I left it there, dropped it among its discarded brethren, climbed into my minivan and drove away, already forgetting it, hoping to come across a large gas grill or something else nice and heavy.

I left it there.

And only now realize I shouldn't have.

That night it was harder getting home than usual. I took wrong turns down streets I'd never seen before, retracing my routes, driving in circles before finally finding my way back to Main Street, where I sighed, a creeping anxiety seeping out of me.

Over the next few weeks, finding my way home got harder.

◇

Seemed like no time had passed until Wednesday night rolled around and I was again cruising for scrap metal. I didn't think anything unusual at the time because it wasn't like much had happened since the previous Wednesday. I worked Thursday, Friday, Saturday and Sunday nights at the Mobilmart, 11 P.M. to 7 A.M., which meant I slept most of Friday, Saturday, Sunday and Monday morning and early afternoon. Monday evening I usually walked one of Clifton Height's many back roads to pick cans and bottles, while I spent Tuesday watching whatever talk show was on, and Tuesday night I'd go to The Stumble Inn, order a plate of hot wings, sit in a corner deep in the shadows and quietly get myself as drunk as I could afford, which usually only amounted to a buzz. Then, the next day was Wednesday, which meant more talk shows and then later that night, scavenging.

My social schedule didn't offer much in the way of milestones to mark passing time, and I'd become accustomed to "slippage." It didn't seem strange that I couldn't recall what I'd done since the previous Wednesday, that was just the way things were, and my memory of finding that impossible copy of *The Illustrated Man* had hidden behind the blurred scenery of my colorless existence.

But that changed when I found the next thing, in front of a small white Colonial with red trim on Acer Street. Soon as I stepped out of my van and saw it, several connections fired in my head. I remembered how hard it was getting home last Wednesday, how afraid I was of being lost, and I remembered with a shiver *The Illustrated Man* I'd given Emily before she died.

A gray Texas Instruments 8010 electric word processor.

Sitting atop a box of old *TIME* magazines.

And it was mine.

I knew this because of the round sticker on the keyboard's cover, of a robot—I think from one of Issac Asimov's robot novels—sitting on a cliff watching a sky turning purple-orange at sunset. The sticker came in the mail with my subscription to *Asimov's Science Fiction Magazine*, one of the many speculative magazines I'd consumed during college (along with *Cemetery Dance* and *Twilight Zone Magazine*) as I pounded out stories on that gray Texas Instruments 8010 electric word processor in my attempts to become a writer.

I forgot to mention that, didn't I? That I'd grown up in love with science fiction, fantasy and horror; that during college all I'd wanted was to write, my degree in English Education a cover to make it look like I had a plan.

And right then I realized I couldn't possibly explain away the word processor's presence because I'd destroyed it twenty years ago after receiving my thirtieth-or-so story rejection. I'd gotten drunk and tossed that word processor out our third-story dorm room window in a fit of rage. It plummeted to its shattering destruction onto the brick courtyard below. Luckily I didn't hit anyone but I still got written up by the Residence Director and fined.

But twenty years later there it sat on a box of moldy *TIME* magazines in front of a red-trimmed white Colonial on Acer Street, and as I stared at it, something broke inside of me. A door opened and loosed the real reason why I'd hurled my word processor to its plastic-shattering and electronics-crunching doom. At the time I'd told myself I'd gotten fed up with writing, disgusted with the endless toil and the sting of rejection, angry that I didn't have the necessary talent, and though maybe all those things were partly true, I realized, standing on that curb, it wasn't the whole truth.

I'd been afraid.

Afraid of my father. Afraid of his continued scorn of my dreams, and I'd grown tired of weathering said scorn and upon receiving that thirtieth rejection letter, I hurled my dreams out the window with that Texas Instruments 8010.

I'd always assumed my rage had come from the bitter realization that I didn't have enough talent to write, but at that moment, staring at that impossible word processor, I realized my rage had come from realizing I didn't have the courage to stand up to my father's scorn; the rage had come from giving up my dreams.

◇

And then I remembered how I'd left behind Emily's copy of *The Illustrated Man* the previous week, so I gathered up that Texas Instruments 8010 and took it to the van. A piece of paper fluttered from its wheel to the ground but I didn't stop to inspect it, even though the masthead looked terribly similar to the masthead on my last rejection letter, from my college literary journal, *The Oswegian*.

Because that would be too much, seeing that same letter twenty years later.

Emily had loved all the speculative genres as much as me. She'd grown up reading Bradbury, Poe, Matheson, L'Engle, Lewis, Tolkien, Dahl and so many others, escaping from her fractured childhood into those mesmerizing tales.

Just like I'd escaped from mine.

That night I did manage to find some scrap metal. Three rusted lawn chairs and a crooked folding chair. But I missed a lot after collecting the Texas Instruments 8010, numbly cruising streets, buildings and houses and telephone poles and garbage piled on curbs blurring past. And I had a very hard time getting home that night. Got lost in the poorer section of town, only blundering by pure happenstance onto Old Barstow Road and the NYSEG Utility Payment center to find my way back to Main Street.

But for some reason I wasn't as afraid of getting lost that night. I just kept driving, ignoring the garbage piled on curbs in front of houses...

Because they didn't have what I *needed*.

And something inside kept pushing me to drive, drive until I found something I *did* need.

After another numb week of working third shift at the Mobilmart and sleeping all day and walking for cans and bottles on Monday and drinking at The Stumble Inn, I found myself—feeling alarmed, this time—blinking awake as I pulled off Main Street onto a side street I didn't recognize, apparently sleep-driving into another night of sidewalk scavenging.

My scalp prickling with unease, my heart pounding the way anyone's does when they jerk awake at the wheel, I nearly slammed on the brakes when—looking out the window for some clue as to which street I'd turned onto—I saw the Texas Instruments 8010 sitting on the passenger seat. For some reason, I'd lugged it back out to the minivan for my Wednesday night metal hunt.

Or, more disturbing: I'd never taken it out of the minivan at all, which then conjured up the fancy that maybe all my blurry memories of the past week were nothing more than echoes of other weeks playing themselves over and I'd never left the minivan at all, never stopped driving, had been driving ever since...

I tried to remember what I'd eaten last night for dinner.

Did I have luck in collecting bottles and cans Monday? What road had I walked?

Nothing. And the kicker? I had no idea what talk shows I'd watched that week.

I felt close to losing it, then. Close to slamming my foot on the gas and sending my minivan careening down that nameless street into the path of whatever came by, be it another car, truck, or kid on tricycle. Anything to snap the colorless, unbroken stream my life had become...

In all the time before I started finding these things, I never once allowed myself to wonder why my life had fallen apart, never let myself ponder where things had first gone wrong. I had repressed those questions, too scared of facing the answers, and where those answers would lead.

Even though that was what I needed the most.

◇

Again, I can't defend what happened between Emily and me. But the pattern seems clear now, doesn't it? Two scarred souls who tried—despite the clear consequences—to heal each other of their festering wounds. And of course I don't know for sure because she kept her plans secret, but I think—hell, I know—Emily killed herself less because of the shame she and I would've had to endure, but more because she'd feared her father's jealous reaction if he discovered the truth.

How do I know she wasn't ashamed of us?

Why else would she address her suicide letter to me?

When I was only twelve years old my alcoholic father came home from another Saturday night with the boys, drunk and raving about the usual: liberal fucking hippy democrats ruining the government, blacks and Hispanics and welfare ruining the economy and how his shrewish, spineless hag of a wife undercut his God-given right to rule the household with an iron fist by letting his faggotty son read comic books and write stupid stories and collect those stupid, goddamn worthless old soda bottles he put on his sissy-ass shelf of worthless shit.

The routine Saturday night run-through, which usually ended with Mom reluctantly letting Dad man-handle her into the bedroom in hopes she could satisfy him enough to forestall him turning his liquor-fueled attentions towards me. It usually worked well enough.

But not that night.

She said something different. I never discovered what because that "spineless" woman packed her bags and disappeared for good the next day. But she said something that broke the routine because I heard Dad roar, heard the smack of a calloused hand on flesh and heard Mom scream, then his heavy Timberlands were pounding their way to my room, where I was, as usual, sitting on the bed writing in one of those black and white marble notebooks, surrounded also by several issues of *Spider-man*, *Superman* and *The Incredible Hulk*.

He kicked my door in so hard the doorknob slammed against the opposite wall and without a word he hauled back and decked me with a hay-maker I can still feel ringing in my jaw when I'm tired.

I sprawled onto the floor, head spinning, bleeding from my mouth and nose, then everything dissolved into a medley of pain and curses and punches, even a few kicks. How I avoided several broken bones and ribs I'll never know.

I don't remember much, save two devastating sights that came back to me the instant I saw those broken soda bottles and ruined comic books lying on the curb. At the height of his rage Dad attacked my flimsy, cheap comic book rack—made by *him* in a moment of kindness, from lumber mill castoffs—and ripped the comics from their plywood slots, tearing and shredding and crumpling pages, screaming and cursing. Then, he methodically snapped each shelf with his meaty hands and tore the shelf from the wall, drywall anchors and all.

Then after that, the coup de grace. He grabbed my Louisville Slugger (which he'd bought for my tenth birthday, despite knowing I hated sports) from where it leaned against the wall, wound up and in one swing cleared my knick-knack shelf of those carefully collected, cleaned and arranged—but goddamn stupid—vintage soda bottles, their shattering like shrill cries in my ears.

And then I passed out to the sight of Dad swinging up and down, pounding those broken bottles into dust, the torn pages of my comic books fluttering around us like dying butterflies.

My father abused me off and on in similar escapades until I escaped to college, leaving behind a man who'd eventually get knifed and killed in a drunken bar fight. I'd like to say that he only abused me physically and emotionally, but that would be a lie.

◇

A sudden urge tugged at my brain, heart and soul. I pulled over to the curb, braked and parked the minivan.

Because the pile of garbage before this yellow Concord with black trim had something I needed. Slowly, feeling distant and far away, I got out and stood before the refuse piled on the curb and saw what I *needed*. Two things, actually.

One: a wooden crate full of smashed vintage soda bottles, circa 1960s. Shards of what looked like Coke, Dr. Pepper, Pepsi bottles and the emerald green bits of most likely a few 7UP bottles. Next to that the wreckage of a homemade, cheap plywood comic book rack, littered with torn and crumpled comic books and comic book pages, all the classics: *Batman*, *The Astounding X-men*, *Superman* and even *ROM: Space Knight*, shredded into ruin.

I stared, my face rigid, when a brisk, non-confrontational but stiff voice asked, "Can I help you?"

I looked up and saw a middle-aged man wearing a white dress shirt and tan khakis, easily upper-middle class, probably disturbed in the middle of dinner by me pulling up to his curb. Sharp, clear blue eyes weighed me, his stance casual... but poised and wary, regardless.

I opened my mouth but remembered that lost-looking man, that scavenger I'd encountered on my curb years ago; remembering his lost, questioning gaze and realized that this man wouldn't see the broken soda bottles and destroyed comics. He couldn't see them. Only *I* could see them.

Because I needed them.

I swallowed thickly, cast my eyes down and whispered, "No, I'm fine." Got back into my minivan and pulled away from the curb as quickly as possible while retaining some shred of dignity.

And waited until nightfall, driving and turning down an endless variation of streets with no names until I somehow returned to that street and collected those smashed bottles, destroyed comic book rack and ruined comic books.

Because they were what I *needed*.

I'm still driving, and I've found lots more since the broken soda bottles and ruined comic books. A box of my G. I. Joe action figures Dad threw away when I turned nine because I was "too old for that baby shit nonsense. Boys don't play with goddamn dolls when they're almost ten, fer Chrissake."

Also, some of my stuffed animals—one of them my beloved Pound Puppy—which Dad had insisted on throwing out when I'd turned five, because "how can you expect ta stop wettin the bed when you act like a goddamn baby?"

And lately I've been finding my old black and white marble composition notebooks here and there. I haven't looked in them (almost afraid to see what I wrote years ago), just piled them in my minivan with all the other things I've found.

See, I don't collect scrap metal anymore. I collect things I *need*. I drive all the time, now. I have no memories of stopping for food or gas or ever going home or back to work at the Mobilmart. It always seems like Wednesday night, and I'm always turning down yet another street I don't recognize, looking for what I need and while I keep finding things, I haven't yet found that thing I *think* I need the most...

A dog-eared copy of *The Illustrated Man*, the one I gave to Emily, with the inscription that seems dreadfully ironic now—LIVE FOREVER!—because I feel like I'll be driving around forever until I find that thing I so desperately needed and *should've* accepted the first time around. Maybe if I had, I wouldn't still be driving around looking for it.

THE WORD

RAMSEY CAMPBELL

NOBODY TRIES TO SPEAK to me while I'm waiting for the lift, thank Sod. Whenever you want to go upstairs at a science fiction convention the lift is always on the top floor, and by the time it arrives it'll have attracted people like a dog-turd attracts flies. There'll be a woman whose middle is twice as wide as the rest of her, and someone wearing no sleeves or deodorant, and at least one writer gasping to be noticed, and now there's a vacuumhead using a walkie-talkie to send messages to another weekend deputy who's within shouting distance. Here comes a clump wearing convention badges with names made up out of their own little heads, N. Trails and Elfan and Si Fye, and I amuse myself trying to decide which of them I'd least like to hear from. Here's the lift at last, and I shut the doors before some bald woman with dragons tattooed on her scalp can get in as well, but a thin boy in a suit and tie manages to sidle through the gap. He sees my *Retard* T-shirt, then he reads my badge. "Hi there," he says. "I'm—"

"Jess Kray," I tell him, since he seems to think I can't read, "and you sent me the worst story I ever read in my life."

He sucks in his lips as if I've punched him in the mouth. "Which one was that?"

"How many have you written that are that bad?"

"None that I know of."

Everyone's pretending not to watch his face doing its best not to wince. "You sent me the one about Frankenstein and the dead goat and the two nuns," I say for everyone to hear.

"I've written lots since."

"Just don't send any to *Retard*."

My fanzine isn't called that now, but I'm not telling him. I leave him to ride to the top with our audience while I lock myself in my room. I was going to write about the Sex, Sects and Subtexts in Women's Horror Fiction panel, which showed me why I've never been able to read a book by the half of the participants I'd heard of, but now I've too much of a headache. I lie on the bed for as long as I can stand being by myself, then I look for someone I can bear to dine with.

We're at Contraception in Edinburgh, but it could be anywhere a mob of fans calling themselves fen take over a hotel for the weekend. As I step into the lobby I nearly bump into Hugh, a writer who used to have tons of books in the shops, maybe because nobody was buying them. Soon books will all be games you play on screens, but I'll bet nobody will play with his. "How are you this year, Jeremy?" he booms.

"Dying like everyone else."

He emits a sound as if he's trying not to react to being poked in the ribs, and the rest of his party comes out of the bar. One of them is Jess Kray, who says "Join us, Jeremy, if you're free for dinner."

He's behaving like the most important person there, grinning with teeth that say we're real and a mouth that says you can check if you like and eyes with a message just for me. I'd turn him down to see how that makes him look, except Hugh Zit says "Do by all means" so his party knows he means the opposite, and it's too much fun to refuse.

Hugh Know's idea of where to eat is a place called Godfathers. I sit next to his Pakistani wife and her friend who isn't even a convention member, and ignore them so they stop talking English. I've already heard Hugh Ever say on panels all the garbage he's recycling, about how it's a writer's duty to offer a new view of the world, as if he ever did, and how the most important part of writing is research. He still talks like the fan he used to be, like all the fen I know talk, either lecturing straight in your face or staring over your shoulder as though there's a mirror behind you. Only Kray couldn't look more impressed. Hugh Cares finishes his pizza at last and says "I feel better for that."

I say "You must have felt bloody awful before."

Kray actually laughs at that while grimacing sympathetically at Hugh, and I can't wait to go back to my room and write a piece about the games he's playing. I write until I can't see for my headache, and after I've managed to sleep I write about the rest of the clowns at Contraception, until I've almost filled up the first issue of *Parade of the Maladjusted and Malformed*, which is what conventions are. On the last day I see Kray buying a publisher's editor a drink, which no doubt means he'll sell at least a trilogy. At least that's what I write once I'm home.

Then it's back to wearing a suit at the bank in Fulham and having people line up for me on the far side of a window, which at least keeps them at a distance while I turn them and their lives into numbers on a screen. But there's the smell of the people on my side of the glass, and sometimes the feel of them if I don't move fast enough. Playing the game of never saying what I think just about sees me through the day, and the one after that, and the one after that. I print my fanzine in my room and mail it and wait for the clowns I've written about to threaten to sue me or beat me up. The year isn't over when among the review copies and the rest of the unnecessaries publishers send to fanzines I get a sheet about Jess Kray, the most exciting new young writer of the decade, whose first three novels are going to give a new meaning to fantasy.

Sod knows I thought I was joking. I ask for copies to see how bad they are, and they're worse. They're about an alternate world where everyone becomes their sexual opposite, so a gay boy turns into a barbarian hero and a dyke becomes his lover, and some of the characters remember when they return to the real world and most of them try to remind the rest, except one thinks it's meant to be forgotten, and piles of similar crap. I just skim a few chapters of the first book to get a laugh at the idea of people buying a book called *A Touch of Other* under the impression that it's a different kind of junk. Apparently the books go on to be about some wimp who teaches himself magic in the other world and gets to be leader of this one. It's nine months since I saw Kray talking to the editor, so either he writes even more glibly than he comes on to people or he'd already written them. One cover shows a woman's face turning into a man's, and the second has a white turning black, and the third's got a tinfoil mirror where a face should be. That's the one I throw hardest across the room. Later I put them in the pile to sell to Everybody's Fantasy, the skiffy and comics shop near the docks, and then I hear Kray will be there signing books.

How does a writer nobody's heard of put that over on even a shop run by fen? I'm beginning to think it's time someone exposed him. That Saturday I take the books with me, leaving the compliments slips in so he'll see I haven't bought them. Maybe I'll let him see me selling them as soon as he's signed them. But the moment I spot him at the table with his three piles on it he jumps up. "Jeremy, how are you! This is Jeremy Bates, everyone. He was my first critic."

Sod knows who he's trying to impress. The only customers are comics readers, that contradiction in terms, who look as if they're out without their mothers to buy them their funnies. And the proprietor, who I call Kath on account of his kaftan and long hair, doesn't seem to think much of Kray trying to hitch a ride on my reputation, not that he ever seems to think of much except where the next joint's coming from. I give Kray the books with the slips sticking up, but he carries on grinning. "My publishers haven't sent me your review yet, Jeremy."

I should tell him that's because I won't be writing one, but I'm mumbling like a fan, for Sod's sake. "Write something in them for me."

In the first book he writes *For Jeremy who knew me before I was good*, and *To our future* in the second, and *For life* in what I hope's the last. When he hands them back like treasure I stuff them in my armpit and leaf through some tatty fanzines so I can see how many people he attracts.

Zero. Mr Nobody and all his family. A big round hole without a rim. Some boys on mountain bikes point at him through the window until Kath chases them, and once a woman goes to Kray, but only to ask him where the Star Trek section is. Kath's wife brings him a glass of herbal tea, which isn't even steaming, and with the bag drowning in it, and it's fun to watch him having to drink that. We all hang around for the second half of the hour, then Kath says in the drone that always sounds as if he's talking in his sleep "Maybe you can sign some stock for us."

I can hear he doesn't mean all the books on the table, but that doesn't stop our author. When Kray's defaced every one he says "How about that lunch?"

Kath and Mrs Kath glance at each other, and Jess Kidding gives them an instant grin each. "I understand. Don't even think of it. You can buy lunch next time, after I've made you a bundle. Let me buy this one."

They shake their heads, and I see them thinking there'll never be a next time, but Jess Perfect flashes them an even more embracing grin before he turns to me. "If you want to interview me, Jeremy, I'll stand lunch. You can be the one who tells the world."

"About what?"

"That'd be telling."

I want the next *PotMaM* to spill a lot more blood, and besides, nobody's ever bought me lunch. I take him round the corner to Le Marin Qui Rit, which some French chef with too much money built in an old warehouse by the Thames. "This is charming," Kray says when he sees the nets full of crabs hanging from the beams and the waiters in their sailor suits, though I bet he doesn't think so when he sees the prices on the menu. As soon as we've ordered he hurries through the door that says Matelots, maybe to be sick over the prices, and I rip through his books until he comes back with his grin and says "Ask me anything." But I've barely opened my mouth when he says "Aren't you recording?"

"Didn't know I'd need to. Don't worry, I remember everything. My ex could tell you."

He digs a pocket tape-recorder out of his trench coat. "Just in case you need to check. I always carry one for my thoughts."

He heard an ex-success say that at Contraception. A sailor brings us a bottle of sheep juice, Mutton Cadet, and I switch on. "What's a name like Kray supposed to mean to the world?"

"It's my father's name," he says, then proves I was right to be suspicious, because it turns out his father was a Jewish Pole who was put in a camp and left the rest of his surname behind when he emigrated with the remains of his family after the war.

"Speaking of prejudice, what's with the black guy calling himself Nigger when he gets to be the hero?"

"A nigger is someone who minds being called one. Either you take hold of words or they take hold of you."

"Which do you think your books do?"

"A bit of both. I'm learning. I want to be an adventurer on behalf of the imagination."

I can hardly wait to write about him, except here's my poached salmon. He waits until I've taken a mouthful and says "What did you like about the books?"

I'm shocked to realise how much of them has stuck in my mind—lines like "AIDS is such a hell you'll go straight to heaven." I want to say "Nothing," but his grin has got to me. "Where you say that being born male is the new original sin."

"Well, that's what one of my characters says."

What does he mean by that? His words keep slipping away from me, and I've no idea where they're going. By the time we finish I'm near to nodding in my pudding, his refusal to be offended by anything I say has taken so much out of me. The best I can come up with as a final question is "Where do you think you're going?"

"To Florida for the summer with my family. That's where the ideas are."

"Here's hoping you get some."

He doesn't switch off the recorder until we've had our coffee, then he gives me the tape. "Thanks for helping," he says, and insists on shaking hands. It feels like some kind of Masonic trick, trying to find out if I know a secret—either that or he's working out the best way to shake hands. He pays the bill without letting his face down and says he's heading for the station, which is on my way home, but I don't tell him. I turn my back on him and take the long way through the streets I always like, with no gardens and no gaps between the houses and less sunlight than anywhere else in town. While I'm there I don't need to think, and I feel as if nothing can happen in me or outside me. Only I have to go home to deal with the tape, which is itching in my hip pocket like a tapeworm.

I'm hoping he'll have left some thoughts on it by mistake, but there's just our drivelling. So either he brought the machine to make sure I could record him or more likely wanted to keep a copy of what we said. Even if he didn't trust me, it's a struggle to write about him in the way I want to. It takes me days and some of my worst headaches. I feel as if he's stolen my energy and turned it into a force that only works on his behalf.

When I seem to have written enough for an issue of *PotMaM* I print out the pages. I have to pick my way around them or tread on them whenever I get up in the night to be sick. I send out the issue to my five subscribers and anyone who sent me their fanzine, though not many do after what I write about their dreck. I take copies to Constipation and Convulsion and sell a few to people who haven't been to a convention before and don't like to say no. When I start screaming at the fanzine in the night and kicking the piles over I pay for a table in the dealers' room at Contamination. But on the Saturday night the dealers' room is broken into, and in the morning every single copy's gone.

It isn't one of my better years. My father dies and my mother tells me my ex-wife went to the funeral. The branch of the bank closes down because of the recession, and it looks as if I'll be out of a job, only luckily one of the other clerks gets his back broken in a hit and run. They move me to Chelsea, where half the lunchtime crowd looks like plain-clothes something and all the litter bins are sealed up so nobody can leave bombs in them. At least the police won't let marchers into the district, though you can hear them shouting for employment or life sentences for pornography or Islamic blasphemy laws or a curfew for all males as soon as they reach puberty or all tobacco and alcohol profits to go to drug rehabilitation or churchgoing to be made compulsory by law... Some writers stop their publisher from sending me review copies, so at least I've bothered them. I give up going to conventions for almost a year, until I forget how boring they are, so that staying in my room seems even worse. And at Easter I set out to find myself a ride to Consternation in Manchester.

I wait most of an hour at the start of the motorway and see a car pick up two girls who haven't waited half as long, so I'm in no mood for any crap from the driver who finally pulls over. He asks what I'm doing for Easter and I think he's some kind of religious creep, but when I tell him about Consternation he starts assuring me how he used to enjoy H. G. Wells and Jules Verne, as if I gave a fart. Then he says "What would you call this new johnny who wrote *The Word*? Is he sci-fi or fantasy or what?"

"I don't know about any word."

"I thought he might be one of you chaps. Went to a publisher and told him his ideas for the book and came away with a contract for more than I expect to make in a lifetime."

"How come you know so much about it?"

"Well, I am a bookseller. Those on high want us to know in advance this isn't your average first novel. Let me cudgel the old brains and I'll give you his name."

I'm about to tell him not to bother when he grins. "Don't know how I could forget a name like that, except it puts you in mind of the Kray brothers, if you're not too young to remember their reign of terror. The last thing he sounds like is a criminal. Jess

Kray, that's the phenomenon."

I'd say I knew him if I could be sure of convincing this caricature that he isn't worth knowing. I bite my tongue until it feels as if my teeth are meeting, then I realise the driver has noticed the tears that have got away from me, and I could scream. He says no more until he stops to let me out of the car. "You ought to tell your people about this Kray. Sounds as if he has some ideas that bear thinking about."

The last thing I'll do is tell anyone about Kray, particularly when I remember him saying I should. I wait in my hotel room for my headache to let me see, then I go down to the dealers' room. Instead of books a lot of the tables are selling virtual reality viewers or pocket CD-ROM players. I can't find anything by Kray, and some of the dealers watch me as if I'm planning to steal from them, which makes me feel like throwing their tables over. Then the fat one who always wears a sombrero says "Can I do something for you?"

"Not by the look of it." That doesn't make him go away, and all I can think of is to confuse him. "You haven't got *The Word*."

"No, but Jess sent us each a copy of the cover," he says, and props up a piece of cardboard with letters in the middle of its right-hand side:

JESS KRAY
THE WORD

I can't tell if they're white on a black background or black on white, because as soon as I move an inch they turn into the opposite. I shut my eyes once I've seen it's going to be published by the dump that stopped sending me review copies. "What do you mean, he sent you it? He's just a writer."

"And he designed the cover, and he wants everyone to know what's coming, so he got the publisher to print enough cover proofs for us all in the business."

I'm not asking what Kray said about his book. When Fat in the Hat says "You can't keep your eyes shut forever" I want to shut his, especially when as soon as I open mine he says "Shall we put you down for a copy when it's published?"

"They'll send me one."

"I doubt it," he says, and he'll never know how close he came to losing the bone in his nose, except I have to take my head back to my room.

Maybe he wasn't just getting at me. Once I'm home I ring Kray's new publisher for a review copy. I call myself Jay Battis, the first name that comes into my head, and say I'm the editor of *Psychofant* and no friend of that total cynic Jeremy Bates. But the publicity girl says Kray's book isn't genre fiction, it's literature and they aren't sending it to fanzines.

So why should I care? Except I won't have her treating me as though I'm not good enough for Kray after I gave him more publicity than he deserved when he needed it most. And I remember him thanking me for helping—did he mean with this book? I ask the publicity bitch for his address, but she expects me to believe they don't know it. I could ask her who his agent is, but I've realised how I'd most like to get my free copy of his world-shaking masterpiece.

I don't go to Kath's shop, because I'd be noticed. On the day the book is supposed to come out I go to the biggest bookshop in Chelsea. There's a police car in front, and the police are making them move out of the window a placard that's a big version of the cover of *The Word*—I hear the police say it has been distracting drivers. I walk to a table with a pile of *The Word* on it and straight out with one in my hand, because the staff are busy with the police. Only I feel as if Kray's forgiving me for liberating his book, and it takes all my strength not to throw it away.

Even when I've locked my apartment door I feel watched. I hide the book under the bed while I fry some spaghetti and open a tin of salmon for dinner. Then I sit at the window and watch the police cars hunting and listen to the shouts and screams until it's dark. When I begin to feel as if the headlights are searching for me I close the curtains, but then I can't think of anything to do except read the book.

Only the first few pages. Just the prospect of more than a thousand of them puts me off. I can't stand books where the dialogue isn't in quotes and paragraphs keep beginning with "And". And I'm getting the impression that the words are slipping into my head before I can grasp them. Reading the book makes me feel I'm hiding in my room, shutting myself off from the world. I stuff *The Word* down the side of the bed where I can't see the cover playing its tricks, and switch on the radio.

Kray's still in my head. I'm hoping that since it's publication day I'll hear someone tearing him to bits. There isn't a programme about books any longer on the radio, just one about what they call the arts. They're reviewing an Eskimo rock band and an exhibition of sculptures made out of used condoms and a production of *Jesus Christ Superstar* where all the performers are women in wheelchairs, and I'm sneering at myself for imagining they would think Kray was worth their time and at the world for being generally idiotic when the presenter says "And now a young writer whose first novel has been described as a new kind of book. Jess Kray, what's the purpose behind *The Word?*"

"Well, I think it's in it rather than behind it if you look. And I'd say it may be the oldest kind of book, one that's been forgotten."

At first I don't believe it's him, because he has no accent at all. I make my head throb trying to remember what accent he used to have, and when I give up the presenter is saying "Is the narrator meant to be God?"

"I think the narrator has to be different for everyone, like God."

"You seem to want to be mysterious."

"Don't you think mystery has always been the point? That isn't the same as trying to hide. We've all read books where the writer tries to hide behind the writing, though of course it can't be done, because hiding reveals what you thought you were hiding..."

"Can you quote an example?"

"I'd rather say that every book you've ever read has been a refuge, and I don't want mine to be."

"Every book? Even the Bible? The Koran?"

"They're attempts to say everything regardless of how much they contradict themselves, and I think they make a fundamental error. Maybe Shakespeare saw the problem, but he couldn't quite solve it. Now it's my turn."

I'm willing the presenter to lose her temper, and she says "So to sum up, you're trying to top Shakespeare and the Bible and the rest of the great books."

"My book is using up a lot of paper. I think that if you can't put more into the world than you take out of it you shouldn't be here at all."

"As you say somewhere in *The Word*. Jess Kray, thank you."

Then she starts talking to a cretic—which is a cretin who thinks they're a critic, such as everyone who attacks my fanzines—about Kray and his book. When the cretic says she thinks the narrator might be Christ because of a scene where he sees the light beyond the mountain through the holes in his hands I start shouting at the radio for quite a time before I turn it off. I crawl into bed and can't stop feeling there's a light beside me to be seen if I open my eyes. I keep them closed all night and wake up with the impression that some of Kray's book is buried deep in my head.

For the first time since I can remember I'm looking forward to a day at the bank. I may even be able to stand the people on my side of the glass without grinding my teeth. But that afternoon Mag, one of the middle-aged girls, waddles in with an evening paper and nearly slaps me in the face with it as though it's my fault. "Will you look at this. Where will it stop. I don't know what the world is coming to."

CALL FOR BAN ON "BLASPHEMOUS" BOOK

I don't want to read any more, yet I grab the paper. It says that on the radio programme I heard Kray said his book was better than the Bible and people should read it instead. A bishop is calling for the police to prosecute, and some mob named Christ Will Rise is telling Christians to destroy *The Word* wherever they find it. So I can't help walking past the shop my copy came from, even though it isn't on my way home. And on the third day half a dozen Earnests with placards saying CHRIST NOT KRAY are picketing the shop.

The police apparently don't think they're worth more than cruising past, and I hope they'll get discouraged, because they're giving Kray publicity. But the next day there are eight of them, and twelve the day after, and at the weekend several Kray fans start reading *The Word* to the pickets to show them how they're wrong. And I feel as though I've had no time to breathe before there's hardly a shop in the country without clowns outside it reading *The Word* and the Bible or the Koran at one another. And then Kray starts touring all the shops and talking to the pickets.

I keep switching on the news to check if he's been scoffed into oblivion, but no such luck. All the time in my room I'm aware of his book in there with me. I'd throw it away except someone might end up reading it—I'd tear it up and burn it except then I'd be like the Christ Will Risers. The day everyone at the bank is talking about Kray being in town during my lunch hour I scrape my brains for something else to do, anything rather than be one of the mob. Only suppose this is the one that stops him? That's a spectacle I'd enjoy watching, so off I limp.

There must be at least a hundred people outside the bookshop. Someone's given Kray a chair to stand on, but Sod knows who's arranged for a beam of sunlight to shine on him. He's answering a question, saying "If you heard the repeats of my interview you'll know I didn't say my book was better than the Bible. I'm not sure what better means in that context. I hope my book contains all the great books."

And he grins, and I wait for someone to attack him, but nobody does, not even verbally. I feel my voice forcing its way out of my mouth, and all I can think of is the question vacuumheads ask writers at conventions. "Where did you get your ideas?"

So many people stare at me I think I've asked the question he didn't want asked. I feel as if he's using more eyes than a spider to watch me, more than a whole nest of spiders—more than there are people holding copies of his drivel. Kray himself is only looking in my general direction, trying to make me think he hasn't recognised me or I'm not worth recognising. "They're in my book."

I want to ask why he's pretending not to know me, except I can't be sure it'll sound like an accusation, and the alternative makes me cringe with loathing. But I'm not having any of his glib answers, and I shout "Who are?"

The nearest Kray fan stops filming him with a steadycam video and turns on me. "His ideas, he means. You're supposed to be talking about his ideas."

I won't be told what I'm supposed to be saying, especially not by a never-was who can't comb her hair or keep her lips still, and I wonder if she's trying to stop me asking the question I hadn't realised I was stumbling on. "Who did you meet in Florida?" I shout.

Kray looks straight at me, and it's as if his grin is carving up my head. "Some old people with some old ideas that were about to be lost. They're in my book. Everyone is in any book that matters."

Maybe he sees me sucking in my breath to ask about the three books he wants us to forget he wrote, because he goes on. "As I was about to say, all I'm asking is that we should respect one another. Do me the honour of not criticising *The Word* until you've read it. If anyone feels harmed by it, I want to know."

I might have vanished or never been there at all. When he pauses for a response I feel as if his grin has got stuck in my mouth. The mob murmurs, but nobody seems to want to speak up.

Any protest is being swallowed by vagueness. Then two minders appear from the crowd and escort Kray to a limo that's crept up behind me. I want to reach out to him and—I don't know what I want, and one of the minders pushes me out of the way. I see Kray's back, then the limo is speeding away and all the mob are talking to one another, and I have to take the afternoon off because I can't see the money at the bank.

Whenever the ache falters my head fills up with thoughts of Kray and his book. When I sense his book by me in the dark I can't help wishing on it—wishing him and it to a hell as everlasting as my headache feels. It's the first time I've wanted to believe in hell. Not that I'm so far gone I believe wishes work, but I feel better when the radio says his plan's gone wrong. Some Muslim leaders are accusing him of seducing their herd away from Islam.

I keep looking in the papers and listening in the night in case an ayatollah has put a price on his head. Some bookshops in cities that are overrun with Muslims are either hiding their copies of *The Word* or sending them back, and I wish on it that the panic will spread. But the next headline says he'll meet the Muslim leaders in public and discuss *The Word* with them.

A late-night so-called arts programme is to broadcast the discussion live. I don't watch it, because I don't know anyone who would let me watch their television, but when it's on I switch out my light and sit at my window. More and more of the windows out there start to flicker as if the city is riddled with people watching to see what will happen to Kray. I open my window and listen for shouting Muslims and maybe Kray screaming, but I've never heard so much quiet. When it starts letting my head fill up with thoughts I don't want to have, I go to bed and dream of Kray on a cross. But in the morning everyone at the bank is talking about how the Muslims ended up on Kray's side and how one of them from a university is going to translate *The Word* into whatever language Muslims use.

And everyone, even Mag who didn't know what the world was

coming to with Kray, is saying how they admire him or how they've fallen in love with him and the way he handled himself, and wish they'd gone to see him when he was in town. When I say I've got *The Word* and can't read it they all look as though they pity me. Three of them ask to borrow it, and I tell them to buy their own because I never paid for mine, which at least means nobody speaks to me much after that. I can still hear them talking about Kray and feel them thinking about him, and in the lunch hour two of them buy *The Word* and the rest, even the manager, want a read. I'm surrounded by Kray, choked by a mass of him. I'm beginning to wonder if anyone in the world besides me knows what he's really like. The bank shuts at last, and when I leave the building two Christ Will Risers are waiting for me.

Both of them wear suits like civil servants and look as though they spend half their lives scrubbing their faces and polishing the crosses at their throats. They both step forward as the sunlight grabs me, and the girl says "You knew him."

"Me, no, who? Knew who?"

Her boyfriend or whatever touches my arm likes a secret sign. "We saw you making him confess who he'd met."

"Let's sit down and talk," says the girl.

Every time they move, their crosses flash until my eyes feel like a whole graveyard of burnt crosses. At least the couple haven't swallowed *The Word*, and talking to them may be better than staying in my room. We find a bench that isn't full of unemployed and clear the McDonald's cartons off it, and the Risers sit on either side of me even though I've sat almost at the end of the bench. "Was he a friend of yours?" the girl says.

"Seems like he wants to be everyone's friend," I say.

"Not God's."

It doesn't matter which of them said that, it could have come from either. "So how much do you know about what happened in Florida?"

"As much as he said when I asked him."

"You must be honest with us. We can't do anything about him if we don't put our faith in the truth."

"Why not?"

That throws them, because they're obviously not used to thinking. Then they say "We need to know everything we can find out about him."

"Who's we?"

"We think you could be one of us. You're of like mind, we can tell."

That's one thing I'll never be with anyone. I nearly jump up and lean on their shining shampooed heads so they won't follow me, but I want to know what they know about Kray that I don't. "Then that must be why I asked him about Florida. All I know is that last time I met him he was going there and he wrote *The Word* when he came back. So what happened?"

They look at each other across me and then swivel their eyes to me. "There are people who came down a mountain almost a hundred years ago. We know he met them or someone connected with them. That has to be the source of his power. Nothing else could have let him win over Islam."

I wouldn't have believed anyone could talk less sense than Kray. "He was like that when he was just a fantasy fan. He's got a genius for charming everyone he meets and promoting himself."

"That must be how he learned the secret that came down the mountain. What else can you tell us?"

I don't mind making them more suspicious of Kray, but I won't have them thinking I tried to help them. "Nothing," I say, and get up.

They both reach inside their jackets for pamphlets. "Please take these. Our address is on the back whenever you want to get in touch."

I could tell them that's never and stuff their pamphlets in their faces, but at least while I've the pamphlets in my fist nobody can take me for a Jess Kray fan. At home I glance at them to see they're as stupid as I knew they would be, full of drone out of the Bible about the Apocalypse and the Antichrist and the Antifreeze and Sod knows what else. I shove them down the side of the bed and try to believe that I've helped the Risers get Kray. And I keep hoping until I see *Time* magazine with him on the cover.

By then half the bank has read *The Word*. I've seen them laughing or crying or going very still when they read it in their breaks, and when they finish it they look as if they have a secret they wish they could tell everyone else. I won't ask, I nearly chew my tongue off. Anyone who asks them about the book gets told "Read it" or "You have to find out for yourself", and I wonder if the book tells you to make as many people read it as you can, like they used to tell you on posters not to give away the end of films. I won't touch my copy of *The Word*, but one day I sneak into a bookshop to read the last page. Obviously it makes no sense, only I feel that if I read the page before it I'll begin to understand, because maybe it can be read backwards as well as forwards. I throw the book on the table and run out of the shop.

At least they've taken *The Word* out of the window to make room for another pound of fat in a jacket, but I keep seeing people reading it in the streets. Whenever I see anything flash in a crowd I'm afraid it's another copy drawing attention to itself. At home I feel it beginning to surround me in the night out there, and I tell myself I've one copy nobody is reading. But I have to take train rides into the country for walks to get away from it—they're the only way I can be certain I'm nowhere near anyone who's read it. And coming back from one of those rides, I see him watching me from the station bookstall.

He looks like a recruiting poster for himself that doesn't need to point a finger. While I'm pretending to flip through the magazine I knock all the copies of *Time* onto the floor of the booking hall, except for the one I shove down the front of my trousers. All the way home I feel my peter wiping itself on his mouth, and in my room I have a good laugh at my stain on his face before I turn to the pages about him.

The headline says WHAT IS THE WORD? in the same typeface as the cover of his book. Maybe the article will tell me what I need to put him out of my mind for good. But it says how he bought his parents a place in Florida with part of his advances, and how *The Word* is already being translated into thirteen languages, and I'm starting to puke. Then the hack tries to explain what makes *The Word* such a publishing phenomenon, as she calls it. And by the time I've finished nearly going blind with reading what she wrote I think it's another of Kray's tricks.

It says too much and nothing at all. She doesn't know if the word is the book or the narrator or the words that keep looking as if they've been put in by mistake. Kray told her that if a book wasn't language it was nothing. "So perhaps we should take him at his, you should forgive it, word." He said he just put the words on paper and it's for each reader to decide what they add up to. So she collected a gaggle of cretics and fakes who profess and that old joke "leading writers" and got them to discuss *The Word.*

If I'd been there I'd have mashed all their faces together. It was the funniest book someone had ever read, and the most moving someone else had, and everyone agreed with both of them. One woman thought it was like *The Canterbury Tales*, and then there's a discussion about whether it's told by one character or several or whether all the characters might be the same one in some sort of mental state or it's showing a new kind of relationship between them all. A professor points out that the Bible was written by a crowd of people but when you read it in translation you can't tell, whereas she thinks you can identify to the word where Kray's voices change, "as many voices as there are people who understand the book." That starts them talking about the idea in *The Word* that people in Biblical times lived longer because they were closer in time to the source, as if that explains why some people are living longer now and the rest of what's happening to us, the universe drifting closer to the state it was in before it formed. And there's crap about people sinning more so their sins will reach back to the Crucifixion because otherwise Christ won't come back, or maybe the book says people have to know when to stop before they have the opposite effect and throw everything off balance, only by now I'm having to run my finger under the words and read them out loud, though my voice makes my head worse. There are still columns to go, the experts saying how if you read *The Word* aloud it's poetry and how you'll find passages almost turning into music, and how there are developments of ideas from Sufism and the Upanishads and Buddhism and Baha'i and the Cabbala and Gnosticism, and Greek and Roman and older myths, and I scrape my fingernail over all this until I reach the end, someone saying "I think the core of this book may be the necessary myth for our time." And everyone agrees, and I tear up the magazine and try to sleep.

I can still hear them all jabbering as if Kray is using their voices to make people read his book to discover what they were raving about. I hear them in the morning on my way to the bank, and I wonder how many of them his publisher will quote on the paperback, and that's when I realise I'm dreading the paperback because so many more people will be able to afford it. I'm dreading being surrounded by people with Kray in their heads, because then the world will feel even more like somewhere I've wandered into by mistake. It almost makes me laugh to find I didn't want to be shown that people are as stupid as I've always thought they were.

When posters for the paperback start appearing on bus shelters and hoardings I have to walk about with my eyes half shut. The posters don't use the trick the cover did, but that must mean the publishers think that just the title and his name will sell the book. At the bank I keep being asked if I don't feel well, until I say I'm not getting my Sunday dinner any more since my mother had a heart attack and died in hospital, not that it's anyone's business, but as well as that I can hardly eat for waiting for the paperback.

The day I catch sight of one there's a march of lunatics demanding that the hospitals they've been thrown out of get reopened, and in the middle of all this a woman's sitting on a bench reading *The Word* as though she can't see or hear what's going on around her for the book. And then the man she's waiting for sits down by her and squashes his wet mouth on her cheek, and leans over to see what she's reading, and I see him start to read as if it doesn't matter where you open the book, you'll be drawn in. And when I run to the bank one of the girls asks me if I know when the paperback is coming out, and saying I don't know makes me feel I'm trying to stop something that can't be stopped.

Or am I the only one who can? I spend the day trying to remember where I put the interview with him. Despite whoever stole all the copies of *PotMam* at Contamination, I should still have the tape. I look under my clothes and the plates and the tins and in the tins as well, and under the pages of the magazine I tore up, and under the towels on the floor in the corner, and among the bits of glasses I've smashed in the sink. It isn't anywhere. My mother must have thrown it out one of the days she came to clean my room. I start screaming at her until I lose my voice, by which time I've thrown just about everything movable out of the window. They're demolishing the houses opposite, so some more rubbish in the street won't make any difference, and my fellow rats in the building must be too scared to ask what I'm doing, unless they're too busy reading *The Word.*

By the end of the week, two of the slaves at the bank have the paperback and will lend it to anyone who asks. And I don't know when they start surrounding me with Kray's words. Most of the time—Sod, all the time—I know they're saying things they've heard someone else say, but after a while I notice they've begun speaking in a way that's meant to show they're quoting. Like the girl at the window by mine would start talking about a murder mystery on television and the one next to her would say "The mystery is around you and in you" and they'd laugh as if they were sharing a secret. Or one would ask the time and her partner in the comedy team would say "Time is as soon as you make it." And all sorts of other crap: "Look behind the world" or "You're the shadow of the infinite," which the manager says once as if he's topping everyone else's quotes. And before I know it at least half the slaves don't say "Good morning" any more, they say "What's the word?"

That makes the world feel like a headache. People say it in the street too, and when they come up to my window, until I wonder if I was wrong to blame my mother for losing the tape, if someone else might have got into my room. By the time the next catch-phrase takes root in the dirt in people's heads I can't control my-self—when I hear one of the girls respond to another "As Kray would say."

"Is there anything he doesn't have something to say about?"

I think I'm speaking normally enough, but they cover their ears before they shake their heads and look sad for me and chorus "No."

"Sod, listening to you is like listening to him."

"Maybe you should."

"Maybe he will."

"Maybe everyone will."

"Maybe is the future."

"As Kray would say."

"You know you're the only one who hasn't read him, Jeremy?"

"Thank Sod if it keeps me different."

"Unless we find ourselves in everybody else..."

"As fucking Kray would say."

A woman writing a cheque gasps, and another customer clicks his tongue like a parrot, and I'm sure they're objecting to me daring to utter a bad word about their idol. None of the slaves speaks to me all day, which would be more of a relief if I couldn't feel them thinking Kray's words even when they don't speak them. I assume the manager didn't hear me, since he was in his office telling some-one the bank is going to repossess their house. But on Monday morning he calls me in and says "You'll have been aware that there's been talk of further rationalisation."

He was talking before that, only I was trying to see where he's hidden *The Word.* At least he doesn't sound like Kray. "Excuse me, Mr Bates, but are there any difficulties you feel I should know about?"

"With what?"

"I'd like to give you a chance to explain your behaviour. You're aware that the bank expects its staff to be smart and generally presentable."

I hug myself in case that hides whatever he's complaining about and hear my armpits squelch, and me saying "I thought you were supposed to see yourself in me."

"That was never meant to be used as an excuse. Have you really nothing more to say?"

I can't believe I tried to defend myself by quoting Kray. I chew my tongue until it hurts so much I have to stick it out. "I should advise you to seek some advice, Mr Bates," says the manager. "I had hoped to break this to you more gently, but I must say I can see no reason to. Due to the economic climate I've been asked to propose further cuts in staff, and you will appreciate that your attitude has aided my decision."

"Doesn't Kray have anything to say about fixing the economy?"

"I believe he does in world terms, but I fail to see how that helps our immediate situation."

The manager's beginning to look reluctantly sympathetic—he must think I've turned out to be one of them after all, and I won't have him thinking that. "If he tried I'd shove his book back where it came from."

The manager looks as if I've insulted him personally. "I can see no profit in prolonging this conversation. If you wish to work your notice I must ask you to take more care with your appearance and, forgive my bluntness, to treat yourself to a bath."

"How often does he say I've got to have one?" I mean that as a sneer, but suppose it sounds like a serious question? "Not that I give a shit," I say, which isn't nearly enough. "And when I do I can use his book to wipe my arse on. And that goes for your notice as well, because I don't want to see any of you again or anyone else who's got room in their head for that, that…" I can't think of a word bad enough for Kray, but it doesn't matter, because by now I'm backing out of the office. "Just so everyone knows I know I'm being fired because of what I say about him," I add, raising my voice so they'll hear me through their hands over their ears. Then I manage to find my way home, and the locks to stick the keys in, and my bed.

There's almost nothing else in my room except me and *The Word*. So I still have a job, to stay here to make sure it's the copy nobody reads. I do that until the bank sends me a cheque for the money they must wish they didn't owe me, and I remember all my money I forgot to take with me when I escaped from the bank.

I'm waiting when they open. At first I think the slaves are pretending not to know me, then I wonder if they're too busy thinking Kray's thoughts. A slave takes my cheque and my withdrawal slip and goes away for longer than I can believe it would take even her to think about it, then I see the manager poke his head out of his office to spy on me while I'm tearing up a glossy brochure about how customers can help the bank to help the Third World. I see him tell the clerk to give me what I want, then he pulls in his head like a tortoise that's been kicked, and it almost blinds me to realise he's afraid of what I am. Only what am I?

The slave stuffs all my money in an envelope and drops it in the trough under the window, the trough that always made me wonder which side the pigs were on. I shove the envelope into my armpit and leave behind years of my life. I'm walking home as fast as I can, through the streets where every shop either has a sale on or is closing down or both, when I see Kray's face.

It's a drawing on the cover of just about the only magazine that is still about books. I have to find out what he's up to, but with the money like a cancer under my arm I can't be sure of liberating the magazine without people noticing. I go into the bookshop and grab it off the rack, and people backing away make me feel stronger. I've only read how *The Word* is shaping up to outsell the Bible world-wide, and how some campus cult is saying there's a different personal message in it for everybody and anyone who can't read it should have it read to them, when a bouncer trying to look like a policeman tells me to buy the rag or leave. I've read all I need to, and I have all I need. The money is to give me time to do what I have to do.

Only I'm not sure what that is. The longer I stay in my room, the more I'm tempted to look in *The Word* for a clue. It's trying to trick me into believing there's no help outside its pages, but I've something else to read. I find the Christ Will Rise pamphlets that *The Word* has done its best to tear up and shove out of my reach, and when I've dragged them and my face out of the dust under the bed I manage to smooth out the address.

It's down where most of the fires in the streets are and the police drive round in armoured cars when they go there at all, and no cameras are keeping watch, and hardly any helicopters. By now it's dark. People are doing things to each other standing up in door-ways if they aren't prowling the streets in dozens searching for less than themselves. I'm afraid they may set fire to me, because I see dogs pulling apart something charred that looks as if it used to be someone, but nobody seems to think I'm worth bothering with, which is their loss.

The Risers' sanctuary is in the middle of a block of hundred-year-old houses, some of which have roofs. Children are running into one house holding a cat by all its legs, but I can't see anyone else. I feel the front steps tilt and crunch together as I climb to the Risers' door, and I hold onto the knocker to steady myself, though it makes my fingers feel as if they're crumbling. I'm about to slam the knocker against the rusty plate when a fire in a ruin across the street lights up the room inside the window next to me.

It's full of chairs around a table with pamphlets on it. Then the fire jerks higher, and I see they aren't piles of pamphlets, they're two copies of *The Word*. The books start to wobble like two blocks of gelatin across the table towards me, and I nearly wrench the knocker off the door with trying to let go of it. I fall down the steps and don't stop running until I'm locked in my room.

I watch all night in case I've been followed. Even after the last television goes out I can't sleep. And when the dawn brings the wagons to clean up the blood and vomit and empty cartridges I don't want to sleep, because I've remembered that the Risers aren't the only other people who know what Kray was.

I go out when the streets won't be crawling—when the taken care of have gone to work and the beggars are counting their pennies. When I reach Everybody's Fantasy it looks as if the books in the window and the Everything Half Price sign have been there for months. The rainy dirt on the window stops me reading the spines on the shelf where Kray would be. I'm across the road in a burned-out house, waiting for a woman with three Dobermans to pass so I can smash my way into the shop with a brick, when Kath arrives in a car with bits of it scraping the road. He doesn't look interested in why I'm there or in anything else, especially selling books, so I say "You're my last hope."

"Yeah, okay." It takes him a good few seconds to get around to saying "What?"

"You've got some books I want to buy."

"Yeah?" He comes to as much life as he's got and wanders into the shop to pick up books strewn over the floor. "There they are."

I think he's figured out which books I want and why until I realise he means everything in the shop. I'm heading for the shelf when I see *The Word, The Word, The Word, The Word*... "Where's *A Touch of Other*?" I nearly scream.

"Don't know it."

"Of course you do. Jess Kray's first novel and the two that go with it. He signed them all when you didn't want him to. You can't have sold them, crap like them."

"Can't I?" Kath scratches his head as if he's digging up thoughts. "No, I remember. He bought the lot. Must have been just about when *The Word* was due."

"You realise what he was up to, don't you?"

"Being kind. Felt guilty about leaving us with all those books after nobody came, so he bought them back when he could afford to. Wish we still had them. I've never seen them offered for sale."

"That's because he doesn't want anyone to know he wrote them, don't you see? Otherwise even the world might wonder how someone like that could have written the thing he wants everyone to buy."

"You can't have read *The Word* if you say that. It doesn't matter what came before it, only what will happen when everyone's learned from it."

He must have stoned whatever brains he had out of his head. "I felt like you do about him," he's saying now, "but then I got to know him."

"You know him? You know where I can find him?"

"Got to know him in his book."

"But you've got the address where you sent him his books."

"Care of his publishers."

"He didn't even give you his address and you think he's your friend?"

"He was moving. He's got nothing to hide, you have to believe that." Having to give me so many answers so fast seems to have used Kath up, then his face rouses itself. "If you want to get to know him as he is, he's supposed to be at Consummation."

"I've given up on fans. The people I meet every day are bad enough."

Kath's turning over magazines on the counter like a cat trying to cover its turds. "There'll be readings from *The Word* for charity and a panel about it, and he's meant to be there. We'd go, only we've not long had a kid."

"Don't tell me there'll be someone growing up without *The Word*."

"No, we'd like her to see him one day. I was just telling you we can't afford to go." He shakes two handfuls of fanzines until a flyer drops out of one. "See, there he is."

The flyer is for Consummation, which is two weeks away in Birmingham, and it says the Sunday will be Jess Kray Day. I manage not to crumple much of it up. "Can I have this?"

"I thought you didn't want to know him."

"You've sold me." I shove the flyer into my pocket. "Thanks for giving me what I was looking for," I say, and leave him fading with his books.

I don't believe a whole sigh fie convention can be taken in by Kray. Fen are stupid, Sod knows, but in a different way—thinking they're less stupid than everyone else is. I'll know what to do when I see them and him. The two weeks seem not so much to pass as not to be there at all. On the Friday morning I have a bath so I won't draw attention to myself until I want to. For the first time ever I don't hitch to a convention, I go by train to be in time to spy out the situation. Once I'm in my seat I stay there, because I've seen one woman reading *The Word* and I don't want to see how many other passengers are. I stare at streets of houses with steel shutters over the windows and rivers covered with chemicals and forests that children keep setting fire to, but I can feel Kray's words hatching in all the nodding heads around me.

The convention hotel is five minutes' walk from the station. After about ten beggars I pretend I'm alone in the street. The hotel is booked solid as a fan's cranium, and the hotel next to it, and I have to put up with one where the stairs lurch as if I'm drunk and my room smells of someone's raincoat and old cigarettes. It won't matter, because I'll be spending as much time with the fen as I can bear. I go to the convention hotel while it's daylight and there are police out of their vehicles. And the first thing the girl at the registration desk with a ring in her nose and six more in her ears says is "Have you got *The Word*?"

My face goes hard, but I manage to say "It's at home."

"If you'd like one to have with you, they're free with membership."

It'll be another nobody else can read. I tell her my name's Jay Batt and pin my badge on when she's written it, and squeeze the book in my right hand so hard I can almost feel the words mashing together. "Is he here yet?"

"He won't be."

"But he's why I'm here. I was promised he was coming."

She must think I sound the same kind of disappointed as her. "He said he would be when we wrote to him, only now he has to be in the film about him they'll be televising next month. Shall I tell you what he said? That now we've got *The Word* we don't need him."

I know that's garbage, but I'm not sure why. I bite my tongue so I won't yell, and when I see her sympathising with the tears in my eyes I limp off to the bar. It's already full of more people than seats, and I know most of them—I've written about them in my fanzines. I'm wondering how I can get close enough to find out what they really think about *The Word* when they start greeting me like an old friend. Two people have offered to buy me a drink before I realise why they're behaving like this—because I've got *The Word*.

I down the drinks, and more when they're offered, and make sure everyone knows I won't buy a round. I'm trying to infuriate someone as much as their forgiveness infuriates me, because then maybe they'll argue about Kray. But whatever I say about him and his lies they just look more understanding and wait patiently for me to understand. The room gets darker as my eyes fill up with the dirt and smoke in the air, and faces start to melt as if *The Word* has turned them into putty. Then I'm screaming at the committee members and digging my nails into the cover of the book. "Why would anyone be making a film about him? More likely he was afraid he'd meet someone here who knows what he wants us to forget he wrote."

"You mustn't say that. He sent us this, look, all about the film." The chairman takes a glossy brochure out of his briefcase. The sight of Kray grinning on the cover almost blinds me with rage, but I manage to read the name of the production company. "And they're going to do a live discussion with him after the broadcast," the chairman says.

I run after my balance back to my hotel. I can hear machine-guns somewhere, and I have to ring the bell three times before the armed night porter lets me in, but they can't stop me now. I haul myself up to my room, snapping a banister in the process, and fall on the bed to let my headache come. Whenever it lessens I think of another bit of the letter I'm going to write. The night and the sounds of gunfire falter at last, and the room fades into some kind of reality. It's like being part of the cover of a book nobody wants to take out of a window, but they won't be able to ignore me much longer.

I write the letter and check out of the hotel, telling the receptionist I've been called away urgently, and fight my way through the pickpockets to the nearest post office, where I get the address of the television channel. Posting the letter reminds me of going to church when I had to live with my parents, where they used to put things in your mouth in front of the altar. As soon as the letter is out of my hands I don't know if I feel empty or unburdened, and I can't remember exactly what I wrote.

I spend Sunday at home trying to remember. Did I really claim I was the first to spread the word about Kray? Did I really call my-self Jude Carrot because I was afraid he'd remember the interview and tell the producer not to let me anywhere near? Won't he just say he's never heard of me? I can't think how that idea makes me feel. I left the other copy of *The Word* in my hotel room as if it was the Bible, and I have to stop myself from throwing the one under the bed out of the window to give them something to fight over besides the trash in the street.

On Monday I know the letter has arrived. Maybe it'll take a few hours to reach the producer of the discussion programme, since I didn't know his name. By Tuesday it must have got to him, and by Wednesday he should have written to me. But Thursday comes, and I watch the postman dodging in and out of his van while his partner rides shotgun, and there's no letter for me.

Twice I hear the phone in the hall start to ring, but it could just be army trucks shaking the house. I start trying to think of a letter I could write under another name, saying I know things about Kray nobody else does, only I can't think of a letter that's different enough. I go to bed to think, then I get up to, and keeping doing those is Thursday and Friday morning. Then I hear the van screech to a halt just long enough for the postman to stick a letter through the door without getting out of his cabin, because presumably they can't afford to pay his partner any more, then it screeches away along the sidewalk. And when I look down the stairs I see the logo of the television company on the envelope.

I'd open it in the hall except I find I'm afraid to read what it says. I remember I'm naked and cover my peter with it while I run upstairs, though everyone in the house is scared to open their door if they hear anyone else. I lock all my locks and hook up the chains and wipe my hands on my behind so the envelope won't slip out of them, then I tear it almost in half and shake the letter flat.

```
Dear Mr "Carrot"
Jess Kray says
```

Suddenly my hands feel like gloves someone's just pulled their hands out of, and when I can see again I have to fetch the letter from under the bed. I'm already struggling to think of a different name to sign on the next letter I send, though since now I'll know who the producer is, should I phone them? I poke at my eyes until they focus enough that I can see her name is Tildy Bacon, then I make them see what she wrote.

```
Dear Mr "Carrot"
Jess Kray says he will look forward
to seeing you and including you in
our discussion on the 25th.
```

There's more about how they'll pay my expenses and where I'm to go, but I fall on the bed, because I've just discovered I don't know what to do after all. It doesn't matter, I'll know what to say when the cameras are on and the country's watching me. Only something's missing from that idea and the absence keeps pecking at my head. It feels like an intruder in my room, one I can't see that won't leave me alone. Maybe I know what I'm trying not to think, but a week goes by before I realise: I can't be certain of exposing Kray unless I read *The Word*.

I spend a day telling myself I have to, and the next day I drag the book out of its hiding place and claw off the dusty cobwebs. I stare at the cover until it feels as if it's stuck behind my eyes, then I scream at myself to make me open it. As soon as I can see the print I start reading, but it feels as if Kray's words and the noises of marching drums and sirens and gunfire are merging into a substance that's filling up my head before I can stop it, and I have to shut the book. There's less than a week before I'm on television, and all I can think of that may work is being as far away from people as I can get when I read the book.

The next day is Sunday, which makes no difference, since there are as many people wandering around the countryside with nothing else to do any day of the week. I tear the covers off a Christ Will Rise pamphlet and wrap them round *The Word* before I head for

Kings Cross, and I'm sure some of the people I avoid look at it to see if it's *The Word*. I thump on the steel shutter until the booking clerk sells me a ticket. While I'm waiting for the train I see through the reinforced glass of the bookstall that most of the newspapers are announcing a war that's just begun in Africa. I catch myself wondering if *The Word* has been translated in those countries yet, and then I imagine a world where there are no wars because everyone's too busy reading *The Word* and thinking about it and talking about it, and my fingernails start aching from gripping the book so I won't throw it under a train.

When my train leaves I'm almost alone on it, but I see more people than I expect in the streets. Quite a few seem to be gathering in a demolished church, and I see a whole crowd scattered over a park, being read to from a book—I can't decide whether it's black or white. All their faces are turned to the sun as if they don't know they're being blinded. As the city falls away I'm sure I can feel all those minds clogged with Kray trying to drag mine back and having to let go like old tasteless chewing gum being pulled out of my head. Then there are only fields made up of lines waiting to be written on, and hedges blossoming with litter, and hours later mountains hack their way up through fields and forests as if the world is still crystallising. In the midst of the mountains I get off at a station that's no more than two empty platforms, and climb until I'm deep in a forest and nearly can't breathe for climbing. I sit on a fallen tree, and there's nothing to do except read. And I make myself open *The Word* and read as fast as I can.

I won't look up until I've finished. I can feel his words crowding into my head and breeding there, but I have to understand what he's put into the world before I confront him. The only sound is of me turning pages and ripping each one out as I finish it, but I sense the trees coming to read over my shoulder, and moss oozing down them to be closer to the book, and creatures running along branches until they're above my head. I won't look; I only read faster, so fast that the book is in my head before I know. However much there is of it, I'm stronger—out here it's just me and the book. I wonder suddenly if the pages may be impregnated with some kind of drug, but if they are I've beaten it by throwing away the pages, because you must have to be holding the whole book for the drug to work. I've no idea how long I've been reading the book aloud, but it doesn't matter if it helps me see what Kray is up to. Though my throat is aching by the time I've finished, I manage a laugh that makes the trees back away. I fall back with my face to the clouds and try to think what the book has told me that he wouldn't want anyone to know.

My body's shaking inside and out, and I feel as if my brain is too. There was something about panic in *The Word*, but if I think of it, will that show me how the book is causing it, or won't I be able to resist swallowing *The Word* as the cure? I'm already remembering, and digging my fingernails into my temples can't crush the thought. Kray says we'll all experience a taste of the panic Christ experienced as we approach the time when the world is changed. I feel the idea cracking open in my brain, and as I fight it I see in a flash what he was trying not to admit by phrasing it that way. He wanted nobody to know that he is panicking—that he has something to be afraid of.

I sit up and crouch around myself until I stop shaking, then I go down through the forest. The glade papered with *The Word* seems to have a meaning I no longer need to understand. Some of the pages look as if they're reverting to wood. The night comes down the forest with me, and in a while a train crawls out of it. I go home and lock myself in.

Now it takes me all my time to hold *The Word* still in my head. The only other thing I need to be aware of is when the television company sends me my train ticket, but everything around me seems on the point of making a move. Whenever I hear a car it sounds about to reveal it's a mail-van. At least that helps me ignore my impression that all I can see of the world is poised to betray itself. If this is how having read *The Word* feels...

The next day the mail-van screeches past my building, and the day after that. Suppose the letter to me has been stolen, or someone at the television company has stopped it from being sent? I'll pay my own fare and get into the discussion somehow. But the ticket finally arrives, which may mean they'll try and steal it from my room.

I sit with the ticket between my teeth and watch the street and listen for them setting up whatever they may use to smash my door in. Suppose the room itself is the trap? Or am I being made to think that so I'll be driven out of it? I wrap the ticket in some of a Christ Will Rise pamphlet so that the ink won't run when I take it with me to the bathroom, and on the last morning I have a long bath that feels like some kind of ritual. That would be a good time for them to come for me, but they don't, nor on my way to the station, though I'm sure I notice people looking at me as if they know something about me. For the first time since I can remember there are no sounds of violence in the streets, and that makes me feel there are about to be.

On the train I sit where I can watch the whole compartment, and see the other passengers pretending not to watch me. All the way to Hyde Park Corner I expect to be headed off. I'm trudging up the slope to the hotel when a limo pulls up in front of the glass doors and two minders climb out before Kray does. As he unbends he looks like a snake standing on its tail. I pretend to be interested in the window of a religious bookshop in case he tries to work on me before the world is watching. I see copies of *The Word* next to the Bible and the Koran, and Kray's reflection merging with his book as he goes into the hotel. He must have noticed me, so why is he leaving me alone? Because passiveness is the trick he's been playing on me ever since I read *The Word*—doing nothing so I'll be drawn towards him and his words. It's the trick he's been playing on the world.

Knowing that makes me impatient to finish. I wait until I see him arrive in the penthouse suite, then I check in. My room is more than twice the size of the one I left at home. The world is taking notice of me at last. I drink the liquor in the refrigerator while I have another bath, and ignore the ringing of the phone until I think there's only just time to get to the studio before the discussion starts.

A girl's face on the phone screen tells me my taxi's waiting. As soon as we're in it she wants to know everything about me, but I won't let her make me feel I don't know what I am. I shrug at her until she shuts up. There are no other cars on the road, and I wonder if there's a curfew or everyone's at home waiting for Kray and me.

Five minutes later the taxi races into the forecourt of the television studios. The girl with not much breath rushes me past a guard at the door and another one at a desk and down a corridor that looks as if it never ends. I think that's the trick they were keeping in store for me, but then she steers me left into a room, and I'm surrounded by voices and face to face with Kray.

There are about a dozen other people in the room. The remains of a buffet are on a table and scattered around on paper plates. A woman with eyes too big for her face says she's Tildy Bacon and hands me a glass of wine while a girl combs my hair and powders my face, and I feel as if they're acting out some ritual from *The Word*. Kray watches me as he talks and grins at some of his cronies, and once the girl has finished with me he puts a piece of cake on a plate and brings it over. "You must have something, Jeremy. You look as if you've been fasting for the occasion."

So does he. He looks thinner and older, as if he's put almost all of himself into his book, or is he trying to trick me into thinking he'll be easy to deal with? I take the plate and wash a bite of the cake down with some wine, and he gives me the grin. "It's nearly time."

Is he talking about the programme I can see behind him on a monitor next to a fax machine? Someone who might be a professor or a student is saying that nobody he's met has been unchanged by *The Word* and that he thinks it promises every reader the essential experience of their life. Kray's watching my face, but I won't let him see I know how much crap the screen is talking until we're on the air. Then Tildy Bacon says to everyone "Shall we go up? Bring your drinks."

As the girl who ought to learn how to breathe ushers people towards the corridor, Tildy Bacon steps in front of me and looks me in the face. So they've saved stopping me until the last possible moment. I'll wait until everyone else is out of the room, then I'll do whatever needs to be done to make certain she can't follow me and throw me off the air. But she says "We had to ask Jess how to bill you on screen since you weren't here."

If she thinks I'm going to ask what he said I was, she can go on thinking. "I'm sure he knows best," I tell her with a grin that may look like his for all I care, and dodge around her before she can delay me any further, and follow the procession along the corridor.

At first the set-up in the studio looks perfect. The seven of us, including Kray, will sit on couches around a low table with glasses and a jug of water on it while Kray's minders have to stay on the far side of a window. Only I haven't managed to overtake the procession, so how can I get close to him? Then he says "Sit next to me, Jeremy," and pats a leather cushion, and before I have time to wonder what he's up to I've joined him.

Everyone else sitting down sounds like something leathery stirring in its sleep. The programme about Kray is on a monitor in a corner of the studio. A priest says he believes the secret of *The Word* needs to be understood, then the credits are rolling, and a woman who I hadn't even realised was going to run the discussion leans across the table and waits for a red light to signal her. Then she says "So, Jess Kray, what's your secret?"

He grins at her and the world. "If I have one it must be in my book."

A man with holes in his purple face where spots were says "In other words, if you revealed the secret it wouldn't sell."

Is there actually someone here besides me who doesn't believe in *The Word?* Kray grins at him. "No, I'm saying the secret must be different for everyone. It isn't a question of commerce. In some parts of the world I'm giving the book away."

The holey man seems satisfied, but a woman with almost more hair on her upper lip than on her scalp says "To achieve what?"

"Peace?"

Good Sod, Kray really does believe his book can put a stop to wars. Or does he mean he won't be peaceful until the whole world has *The Word* inside them? The woman who was given the signal leans across the table again, reaching for Kray with her perfume and her glittering hands and her hair swaying like oil on water. She means to turn the show into a discussion, which will give him the chance not to be watched all the time by the camera. I'll say anything to bother him, even before I know what. "It's supposed to be…"

That heads her off, and everyone looks at me. Then I hear what I'm going to say—that the secret of *The Word* is supposed to be some kind of eternal life. But there is no secret in *The Word,* that's why I'm here. "Jeremy?" Kray says.

I'm wondering if *The Word* has got inside me without my knowing—if it was making me say what I nearly said and that's why he is encouraging me. He wants me to say that for him, and he's talking about peace, which I already knew was his weapon, and suddenly I see what everything has been about. It's as if a light is shining straight into my eyes, and I don't care if it blinds me. "He's supposed to be Christ," I shout.

There's some leathery movement, then someone I don't need to see says "All the characters are clearly aspects of him."

"We're talking about the narrator of *The Word,*" the television woman explains to the camera, and joins in. "I took him to be some kind of prophet."

"Christ was a prophet," says a man who I can just about see is wearing a turban.

"Are we saying—" the television woman begins, but she can't protect Kray from me like that. "He knows I didn't mean anyone in his book," I shout. "I mean him."

The words are coming out faster than I can think, but they feel right. "If people don't believe in him they won't believe in his book. And they won't believe in him unless he can save himself."

Ideas are fighting in my head as if *The Word* is trying to come clear. If Christ came back now he'd have to die to make way for a religion that works better than his did, or would it be the opposite of Christ who'd try to stop all the violence and changes in the world? Either way… I'm going blind with panic, because I can feel Kray close to me, willing me to… He wants me to go on speaking while my words are out of control—because they're his, or because I won't be able to direct them at him? Then I realise how long he's been silent, and I think he wants me to speak to him so he can speak to me. Is the panic I'm suffering his? He's afraid—afraid of me, because I'm…

"I think it's time we moved on," the television woman says, but she can't make anything happen now. I turn and look at him.

He's waiting for me. His grin is telling me to speak—to say whatever I have to say, because then he'll answer and all that the world will remember hearing is him. It's been that way ever since the world heard of him. I see that now, but he's let me come too close. As I open my mouth I duck my head towards him.

For a moment it seems I'm going to kiss him. I see his lips parting, and his tongue feeling his teeth, and the blood in his eyes, and the fear there at last. I duck lower and go for his throat. I know how to do it from biting my tongue, and now I don't need to restrain myself or let go. Someone is screaming, it sounds as if the world is, but it can't be Kray, because I've torn out his voice. I lift my head and spit it back into his face.

It doesn't blot out his eyes. They meet mine, and there's forgiveness in them, or something even worse—fulfilment? Then his head falls back, opening his throat so I'm afraid he'll try and talk through it, and he throws his arms wide for the cameras. That's all I see, because there's nothing in my eyes now except light. But it isn't over, because I can still taste his voice like iron in my mouth.

Words are struggling to burst out of my head, and I don't know what they are. Any moment Kray's minders or someone will get hold of me, but if I can just… I bang my knees against the table to find it, and hear the glasses clash against the jug. I throw myself forwards and find one, and a hand grabs my arm, but I wrench myself free and shove the glass against my teeth until it breaks. Now the light feels as if it's turning into pain that is turning into the world, but whose pain is it—Kray's or mine? Hands are pulling at me, and I've no more time to think. As I make myself chew and swallow, at least I'm sure I'll never say another word.

WELCOME HOME, ALL YOU UNINVITED

ERIK T. JOHNSON

"Without attempting to explicate something for which there are likely no words, I simply state that at a single fell stroke, I have lost any tranquility and peace of mind which I ever achieved. I stand face-to-face with nothingness..."

- Gustav Mahler, letter to Bruno Walter [1909]

I. WHAT THE TOILET TELLS ME

Mornings had been bad for the past half year, since the night Wilson got the ass-kicking of his life. It was like this: First, Wilson would wake up but couldn't manage to open his eyes. Instead, he'd vividly imagine—a vision of hearing—the first stalking bars of Mahler's 10th Symphony, which death had distracted the composer from finishing.

Tentative, 1911 violas would probe the *andante* darkness of Wilson's skull, like the fingertips of a man buried alive as they trace coffin's lid—almost, but not yet ready, to dare acknowledge the possibility of his predicament...

And then, this day [as every other], Wilson would open his eyes, with a weak, clairvoyant taste in his mouth, too distilled with spit for interpretation. Who knows? Perhaps it meant he would compose again...in the meantime, it was no surprise that the only music in his head was courtesy of Gustav Mahler.

It was the legendary late-20th century composer, Androsaur Flekt, who'd introduced him to Mahler's works; and it was the symphonies that most inspired Wilson to push the conflicting boundaries of his own, ineffable compositions. Over decades of intense study he'd learned to *watch* Mahler's music, observing predatory tension within the spectrality; certain passages—the opening of the 3rd Symphony, for example—resembled nothing so much as a movie-monster that, slowly unveiled by dispersing murk, lies on the ground—surely it's dead?—but there are 25 minutes left until the credits ... you couldn't turn your back on these orchestrations; they threatened to incarnate. They would have Nephilim bones and stampeding plans.

Perhaps Wilson was conceited in thinking that he alone had the key to this secret agenda of Mahler's music, though you couldn't blame him for thinking so: If, as Wilson believed, Mahler's music was a struggle to fight its way into corporeality, then he and Wilson shared something remarkably rare: The attempt at impossible transformation—though Wilson's efforts were made in the opposite direction, for Wilson's mission was to convert his anatomical malformations into music as far from flesh as stars are from questions.

... Bleary and hemorrhaging borrowed, unfinished masterpieces ... nothing but his bladder's insistence got him out of bed ...

Androsaur Flekt had been equally irrepressible, and as close to an internal organ as anything outside could be, that drives you nuts but also gifts supreme relief; and besides—and most importantly—you need it. He missed his mentor and friend—no mere appendix—his only *human being*, really [every other person was too flat, the joyful ones the worst—boring and insipid and popular as dancing Keith Haring figures].

Flekt would've known [or commanded] what Wilson should do now, and if Wilson pointed out that Androsaur never took his own advice, he'd just laugh and his eyes would shine like coronation crowns beneath the befurred rim of his faux-Yeti hat:

"There's nothing hypocritical about being hypocritical, eh, Feffy?"

Most of all, Wilson yearned for those occasions when, against all reasonable probability, he and Androsaur would separately conceive of and blurt out the same odd thing at the same moment; quite simply, it made him be not alone in the world—a rare feeling. Like the time Xenakis asked them, at the premiere of one of his monotonously "immersive" installations, what they'd thought. To which Flekt and Furst replied, stereophonically:

"Shit sandwich without the bread!"

He'd been dead—what? 10, 11 years ... lately, Wilson felt a recent *departure* of Flekt—a sense of his having-just-left after a visit; and he'd look around to see if he'd forgotten anything—much the way one returns to open an empty refrigerator over and over. The feeling could be so uncanny at times; he had even briefly wondered if Flekt might be haunting him. But that was too idiotic for serious consideration—it being hard enough to believe in life *during* life.

Wilson's right hand burned with 1,000 phantom limb violations. He refused to pay it any mind, instead observing the lack of his impression in the rumpled bed sheets, sodden gray as the bloated sky pressed against the vaulted windows. A shower was likely, but would offer no relief in this Chinatown summer, when the rain smelled like street-piss and the pissed-on streets smelled like shit ... enough, bladder! He stumbled through a paradoxically barren mess, reminiscent of the last stages of garage sales, junky miscellanies hauled curbside [PLEASE TAKE! FREE!], and he tiptoed over green-schmeared bagels and a gated community's worth of holiday junk mail—since the attack, he'd dreaded clean-up so much that he'd even stopped masturbating.

At last Wilson reached the seven solemn cairns of stale clothing, beyond which lay the bathroom, clean and yet dingy in an Eastern Bloc fashion. He sat on the toilet, elbows to thighs and forehead tipped in hands, sinking and insufferable and beyond heartbreak, a faithful widow remembering her wedding vows.

An old, rolled-up copy of *Art Now! [Outsider Art Special]* stuck out a bag of popcorn kernels. He shook it loose; opened to a dog-eared page representing an early press "appearance." Maybe his music was gone, but his memory was strong—viciously so, perhaps—and he didn't really look at the 1-page feature as he read:

HE SINGS THE BODY ECCENTRIC

Sterling Prizewinner Wilson Furst completes
the *Art! Now!* Questionnaire

Q: What exactly is your fefhorn?

A: As far as I know it's unique. I suppose you
could say it resembles something out of Hierony-
mus Bosch. I'm a private person, if that's what I
am, so I won't describe it in detail, but it is basical-
ly a part of me, a musical instrument that's sprout-
ed out of my back, midway between the shoulder
blades. There's no medical name for it, but Androsaur Flekt decided to call it a *fetus ex fetu,* and
over the years that got shortened into fefhorn. I
liked it, because it reminded me of the posthorn
which Mahler used to such evocative effect.

Q: How do you play it?

A: I'm private as my parts, and all I can say is
I have to use my right hand. I'm right fefhorned.

Q: What does it feel like?

A: Nothing. It's like it has no nerve-endings.
I've played it a million times but just as you would
an instrument of wood or brass.

Q: Are you a misanthropist?

A: Can a monster be a misanthropist? I don't
know.

Q: How does it feel now that *Welcome Home,
All You Uninvited* was awarded The Sterling Prize
for Most Compelling Composition of the Year?

A: None of my business.

Q: How do you respond to those critics who
claim your work is nothing more than an ingen-
ious form of ventriloquism?

A: I think all music is ultimately ventriloquism. And as for music critics, I think that their

criticisms are sad expressions of the critic's inability to project his voice from anywhere but himself.

Q: Why did you refuse to accept The Sterling Prize in person?

A: Too many people. There's no greater lie than the more the merrier. Just think of Pompeii. Auschwitz. Woodstock.

Q: What composer has had the great influence on your own work?

A: Gustav Mahler.

Q: Why?

A: Mahler and I share a lot of things. Of all composers, he's come the closest to expressing my experience of the world. For example, I can only compose in absolute solitude, and Mahler sequestered himself away at Steinbach, each chance he got. Maybe that's a common feeling. More significantly, I believe Mahler and I share expertise in our relations to impossibility. He carried impossible music in his head—the anguish and joy in his works express the beautiful agony of flailing about, trying desperately to express this impossible music—like a man trying to do more than develop womb, and more than giving birth, who also insists on fertilizing it himself.

Q: What would you like to achieve with your music before you die?

A: To finish Mahler's 10th Symphony—for real. Not like the Deryck Cooke version, which is about as exciting as pushing all the buttons in an Empire State Building elevator and listening to the beeps up to the top. I mean *really* complete it. I don't know how, but I don't know a lot of things. Whether or not I'm a misanthrope for example.

Q: Anything else you'd like to let our readers know?

A:

Wilson dropped the magazine and watched the toilet mock-flush. He looked in the mirror and observed a wide-eyed, grotesque expression—Louis Armstrong tasting a bad trumpet. He returned to the loft's obnoxious expanse. Rent was a luxurious $3,000 monthly, but it had a refugee center Feng Shui—a place hastily constructed in response to unexpected disaster.

The storm began. At the great vaulted window Wilson watched the rain falling in tongues. The homeless man stood at his usual station across the street, wearing his blank advertising placard, plywood boards sheathing torso and back, a sort of not-much-proof vest. He had a Harry Partch percussion instrument quality—hints of unlikely utility, hidden microtonalities. He was coarse and public as the vacant lot beneath his bluescuffed boots; and behind and high above him always loomed the windowless back of an anonymous building, hideous gray as cheap dental fillings.

In recent days, Wilson had developed a mild fascination with this character. He often fantasized the details of his childhood: Formative years as a human sandwich, advertising a Dry Cleaning business or Delicatessen or Nail Salon; a tiny strolling sign, ignored and pacing endless between the opposite poles of one dreary block, each day identical in length and tone and feeling as an insect's belly-segments ... and, as the peripatetic placard aged, the plywood boards, which hung over his shoulders with handleless jump-ropes, grew with him, anatomical extensions [like Wilson and his fefhorn]; and when the business he paced for closed down he wandered off ... the decades of reckless divagation eroding SALE! and %OFF! from his placards ... and now he was his own man and didn't need to pace or advertise anymore. Now he'd realized his dream of immobility, across the street from Wilson's loft ... here Wilson got tired of his imaginary biography.

Every few minutes, white-belted white people—who sipped "infused" beverages and would not under any circumstances play Russian Roulette without locally recycled bullets—walked by the blank man/sign, dung beetles passing a beetle without dung.

Today there were less of these gentrifiers, and umbrellas hid their casual smugness. As usual the man/sign just stood there getting soaked, a sentry unable to leave his post.

The phone ringing took Wilson by surprise. Who wanted to talk to him? Nobody cared any longer. Critics claimed his work had become overly redundant—like breathing, he supposed.

"Yes?"

"Hullo, Dash here. How's the piece going?"

"Fine, it's going fine. Thanks forch…"

The homeless man was staring up at Wilson's window, right at him, though possibly not seeing him; the rain now snapped like gravel at the panes.

"For checking in?" Dash asked.

A flash of static came and went, after which he still heard Dash speaking but the phone line had crossed with his past; and as Squall waited for a reply Wilson eavesdropped on a conversation he'd shared with Androsaur Flekt 10 years ago:

"Feffy, have you always hated people?"

"Uh, Dash, I'm sorry?"

"No, I haven't always existed."

"You said *forch*—thanks for calling, I'm sure you meant. Are you OK?"

"Don't worry Feff. They all die in the end."

"Yes. Thanks. Yes, thanks for checking in and … for this opportunity."

"You know what I say, Androsaur…"

"My pleasure. When do you think I can hear a bit? I don't mean to prod, but as the key piece in our 20th Anniversary Celebration you can understand I am a tad more anxious than usual. Not trying to rush you—but the event is next month."

Simultaneously, the friends raise their glasses and shout:
"All's well that ends!"
"Soon, Dash. I promise."
Serrated, comforting laughter…
"Soon?"
"You know how it is making art, Dash."
"I only wish I did. But I know how to make a deadline."
"But doesn't making art hurt? It's self-mutilation. But, it's like this: If you are compelled to painfully rip the hairs out of your head 1-by-1, you might as well make a pretty bloody pattern on your scalp while you're at it. Something people can clap at."
"I trust you won't let me down."
"Do you really think it's bad as all that, Androsaur?"
"Sure," Wilson said.
"I think the truth only hurts if you care about it."
"Great, talk soon Wilson."

Dash was Director of the New York Anti-New Music Symphony Orchestra, and one of the few influential figures who still championed Furst as an important composer. His phone call today had been the first time they'd spoken in half a year, when Squall commissioned Wilson to compose and record a piece, to be released in a limited, autographed vinyl edition exclusively for the top financial supporters of the Orchestra, in celebration of its second transgressive [but cultured] decade. Squall was particularly keen on the idea because the first piece they'd ever presented had been Furst's own *Welcome Home, All You Uninvited.*

At their winter meeting over sushi and sake, Wilson had leapt at the chance to compose a new piece in exchange for a generous sum of much-needed money, and the possibility of future commissions and acclaim.

He returned to the placard, blank and coughing in the rain.

What am I thinking?

Maybe I should help that man. Maybe I'm like that man.

Yes. No.

Then why am I watching him? What am I thinking?

I'm thinking he should really get an umbrella.

Nothing else?

No.

Wilson disconnected the phone. He thought about the incidents of the mugging, in vivid sequential detail. It was like he'd lost an important key and the only hope of retrieval was diligent, retrorse tracing of his day. It was also like going back in time and finding out the past was worse than you remembered it.

II. WHAT THE SNOW TELLS ME

Wilson had left the dinner with Squall a little past midnight in a glorious, C major dithyrambic mood. He'd even forgotten about those obscene, reveling anonymassholes at the table adjacent. It had been someone's birthday, and attending their gynecological celebration were the most unthinkably idiotic, laughing twat-dropped creatures, all pleased and oblivious as air-conditioned tourists in some shitty desert land—you *know* them—and you *know* the one.

Ah, but now Wilson had the intense pressure and consequent focus that were the silver linings of hard deadlines. It was just what he needed to get out of a recent creative funk and force a breakthrough; and he had until summer—6 months was sufficient to compose a fine piece of music.

Heavy snow had smoothed the city's sharp things, defunct antennas and barbed-wire fences, shattered beer bottles and even the shoutspeak of poor people who used windows for telephones. The buildings and cars merged, like mating worms into a single pale obesity; Wilson felt *scherzo*-like in a Mahler's 7th kind of way. 6 illegally intoxicated teenagers traipsed toward him like evacuees from a flooded city, singing the latest pop-puke [I've got 9 hearts and don't you forget it or I'll push you in the pool with my electric ferret]; they passed him with their cruelty and cell-phones and Wilson hummed a cute little *Kindertotenlieder* as chilly murk embraced him.

He took a half-assedly shoveled shortcut through diatomite curves, following sodium orange cones of streetlight through a hollow park, cold quiet broken now and then by a colder circling wind. Ahead, the sinister gathering of lumpy dwarfish figures under an icy moon turned out to be nothing but deadbeat snowmen.

He stumbled onward, alcohol and blazing-phoenix future setting his blood soaring…

"Shut up, Feffy and listen. Here is the great secret: Music is none other than The Uninvited."

"Meaning?"

"Not so much meaning, as telling-it-like-it-is, Feffy. The Uninvited is a special instance of appearing; it is an arrival which is not possible to claim is on time or late; it cannot even be unscheduled…Now, that which is Uninvited can be either Recognized or Unrecognized—an acquaintance or a stranger; and the acquaintance or stranger can be either Welcome or Unwelcome."

"Supposing that's true, what does that have to do with music?"

"Not music so much as the composer. Our role in life is serious, Wilson. Our aim is to Double-U-W: Cause The Uninvited to appear, in an Unrecognized form—and to Welcome it as though we had been expecting it all along and were delighted at its arrival."

"Double-U-W? That's a World-War prefix."

"Ha, I hadn't noticed. That only makes it more interesting. Didn't Mahler tell Sibelius the symphony must contain the world?"

"Yes, but your theory sounds like total bullshit."

"Do you have a better explanation?"

Wilson does not.

Now the loft was just a block away, the street empty as a bookstore; and Wilson felt like Mahler, implacably world-striding to his very own composing hut at Steinbach. He nearly slipped on a patch of ice, and as he gigglingly steadied himself a gun pressed into his back, mere centimeters beneath his flaccid fefhorn tip.

Suddenly, things were getting very 6th Symphony hammer-falls.

"All of it...wow nice shoes."

The voice was slurred and gravelly, frighteningly hopeless, yet oddly, timidly cultured—an unemployed professor of musicology?

Instinctively, Wilson reached his right hand behind his back to protect the fefhorn.

The hand was quickly seized and brutally crushed.

Too quick to be gentle or violent, and reptilian as he'd always imagined a lover's kiss must feel, the gun-muzzle mouthed the nape of Wilson's neck. His attacker kept Wilson's fefhorning hand in his lethal grasp and Wilson awkwardly emptied his pockets with his left hand, wallet to concrete, coins scattering. The man ordered Wilson to kneel and pulled off his John Lobb shoes, scraping his heels and undoing silken socks. Chunks of rock salt and inadequately melted ice ate at his knees.

The grip on his right hand loosened; now the pain flowed more freely. It was impossible to believe this agony didn't stretch to the unseen horizon and would literally drown him.

"That's everything," Wilson managed.

"The ring, clitshit."

Androsaur had gifted Wilson the faux Yeti-fur-lined ring, that one time in Rome, when they argued about Scott Walker during that amazing lightning storm; the trip during which he'd said all the wrong words to Androsaur as he lay on his deathbed.

"I can't."

"Aw, do I smell poop in your diaper?"

"It's not a diaper."

Wilson's fingers broke quietly and stolen ring dimly clinked on the ground like a counterfeit penny flung into a begging cup.

There was shit in his pants but he couldn't smell it. Why did that make things more nightmarish?

"Lately I fantasize the most shocking things—my imagination leaves nothing to the imagination..."

Yet he was no longer afraid—for his life, anyway. His brain was too busy fumbling for meanings and hopes related to the mauled hand, like a tongue which prods a hole in a tooth and mis-perceives its shape, depth and location, unable to confirm the actu-al affairs of its sponsor mouth…

"Enough with this thinking for yourself bullshit—how about learning to feel for yourself!"

Probably the butt of a pistol slammed the base of his skull. As he began blacking out in an altered dominant-9th haze, Wilson managed to glance up. He glimpsed half the face of everyone, from a dogshit's view…

Wilson woke to an inconsiderate polyphony of intersecting streams of nearby traffic, reminiscent of the 1st Symphony's *Todten-marsch*. The snow had stopped falling and the sky sprawled blue. Without warning a hot stream of piss followed the margins of his inner thighs and warmed bare, frozen feet.

He sat up in his excretions. The fefhorn was OK. The right hand was roadkill. On either side of him, the recent boot tracks of the indifferent white-belted.

Insouciant, stern Flekt's voice flickered between the emaciated scraping of gutterblown tabloids.

"At a certain age, you discover the only way to deepen your knowledge of life is to learn new jokes about it…"

… and Flekt on his cot, his serrated laughter, attenuated body draped in bearskin; and on the nightstand the surprising gravitas of grainy pulp curdled on the floor of an untouched glass of lemon-ade.

Whispering:

"Come closer, I have a new secret: Cancer is the awkward age between childhood and death, adolescence and death, adulthood and death, and old age and death."

"What do you mean?"

"Well, what do you want to be when you turn cancer?"

It was somehow more than nonsense.

If only because they were his last words.

III. WHAT THE DEAD TELL ME

The phone disconnected, Wilson watched the soggy homeless man schlep eastward, gutter for road. Without intending to, he examined his right hand. The fingers were twisted and bent, totally fucked. He wouldn't be playing the fefhorn any time soon—if ever. At least the instrument itself was not injured.

Does that matter?

If I'm disabled, so is my music.

Even if my hand heals, the fefhorn might fall off like a frozen wart, or develop a disease.

Am I even a human being? I've never been to a doctor, so who knows?

Have I turned cancer?

Who can I be, if not myself?

Body.

That night Wilson wolfed sleeping pills with a glass of what should not have been vinegar. He woke next afternoon, all *andante* fingers tapping coffin ceilings and tongue stuck to the roof of his mouth with clueless paste. Carefully moving through the solemn cairns of stale clothing, he reached the bathroom and regarded the mirror, disgusted; he was filthy, his mentionables were unmentionable. His reflection suggested a humorless mash-up of Groundhog Day and The Metamorphosis.

Hanging on the wall behind him was an 8-x-10 askew photograph of Mahler's composing hut at Steinbach, where the master had composed his titanic worlds with astounding discipline, precision and visionary abandon. Wilson used to look at it when he crapped.

He straightened the picture. He dressed quickly and, not really sure what he was doing, went downstairs. The sky was barely trying, a half-assed gray, the nearly no-color of paper towel sopping up more water than it can handle. The hot sun pissed all over the city, everyone plodding about guardedly, remembering and plotting interrogations.

He crossed the street toward the homeless man.

Why him?

I never have to awkwardly decline an invitation to his house.

And?

And that's it.

The man/sign was staring intently at something spherical in his hands, as though watching and waiting for a lottery number to appear. It was about the size of the huge boil on Sigmund Freud's testicles, which he describes at length in the *Interpretation of Dreams*.

A bruised apple.

The cracked, fat hands cradling the dead fruit, set against the rectangular white background of the placard made a striking image, creating the Magrittesque illusion he was concealed behind a painting that appeared part of his person/environment.

"Hello sir, I hope you don't mind me bothering you—my name's Wilson, how are you?"

"Hungry," he said with a swollen, careless voice. He didn't bother looking up.

"Great Glob, Feffy—You have no social graces. Had you no childhood friends?"

"You need a childhood for that."

"I can help you with that—I want to help you. I will help you, I'm not saying I'm withholding food I could share with you unless you do me a favor, too," Wilson said, feeling faint, slightly nauseous as when you get a spot to sit in a crowded subway car, and experience the assheat signature of the fat person who exerted himself from the seat seconds before you sat down, and you wonder if resting your legs was worth it.

"I almost burped."

"Sir, I have a job if you are interested, and I've got all the food you could want, and I insist we would work out a monetary payment. It's a weird job—not *that* kind of weird, but ... I'm an artist;

we're eccentric I guess..."

"Well do at least make an attempt at schmoozing. Remember you cannot fail if you don't try first..."

"You rich?"

He looked up, eyes lost and no fare to get back. His face was puffy and pocked and erratically bearded; and he should probably have been in a hospital for any number of conditions.

"Oh—there's a worm in there."

The man returned to the apple with a yellowy smile and carefully turned it upside down so a maggot fell in his hand. It wriggled. He ate it and tossed the apple away.

"You rich?"

"Not too much," Wilson said, going on as he had to, as if this were all a dream, with no consequences and no taboos, the most hideous acts merely symbolic. "No, not rich but you could, uh—you could finally get a new set of boards or a suit, some good shoes, a fine hat or umbrella to keep the rain off your head. A room to rent and hot food, maybe. What do you say?"

"I'm Kenneth?"

"Good to meet you ... You're not allergic to latex, are you?—that sounds bad...but it's not what it sounds like."

"What it feels like?"

"I mean latex gloves of course. It's hard to explain. I have to show you. Do you mind? I mean, I could really need you..."

He grunted and coughed.

"You rich?"

One minute they were on the street, and the next, Wilson sat backwards and shirtless on a chair, arms hanging over the back, head propped straight and still as mounted taxidermy, looking at he and Kenneth in the oblong mirror he'd propped up before them.

Kenneth remained in his blank, frayed placards, having looked at Wilson as though he were the devil when he offered to put them somewhere safe.

"You're sure you are OK with this? We'll have to do this a lot—there's only a month before the music must be written and recorded...there's a lot you have to learn quickly. "

Kenneth shrugged, grunted, tugged at the surgical gloves Wilson had instructed him to wear.

What am I doing? You know what you're doing.

You know.

I know, I know.

Variations.

"OK, here's the part I told you about. It's all about that bumpy object on the thing on my back—all right; I hope it doesn't disgust you..."

"Part of being human is being inhuman, eh Feffy?"

"I suppose so."

"So cheer up Feff."

"But I feel so lost, I can't find the wrong way to go."

"That's easy," Flekt says, doing his best Ray-Bolger-at-the-yellow-brick-crossroads impersonation.

"That a wing, right?"

"Do you think so?"

"Big chicken wing?"

Kenneth grunted, shrugged:

"You're pretty rich?"

"Remember: Double-U-W."

"No really I'm not OK, let's start. Just move your hand along the right-side ridge. Do it gently. I just want us to get a feel—"

—It wasn't pain exclusively or even exactly—a peripheral, if striking phenomena, like the light of burning fire; Wilson convulsed and his eyes twirled up to spy into his inner-face—

—A clattering, loud and world-like, drew his eyes back down from his head.

In the mirror, he could tell the man/sign had tripped over a pile of dishes and flatware and God knows what else and had slammed backwards into the wall. But why was his expression full of discovery? What sale was the flat surface of his board now advertising? Wilson tried to read it but the words were in some ancient language, all swirly and drippy wet reds. What was in Kenneth's hands?

The fefhorn! He'd ripped it off Wilson's back and was examining it with a child-like disinterest in warnings—tapping and sniffing it, sticking his hand in up to the jolly elbow.

It was hollow.

Wilson heard, then saw the blood dripping off his body to the floor behind him. It meant nothing. He was transfixed by his impossible, outsider's view of the fefhorn.

He wanted the man/sign to turn it more slowly so he could get a thorough look. He was too tired to express this, or anything else.

Then Kenneth lifted the fefhorn above his head and looked up inside. He shook it, as though trying to dislodge something. He brought it down and peered into its conical hollow, grunted and frowned in a puzzled way, raised the fefhorn again, shook it, grunted, shrugged, and put it on his head.

It fit perfectly.

Only now did Kenneth look at the mirror. He stood over Wilson's slumping form with a very serious face and adjusted the fefhorn just a tad. He nodded, satisfied. Suddenly, his eyes met Wilson's in the mirror. Until then he seemed to have forgotten Wilson was in the room with him. He grunted and came round from behind Wilson and crouched before him. Wilson's blood streaked his placard and spotted the folds of his neck. He grasped Wilson's shoulders and hauled him up, straightened him out so he didn't slide onto the floor.

Wilson kept his eyes open. It was difficult to do, but Kenneth's face was a mass of worries and he knew that to look away would be to confirm the man's worst fears. Why that should matter to him, he didn't know. This guy was just another anonymasshole—but it was somehow more than nonsense when he offered Kenneth a smile, to reassure him.

Kenneth returned an ochre grin.

Then he pointed at the fefhorn on his head:

"This waterproof?"

"Do you know that story about Mahler," Androsaur is saying, "how, one summer in 1908, while he and Alma were away from Steinbach, actually—in Tyrol, I think—he came running up to her, all breathless and shaken?"

"No, tell me," Wilson says. "This was when he was working on Das Lied von Der Erde?"

"I imagine so. Ah this is a good one. So Gustav comes racing over the green grass to his wife. He is covered in perspiration, his eyes are wild and red, his hair a greater disaster than usual and he can hardly get out a breath. He tells Alma that, in the seclusion of his composer's hut, he suddenly felt the eye of Pan upon him with all the grotesque, hateful plans which the natural world has for the nature-lover in it. Then he says he needs to get away from the presence of the Goat-God. He goes into the house and is only able to get on with his composition in the company of other human beings."

"Seems a bit mad, even for Mahler. With the Goat-God and all."

"But there are Goat-God costumes. Mahler's was a time of disguises—you know his confession of triple-homelessness: he was a Jew in Catholic's clothing, a Bohemian in Austria, and an Austrian among Germans. Everywhere an intruder—welcomed nowhere—uninvited."

"But eye of Pan?"

"Do I have to point it out? The uninvited had slipped through a space as it opened between the covert shuffling of things."

"And?"

"It was disguised as a Goat-God."

"Could it come dressed as anything at all?"

"Of course."

"Then it could be dressed as you—or me, or anyone."

"It could've been a hat-rack."

"A bottle of brandy!"

"Yes. Keep it down."

"A fig! Underpants! A mirror!"

"Yes. Enough already, Feffy."

Wilson knows when to stop pushing Androsaur; he has that sealed jam-jar stare and his mouth has compressed into a frown that could hold back the Cossacks. The carefree mood broken, they sit somewhat awkwardly for a while, quiet, each occasionally sipping at his brandy, leaving the rim of the glass against the mouth a tad too long before putting it on the café table, desperate to use whatever poor resources at hand as an excuse to not speak.

Until suddenly—surprisingly, neither expecting it—they raise their glasses and shout together:

"Music!"

THE GEMINIS

JOHN PALISANO

I KNOW LOVE. It whispers in my ear at night. In a dream she steals a kiss. Her voice on my phone. I feel her against me, if only in my thoughts. Her arms and body wrap around me. Her belly on mine. Her mouth hangs slightly open. Her face twisted in pleasure. Her lips move slightly askew. I have not felt this way in ages— thought my heart cold and cynical and forever gone. Why is it the unexpected ones?

When I see her I feel light.

When I leave I am hollow and my heart feels drawn back. My blood curves inside, going left then right like the snake-shaped roads leading to her house.

This is good enough. To know I can feel again. To know my heart can stretch. To know I've finally healed. It's plentitude. But, wow, did it take time. Of course I'm deeply involved with another, as is she. And so what? A gentle word, a small touch, gives me enough. Our love will not be ruined through familiarity. Our love remains true and unbroken. Love has awoke. Life will follow.

I know her and she knows me. She has luscious dark and wavy hair. A soft face, similar to mine. We were even born close together: her on the 13th of June, and I, the day after. Same year. Hours apart. Both in New York City, although we've met decades later in San Diego. Lia was drawn west like me. The call. The bug. The creative pull. Neither of us have seen our original, youthful dreams through, but we've managed more appropriate dreams. Her a designer. My filmmaking. Now our music. Such cascades of sound. Rhythm. Bass. Counterpoint. Such beautiful melodies. Our voices blend. Her piano. My electric guitar.

It drives away the darkness.

In this sunshine, in the shadows under the greens, hate filled things linger. They burrow inside your mind. They push you toward the edge, and then shove you over.

Take you.

Take yourself.

That's what they say inside my head. They're trying to draw me into their abyss, but I won't go quietly.

What is it that causes love? The years of attraction we program into our thoughts? The way someone looks? The beauty of another human being? Are we attracted to those who are not like our parents? Those unlike those our parents like?

Lia looked up at me from behind her keyboard. "That's a neat riff," she said. "Very catchy. I think we're on to something."

"Sure," I said. It was all I could muster. The jam had felt good. My entire life I've been searching for someone who clicked perfectly with me. So many false starts in all those bands, and all those partners, trying to make films. Nothing was ever a hundred percent. It was always compromised. That's the big problem I've always had. Nothing was easy. The collaborations were forced, most out of necessity. There weren't a lot of options. That, and I didn't always believe in myself or have the confidence to step up and take charge, nor did I have the heart to tell people when they, or I, weren't working. The one time I asked a singer to leave a band, as he never hit the right notes, well, that turned into a disaster. The other members rebelled against me, and I found myself out of the band I'd started. They carried on gallantly, but never found much success. I ventured into obscurity.

This does not make me bitter. Not anymore. Finding Lia has made me realize it was all for a reason, and a bigger plan was laid out in front of me. One I could never imagine or predict.

My white Stratocaster caught some gleaming sunlight. It was a new instrument, which I found necessary. I'd needed to separate from my past in order to start something new without the baggage I'd gathered on my older guitars.

"Do you think we should check the recording?" I said.

She nodded. "Yes. Great idea. I don't want to forget what we just did." She winked. "Shut your eyes and remember, though, just in case it didn't take."

I did.

The high B echoed throughout her living room, plucked by me on the A string. Simple, and the repeating pattern soon caught on. Lia joined in, adding a diminished chord from her keyboard. She filled it in with a droning bass pattern with her left hand.

Expression.

Channeling.

Connecting.

My memory of the jam blended with the recording, which she played through her phone and her keyboard's external speakers.

She was my other half. Not a perfect mirror, mind you, but the other side of me. Where I flew, she came. If her improvisational choices went too far, I caught her. If mine were too safe, she urged me outside my comfort zone. We did this without talking, without looking, and only through the spirituality inside our playing.

Harmony.

Synchronicity.

The sound and movement of Love and Spirit flowing.

And were we only doing it for ourselves?

No.

We didn't know so.

Not until later.

Sexuality is the curve of a body. The feel. The body has limits. We all look similar. How many variations? Hairstyles? Grooming? Body types? Orgasms are centered in thoughts. So why is it only expressed physically? Can people love without touch? Does it always need to become primal. There's little of that left inside me. I cannot express myself solely through sexuality. Bonding through music feels more intimate, more inside… sex is only on the outside…

◇

The top of Arrowhead road blossomed out into several smaller mountain streets. The houses got bigger. The gates became taller. The roads more rarified. My daily walk with Charlie, her pit, always brought me great inspiration. We were high up off the valley basin. The air was cool and fresh, even in the summer heat waves. There was a lot less traffic, and a lot less people, which I preferred. I liked the relative solitude it brought. Charlie enjoyed the scents.

I saw a pattern.

In the side of the mountain there seemed to be a dark edge running from the bottom of the crest, near to the top. This jagged line was nearly a foot wide at its fullest, but often shrunk down to only a few inches. It ran behind the houses and picked up on the un-built spaces between.

At first I believed it was only a natural sediment layer, naked and revealed. On top of Arrowhead, despite the houses, most of nature was untouched. There weren't gardeners pruning and planting the area into joyless sameness. No. You could still see nature the way nature grew. No imported grass. No extra plants. No palm trees. Just raw earth.

On my third day of recognizing the pattern, I decided I'd go up for a better look. Why not? Maybe I'd see some kind of fossil. I was kidding myself in that regard, but my curiosity bested me.

"Come on, Charlie," I said, as we veered off the edge of the road and made our way between two sand-colored houses. There was a particularly good and thick section. The closer we got, the more detail I made out. Small granules glistened. They appeared organic to the layer. When we made it only a few feet from the strip, it moved, expanding horizontally, top and bottom, by a foot.

For a moment I believed it'd been some kind of optical illusion or trick of sunlight moving across it.

The strip expanded again and it moved outward toward me. "You see this?" I said to Charlie, but he was looking elsewhere and not interested in the slightest.

Small rocks and sandy soot fell. The strip widened. There was a low rumble, and I swear I heard voices.

I shoved back.

More sandy soot and rocks poured down.

"Come on," I said to Charlie.

It had to be an earthquake. I'd had terrible timing. Scanning the street, I didn't see anywhere perfect to go. If the houses came down, me and Charlie would be right in the crossfire. There were other hazards on the street.

The ground shook.

Charlie whimpered.

Strangely, everything appeared blurry to me. That must have been my adrenaline.

We made it to the middle of the street.

As we ran, I heard a horn.

A white van slammed its brakes.

I pulled Charlie back as fast as I could. Both of us looked toward the van.

The driver, a stout Latin man, said, "What's wrong with you?"

"Quake," I said, and realized it'd stopped.

He regarded me for a moment, shook his head a little, and drove on up Arrowhead.

"That could've been bad," I said to Charlie.

As we walked away, I looked back at the strip. It'd widened considerably. In one place, I swear I saw an obsidian eye.

Sleep came easy. My trusted eye pillow cushioned my eyelids, a gift from Lia. Colors swirled like a million galaxies in my dreams. Dread filled my gut. The worries of my waking life seeped through. Money was always an issue, as was my heart. Both were always on the verge of collapse. This was entirely due to a genetic predilection against normal work and normal people. Why dedicate over forty hours a week to tasks I could do in a few hours? Only for money. Commerce. Why spend time with someone you don't love? These philosophies led me to near ruin. Instead of settling for a decent job and a comfortable wife with her own cozy job, I wanted more. Explore the outer reaches. Bask in creation. Live for the unraveling. But this unmade me. Had it not been for Lia's generosity, I'd be in serious trouble. As it were, the worst was feeling guilty.

That dream, though, unleashed something else. A deep, fatalistic melancholy that infused my heart. I felt guilty for being alive. Humanity held promise, but ultimately failed. Why did I choose to be born as man?

Choose.

There weren't voices in my head, per se, but thoughts delivered. These weren't of my own imagination. I felt them arrive as clearly as someone knocking on the door. They were coming from somewhere.

The colors turned darker and darker until it was an enormous spinning black mass of organic matter. I travelled toward it, its vastness and freezing temperature slowly overtaking me. This was my destiny. Purpose. Chosen way.

And I remembered the eye looking out at me from the obsidian strip between the houses.

Hundreds of small yellow orbs floating through the air. Where they go they bring death to every living thing. Nothing escapes. I see them pour from the slit in the mountain.

I woke with tears dried to my face.

Lia opened the glass bay doors. Outside, the canyon stretched for miles in every direction. It looked like a sea of green. There were a few houses below, but the steepness and sandstone made developing most of the canyon too treacherous to develop.

"I want to hear our music sing to nature," she said.

We'd already positioned our amps and speakers so they faced outside.

This I knew would be good.

I plugged in my Stratocaster and set the dials on my amp. It didn't take me long to find my sweet spot. Lia tuned up her keyboard. She found the patches she liked and started playing. I followed along. This time in A minor. The notes cascaded throughout her vast living room. I pictured them as colors ringing off the walls and flowing slowly outside. I felt transformed into an otherworldly conduit. There's something surely magical about making music. It's the closest thing you can get to finding God on earth. That's what I've always believed. No other art forms I've practiced have gotten that close. Perhaps writing, when in the zone. Music forces the listener to be in the moment. It's very difficult not to be.

It's hard to say how long the song went on. I didn't slight to the rhythm. My fingers didn't feel like they were my own, but guided by other hands. Nothing else mattered. I felt electric and pure.

Our spirits melded together. It was as if we had joined somehow in the ether. The music echoed outside of the house and we could hear it flowing into the canyon. This was a new audience for us. Even if there were no people there were other things listening to what we were creating.

Something made me look out across the canyon to the top of the other hill. Something primal inside.

About three quarters of the way to the top of the adjacent hill I swear I saw trees and vegetation moving. It was as if the mountain were about to split. What was I seeing? Was this another earthquake? Wind? My instinct told me it was something else.

I shut my eyes and played.

Other than my hands, I barely moved. I felt hypnotized.

Don't stop.

Almost there.

Feels so right.

◇

When I first became friends with Lia, I felt a pull inside I thought I'd never feel again. I thought I was too old to fall madly in love. We didn't even have to say much to one another. There was a magical connection. I'd drive away down the curving mountain roads and could barely hold my breath. My head spun, hands shook. I could barely focus on the road. I played love songs on the iPod through the stereo. It hurt; I hurt, in that most magnificent and wonderful way.

Back home I had to go through the motions. I wasn't in love with Theresa. I cared for her. Deeply. I loved her. But I wasn't *in* love. Not like I was with Lia.

Many counseled me. Mature love doesn't have to come on strong, they'd say. It's better if it doesn't. It'll be stronger. I didn't believe them, despite my nods, despite my thanks. No. Especially not after my feelings for Lia erupted.

Love is more important than it may seem. Love kept me going back. Love guided me to Lia. Love drove the music. The music drove away the darkness.

Our thoughts meet our souls embrace and our inside worlds run free creating shades and colors and sounds our bodies on autopilot transcribing what they can through their hands and bodies does it make it through and sound true who can know for sure blue is everywhere like a tinted glass then orange then purple then everything sounds like a million voices.

I can't play it safe anymore. Not if I think I can really get off. I need things to be new. Different. Taboo situations. My brain has to be charged. On fire. Sex is so damn mental. You just know what people are doing. The same old rhythms. Tricks. Positions. Bathroom mouth. Not clever or sexy. It's often ruined with National Geographic like close-ups of anatomy. Why? It's all inside. The eyes. Kissing. The sexiest part. The touching. Feeling someone close to you. It's not all about the genitals. Those are only one means of expression of love. And it's been reduced to something about as attractive as going to the bathroom. It's not sexy seeing girls being abused or their faces used as targets.

It's gross. Sickening. Who wants to see that? Romance is a dying art. Pornography is killing it. Broad daylight. Aerobics with body fluids. No fun. Not romantic. Not special. Let's not even cross that line.

Let's just let it melt away until there is only spirit. Let the sounds free us from our bodies. Let the husks fade to dust. Only the humming of our souls, like a drum hit that doesn't decay or fade, but stays on for several minutes.

That's when the soul hums.

That is how it sounds.

They spoke to me, their voices like discordant bursts through the music. I looked down at the amp, convinced something had gone wrong. Lia didn't notice. She was still in a trance, her chin up, eyes closed, dark hair cascading.

What was it, then?

Klaat somi Dow / Klaat somi Dey

The exotic, unfamiliar words came through, bundled in static and volume.

Who spoke them? What did they mean? Why me?

A vision, then:

The mountaintop opens. Obsidian limbs find purchase. Their lengths lined with orifi, tasting the air. Protective layers peel away. Small, round things are freed. They'd been cradled within the limbs. Babies? They roll, then crawl, then roll, like smooth, black baseballs. Rows of small thorns circle their diameters. They give off a sweet smell that I instinctively know is poisonous. They roll toward the houses. I see people—everyone, in fact—on the ground. Everyone paralyzed by the scent. Still alive. Still conscious. Still feeling when the orbs unfold and their thorns grow outward, hungry for the kill. No one can scream when the orbs rip into them. Blood. Tissue. Shredding. Slowly. Painfully. Above, a shadowed thing blocks the sun. The dying see glimpses.

Klaat somi Dow / Klaat somi Dey

The city will pay. This city will pay. These people will pay.
And this will only be the beginning.

"That was wonderful," Lia said. "We keep getting better and better. I wish I knew you back in New York when I was just starting out. We both would have probably been much further along. It just feels like I've known you forever. We just click. Where've you been all my life?"

"I don't know," I said. "Wasting my time with other people?"

I turned the volume down on my guitar so we didn't have to hear the 60-cycle hum.

Lia nodded. "I know what you mean. How long do you think we were playing?"

I shook my head. "Ten minutes?" I said.

"Try close to half an hour," Lia said. "I can't believe we lasted that long."

"Wow. Me neither. That's crazy."

She said, "Want to go again?" and smirked.

"How can I say no?"

"How about we do D minor this time?" she said.

"Sounds good to me. Just make sure that recorder is going."

Lia pressed a button. "Rolling," she said.

Words. Devastating, cruel. It's what drove me forward. The other one insisted on devolving into abuse. When we first met, she loved me. Her eyes lit. Her face lit. But like so many relationships, things went south. Her sloth became overbearing. Her tongue grew critical and sharp. She found faults where once she found redemption.

I became litmus for her to get back at all the men who'd done her wrong. She became so cold she literally turned her back on me when my kidney disease flared. Instead of loving me, she picked a fight, accusing me of terrible things. I was the stand-in for her to say and act toward those who'd hurt her, unfair as it seems.

This is so you know what I realized. A larger current pushed me. I may never have become close to Lia otherwise. I'd never have asked her to play music. I needed escape. We needed to come together. Only pure connection... pure spiritual love... would have been enough. Faking it wouldn't work. It had to be authentic beyond any doubt.

The thing inside the mountain would know.

The house shook. My head felt suddenly filled with small holes, like a piece of corral. Inside these gaps I felt fluid swoosh in and out. It didn't hurt, although it was extremely unpleasant.

Lia looked uncomfortable, more so than me. She stood from her keyboard and made it to her couch.

The house shook again. It threw me off.

"Quake," I said.

Lia didn't notice. She was stretched out across her white sectional, an elbow over her eye. I ran to her with my guitar.

"What's going on?" I said. "Lia?"

The guitar came off; I rested it against the couch.

Her eyes didn't look right.

There was an odd, smokey smell that overtook the house. The air seemed cloudy. My throat went dry. "Something's going on," I said. "I think there's a fire."

Lia barely registered what I'd said through her tears.

Then she looked to me.

"It's horrible," she said. "The thing in the mountain."

My mind raced.

"I saw it just now," she said. "In my thoughts. Very dark. Eyes everywhere. Mouths."

As she saw, I saw. Pictures formed in my mind. She, my other half, trembled.

"It has long legs with holes in them. Lots of little holes. They all move, too. And it's inside at the top of the mountain. It wants to kill us all. It's just waiting. Extinction. The little black orbs it releases... they give off some kind of smoke..."

We both looked up

Several orbs were on the ceiling.

That was where the strange smell came from.

Ringing sounds and indistinct words.

Klaat somi Dow / Klaat somi Dey

I heard not through my ears, but somehow through vibrations in my bones. Unlike anything I'd ever sensed. Cacophony. Noise. Disjointed. Not rhythmic at all.

The orbs tore into the ceiling, causing cracks. Their sounds became worse.

Lia screamed.

That, too, made their noises worse.

"I know what we have to do. There's only one way we can get out of this."

I'm not sure what made me think of it. I knew she wasn't able to walk to the booth. And I didn't have the strength to carry her. Somehow my instinct took over. I hurried to the keyboard, found the box, and pressed the red triangle on top.

Our music filled the room. It blended with the noises coming from the orbs. We realized it all fit together.

Feels like static electricity inside, curling around like waves. Currents carry us, intermix us, our energies move in and out if one another like two cloudy mists, only they're not mists, but countless atoms circling.

It didn't make sense at first, but their terrifying notes and sounds blended perfectly and systematically with the music we had been creating. We'd channeled them without realizing it.

All those memories and experiences turned off. Gone. The world inside fades to nothing. It can't all be for nothing. How can we have this consciousness evolved from nothing. There is meaning. There is reason. There must be a place where all this ends up.

Tears streamed down Lia's face. She gave a slow nod. At that moment my heart broke into a million pieces. I don't know how it had come to this. I loved her so much, but there was very little I knew I'd be willing to do to express that. Many times I thought through a possible relationship with her. I had scanned all the milestones. First date. First kiss. Love making. The proposal. Settling into a routine. Then twins. A boy and a girl. Their hair a mixture of ours. My blonde and her dark hair mixing together. I saw the happy faces. I almost needed their names.

But then I looked down at her and wasn't sure it would ever happen. She'd know me from this now. From these things. And our music was magic. What our love made together was some sort of shield against the thing inside the mountain. I knew it in my heart. We needed the passion. We needed our truest feelings. Yet passion and feelings fade over time, even with lovers who are crazy about each other. We couldn't risk that happening.

"I see these things," she said. "There's another across from us, too. Maybe more." She gestured out the bay doors.

She was right.

The top of the mountain moved. There was another thing living inside. We must've woken them. Stark limbs pushed through dirt and rock, setting aside trees and vegetation.

"They won't stop with us," Lia said.

The orbs on the ceiling rolled toward the door. Within moments they left. Their part of the music faded. We waited, our eyes trained on the hill across from us. When the recording stopped, it appeared that the things in the mountain faded back within their hiding place.

No trace of the orbs. A faint smell lingered. I found the courage to sit on the couch next to Lia. I put out my hand, and she held it. Where would we go from here?

"What now?" she said. "What are we supposed to do? Staying in this room forever? Are we supposed to play new music forever, or do we play the recording over and over and over again?"

"I think we'll have to follow our instincts."

"How are we going to know when they come back? How are we supposed to live our lives now? Are we supposed to wait here?"

"Yes. I think one of us is always going to have to be here, waiting. Just in case. If we're not here when they come calling, that could be bad."

My throat hurt. My head ached. I wanted to sleep. To forget all I knew and saw. To forget what had happened.

"What if we're hallucinating?" she said. "What if none of this is real?"

"I've been thinking the same thing. Second-guessing myself. This can't be real. Things in the mountain. Black orbs in the neighborhoods killing people. Doesn't make any sense."

"I was hoping for so much more," she said. "I knew there was something special when I met you. But I thought it was something else. I thought they were something personal."

"This is personal," I said. "You're the left hand and I'm the right. We need each other to be whole. We need each other to make the music. Treble clef and bass clef. We're each playing half the melody. You play a phrase and I play a phrase."

"That's it then. We found our destiny. Each other. And those things. Those things in the mountain. They'll be listening."

"Forever."

"Forever."

She patted her abdomen, where a small bump rose. "Twins," she said. "Ours."

A GUIDE TO ETIQUETTE AND COMPORTMENT FOR THE SISTERS OF HENLEY HOUSE

EMILY B. CATANEO

1

EACH OF THE SISTERS of Henley House will use recreation time to pursue a particular activity.

Grace will handle the arrangement of the tinsel. Bell will amuse herself with her magnifying glass. I will write the etiquette book.

2

Days for the sisters of Henley House will be orderly and regimented.

Each day, we Henley sisters awake and proceed to the Elephant Room, where we sit in a row before the elephant, an ebony statue whose tusks are white and who leans to one side because his front right foot has been broken off. After this hour of reflective matins, I lead calisthenics: ten minutes of jumping rope with the cord dredged out of the corrugated mud in the hallway, then five minutes of touching the toes, then ten minutes of ballet—pliés, first position through fifth position.

Then comes dinner hour. Bell, Grace and I sit around a table that we found tossed on its side beneath a tangle of pans, dead un-potted plants, drowned stuffed animals and sodden inky paper. There is no food in Henley House, but that is not a polite topic of conversation for dinner hour. What do we discuss? We find shapes in the pattern made by the receding wallpaper. We discuss Grace's plans for creating a mosaic out of the trapezoids and rhombi of china that strew the ground beneath our feet. We speak of how Christmas is coming, and how Grace is gathering tinsel to decorate.

Bell may mention her magnifying glass—she may even take it out and place its condescending eye, its fat brass handle on the table—but only if she remembers to do so in an uncontroversial way.

We then retire to the Recreation Room to amuse ourselves with our own pursuits for several hours. Then we once again reflect before the elephant; we have dinner hour; we wipe our faces with towels and retire to bed. The three of us sleep together in the great white porcelain tub in our bedroom. Bell is a year younger than I, but she is the tallest, and her toes curl around the faucet when she sleeps.

On the second day, Bell said that the light outside the curtains never changes, so how is it possible for us to keep track of time? But I pointed to a horned amber insect crawling along the side of the uprighted table. I placed a cracked drinking glass over the insect and told Bell when the insect dies, one day has passed. Every morning I place a new insect under the glass, and a new day begins.

3

On occasion, the sisters of Henley House are troubled by unsettling dreams. It is considered impolite to speak of these dreams, and so it is forbidden.

It was afternoon recreation time on the fifteenth day, and Grace was stroking her bedraggled and shredded silver tinsel. I was picking through a pile of books on the floor—the pages were warped and wavy, but still I ran my finger along the pocked leather of the spines, found the first word in each title, and stacked them in alphabetical order.

Then I saw that Bell was sleeping on a floorboard that had come unmoored, stuck up at a 20-degree angle from the floor. I tossed my book aside and lunged towards her, about to shake her awake and scold her for sleeping during recreation time.

Then she howled.

Grace dropped her tinsel and looked up, her blue eye a combination of hurt and annoyance.

Bell writhed, kicked one foot in the air, and opened her eyes.

"No." Her fingers locked around my wrist. "No, no, no. *Nononono.*"

"Keep your voice down," I said.

"It wasn't always like this." Whites gleamed around Bell's pupils. "I saw something, in my dream—before, in this room, everything glowed gold, and the curtains were whole." She gestured at the periwinkle curtains, which were stained with black splotches. "But then all this dust blew in through the windows, and it got into my nose and eyes and I felt as though... as though my insides had been hollowed out." She sat up and seized my other wrist. "What happened, Elisa? Why can't we look out the windows? Why can't we go up the stairs in the hallway?"

I clapped my hands over Grace's ears and told Bell to stop asking such disturbing questions.

"I'm going to find out." Bell scrabbled away from me, her magnifying glass sticking out of her overalls pocket. "I'm going to make it outside this house, and then we'll see what happened."

I told Bell not to mention her dreadful dreams again, but she skittered away into the Elephant Room.

4

It is rude to remark on idiosyncrasies in the appearances of the Henley sisters.

There are unmistakable marks of a Henley sister: a forest of mousy brown curls; blue eyes, although Bell's are more gray, Grace's dark and mine sapphire; a longness of limb and a slump in the shoulder; moles peppering our forearms.

There are also several peculiarities in our appearances, but it is rude to point these out.

On the eighteenth day, Grace sorted through shards of pottery patterned with cornblue flowers. Bell prowled along the far wall of the Recreation Room, frowning through her magnifying glass at the curtains and muttering to herself.

Bell grabbed Grace and placed her magnifying glass over the black hole standing in for a right eye on our youngest sister's face.

"Does it hurt?" Bell pulled Grace's head towards hers and squinted. Her index finger skirted the edge of the hole—its edges were puckered like chapped lips.

"Leave me alone." Grace twisted away from Bell. Bell repositioned the magnifying glass and held Grace still with one hand. Grace wriggled and screamed.

"Bell Henley, what're you doing?" I said. "Stop bothering her."

"Don't tell me what to do," Bell said.

"Grace has to prepare for Christmas. It will be any day now."

"Really? We've been here for nineteen days—"

"Eighteen days."

"—and you keep saying that. I don't think you have any idea what you're talking about, and I think you're making up that," she jabbed her finger at this etiquette book "as you go."

I slapped Bell's finger away. You see, this is what comes from remarking on such things as Grace's eye. This is why it's impolite to point out the ring of livid purple bruises on Bell's long neck, or the gash smiling on my arm.

5

If you are not a Henley sister, you may not visit our chambers.

On the twentieth day, I awoke in the tub with my cheek pressed against Grace's shoulder blade. Bell was nowhere to be seen.

I crept out of our bedroom, careful not to disturb Grace.

In the hallway, Bell crouched in front of a door opposite our bedroom, running fingertips over the door's peeling white paint.

"What on earth—"

"Shh," Bell said. "I woke up and I heard—"

Something shuffled on the other side of the door, and a smell like a cave breathing crept into the hallway.

"Bell, get away from there."

But Bell's fingernails scratched against the wood, and her hands moved as though peeling open an invisible barrier covering the wooden door.

I pressed the back of my hand against my nose as the stench grew stronger.

Then the door creaked open, and a woman stepped into our hallway. Her lined face might have once been nut-brown but it had taken on a gray pallor, hair matted in clumps of sticky darkness.

She extended one hand and croaked, "You helped me get out."

"Stay away from my sisters," I said. "Don't you hurt them."

"Stop, stop," said the woman. She coughed something sticky and wet into her hand. "I'm not going to hurt you," she said. "I'm Adriana. I think..." Her fat face crinkled around the words. "I think I used to watch over you... you little ladies. You look..."

"Where did you come from?" Bell said.

"Below." Adriana pointed at the warped floorboards. "There was a staircase, like that one." She gestured at the staircase leading up out of the hallway.

"You came up the staircase?" Bell turned to me and Grace, who had emerged from the bedroom and stood with her tinsel dragging from her hand and her eye blank and annoyed. "You know what this means?"

"It means it's time for matins," I said.

"If you climbed those stairs, that means we should be able to climb our stairs," Bell said. "I've been trying to get out the windows—that's what I've been trying to do. But the stairs—maybe I should have tried the stairs."

"It's time for matins." I grabbed Grace and pulled her into the Elephant Room, where I sat her in front of the elephant, bowed my head and pressed my hands together. But Bell didn't follow.

"I've been using my magnifying glass." Bell's voice trailed into the Elephant Room from the hallway. "I can't find a way out."

"I used something that looked like that, little lady." Adriana insists on calling us little ladies, which I find impertinent. I peered around the doorjamb and watched her rummage in her pocket and produce a pair of bent-framed spectacles. She balanced them on her nose. "They helped me find my way up the stairs."

"But how?"

Adriana told Bell that she had stood on the second-to-top stair, ankle-deep in mud, and felt every inch of air with her fingers, groping for an edge, a hinge, some crenellation that she could pry open. She had held the spectacles to her nose and scrutinized the space in front of her, looking for a glimmer of light, of air, for a doorway.

She didn't know how much time passed during her search, but finally a seam in the air caught her eye. It was no thicker than sewing thread, but it gleamed a lighter gray than the dank air around it.

She scrutinized the seam, breaking her nails on its sharp edges, trying to pry it open, until she heard someone moving on the other side. She shouted at the person to find a crack, to pull, and this time, when she dug her fingernails into the crack, the darkness folded back like a shutter. She caught a breath of fresher air, then she stepped up to the door, creaked it open and emerged into our hallway.

"We have to find the same kind of opening in this staircase," Bell said. "Then maybe we can figure out what happened."

"I thought we were supposed to spend matins looking at the elephant, Elisa," Grace said.

"You're right, Gracie," I said. "We are."

6

When crossing the hall from the Recreation Room to the Elephant Room, extend your arms for balance, and circumnavigate the tangle of coats and reeds and offal by placing one foot in front of the other, heel to toe, heel to toe. Climb carefully over the grandfather clock leaning against the wall. Do not pause by the staircase.

"Bell," I shouted. "Adrianna. Grace."

I heard them rattling around in the Elephant Room.

"You'd better not be bothering Grace with your foolish ideas."

I hurried out of the Recreation Room into the hallway. I put my left foot at an angle between the jagged edge of a picture frame and the leg of an upturned stool. I spread my arms for balance and I placed my right foot between the swampy mess of coats.

The black beam of the grandfather clock loomed before me, and I was about to slip my hands over its edge and then swing my legs over and continue on to the Elephant Room, when I looked at the staircase.

I stood frozen, my arms extended and one foot trailing off the ground. Twilight, bordering on darkness, leaked over the colorless runner on the six stairs I could see.

Something is up there, I thought. And questions lit up my mind: why is the light outside always in the gloaming? Why does Christmas never come? How did we get here? Did we always worship that elephant?

But I shook off this creeping feeling, climbed over the grandfather clock and walked into the Elephant Room. Such questions, such feelings, would only lead to trouble.

This is why a sister of Henley House should never pause by the staircase: because it will lead her thoughts down dark and dangerous paths.

7

Magnifying glasses, spectacles and any sort of special glass should be used only to examine horned beetles or interesting pottery—never for any sort of larger quest. If they are used for other purposes, they will be confiscated.

I sat in the Recreation Room on the twenty-fifth day, listening to their low voices—Bell's insistent and shrill, Adriana's still raspy—as they searched the staircase. Grace had fallen asleep, and I shook her shoulder—it was recreation time, after all—but she grunted and didn't wake.

I walked into the hallway. Adriana leaned against the drooping, peeling wallpaper, holding her spectacles. Bell wielded her magnifying glass as she bent over, examining the air for some kind of gap.

"Bell, you're not allowed to use your magnifying glass for that."

"I smell something along here."

Bell squinted through her magnifying glass at the air just above the third step.

"Do you need my help, little lady?"

"Don't call her that. Bell, I order you, give me the magnifying glass." I tugged on the wooden handle; Bell tightened her grip and leaned away.

I yanked it out of her hand.

"Give it—"

I smashed it against the wooden railing. The handle shuddered and a maze of cracks spread through the glass.

"No," Bell shouted, punching me in the shoulder. "Elisa, what the *hell*—"

"Don't you speak to me that way. It's for your own good."

"Don't worry, little lady, we still have the spectacles," Adriana said. "Elisa, apologize to Bell for breaking her magnifying glass."

"No. You're not even supposed to be out here. It's recreation time." I stalked back to the Recreation Room and tried not to listen to their muttering in the hallway.

I remembered when Bell's magnifying glass had stayed in her pocket, when it had been just us sisters, sitting before the elephant, examining pottery, braiding our curls, and falling asleep together in the tub, before this obsession with the staircase began, before Bell started asking questions.

8

If Henley sisters raise their voices to each other, they will be banished from our bedroom. They will no longer be considered sisters of Henley House.

Grace and I were curled in our white marble tub when the bedroom door opened and Bell stormed in, her face drawn and her hands trembling.

"What do you want?" I said.

Bell threw herself onto the floor and splayed out her long legs. "Adriana's still looking, but she told me to come in here and rest for a while."

"You should be sleeping," I said. "It's past bedtime."

"Oh my *gosh*, Elisa, are you serious? We have more important things to worry about now, you know. Adriana and I are going to find the way up the stairs—"

"And then what?" I shouted. Grace grunted awake and fixed me with one indignant blue eye, but I ignored her. "What then? What do you think is going to be up those stairs, exactly, Bell?"

"The truth about why we're—"

"The truth about what?" My voice echoed off the tile.

"Will you keep it down, please?" Grace said.

"The truth about why we're stuck here," Bell said.

"We're not stuck. We have a perfectly good—"

"All lies, lies and fake rules you made up to try to keep me and Grace under control," Bell said. "Not anymore. I'm going up those stairs, and Adriana and I are going to find it tonight, you'll see."

"Find what?" Grace said.

"Get out." I advanced on Bell. "Get out of our bedroom. Don't you dare—"

Bell's bare foot kicked against my shin. I shoved her towards our bedroom door.

"I'm done with you—you're not a Henley sister. Stop trying to corrupt us."

"Fine. I don't want to be in here, anyway. Adriana's a better sister than you are." Bell stalked out of the hallway and shouted, "But when I find a way up, I'm taking Grace with me."

I slammed the door, and an already crooked lithograph of potted flowers broke free from the crumbling plaster and shattered on the floor.

Now Bell and Adriana are stomping out on the stairs. I hear them muttering, hear footsteps creaking on the wooden boards.

Bell is now a lost cause. She's gone over to Adriana's side, and she's no longer one of us.

But if she thinks she's going to bring Grace through her horrid door, she's very much mistaken.

9

There are no more rules.

I had only left Grace for a moment, to step into the kitchen to replace the horned beetle under the drinking glass, when I heard a shriek from the staircase, followed by a guttural sound of approval. I dropped the glass—it shattered on the floor—and then I ran into the hallway.

"Adriana, I couldn't have done it without you!" Bell shouted, one arm slung around Adriana's shoulders, the other hooked in midair as though Bell were holding a door open.

Adriana shook Bell's shoulders. "Well done, little lady."

Bell placed her right hand next to her left. Her shoulder blades contracted and her fingers scraped along the invisible hinge. Then the air rippled, and she stumbled forward, gasping.

"What's going on?" Grace had appeared, her tinsel trailing behind her.

"Nothing, Grace. Go back—"

"Grab her," Bell said. Adriana snatched Grace and set her down at the entrance to Bell's door.

"Don't you dare—" I lunged towards them, shoving past Adriana, but Bell was already racing upwards, Grace in tow.

"Stop. I'm ordering you to stop. Bring her back."

Bell and Grace disappeared at the top of the stairs.

I raced after them, emerging into a hallway that stank of dirt, but where the carpet was clean and pictures hung on pristine wallpaper: pictures of a woman, with cropped hair and Bell's freckles, and a man, with Grace's eyes and a fat mustache.

I stumbled against the wall: I had met that woman, who was called Mom, and that man, called Dad, in this hallway before.

"Bring Grace back down." I hurried after them to a room at the end of the hallway. Bell was shoving a chair beneath a skylight; weak silver sunrays poured onto her curls.

"Stop," I said, but memories bloomed, unleashed by the second floor:

The man called Dad hanging the painting of pastel flowers above the bed in this room, Mom spraying herself with the fluted perfume bottle on the dresser. Adriana vacuuming the unstained beige carpet and telling Bell to stop jumping on the blue paisley-covered bed, and Bell sniping that we were too old for a babysitter.

We had lived in this house with Mom and Dad and Adriana: we had eaten stew for dinner, and played checkers, and thrown tennis balls for our dog Jake on the lawn. It had been almost Christmas.

Bell lifted Grace onto the chair, climbed next to her, cranked open the skylight and lifted Grace through, onto the roof. Then Bell's legs disappeared off the chair as she clambered up after Grace. I followed them, pulling myself towards the warmth of sunlight, squinting against the view: flat sunblade at the horizon, a sheen of water to our left, and sagging house after sagging house stretching off towards a line of barren trees and dark pines.

The roofs before us were a parade of smashed-in, broken shingles and exposed rafters. Broken boards, shattered trees, abandoned car tires littered the sunlit streets.

It had been almost Christmas, and there had been a storm. The announcer

said on the radio that we'd be all right if the dam held, and the dam was ex-
pected to hold.

Mom had brought home a box of books from the library, and I had leafed
through an old manners guide, and I'd said I liked all these rules, and Dad
said of course I did, and he told me that people invent rules to keep back the
bad things under the bed, to prevent chaos. I didn't understand. Mom and Dad
had gone to bed upstairs, and Bell and Grace and I had spread our sleeping
bags on the floor of the living room, as we did sometimes.

"No," I said on the roof. Grace's single eye swept the landscape, and Bell looked at me with horror written in her wide eyes.

The water had been heavy. A roar leapt into my sleep, and I was shaking
off my dream when the windows broke, and I rolled over onto Bell and tried to
breathe and found only liquid, only cold muddy water, and then so much water
was slamming into me that breathing became a secondary concern, and I
couldn't move, and I writhed there waiting for the water to stop and somehow
knowing it never would...

"Mom? Dad?" Grace said, as the sun inched further up the
horizon, and found the bruises that covered her cheekbones.

"Elisa." Bell slipped her hand into mine. "I am so sorry, so, so
sorry—I never should have..."

"No, you shouldn't." I fell with a thud back into the bedroom
and shoved past Adriana. I walked down the stairs to our former
haven, now our coffin. I climbed over the grandfather clock and
walked into the Elephant Room.

I remembered now: the elephant, our silent god, was nothing
more than a statue Dad had brought home from a business trip.

I looked at its laughing eyes, the joyful curve of its mouth, and
I swiped it onto the floor, where its head snapped from its body
and one tusk rolled away under the kitchen table.

This will be my last entry in this etiquette book. Because what
good are rules for three dead girls? How can an elephant-god make
us forget our sister's missing eye? How can we spend nights in the
tub when we once had beds, and slippers, and stars outside our
windows?

THE RIGHT THING

JACK KETCHUM

"I'M NOT SURE I CAN DO THIS," she said.

"You knew it was going to be hard," he said. "We both did. But we've tried everything, haven't we."

"I don't know. Have we?"

"You know we have."

"I can't help feeling that something…"

"Tell me what. Tell me one thing. A single thing we haven't tried."

She stared at him and they each knew there was no answer for that.

Their living room was suddenly very large he thought. And very still. No sounds from the street. No passing cars. No neighborhood kids playing ball outside. Their house was holding its breath. Waiting.

"Nine months," she said.

"I know," he said.

And again the silence. So that when the doorbell rang it might have been a shotgun blast fired into the room.

He got up. She stayed where she was. Sitting with clasped hands at the edge of their sofa, like a woman on the unyielding chair of a hospital waiting room.

"I'm Mrs. Kaltsas," said the woman in the doorway. "Department of Social Services."

When they were finished with the paperwork she asked them at last why they were doing this. You have a lovely home, she said. You have a good job. I know it's really none of my business. But I confess I don't understand.

We're unfit parents, he said.

She frowned, puzzled.

Unfit? I don't understand. How so?

So he told her.

While in the crib upstairs little Caroline began to cry.

When they were gone his wife cried too and he held her in his arms on the sofa and in the now even vaster silence, told her that there was nothing else they could have done, they had done the right thing finally, she knew they had and she said that yes she did, of course she did. It was a matter of loyalty wasn't it? A matter of eight long years and not just months. But it was terrible. Terrible. He told her that he knew that too. Until at last her tears subsided.

Good cats seem to know somehow when the humans they share their lives with are in need of comfort and George had gone to her lap nearly as soon as her crying began and lay curled there, purring steadily. Gazing up at her for the duration. She petted him and scratched his chest and chin until a small tuft of tabby-fur fell off her fingers and drifted to the floor.

It was no longer a problem.

PASSING AFFLICTION

PATRICK O'NEILL

WELL, HERE IT IS: my account as foster carer for the child, Anna Pinter. It won't make for easy reading but then you asked for it, as I knew you would. That's what you social workers do, isn't it? Get it on the record, seal the cracks and make it watertight; a neat little report outlining what occurred, how it all went so wrong and why, but not in your words—mine—so there can be no comeback. You are simply a bystander collating facts; an impartial witness observing events.

I will sign at the bottom of the page and you will file this away amongst the other fragmented chapters—another misfit piece of the unsolvable puzzle; another instalment in another child's disjointed existence in the care system. But this is different and no doubt you will think me insane once you have read it, and with good reason, but it changes nothing. I will recount this chapter exactly as it occurred, regardless of your views.

I wasn't surprised to be selected for Anna's placement. There can't be many foster carers with a track record like mine: 53 placements of varying longevities and complexity, all successfully completed without breakdown, until now. And as for personal experience, having been a wife, mother, widow and childless all before the age of 45 could only have strengthened your case. I'm the one who can cope with problems. I'm the one who can cope with Anna, where everybody else failed.

And how many failed?

I heard that mine was to be her sixth placement with foster carers in as many months; an appalling record for the Borough by any standards. After all, Anna is only 6. But then of course you knew the extent of her difficulties, did you not? Far more than you told. So perhaps your hands are not so clean after all. Your understated summary of her affliction stays with me even now:

"Anna is a quiet child from a difficult background. She simply suffers from an unusual disorder. Shelley, trust me, you are more than capable of caring for her."

The slender file you prepared before her arrival was of equally meagre content; nothing more than a half-filled page.

Name: *Anna Pinter*
Age: *6 years 2 months*
Hair Colour: *Light Brown*
Eye Colour: *Blue/Green*
Background/Circumstance: *Neglect*

Anna is in good physical health although rarely speaks and generally uses nodding and headshaking as a method of communication. Anna was taken into care 6 months ago following removal from the family home under Section 46 of the Children's Act 1989 due to significant concerns around her well-being and of her mother's ability to care for her. Anna's mother is a self-confessed heroin addict and conditions in the family home are of a poor standard. Neglect was clearly apparent. To date Anna has made no mention of her mother, or expressed desire to return home.

And that was it. Not very helpful. I wonder if you agree now.

It is of no consequence but I remember the morning of Anna's arrival all too well. The house was quiet, unnaturally so, the expectant silence broken only by the monotonous ticking of the grandfather clock in the living room and the distant moaning of autumn wind straining around the brickwork of Bowden Hill.

I have lived in this old house for over two decades now, ever since the car accident that left my life bereft of all meaning, but I have never known a silence like it; as though every brick, wall, ceiling and floor were listening and waiting patiently for her arrival.

I spent the morning making up the long room in the attic; the one that overlooks the lawn to the south. The children always love it here. The walls are yellow and patterned with turquoise and red butterfly print. On the ceiling there are stars that shine and glow through the darkness of night. There are no ominous cupboards or gloomy corners, and in the early evenings red kites glide far above the grass in perfect circles. Sometimes they fly close enough to the leaded windows that you hear their haunted callings. It is a happy room, or at least it was.

Later that morning as I sat waiting, with only the heavy ticking of the clock for company, I gazed out towards the woodland and wondered—as I had wondered so many times before—what it must be like for a child to arrive at this place, so far from any-where. The potholed driveway, flanked with gnarled almond trees on the approach, must be as daunting as the house itself: red brick against spindly larch trees. Most of the children who have passed through these doors have come from a world where the street is their only knowledge and comfort. They are powerful in their own territory and possess the skills to survive. But here, in the tranquilli-ty of Berkshire's greenbelt countryside, they are suddenly out of their depth, in the beginning at least. It must be hard.

I always try to visualise the children before they arrive and with Anna, it was no different. It is in our nature to second guess out-comes, to speculate, even presume what the future will bring. We simply cannot help ourselves; but how wrong I was with her.

As I opened the front door she peeked up for a fleeting sec-ond, just long enough to fix me with her eyes: the right, a luminous turn of pale blue (much like my own), the left, an impossible shade of pea green. Her hair, just as you said, was light brown in colour but so tightly cropped to her pale little head that she appeared bald at first glance.

Her young skin was smooth and without flaw but pallid and translucent; no more than a thin membrane stretched across elf-like features revealing a dark network of tiny veins beneath. I could sense the fear within her as she craned her neck slightly, first to the left, then to the right, to see past me and into the corridor beyond.

"It's alright," I said quietly. "It's nice here. Come in."

I turned my attention to the social worker who had brought Anna; a shabbily dressed effort in his twenties, perhaps the age Benedict would have been had the car accident never happened.

"You can leave us now. Thank you for bringing Anna."

I saw his expression change, as I knew it would. He was hoping to have been invited inside to aid Anna's transition to Bowden Hill. Social workers detest relinquishing authority but in my experience their very presence unsettles the children. Through their young eyes, you are the carriers of change, the bearers of uncertainty, and who could blame them? After all, it is you that arrives to 'remove' them from one situation and 'place' them in to another. It is you that threatens their security by forcing decisions that they have had no hand in. They are not stupid. They are children.

I alone decide who steps foot in this place and so, five minutes later, with the wind howling outside and the chiming of the grandfather clock striking the hour, Anna and I were alone.

"It's fine," I beckoned her towards the kitchen. "Follow me."

For the longest time Anna stood motionless on the doormat—eyes downturned, hands dangling to her sides—but finally, with nervous breath, she began her careful journey across the hallway, making sure to step only on the smooth grey flagstones and avoid contact with the grout work and cracks in between. Halfway, she stopped—perfect black shoes aligned in the centre of a pave—and tapped her palms twice against her hips before continuing.

In the kitchen, she tip-toed cautiously across the tiles and perched herself neatly on a wooden chair, resting her little hands on the table and tucking thumbs out of sight before splaying eight fingers in perfect symmetry across its surface.

Her digits were neatly manicured but the nail on each forefinger had been left to grow and sharpened to a point, like the talon of a small bird. *Why?*

"Are you hungry?"

She shook her head.

"Thirsty?"

Nod.

"Water?"

Nod.

I watched her clasp the glass evenly in both hands and gulp it down. When finished, she returned her hands to the table with spread fingers once again, and smiled a little elfin "thank you."

It almost brought me to tears. She was so utterly trapped. You should have told me. You should have explained and then maybe none of this would have happened.

"Come along. Come and see your new bedroom."

They have a name for it: Obsessive Compulsive Disorder—OCD, an anxiety disorder characterized by repetitive behaviours aimed at reducing fear. But then they have a name for everything, don't they?

The condition is commonplace amongst children who have suffered trauma and neglect, as you well know. And in a way it makes perfect sense. When all else descends into chaos and uncertainty, the establishment of an unwavering routine creates a climate of security; something at least in a world of disorder that is predictable and comforting; an invisible shroud of harmony that, although requiring continual lacing to prevent rips from appearing, fashions a sense of safety.

I could see immediately that Anna's affliction ran far deeper than simple routine though and that her shroud had hardened to an impenetrable barrier between herself and reality; making her captive in a hellish landscape of forced symmetry. Every movement, every action she took was restricted mercilessly by its influence. How I felt for her.

That first night, around midnight, I crept to the attic room to check on her. Moonlight streamed into the darkness and across the butterfly print on the walls. Anna's gentle breaths whispered through the silence at perfectly regular intervals. I had been expecting her be tucked warmly beneath the covers but instead she lay on the made bed, arms crossed over chest, bare feet in faultless formation, crispy white pyjamas immaculately pressed, as motionless and pale as a corpse.

Later, I took up a tartan blanket and rested it over her delicate form, but when I returned the following morning, Anna was sitting on the bed, arms linked around knees like a little pixie, gazing through the leaded windows and down at the lawn. The tartan blanket was now draped neatly over the mirror on the dressing table, concealing its glass.

"You don't like mirrors?"

Anna shrugged her shoulders and continued eyeing the garden far below.

"Why not?"

She turned then, fixing me with a blank and unreadable mask. October sunlight shone across her pale features, exaggerating further the stark difference in her eye colours. And suddenly I understood: zero symmetry. Why would she possibly want to see that?

"Wait here," I told her. "One minute."

When I returned, I sat gently on the bed and passed her a pair of small mirrored sunglasses. She took them and unfolded the black plastic arms, in and out, in and out, four times, before sliding them on to her face.

"Now come and see."

I stood her before the mirror and rested my hands on her willowy shoulders.

"Trust me."

Her taut little muscles trembled as I reached up and pulled the blanket away.

Silence fell around us like a tangible, vibrant presence and for a moment, as Anna's shoulders tightened to concrete beneath my touch, I thought she would scream, but quite suddenly she smiled: a bright, wonderful, brilliant smile lined with perfect white teeth.

"You see," I said. "You are beautiful. Anna is beautiful."

I spent the next few days in quiet observation, only sporadically including myself in Anna's games, which usually involved the careful arrangement of toys in neat, military rows to either side of the living room in faultless parallel formation. She sometimes drew butterflies too, but then became anxious if a marking on one wing did not correlate exactly with its counterpart. This always ended with the contaminated picture being folded in half again and again and finally cut in to precise, equally-sided triangles which were then consigned face down to the floor into orderly rows or immaculate patterns.

Having made headway with the mirror incident, I was close to winning Anna's trust, but knew that it was a fragile, hesitant confidence that could fall away at any time. I knew that if I could help Anna find her voice, there would be no turning back. Her speech would be the key. But for now, patience would need to prevail.

I steered clear of bedtime rituals too—even when the distant hum of the electric razor sounded from the attic room.

The head-shaving was an integral part of her routine and, though it went against all my instincts, I knew it would be a mistake to intervene at such an early stage of the placement. I knew how important it was to her. Whilst her eyes were different colours, she could still control the symmetrical appearance of her head. Ironically, I had inadvertently helped her with this particular rite as she was now able sit in front of the mirror, clad in sunglasses, and see exactly what she was doing.

The afternoon that everything changed was much the same as any other that first week; autumn wind continued to wail around the house like a lost child calling for its mother, spitting rain angrily against the windows. Leaves continued to fall from the beech hedge at the end of the lawn and from the apple tree where the empty wooden swing creaked back and forth. The red kites continued to circle the gun-metal skies far above Bowden Hill and the old grandfather clock continued to tick the seconds away.

At around six o'clock I entered the living room to find Anna sitting at the table by the window, her fingers splayed out evenly across its polished wooden surface. Every so often she would slowly lift her sharpened forefingers in unison, wave them to the left and to the right, and then rest them down again in line with the others.

I took the seat opposite and together we sat for a few moments. Outside, shadows were gathering at the corners of the lawn and a small brown rabbit hopped across the grass and disappeared beneath the darkness of the beech hedge. The grandfather clock chimed the hour.

"Anna, I want you to try something. Something new."

She looked up from her forefingers with interest.

"I want you to turn one hand over, very slowly, and lay it back down on the table. But leave the other one just where it is. Do you think you can do that?"

In a second, Anna's expression changed from interest to fear, her jaw tensing and the glow around her cheeks draining to pallor. Skin tightened across her pointed features and as she shook her head, a small blue vein throbbed at her temple.

"What do you think would happen?" I asked gently. "If you did it?"

Anna swallowed into the quietness and shifted uncomfortably in her seat, first one way and then the other.

I looked at the scene beyond the window. Darkness was forming properly now, gathering in strength in the woodland beyond the lawns. A chill went through me as Anna whispered into the quietness.

"Bad things."

It was the breakthrough though. Finally, she had found the strength to use her voice, the voice that would bring her from captivity to freedom. I could have jumped to my feet in elation. Instead, I kept my nerve.

"Anna, you need to trust me now. You are safe here, in this

house. Nothing can hurt you here. I want you to try and turn one hand over. Just try."

Tears brimmed in her eyes. She gulped again, louder this time, her talon-like forefingers tapping nervously in unison on the table. She took a deep breath, crumpled up her delicate features, and turned her right hand on its back.

Silence settled over the room; the same eerie silence that I had felt before Anna's arrival here. But it was more than that, much more, and it took me a moment to understand what had happened, what had changed. But then I saw Anna's eyes turn to the wall behind me, to the grandfather clock. It had stopped ticking. I will admit it was odd, as though time itself had suddenly become redundant, meaningless, and that all that was left was Anna and I, struggling to breath in the tense, overbearing atmosphere of the living room.

And then she screamed; a chilling, high pitched shriek that froze every muscle and sinew in my body. I could only watch as Anna clasped her hands over her ears and the sound rose to a terrifying crescendo.

I cried out as something bulky and dark thudded against the window beside us, almost shattering the pane. In the same moment, Anna stopped screaming and ran from the room. The grandfather clock began ticking once again.

Later, I realised it had been a bird. I found its lifeless body, twisted and ruffled, on the grass outside. A red kite.

Throughout that evening I tried repeatedly to convince myself that it had all been coincidence but each time I was left with the same distant sense of unease. What if it hadn't been? What if Anna was right—that 'bad things' would happen if she did not conform to the symmetry? It was ridiculous, I know, but the feeling would not leave me.

As I was slipping on my dressing gown before bed, Anna entered my bedroom with her head held low.

"Sorry," she whispered. "I killed a bird."

"Come here." I put my arms around her. "No you haven't. It was just coincidence. Birds always fly into things. You've done nothing wrong."

I held her for some time. She trembled like a small animal beneath my embrace.

"What happened," she asked quietly into my shoulder, "to your face?"

Caught off guard, I tensed at the memory—bloodied glass and twisted metal, white hot flames and screaming—but then relaxed again, realising that Anna had obviously been wanting to ask me since her arrival. And why wouldn't she? The children that come here always do.

"It was an accident," I said. "In a car. There was a fire."

That night I dreamt of a church, or rather a place beneath a church, far below the surface; a crypt of some kind where an endless corridor of arches stretched out before me and where shadows slid and danced in candlelight. A shape came into view, the pale form of a naked child stepping out from darkness. Anna.

As I approached she raised her face. In the amber glow of the candlelight her eyes were blacker than night. She grinned to expose a perfect set of razor white teeth, glinting with fresh saliva. Pale wings opened in unison around her, their translucent surface mapped with dark veins and ribbed with spiny little bones.

I awoke screaming to the sight of Anna standing over my bed. She was sleepwalking.

She remembered nothing in the morning. Sleepwalkers rarely do. When I went to the attic room she was sitting on her bed staring out of the window at the red kites circling overhead.

"Sometimes in my dreams," she said quietly, "I have wings."

A chill crept down my spine, and though it is terrible to admit, in that moment I wished that she had never started to speak again.

It is difficult to explain the atmosphere that dwelled in the house over the next few days. Anna rarely spoke and we fell back into our routines, almost as though nothing had happened. Only now I sensed the presence, an invisible void between us, an unspoken barrier that could not be breached. I had attempted to move the situation forwards but that was over now and Anna had retracted into herself once again.

But the retraction was contagious for I too became lost in my thoughts during those long days. Much of the time I found myself staring at the photographs on the mantelpiece in the living room, the ones of Benedict and Charles, mulling over the car accident and everything that I had lost.

Anna continued to play her intricately structured games and to draw butterflies, all predestined for destruction, but I was no more than a spectator on the side lines again. And all the while, with each hour that passed, a quiet but irrefutable tension was steadily building between us.

I was folding clothes in the attic room in early afternoon when I heard the glass smash in the kitchen far below. At first I thought I had imagined it, until I heard Anna scream in pain and begin whimpering into the quiet.

I burst into the kitchen to find her standing on a chair and leaning over the sink with both hands clasped tightly together. She had broken a glass whilst getting a drink, cutting her right forefinger just above the knuckle. Blood dripped through her rigid grasp and onto the clean ceramic surface in large crimson globules.

"It's all right." I peered over the sink. "It's just a scratch. It's not bad."

I should have known not to leave her then—I should have realised—but having seen the cut, which was relatively deep and a borderline case for stitches, I knew I needed the First Aid Kit from the bathroom, and so I left the kitchen.

When I returned, Anna no longer stood at the sink but was hunched over the now-bloodied kitchen table. The shard of glass in her grasp—poised above the knuckle on her left hand—glinted in the pale sunlight as she went to make the cut.

"Don't you dare!"

But it was too late, of course. She paid me no attention as she sank the splintered glass deep into her left forefinger and dragged its razor edge sideways across the digit to complete the necessary incision in all its bloody glory.

It was not my finest hour as a carer, I will admit, because in that moment I simply exploded—as though all the tension that had built in the past few days had finally burst through the vents and found a way into the open.

I called her 'stupid' and 'bad' and 'ridiculous'. All of the things one should never say to a child. It was a terrible, violent and unforgivable verbal attack of which I am deeply ashamed.

Afterwards, I apologised profusely and washed and bandaged her little fingers with gorse and tape to stop the flow of blood, but I could see that it was no use. Anna had withdrawn into herself further still and I knew that this time it would be virtually impossible to coax her back out again. What little trust I had built, was gone. She could barely meet my eyes.

As I sat in the living room hours later, watching Anna swaying back on forth on the swing beneath the apple tree outside—with perfectly aligned hands on the chains—I cried.

Though she had her back to me as she rocked to and fro and was facing the hedge at the end of the lawn, I felt somehow she knew I was watching. Every now and then she would lift two bandaged fingers in perfect symmetry and then rest them down again as she swung.

I sat there for some minutes, mesmerised by the motion of the swing, by her small silhouette swaying in the shadows of the gnarled branches but then, it began.

Anna lifted her right arm horizontally, using the other to hold the swing steady. As she swung, asymmetrically, the grandfather clock stopped.

Coincidence, surely. But as Anna lifted her leg out straight before her and tucked the other beneath the swing, the living room door slammed into the silence and the photograph of Benedict and

Charles fell from the mantelpiece and shattered to the floor.

Outside, the wind picked up as Anna swung higher and higher. She had pulled the chain hard on one side to make the swing twist unevenly as she rode. The larches on the edges of the lawn creaked and bowed. Dead leaves blew out from the woodland and danced on the grass before her. Through the gale, and just as the window beside me shattered, I thought I heard the shrill sound of her laughter.

A terrible realisation: it was not the affliction that controlled Anna, or the fear, but rather that Anna was in complete control and always had been. Not the slave, but the master.

But enough was enough.

It took only moments to crunch across the broken glass of the living room and yank open the door to the garden. Head down to the wind, I tore across the grass and wrenched Anna from the swing.

She wriggled and kicked and screamed in my arms as I bundled her roughly back to the house and forced her to sit at the kitchen table.

"This stops here," I yelled, ripping a chair across the floor for myself. "Right now."

Anna fixed me with a fierce stare, laced with malice, and, as I sat before her, something in her bizarre and wild eyes sent an icy chill to my soul; not the eyes of a child, but the eyes of something else altogether.

"You can't change me," she whispered loudly. "Just the same as you can't change that you were driving the car that day."

I stopped then because, suddenly, I had nothing more.

The shock of what she had said cut deeper than any knife could have. She was right of course, but to hear it like that… There was no way she could have known.

"But I can change *you*." She grasped my limp hands and grinned at me as the razor nails of her forefingers pierced the skin of my knuckles and drove down into the bone.

It is difficult to recall, but I do remember the coldness rushing up my arms, my neck, through my blood and around my body until paralysis set in. I thought I heard wings flapping about me, and a terrible screeching noise that made me think of the red kites above the house. Was it me screaming or something else?

But it is all finished now. The placement has failed and no doubt you have secured the services of another carer for Anna. I wonder if you provided the same inadequate information to them, or whether you thought it right to explain in detail this time. I'd put money on the former.

As for me, I am becoming used to it now; the rules and boundaries to which I must abide. The importance of symmetry and routine are supreme and overriding. I know exactly what I must do to keep disorder from creeping in. The affliction has been passed in its entirety. Mirrors are becoming difficult. My left eye is changing—an impossible shade of pea green—and when I stare into the glass the lack of equilibrium is creating problems. Sunglasses help but the facial scarring from the accident is not so easily rectified. I have made new incisions and burns but it could be years before the results become acceptable.

I am a mere novice but I will learn as time passes, perhaps even control in the end, the force that waits to be unleashed.

So go on, file this away with the other chapters, as you will. But do not send any more children here. It is not safe.

THE GREAT PITY

GARY A. BRAUNBECK

"...all those bodies which compose the mighty frame of the world have not any subsistence without a mind—that their being is to be perceived or known."
- George Berkeley (1685 – 1753)

"The great pity will occur before long,
Those who gave will be obliged to take:
Naked, starving, withstanding cold and thirst..."
- Michel de Nostredame

PRELUDE: CHALK GRIPPED IN EACH HAND

Later, of course, no one is watching when the little girl stumbles out of the burning house and toward the middle of the street, a piece of chalk gripped in each hand. One piece is white, the other is red. She finds a section of the asphalt that is without potholes or cracks and kneels down, brushing away some of the dirt and pebbles so that the surface is as smooth and clear as it can possibly be. She looks at the house she has just left but if she is thinking anything, remembering anything, hoping for or regretting anything, it cannot be seen on her face. The flames that were only a second ago causing the house to screech like some prehistoric beast being pulled into a pit of tar freeze in place, so very still, looking almost artificial; even what remains of the roof pauses in the midst of buckling, snapping, and collapsing inward. When the flames resume their feast, less than one-tenth of a second will have passed; but, for now, time, place, here-and-now, back-then, all of them are no longer fixed in place; this is how she wants it, this little girl. For now, at least.

Leaning forward, she begins drawing a long, unbroken, often-curving line with the white chalk until the basic shape of the fallen body—a woman, in her late twenties; yes, that's it—is complete. Switching hands, she begins to add the blood; a splash near the stomach, a trickle down one leg, a massive fountain on the left side of the head. Leaning her own head to one side so as to afford a different if not better view, the little girl smiles at the parallax effect achieved by this slight change of vantage point. She scoots to the side, brushes away some more dirt and pebbles, and begins working on the shape of the second body. A young boy, this one, with a clubfoot and a jagged maw where the lower portion of his face used to be. It's a good thing the sticks of chalk are brand-new; she has so many figures to outline, so much red to splash, spatter, and spray about. It's nice that no one is watching the house now, not like before. She doesn't like it when people look, when people watch, when people stare; the lookers, the watchers, the staring ones, they never say anything, but, oh, the things they *think*; the things they do think.

Luckily, for us, she does not choose to look up from her task. Not that she would see us, but, still, it's best we remain as we are.

1. AND BY EXTENSION

Not just anyone can be one who only looks: if the person being observed looks back, the observer becomes the one who is being looked at, and the guise of safety, of an action unnoticed and therefore secret and therefore somewhat holy, is shattered; the moment is unalterably affected. Still, one cannot help but wonder: if the being at whom one stares is something akin to a ghost, a spirit, or phantom, does the moment—and, by extension, the observer—remain unaffected? It will be important for us to remember this as we turn our attention to the moment at hand, the moment that is being sculpted from nothingness into a life-like shape, the moment that does not know it's being observed from a safe vantage point; in doing so, like the sculptor confronting the virgin marble or clay or a child who will soon be drawing chalk figures on the street, we will use our words and trust they will speak accurately to who- or whatever is watching and listening. Should we fail in this task, we risk conjuring deaf idols if we take too literally our descriptions of the sculpted scenes, for not just anyone can be one who only looks: if the person being observed looks back, the observer becomes the one who is being looked at.

2. GEOMETRIC EXACTNESS

It is necessary—insomuch as anything can be said to *be* necessary—that we establish certain precincts, particular margins, commonplace boundaries before going any further; let us begin with the *when* of it: right now, in the graceful flow of the present. Now, the where of it: we are hidden here, in the blank spaces between words, paragraphs, pages; we are only *now*, right now, here in this story, here on this page, here in this sentence. And from this place of safety we watch as a young man (not the little girl with the chalk in her hands, she hasn't shown herself yet, and with good reason)—a young man in his early twenties, walks down a street that looks like a lot of other streets, passing houses that look very much like all the other houses. We don't know this young man's name, no one living on this street knows his name, and so, as we observe from our unnoticed and therefore holy vantage point, his identity is of no consequence. What *is* of consequence, what we absolutely must concern ourselves with, is the bouquet of flowers he carries in his left hand, the hand that is, at the moment, facing the house he is passing.

Watch carefully. The young man's face is tight and red. There are streaks down both of his reddened cheeks, but if there were any tears, they have already dried. Is he angry? Hurt? Brokenhearted, perhaps. It doesn't matter; what matters is that he is coming to a stop in front of one of the houses, his entire body shuddering from the anger or broken-heartedness. He closes his eyes, pulls in a slow, deep breath that steadies him, and—bringing to bear a surprising amount of force—tosses the bouquet aside. They land, still neatly wrapped in green tissue paper, on the second of the three stone steps that lead up to the front porch. The young man wipes his eyes, pulls in another deep breath, nods to himself (perhaps having made a decision to which we are not privy), and walks away, his part played, his purpose served, and leaves our story while we remain here, in front of the house, looking at the bouquet of flowers.

We sense more than realize there is something odd about this image. We squint, blink, and stare. It takes a few moments but at last it becomes so obvious that we momentarily feel foolish: there is a certain, almost geometric *exactness* to the position in which the bouquet has landed. Moving closer, we decide that, yes, yes, most definitely, they *do* look as if they were placed in that position on the second stone step *on purpose*, don't they? Absolutely. And with this image of the bouquet firmly set in our memory we can move forward a few hours, unnoticed, undifferentiated, shape- and shadow-less, here on this page, at this paragraph, in this book.

3. THE COMPANY AND FRIENDSHIP OF SHADOWS

The first person to notice the flowers is fifty-eight-year-old Eugene ("Gene to my buddies") Benson, a man who discovered only this morning that the cancer was *not* totally removed along with his prostate, that some of it, like an undetected fragrance, has found a new and metastasized home in his liver, his lungs, and—very soon—his brain. Gene—as we now know him, for what person would refuse the company and friendship of shadows at a time such as this?—has been walking for hours, forcing himself to notice all things he'd taken for granted during his thirty-one years working the graveyard shift at Miller Tool & Die, his attention and skill focused not on the world beyond the factory cell but instead on metal forming rolls, lathe bits, milling cutters, and form tools. He wonders why he never married, never raised a family, never did any of the thousands of things, be they special or everyday, that mark the passing moments of one's life so that some sort of memory will live on.

He stops when he sees the bouquet on the second step of the house he was about to pass, and for a minute he simply stares, wondering who would leave such a thing, and why; then remembers stories he's heard on the radio or read about in the paper or seen on the evening news, stories about people—family, friends, even strangers—who assemble at the site of some domestic tragedy to leave gifts, cards, pictures drawn in crayon by children, toys, flowers, trinkets, handwritten notes, photos that mean nothing to anyone except the one who kneels down, makes the Sign of the Cross, and tearfully places it beside any of the dozens of motif candles arranged in odd, geometrically exact rows (as if the positioning somehow ensures that the iridescent light will continue to burn, as if the act of placing these things at the site of a domestic tragedy somehow lifts the burden of accountability from the shoulders of the neighbors and friends who gather to sing church hymns, weep openly, and crane their necks to offer prayers both silent and shrill to a sky where no one looks down, all the time trying to convince themselves and others that they *didn't know* or *didn't want to interfere with other peoples' business*).

Gene has always been secretly sickened by such stories. What the hell good does any physical item do for the person who's now dead? Why amplify the suffering of that person—unless it's simply a way to draw attention to yourself? It makes no sense to him. But now, for some reason, he finds himself unable to look or walk away from the flowers. He feels something on his face and reaches up to discover that he's begun to weep—but whether it's for the person who's died or for himself, he can't decide.

Then he does something that surprises even him; he reaches into his back pocket and removes his wallet, flipping through the credit cards in their clear plastic compartments (cards he doesn't have to worry about paying off now) until he comes to the single photograph he's carried with him for God-only-knows how many years: the photo that came with the wallet. It's of a little girl, maybe six years old. She smiles at the camera that has captured her image on a perfect autumn day. She is the little girl every married couple wants. (Had the photo been of a little *boy*, he would have been the little boy every married couple wants.)

With his thumb Gene touches the cheek of the little girl, realizing that her face has faded over the years. He can make out her strawberry-blonde hair, her light windbreaker, part of her smile, and her left eye. He tries to remember what she looked like when she was new; he tries to remember why he purchased this particular wallet; and, lastly, he wonders why he did not remove this photo of the little girl who never was. Slipping it from its protective sleeve, he stares at her discolored and washed-out face, feeling a rush of grief he's not experienced since the death of his parents. He pulls in a slow, deep breath that steadies him (not unlike the nameless young man in the moment before he tossed the bouquet), and walks over to the house, kneels before the second step, and gently places the picture of the little girl among the roses and baby's-breath, taking a moment to make certain that she's looking out at those who may pass by once Gene himself has left.

We float, first this way, then that, whispering around him, pondering the anomalous tableau. Why is he doing this, making a gesture that he's always thought to be ineffectual, offensive, and hypocritical? We consider entering Eugene Benson's mind to find the answer, but then he speaks, something in the back of his voice sounding of corroded nails being wrenched from rotted wood:

"May as well give you a name while I'm at, huh? I always kinda thought that Leigh was a really pretty name. L-e-i-g-h, not L-e-e. So why don't we call you 'Leigh,' then? I'll bet whatever your real name is, you're probably all grown up now with a family of your own, but maybe you still model for photos that'll go inside of wallets and picture frames and... whatever else it is they put them kinds of pictures in these days.

"Oh, hon, you ought to see some of the things people have come up with. They got these picture frames now, they're electronic, and you can hook 'em up to a computer and load it with hundreds of pictures, then you turn it on and it'll change pictures every five minutes or so. I guess how long it shows any one picture is something that you have to decide for yourself. I wish I'd known how to use a computer, maybe I could've got on the Internet and found more pictures of you and..." The words trail off, lay fallen at his feet. We drift nearer, closer now than the space between his breaths, and murmur: *and what? Create a daughter who never existed, not in the same sense that—*

"—I exist," says Gene. "I mean, I know that *you* exist, you're right here in the picture, but that's where it sort of *ends* between you and me, isn't it? You look like the daughter I wish I'd had but never did, so what's wrong with wanting to watch her grow up, even if it's just in pictures that I'd find out there in other wallets, other frames? Maybe that's how she stays in touch with me, popping up in them places like that so that I can see that she still has that great smile and her hair still has that terrific shine and her skin still has that... that *bloom*, just like her mother's, and..." The words do not fall at his feet this time; instead, his left hand snaps up to cover his mouth and trap the rest of them within as he turns quickly away from the picture and the flowers; whatever he was about to say will remain unspoken: we can see as much in his eyes, eyes no longer narrowed against the sight of the surrounding world, eyes that are now wide and glistening at the corners and staring at something we are forbidden to look at from the place where we hide, something only he can see, perhaps a thing of heartbreak or madness, quiet fury or ravenous regret, born from a loneliness that whispers of a life misspent, that any and all chances to find something of joy or meaning or permanence have long since passed by, unrecognized, untaken, now unattainable; and as we try to imagine what physical shape this thing only Gene can see might assume— that is, if it were sentient enough to give itself form—questions must be posed;

have you ever:

passed by an ill-kept house where those inside are screeching profanities at one another and notice there is no fence to block your view of the backyard; and did you, despite yourself, look to see brown, brittle grass covered in many places by broken toys and empty beer cans; looking a bit longer, did you catch sight of the crumbling doghouse back there, and did you observe the dog itself: a too-thin, shuddering, frightened, whimpering vaudeville of what it should be, rheumy eyes focusing on you, pleading for a few moments of kindness because kindness does not gift with scabs and scars crisscrossing the body; kindness does not leave the unwashed bowls empty for days on end, until you are so hungry and so thirsty it takes all of your strength to simply lift up your head and lap at the tepid, dirty liquid or nibble at the mashed and moldy heap; it does not rip away chunks of fur, leaving these raw, glistening, red patches of slowly-healing flesh; it does not swing the belt that leaves one eye forever blinded; kindness does not kick the frail bones and laugh at the sound of their breaking; does not allow those broken bones to remain un-mended; it does not laugh at you when you try to fetch the toy but cannot—the deformities left by the broken bones have shortened one leg and rendered useless another; kindness does none of these; and kindness, even a moment's kindness, is all it asks of you, but as you begin to step closer you see that the dog is not chained to a pole or the front of the doghouse, there is nothing weighing it down or forcing it to stay put; and at that moment, safe and unobserved by the screeching people in the ill-kept house, did you wonder why the dog, seemingly of its own free will, *remains there*, where all it knows or will ever know is mockery, starvation, abuse, and loneliness;

have you ever:

watched the shabby vagrants who gather outside the bus station on Friday night, the way each one tries to make him- or herself a bit more presentable before approaching the sore and weary travelers; have you watched as they put on their best smile, the only one they possess, the one that is kept in cold storage and taken out only to ask for a bit of kindness, a little spare change, have you noticed how these smiles—some straight and bright, others displaying teeth that are crooked and broken and yellowed, jutting up from blackened gums—always show for an instant, just a flash, blink and you'll miss it, an echo of the person they used to be; and, in taking note of this, have you ever wanted to approach one of them (especially the worn-out women with bruised faces who hold the hands of small, shivering children), have you ever wanted to touch their cheek and whisper something of genuine comfort, words that will still have value long after the pocket change you drop into their grateful hands has been spent on liquor or drugs or food for the little ones, something like *anytime you feel lost, call my name and I will carry you back across to the place where you can remember what it felt like to still have human dignity*;

have you ever:

walked into a roomful of people and immediately sensed that something important, maybe ugly, possibly profound, has just occurred, and have you then forced a smile onto your face as you make the rounds, trying to discern what has happened by the way the others behave, the tones of their voices, the manner in which they carry themselves, avoiding too much eye contact, but there you are, digging for clues like some second-rate detective just so you can discover what occurred while you were out of the room;

have you ever:

found yourself weeping for no reason, be it at the office or at home or when you find yourself stuck in traffic with nothing to do but *sit there* and wait for everything to start moving again, and while you wait your mind—without your knowledge or assistance—

scrounges through the place where you've stored memories of pain, regret, sadness, despair, guilt, and digs deep until it finds a particularly terrible memory; but instead of throwing that memory into your mind, it sends only the feelings that you experienced at that moment, the ones you hoped you would never experience again; and have you ever

wondered about the purpose of pain; and have you ever

in dreams never spoken of, drank the sky from a silver chalice, reigning over a kingdom where there is no more sorrow, or hunger, or broken spirits; and have you ever

felt your heart skip a beat at the sound of a child's scream because, for just a moment, you can't tell if it's a scream of joy, meant to travel the world, or if it's the scream of absolute terror because someone is doing something *terrible* the child, only you can't see *where* it came from;

and have you ever

railed against the existence of God;

or why it is that movies with happy endings always leave you cold and resentful and wishing you could reach into the film and strangle all the actors;

have you ever

wondered why it is that those who, for some reason, love you, are always forgiving of your mistakes, no matter how cruel; and, in the end;

have you ever asked anyone, say, a little girl drawing chalk outlines on the street, if anything you do or say or hope for or strive toward or dream or regret ultimately matters, or is it all just some protracted, contemptuous, obscene delusion?

Shhh; there-there; it's not necessary for you to have an answer. But we did have to ask if there is enough pain, if there is enough grief, if there is sufficient desperation and hopelessness, and if they are focused intensely enough, with an adequate amount of belief, on a single point and at a single subject (much as the unseen observer watches from his/her/their place of safety), how could you not accept the idea that something that was *not*, suddenly *is?*

We leave Eugene Benson for just a few moments, rising on the breeze toward an upstairs window. Looking in, we see that there is no furniture in the room. Dust covers the badly-scuffed hardwood floor. But as we continue watching, the dust is being disturbed by something unseen; it swirls in the air like snowflakes until it all twists and turns toward the same spot in the middle of the empty room; here, it becomes a small funnel-cloud that, from its behavior, is trying to drill through the floor. Instead—and it takes us a few seconds to realize this—it is trying to pull something up through the floorboards, and, soon enough, we see the semi-gelatinous substance that is leaking upward from the cracks between the boards; at first it looks like mud left on the hillside after rain, but as the funnel continues to churn and more of the mud leaks upward, it takes on the color and consistency of raw liver, all of it combining to form something like a cocoon made of spoiled pork. There is a soft snapping noise from inside the cocoon, and it begins to split apart on one side, a mouth disgorging something unpleasant, and with a series of wet, tearing sounds, a small, slick knot pushes outward. After a few more moments the knot begins to split apart, fingers uncoiling, flexing, and then clawing at the side of the cocoon, ripping away chunks of meat that fall to the floor with heavy splattering sounds.

We turn away from the window and drift back down to Gene, who is now looking across the street where a middle-aged woman has been watching him for who-knows-how-long, her narrowed eyes filled with suspicion.

Gene suddenly feels embarrassed, foolish, insufficient, and inept, so he glances once more at the flowers and the picture of Leigh and whispers a farewell before walking on, eventually going back to his house where he will order a pizza for dinner, watch the DVD of his favorite movie, *The Shootist*, the one where John Wayne plays an ex-gunfighter dying of cancer, and when it's over, Gene will smile at the television, reach over to the small table beside his chair, pick up the gun, shove it in his mouth, and squeeze the trigger. It will be ten days before any of the neighbors notice the stench in the air; twelve days before any of his friends become worried enough to check on him.

INTERLUDE: STILL-LIFE(S) IN WHITE AND RED

With nearly all of the figures completed (there will be twenty-seven once she has finished with them) and the little girl stops with the red chalk, now worn down nearly to a nub, held tightly in her grip. Her brow furrows, creating wrinkles in her face and on her forehead that look as deep as scars, momentarily ageing her by decades. She stands and turns in the direction of the first figure (now several yards down the street), her glance tracking from left to right, examining all of the chalk outlines until she is looking down at this final form at her feet. She considers something—what, we cannot tell—nods her head, and skips a few feet away from this final figure. Looking down the gallery of her chalk ghosts, the little girl raises one arm, pointing straight out, reshaping her hand into an imaginary gun that consists of thumb and index finger. "Bang. Bang. Bang," she whispers. Her brow relaxes, her flesh becomes smooth once again, no longer marked by ageing scars; she is only a little girl, holding nubs of chalk in each hand. She kneels down and begins drawing a new figure, different from the rest; this one—a man in his late thirties, yes, that's it, that's exactly right—is given much more detail than any of the others; he has a recognizable face, a knowing expression; he has clothes—work boots, khaki pants, a tee-shirt, a denim jacket, a work cap, all of them stained by machine grease from a factory floor. He is standing, full of purpose. He begins to move with confidant steps, not too fast, not too slow, just enough that one can take a look at him and know that he will not be deterred from his destination or his task. The little girl smiles at him. He smiles back at her. "Shouldn't I be carrying something?" he asks. The little girl nods her head. A few moments later, he is holding something sleek.

"Hold on," says the little girl. "I gotta finish something on the last person."

"Man or woman?"

"Huh? Oh, geez, I don't know."

"Make it a mother holding her newborn baby."

The little girl considers this for a moment. "I'll have to draw it over again. You'll have to wait."

"That will not be a problem."

"Good."

"That's an impressive fire, by the way."

"Uh-huh."

"It would certainly make *me* want to come outside to watch."

"Well... they started it."

"Yes. That they did. Hey, Leigh?"

"What?"

"Who am I?"

"*Huh?*"

"Give me a name. Tell me the story of my life. I don't care how much of it is left or what I never had of it to begin with, just... tell me. Tell me about me."

"Like *they* told me about me?"

"Something like that, yes. Please?"

"That's fair. Okay... let me... let me think..."

"Will it be a happy story, or a sad one?"

"I don't know yet. Just wait a second."

"Take your time. Make it a good story, this story of my life..."

4. A TERRIBLE THING

We turn our attention to the middle-aged woman across the street. She wears a shabby housecoat and even shabbier slippers, but this does not stop her from coming down off her front porch and crossing over to see what that strange man was up to.

She sees the carefully-placed flowers; she sees the photo of the little girl whose face is no longer smudged and worn down, but clear and bright. For a moment the middle-aged woman—Virginia Thompson, "Jinny" to her friends, recently laid-off from the hospital where she worked as a cafeteria cook—stares at the flowers and the photo. The little girl looks oddly familiar, yet Virginia can't quite place her. It takes her a moment longer to realize what this means, and when the realization hits, she shakes her head, turns around, and heads back to her house where she immediately calls her best friend, Arlene, and tells her all about it.

—I knew it must have been a terrible thing that made them move out in the middle of the night like they did.

—But that was so long ago, wasn't it? Are you sure it's the same house, Jinny? Why would any of them come back? That don't seem like such a smart thing to me.

—Maybe he was feeling guilty and that's why he left the flowers and the picture. Oh, Arlene, you ought to see what this little girl looked like. Poor little thing.

—Did you call the police? I would call the police, Jinny. If he's still nearby, he might hurt some other little girl. You never know.

—And what am I supposed to tell the police? That I seen some strange man leave flowers and a picture on the steps of a house ain't no one lived in for a good two years?

—Well, you know the *names* of the folks who used to live there, right?

—Hell, no! Nobody knows anybody else around here. Everyone minds their own business.

—Don't sound like it's much of a neighborhood.

—It ain't, but the house was the right price. If Herb gets laid off from the plant, I don't know how we're gonna keep up with the mortgage payments, I really don't.

—Hey, Jinny?

—Yeah?

—I just had an idea about that little girl...

By seven-thirty that evening, having phoned most of the people either of them could call a genuine friend, Virginia and Arlene stand on the sidewalk, facing the house where the flowers and photograph have now been joined by dozens of small lighted candles, sympathy cards, children's toys, hand-drawn pictures, figurines of Christ and the Holy Mother, several rosaries, photographs of other dead or missing children brought there by family members. Word has spread quickly about the vigil (we smile to ourselves as we observe this night watch, somewhat dumbfounded that two or three phone calls have set into action this chain of events), and there are easily two dozen people milling around the front of the house, many of whom have never met before. A man we have never seen before (and will never see again) turns to the woman beside him.

—I heard Channel 10 might be sending a news van tonight.

—Really? God, if I'd've known that, I would have fixed my hair. I can't have people seeing me on television looking like this.

Arlene has come prepared, and walks around handing everyone a sacramental candle (they had been on sale at the religious bookstore downtown, three dozen for ten dollars, and Arlene was not one to pass up a bargain); after everyone has set flame to the wick of their candle, the crowd becomes more orderly, forming a lengthy half-circle in front of the house.

—What was her name? someone asks.

—Leigh, replies Virginia. I think I heard the man call her Leigh when he left the picture.

—It must have been a terrible thing, to weigh on a man's conscience like that.

—Do you suppose she suffered much? asks someone else.

And like a curved row of falling dominoes or a grade-school game of Telephone, the speculations begin running down the line and then back again:

I hope he didn't beat her to death, that would have been an awful way to die; think I heard something about a shooting here a couple of years ago, but I don't remember the little girl's name; heard she was strangled with one of her own belts; he tied her hands behind her back and hung her up by her neck in the closet and just left her to choke to death no it was the flu bet you anything it was the flu it's just been terrible this year just a terrible thing the mother poisoned her a little bit each day y'know like in that movie with the little boy who says he can see dead people got pushed down the basement stairs and it broke her neck they both held her under the water in the tub until she drowned a divorce thing the mother had custody and the father got drunk as hell and decided that if he can't have his kids no one can have to wonder why didn't she scream or cry out for help bet she was terrified the whole time her last minutes on this earth were horrible being beaten like that poisoned like that hanged like that strangled like that raped and stabbed like that starved like that pushed down the stairs like that burned like that starved like that hacked up into pieces like that tortured like that what makes a person do such horrible things to a child or anyone for that matter kind of sick person has thoughts like that anyway...

On and on it goes, until, at last, they compare notes and decide they have their answers.

SECOND INTERLUDE: THE STORY, IN MOSAIC, OF THE PURPOSEFUL MAN, WHO IS STANDING

His name was Frank Thomas and for as long as he was alive he acted like a man who was always looking back in hopes that something joyful from his past would come running forward, jump up, and piggyback him into the future, happier life. But that's not quite how it went.

It happened like this:

He finished high school, did his stint in the military, and then went home to help run the farm. He found a good Christian woman to marry and started a family. His parents retired to Arizona on Social Security and passed the farm and its debts to Frank. Everything seemed to be working out just that way it was supposed to.

One night shortly after his parents moved away, Frank remembered telling his wife as she sat at her piano, "I feel powerful, Betty. I'm a man, living in the strongest nation in the world, and I got all that goes along with that; a good home, a good wife and family, plenty of good food. If I work for it, I can have just about anything I want."

But that's not quite how it went.

As his children, Nadine and Rachael, grew up, he found them to be a burden. "It's your fault they grow up so lazy and disrespectful," he told Betty. He did his best to swallow his anger, but when it got the best of him, he told them all just exactly what he thought of them. Betty was a "fat cow" who "…didn't have the backbone to stand up to her brood and teach them what was right and proper." Nadine was a "slovenly ne'er-do-well" who, if she didn't get better grades, would "…grow up to be trailer trash on welfare surrounded by ten screaming children." Rachael was "sickly," and Frank let it be known he resented the special care and expense necessary to support her. As far as he was concerned, none of them had any gratitude for the life he provided for them.

As a young teenager, Nadine got into drugs and sex. She beat up her mother a couple of times and became useless around the farm. One day she was gone and didn't return.

"I'm glad she's run off," Frank told Betty. "I couldn't love nobody who'd do the things that young girl did."

"She grew up like that because you are a heartless bastard," Betty told him. It was the only time she'd ever stood up to him.

The next day, as punishment, Frank sold Betty's precious piano. He enjoyed watching her cry as it was hauled away.

She never gave him any lip again. But she did take up with another man. Frank knew that he should have felt hurt, but he didn't. On some level that he was never really willing to admit to himself, he didn't blame her, but he never visited that level too often and so it was easy to ignore.

He took to forcing himself on Betty some nights, just to see if she'd refuse him.

She never did. Never much enjoyed having him on top of her, either, for that matter, but Frank got to shoot his wad and that was all he cared about—that, and teaching her that there was a price for spreading your legs for another man when you were Frank Thomas' wife.

Eventually Betty died in a car accident on her way to one of her disgraceful, adulterous meetings. There was some question as to whether or not it was an accident; it seemed that there were no skid marks on the road near the tree she'd hit. "Have you noticed if your wife had seemed depressed lately?" one of the investigators had asked him.

Frank stuffed his resentment down deep inside.

So he found himself middle-aged, not as strong as he once was, and without help running the farm. Money was tight. Frank couldn't afford to hire help. Although he'd worked hard all his life and chipped away at his father's debts, he'd never made much of a dent. Rachael, with her mysterious seizures and the drugs she took for them, couldn't be expected to help out much.

The debts piled up.

The farm started to show signs of neglect and ruin.

Younger debts came along to keep the older ones company.

He was forced to sell off half his property.

But he kept the anger and frustration buried deep as the bodies in his front yard.

All too soon there wasn't enough farm *left* to farm. He got a job at the recycling plant, sorting plastic bottles. He was mired in rancid soft drink residue eight hours a day five days a week. Hank Fenster, who drove a forklift at the plant, befriended Frank. With two weeks on the job, they were relaxing one evening after work at the Echo Hollow Tavern.

"Nothing but a bunch of kids running that plant," Frank said, draining half his beer. "Every one of them got a college degree, but no common sense. They push us around like we're nothing. It's like they think I got no pride, that I'll just take anything offa them."

"Ain't it the truth, though?" Hank asked through a mouth full of beer nuts. "I mean, you're just like me, ain't you? I know I couldn't afford to lose that job."

Frank thought about quitting, but with Rachael's medicines and doctor's bills, the repairs to the plumbing and the antiquated tube-and-knob wiring in the farm house, not to mention the debt his father had been so generous with, he knew Hank was right: like it or not, he was stuck.

Frank stared into his empty beer glass and whispered: "One day I'm going to take my hunting rifle down to the plant and blow all them snot-nosed kids away." He was kidding when he said it and laughed, but when he stepped out of his car with his hunting rifle a month later to actually do it, Frank was a man possessed by a lifetime of anger denied. In the mail that morning he had received a letter from his supervisor, explaining how his wages and benefits would have to be cut back or they'd have to let him go.

The bastard couldn't even say it to my face, Frank thought.

His actions that morning were mechanical and dream-like at the same time: before leaving for work, he went into Rachael's bedroom, kissed her on the forehead, put a bullet through her skull, and then headed for work. Hank, just arriving for his shift, saw him in the parking lot, tried to reason with him, and finally tried to stop him. After shooting Hank, Frank paused long enough to register the surprise on his friend's face, surprise that he realized he shared.

What the hell have I done? I should go home!

No—the bastards had to die, if only to pay for Hank's life.

Frank burst through the front entrance to the plant, headed for the administrative offices.

Alerted by the shots fired in the parking lot, the security guard stood just inside, his pistol drawn. Frank had forgotten about him.

"Drop it," the guard demanded.

If I stop now, Frank thought, *maybe I won't get into too much trouble.* Then he focused on the pistol in the guard's hand. It was such a pitiful little thing, not nearly as powerful as his deer rifle. He raised the barrel toward the man and put a hole in his stomach.

Frank killed three more people on his way to the administrative offices; once he reached his destination, he shot everyone who stood between him and the supervisor's office.

The supervisor got special treatment; Frank blew apart both the man's knees, and then stood over him and shoved the barrel of the rifle into the man's mouth.

"A man works his whole life away," Frank spat at the supervisor, "he reports to work on time and punches the clock and works without complaint and doesn't never call in sick no matter how bad he feels, and what does it mean? Can you tell me that, boss-man? What does it amount to when little snotty-ass college pricks like you make him feel embarrassed by what he is, ashamed at his lack of education, humiliated because he can only provide his family with the things they need and never things they *want?*"

The supervisor had wet himself, red-faced, and shook his head as his eyes filled with tears.

The terror in the man's eyes made Frank feel good; for once in his life, he wasn't powerless.

"It ain't so bad when you're in here," he went on, ignoring the supervisor's whimpering. "It's when you're outside that it bothers you, you know? Because you're *marked*, if you know what I mean. You might be all dressed up at a nice restaurant or buying groceries or out getting your mail and folks, they look at you and know right away what you are, what you've always been, and that's a worker, a laborer all your life, and they know this because you're marked. The work marks you, the not-enough money marks you... and little college shits mark you because they look down their noses at you and make you feel like dirt, and soon enough you start acting like dirt and then you wake up one morning and find out that dirt's what you've become... and that's just what you want, ain't it?"

The supervisor shook his head as much as he could; Frank pressed the barrel down harder and heard some of the man's teeth crack.

"...ittle ...rl..." mumbled the supervisor through what was left of his mouth.

"What?" Frank pulled the barrel from the other man's mouth. "What'd you say?"

"The little girl."

"What little girl?"

"Leigh."

"I don't know no little girl named Leigh."

The supervisor nodded toward a window. "Sure you do. She's right out there in the street."

Frank looked over there, as well. "You mean in front of the house that's burning up?"

"Yes. Do you see her?"

"I see her. She's drawing something with chalk."

"Bang. Bang. Bang," said the little girl.

Frank looked at her, looked at the figures she'd outlined in chalk, looked at the burning house where the flames now stood frozen, and then, finally, looked at his empty hands.

"Shouldn't I be carrying something?" he asked her.

5. SO IT WAS DECIDED

Her name was definitely Leigh. She was eleven years old when her father raped her, beat her unconscious, and then tied her hands behind her back with duct tape before wrapping an electrical cord around her neck and hanging her in her bedroom closet. He then killed his wife but the police still haven't found the body. He threw a bunch of stuff into the trunk and backseat of his car and high-tailed it out of town. It was all such a terrible thing.

It is nearly ten P.M. now and many of those gathered here are getting tired. Each person extinguishing their sacramental candle, the group begins to disperse, all of them still thinking about the last horrifying minutes of Leigh's life, poor little thing, and maybe those who gathered here will arrive home and hug their children a little tighter than usual, wanting to never let go, and maybe these children will hug back and kiss Mommy or Daddy's cheek and say *I love you, too.*

Virginia says goodnight to Arlene and the two women go their separate ways.

No one has thought to extinguish any of the candles on the steps and porch of poor little Leigh's house. Soon enough the scene is deserted, excepting us, and we move away from the candles and toys and cards, rising toward the upstairs window once again. Looking into the empty room, we note that the funnel cloud of dust is gone, as is the meat cocoon. But from somewhere in the shadows we hear a soft but nonetheless distinct sound: that of a child crying.

A gust of wind, and beneath us the tissue paper around the flowers flutters backward, just enough so that a small section of it dips into the burning candle beside it. Moments later, the flowers are aflame, and it takes little time at all before all of the candles and toys and cards of sympathy are all burning bright.

We look back into the empty room and are startled to see Leigh standing a few feet back from the window, staring directly at us. She is trembling, her body covered in a sheen of afterbirth that both catches and reflects the light from a streetlamp, making her appear nearly translucent. Her saturated strawberry-blonde hair hangs off her scalp, straggling down to her bony shoulders, and when she moves closer to the window, we see that her skin is the color of a gravestone. The fury in her eyes is unmistakable. And we know she can see us. We are no longer those who can only look.

From somewhere down the street, we hear the sound of a loud automobile engine. The car reveals itself a few moments later; it is an older model Mustang, a convertible with its roof down. Two teenaged boys are sitting on the back of the car, their feet cushioned on the backseat. The driver is alone in the front seat. The car slows, pulling up to park in front of the house. The three teenagers get out but the driver leaves the engine running. He is carrying something is his right hand, something red and square and—judging by the way he keeps adjusting his shoulder—rather heavy.

—So this is it, huh? The house where that little girl was killed.

—She was raped first, is what I heard.

—Me too.

—Well, at least some of this shit's already burning.

A sloshing sound, drunken words, and we watch in fascination as the driver hoists the gas can up onto his shoulder and then throws it forward. It shatters the downstairs window, splashing a trail behind it that the flames are only too happy to follow. One of the girls in the backseat hops out, pulls something from her purse, and scribbles the words FUCK DEATH on the sidewalk in front of the house; FUCK is written in white chalk; DEATH is written in red. She throws the chalk aside and joins the others as they run back to the car and, with the sound of squealing tires and the stench of burning rubber, flee the scene.

Three minutes later the house is nearly engulfed in flames. Leigh is still standing at the window, staring at us, her eyes beckoning, commanding us to observe what is in her mind and heart.

This isn't fair, she thinks. *It isn't fair that all of you went away.* You *were the ones who beat me.* You *were the ones who drowned me.* You *starved me.* You *choked me.* You *raped and burned and tortured me.* You *wrote the stories of my life.* You *gave me life only to kill me over and over again.*

She is not of the dead, nor is she of the living; she is a thing created wholly out of perception, grief, anger, and belief. She is a small fracture in the structure of the multiverse. She has no identity save for that given to her by the vigil group. Her past—*pasts*, we should say—was also given to her by the vigil group.

You gave me life only to kill me and then give me life and then kill me over and over again. And it isn't fair. I never knew what it was like to be alive, to run and laugh and fly kites and blow out birthday candles and hold my first puppy and blush after my first kiss, you took that from me, and then you went away.

The smoke and flames surround her, and at last we hear the sound of sirens.

Leigh smiles.

I'll show you what it's like, she thinks. *You'll know how it feels. I know all of you, I know your children's names. You did this to me. Now it's my turn.*

The flames do not harm her. She seems to draw strength from them. We cannot move away quickly enough. We must now find another place from which to watch and observe what Leigh will do to those who so unfairly did this to her.

Now it's my turn.

Perhaps we can find refuge on another age, in another story, in a different book. Somewhere in the white spaces between words. We can watch safely from there.

You gave me life only to kill me over and over again.

We whisper goodbye to her.

I'll show you what it's like.

And it is here that our part in the story comes (almost) to an end.

Should you believe any part of this to be untrue, then perhaps you are one of the people who, one night not so long ago, stood outside an abandoned house holding a lighted sacrament candle and creating a wretched, ugly, painful, and perpetually unfair past for a little girl who did not exist until you gave her a name, gave her death (which was her life), and then gave her life (which was her death).

We can watch what happens to you. But you will not see us. As for yourself, you can only listen now…

REQUIEM: AUDIO SNUFF FILES

Before each call is replayed, there are these words from the dispatcher: "Nine-one-one, where is your emergency?"

...house across the street is on fire and someone's screaming – there's a fire and it sounds like somebody's shooting a gun – can see him walking through the smoke, sweeping his arms from side to side – little girl in the street, she's laughing and dancing in circles – the fire's so bad the whole goddamn thing's collapsing – ash and sparks and smoke everywhere – Jesus Christ he just killed two little kids, just walked right up to them and shot 'em in their heads and now he's heading toward the house next door – where are the fire trucks – how long does it take for a fuckin' ambulance to get here – the signing girl, she's... ohgod... she's picking up part of a little boy's body and she's... she's *dancing* with it – still shooting, I think it's some kind of semiautomatic, maybe an AK-47 or something like that – old woman is still alive, she's crawling across the lawn and she looks so bad – some of the fire is spreading to the other houses and everybody's running into the street – running around – so much noise – can't see anything – bangbangbang is all I can hear – ohgod, please don't shoot me, please don't – believe something like this could happen here – get some help here, please – he walked right past the little dancing girl, he didn't shoot her – singing's getting louder and her laughing is even louder than the gunshots – help us help us help us – people are falling dead in the street – goddamn chalk outlines, people's dead bodies are dropping right into these goddamn chalk outlines and they land just like the outlines are shaped – so much noise – so much gunfire – so much blood – so much screaming – can't breathe from all the smoke – so much smoke – so much death – helpushelpushelpus – how – why – can't believe this is happening – just killed my husband right in front of our house – can't believe this – why – we're good people – decent people – we didn't do anything – why – two little kids on fire, they just bolted into the street and the ambulance ran right over them – scattered in pieces – a hand on my lawn and its fingers are moving, burning – where's Mom, where is she – we're good people – we didn't do anything to deserve this – we didn't – we didn't – we didn't do anything – can't imagine what would make someone do this – can't imagine why – can't imagine what would make someone

OUTRO
MICHAEL BAILEY

TAKE A BREATH. You deserve it. You have made it to the end. Well, almost the end. I began with an intro, so, to keep everything chiral, I hereby leave you with an outro, in case you are curious about the twenty-eight writers involved in my creation: who they are; what else they write; where else you can find their work. And other fun tidbits of information you may or may not be interested in reading. It is up to you. You can close me now and wipe away those fingerprints on my glossy cover, if you so choose, or you can keep going and leave them on for a while longer. Perhaps this can be the big wind-down; after all, that was some heavy stuff you've been reading. And you've held me this long (or I have held onto you, depending on how you look at things), so why not keep going? Just a short while longer, I promise.

Now, some of the writers whose work fill my pages you may have recognized because they are in fact living legends. There are *Bram Stoker Award*® winners and nominees, as well as winners and nominees (multi- in multiple cases) of the *International Horror Guild Award*, *British Fantasy Award*, *World Fantasy Award*, the *Edgar*, the *Anthony*, and the *Macavity*; not to mention the *Pushcart Prize*, the *DeMarco Prize*, and the *Emerson Fiction Award*. Included are recipients of the International Thriller Writers Association's *Thriller Masters Award*, and Horror Writers Association's *Grand Master Award* and *Lifetime Achievement Award*. And, if I can toot my own horn a bit, since eleven of the twenty-eight from the table of contents of my predecessor (we're still calling her CM1, for short) have returned for yours truly, aka CM2, I'd like to mention her accolades as well: she was a Grand Prize Finalist for the *Eric Hoffer Award*; winner of the *International Book Awards*; winner at the *London Book Festival;* shortlisted for Foreword Reviews' *Book of the Year;* runner-up for *Anthology of the Year* by This is Horror; finalist for the *USA Best Book Awards* for fiction anthology and cover design; finalist for the Halloween Book Festival; and finalist for the *Indie Book Awards*. One of the stories even made it into Ellen Datlow's *Best Horror of the Year*. CM1's gotten around, had some good reviews and praise and whatnot. People seem to like her, and I hope people will like me, too. Why do I mention these accolades? Is it for *my* sake, or to boast? No. I mention these accomplishments to note the credibility of the writers whose names you may have *not* recognized.

My table of contents includes a mix of well-known, known, and un-known writers. I mention this for one reason: every story / writer within my 424 pages (I'm sure CM1 would agree, regarding her contents) is of similar caliber. The well-knowns, you may be familiar with their names, you may have already sought them out; the knowns, you may have them on your radar (they are emerging and rightfully so); and the unknowns... well, I hope they've gotten your attention and you consider them known from here on out, because for some, this is their first publication (noted in the bios that follow). The stories printed on my pages are some damn fine works of literary fiction by some damn fine writers.

Whether you consider me to be psychological horror, straight-up horror, or speculative fiction, know that I consider myself litera-ture. I'll admit to that. *Chiral Mad*, whether referring to volumes past (CM1), present (CM2, me), or future (let's just say CM3-X) is Dickens-like. Similar to the great horror novella, *A Christmas Carol* (yes, horror, and yes, novella), the *Chiral Mad* volumes contain not ghosts, but *Works of Literary Past, Present, and Yet to Come*. The writ-ers within my pages have shaped contemporary fiction (horror or not), these writers are shaping it today, and these writers will con-tinue to shape it 'yet to come.' So, I urge you to follow along in Ebenezer's footsteps and pay close attention to all three tenses.

Wholeheartedly (yes, I have a heart, and it beats to the rhythm of the beautiful words on my pages), I thank you for your time, and for making it to these final pages. And I also thank the following...

MASON IAN BUNDSCHUH – Emerging talent and author of speculative fiction "because it's easier than saying sci-fi and fantasy and horror and things that are literary but with a twist and stuff." Look for more of his fiction in *Historical Lovecraft*, and *Strange Tales of Horror*.

JAMES CHAMBERS – Emerging talent and author of horror, crime, fantasy, and science fiction. Recipient of the *Richard Laymon Award* from the HWA for his dedication to helping the horror community. Required reading: *Corpse Fauna*, which *Publisher's Weekly* calls "chillingly evocative."

MAX BOOTH III – Emerging talent and "author ~~liar~~ of speculative fiction." Required reading: *True Stories Told by a Liar*, and *They Might Be Demons*. Look for his future novels: *Toxicity*, *The Mind is a Razorblade*, and *The Catch-Lie People*. His mom thinks this book is called *Mad China*.

MORT CASTLE – Award-winning horror author and writing teacher with more than 350 short stories and dozens of books to his credit. Required reading: *The Strangers, Shadow Show: All-New Stories in Celebration of Ray Bradbury, New Moon on the Water*, and *Cursed Be the Child*.

JOHN BIGGS – Award-winning author whose work is saturated with as much Oklahoma as it will hold. Look for his work in *Ruin Cities*, and *Dark Side of the Moon*. "John's unique take on everyday events will stay in the readers mind for a very long time." – Regina Williams

ANDREW HOOK – Emerging talent and author of slipstream fiction, the genre that bends the others, with over 100 publications. Required reading: *Residue, Slow Motion Wars*, and *Nitrospective*. "Andrew Hook is a wonderfully original writer." – Graham Joyce

DUSTIN LAVALLEY – Emerging talent, screenwriter, and author of speculative fiction. Required reading: *Lowlife Underdogs, The Bleeding*, and *Odds and Ends: An Assortment of Sorts*, which Thomas Ligotti calls "Extraordinary. Hauntingly poignant."

THOMAS F. MONTELEONE – Award-winning author of science fiction and horror, and shaper of fiction writers. Responsible for the prestigious *Borderlands Press*. Required reading: any *Borderlands* anthology, *The Blood of the Lamb*, and *The Mothers and Fathers Italian Association*.

GENE O'NEILL – Award-winning author of science fiction, fantasy and horror fiction, with over 120 works in print, most of which can be found in his short story collections. Required reading: *Jade, The Burden of Indigo, Taste of Tenderloin*, and *Dance of the Blue Lady*.

LUCY A. SNYDER – Award-winning author of science fiction, fantasy, humor, horror, nonfiction and poetry, with over fifty of her short stories appearing in various magazines, anthologies and collections. Required reading: *Blood Magic, Chimeric Machines*, and *Orchid Carousals*.

DAVID MORRELL – Award-winning author of *First Blood* and creator of Rambo; he is known as the "father" of the modern action novel, and is a co-founder of International Thriller Writers. Required Reading: *The Totem, The Brotherhood of the Rose*, and *Murder as a Fine Art*.

ANN K. BOYER – Emerging talent and newcomer to horror fiction and dark fantasy. This is her first publication, but also the first of many. Look for more of her work in *Horror D'oeuvres, Blood Reign Lit Magazine*, and *Nightmare Illustrated*. Ann is going places.

JOHN SKIPP - Award-winning splatterpunk horror and fantasy author, anthology editor, songwriter, screenwriter and filmmaker. He is slightly responsible for giving us *A Nightmare on Elm Street 5: The Dream Child*. Required reading: *Conscience, Book of the Dead*, and *Jake's Wake*.

E. L. KEMPER – Emerging talent and author of horror fiction. "It happened by accident (or did it?)" Look for more of her work soon in places such as *Shifters, Zombies: Shambling Through History, Handsome Devil*, and *[Nameless] Magazine*.

JON MICHAEL KELLEY — Emerging talent and author of speculative fiction. Required reading: his first novel, *Seraphim*, and all his short fiction you can get your hands on. Look for more of his work in *Miseria's Chorale*, *Midnight Train*, *One Hour*, and *Father Grim's Storybook*.

RICHARD THOMAS — Award-winning author of neo-noir, horror, transgressive, and speculative fiction. Required reading: *Transubstantiate*, and his short story collections, *Staring Into the Abyss* and *Herniated Roots*. Look for more of his work in *Cemetery Dance* and *Pantheon Magazine*.

PHILIP C. PERRON — Emerging talent and newcomer to horror fiction, and one of the voices behind the *Dark Discussions* podcasts. This is one of his first publications, yet one of the firsts of many. Look for more of his work in *Canopic Jars: Tales of Mummies and Mummification*.

USMAN T. MALIK — Emerging talent and graduate of the *Clarion West Writers Workshop*. This is one of his first publications and, such as with the other newcomers in this anthology, this is just the beginning. Look for more of his work in *Thirteen Stories*, and *Daily Science Fiction*.

P. GARDNER GOLDSMITH — Emerging talent and graduate of the *Borderlands Press Boot Camp*. Look for more of his work in *Chiral Mad*. Required reading: *Bite*, a gripping novella. "Goldsmith's prose is like the edge of a knife. Definitely a writer to watch." – Brian Keene

GARY McMAHON - Award-winning author of several novels, collections, and numerous short stories. Required reading: *Pretty Little Dead Things*, *Dead Bad Things*, and *The Concrete Grove*. "Firmly in the front ranks of the new wave of British horror." - The Guardian.

KEVIN LUCIA — Emerging talent and author of speculative fiction. He is a graduate of the *Borderlands Press Boot Camp*. Look for more of his work in *Shroud Magazine*, *Horror Library 5*, and *Hiram Grange*. Required reading: his most recent fiction collection, *Things Slip Through*.

RAMSEY CAMPBELL – Award-winning author and legend of uncanny, weird fiction. Required reading: *Ancient Images, Midnight Sun, Alone with the Horrors,* and *The Long Lost.* "Britain's most respected living horror writer." - *Oxford Companion to English Literature*

ERIK T. JOHNSON – Emerging talent and author of FS/FHH (Funny-strange/Funny Ha-Ha) fiction. Look for more of his work in *Box of Delights, Song Stories: Volume 1, Pellucid Lunacy, Chiral Mad, Mortis Operandi,* and *Dead But Dreaming 2.* Look for all of his stuff, really.

JOHN PALISANO – Emerging talent, Bram Stoker Award ® nominated author, screenwriter, songwriter, and *Borderlands Press Boot Camp* graduate. Required reading: *Nerves.* Look for more of his work in *After Death, Bleed,* and his novella, *The BiPolar Express,* coming soon.

EMILY B. CATANEO – Emerging talent, freelance writer, and graduate of the *Odyssey Writing Workshop.* This is her first publication, but also the first of many. Look for more of her work soon. She was recommended for *Chiral Mad 2* consideration by Jack Ketchum.

JACK KETCHUM – Award-winning author of over twenty novels and novellas, and some of the darkest fiction imaginable. Required reading: *Red, The Girl Next Door, Peaceable Kingdom,* and *I Am Not Sam.* "Who's the scariest guy in America? Probably Jack Ketchum." – Stephen King

PATRICK O'NEILL – Emerging talent from the United Kingdom and author of horror fiction. Look for more of his work in *Chiral Mad, Fear: A Modern Anthology of Horror and Terror,* and *The Darkness Within.* "Patrick O'Niell's words carry emotion and power." – Michael Bailey

GARY A. BRAUNBECK - Award-winning author of over twenty books and 200 short stories. Required reading: *In Silent Graves, Mr. Hands,* and *To Each Their Darkness* (nonfiction). "Braunbeck knows what scares us, and what hurts us too. And it hurts so good…" - Brian Keene

29568092R00255

Made in the USA
Charleston, SC
16 May 2014